The Pioneer

A Tale Of Two States

by

Geraldine Bonner

Double 9 BOOKS

The Pioneer

A Tale Of Two States

by Geraldine Bonner

ISBN: 978-93-71813-12-9

Published by

DOUBLE 9 BOOKS
2/13-B, Ansari Road
Daryaganj, New Delhi – 110002
info@double9books.com
www.double9books.com
Tel. 011-40042856

ABOUT THE AUTHOR

Geraldine Bonner was born on Staten Island, New York, into a literary environment shaped by her father, John Bonner, a journalist and historical writer. Her early years were marked by a significant move to Colorado, where she experienced life in mining camps, a setting that would later influence much of her fiction. After relocating to San Francisco, she began her professional writing career at the Argonaut newspaper in 1887. Bonner's writing extended beyond novels into short stories that appeared in prominent periodicals such as Collier's Weekly, Harper's Weekly, Harper's Monthly, and Lippincott's. Her literary contributions reflect a deep engagement with themes of social structure, isolation, and the American experience, particularly within mining and frontier communities. Geraldine Bonner died in New York City on June 18, 1930, leaving behind a diverse body of work shaped by both rugged landscapes and human complexity. Her parents' names include John Bonner and his spouse, though her mother's name is not recorded.

CONTENTS

BOOK I
THE COUNTRY

CHAPTER I
THE SQUATTER

It had been five o'clock in the clear, still freshness of a May morning when the Colonel had started from Sacramento. Now, drawing rein where the shadow of a live-oak lay like a black pool across the road, he looked at his watch—almost five. The sun had nearly wheeled from horizon to horizon.

During the burning noon hour he had rested at Murderer's Bar. Except for that he had been in the saddle all day, slackening speed where the road passed over the burnt shoulder of the foot-hills, descending into sheltered cañons by cool river-beds, pacing along stretches of deserted highway where his mounted figure was the only living thing in sight.

Stationary in the shade of the live-oak he looked about him. The rich foot-hill country of California stretched away beneath his gaze in lazy undulations, dotted with the forms of the oaks. The grass on unprotected hilltops was already drying to an ocher yellow, the road was deep in dust. Far away, hanging on the horizon like a faded mirage, was the high Sierra, thin, snow-touched, a faint, aërial vision.

The sleepy sounds of midday had died down and the strange, dream-like silence so peculiar to California held the scene. It was like looking at a picture, the Colonel thought, as he turned in his saddle and surveyed the misty line of hill after hill, bare and wooded, dwindling down to where—a vast, sea-like expanse swimming in opalescent tints—stretched one of the fruitful valleys of the world.

Kit Carson, the finest horse procurable in the Sacramento livery stable the Colonel patronized, stamped and flicked off a fly with his long tail. His rider muttered a word of endearment and bent to pat the silky neck, while his eyes continued to move over the great panorama. He had traversed it many times. The first time of all rose in his mind, when in the flush of his splendid manhood, he had sought fortune on the bars and river-beds in forty-nine. Forty-nine! That was twenty-one years ago.

Something in the thought clouded his brow and called a sigh to his lips. He made a gesture as though shaking off a painful memory and gathered up the hanging rein.

"Come, Kit," he said aloud, "we've got to be moving. There's fifteen miles yet between us and supper."

The road before them mounted a spur at the top of which it branched, one fork winding up and on to the mining towns hidden in the mountain crevices. The other turned to the right, and rising and falling over the buttresses that the foot-hills thrust into the plain, wandered down "the mother lode," the great mineral belt of California.

As they rose to the summit of the spur, the brilliancy of the air was tarnished by a cloud of dust, and the silence disrupted by sounds. The crack of whips cut into the tranquillity of the evening hour; the jangling of bells and voices of men mingled in strident dissonance. Both Kit and the Colonel rose above the curve of the hilltop with the pricked ears and alert eyes of curiosity.

The left-hand road was blocked as far as could be seen with a long mule train, one of the trains that a few years before had crossed the Sierra to Virginia City, and still plied a trade with the California mountain towns. The dust rose from it and covered it as though to shut out from Heaven the vision of the straining animals, and deaden the blasphemies of the men. Looking along its struggling length, the end of which was lost round a turn of the road, the Colonel could see the pointed ears, the stretched necks, and the arched collars of the mules, the canvas tops of the wagons and over all, darting back and forth, the leaping flash of the whips.

A forward wagon was stuck, and, groaning and creaking from an unsuccessful effort to start it, the train subsided into panting relaxation. From the dust the near-by drivers emerged, caught sight of the rider, and slouched toward him. They were powerful men—great men in their day, the California mule drivers.

They passed the time of day, told him their destination and asked his. Going on to Foleys, was he? Mining? Supposed not. Not much mining done round Foleys now. Like Virginia, pretty well petered.

"Virginia!" said one of them, "you'd oughter see Virginia! I've taken my sixteen-mule team over the Strawberry Creek route and made my ten dollars a day in Virginia, but it's as dead now as forty-nine."

Then they slouched back to their work. Through the churned-up dust, red with the brightness of the declining sun, men came swinging down from the forward end of the train, driving mules to attach to the stalled wagon. About it there was a concentrating of movement and then an outburst of furious energy. A storm of profanity arose, the dust ascended like a pillar of red smoke, and in it the forms of men struggled, and the lashes of the whips came and went like the writhing tentacles of an octopus. The watcher had a glimpse of the mules almost sitting in the violence of their endeavor, and with a howl of triumph the wagon lurched forward. The next moment the entire train was in motion, seeming to advance with a single movement, like a gigantic serpent, each wagon-top a section of its vertebrate length, the whole undulating slowly to the rhythmic jangling of the bells.

The Colonel took the turning to the right and was soon traversing a road which looped in gradual descent along the wall of a ravine. The air was chilled by a river that tumbled over stones below. Greenery of tree and chaparral ran up the walls. A white root gripping a rock like knotty fingers, a spattering of dogwood here and there amid the foliage, caught his eye.

Yes, Virginia had unquestionably "petered." It had had a short life for its promise. Even in sixty-eight they still had had hopes of it. This was May, the May of seventy, and their hopes had not been realized. Fortunately he had invested little there. California the Colonel had found a good enough field for his investments.

He rode on out of the ravine, once again into the dry rolling land, his mind turning over that question of investments. He had not much else to think of. He was a lonely man, unmarried, childless, and rich. What else was there for a man, who had passed his fifty-fifth year, who did not care for women or pleasure, to concern himself about? It was not satisfying; it brought him no happiness, but he had had no expectation of that.

Twenty-one years ago the Colonel had waked to the realization that he had missed happiness. She had been his, in his very arms then, and he had thought to keep her there for ever. Then suddenly she had gone, without warning, tearing herself from his grasp, and he had known that she would never return. So he had tried to fill the blankness she had left, with business—a sorry substitute! He had spent a good deal of time and thought over this matter of investing, and had seen his fortune accumulating in a safe, gradual way. It would have been much larger than it was if he could have cured himself of a tendency to give portions of it away. But the Colonel was a pioneer, and there were many pioneers who had succeeded better than he in finding happiness, if not so well in gaining riches. As they had been successful in the one way, he had tried to remedy a deficit in the other, and his fortune remained at about the same comfortable level, despite his preoccupation in investments.

This very trip was to see about a new one in which there were great possibilities. He had a strip of land at Foleys, back of the town, purchased fifteen years ago when people thought the little camp was to be the mining center of the region. Now, after he had been regularly paying his taxes, and hearing that the place annually grew smaller and deader, a mineral spring had been discovered on his land. It was a good thing that something had been discovered there. The hopes of Foleys had vanished soon after he had come into possession of the tract. His efforts to sell it had been unsuccessful. Some years ago—the last time he was up there—you couldn't get people to take land near Foleys, short of giving it to them. But a mineral spring was a very different matter.

As Kit Carson bore him swiftly onward he reviewed the idea of his new investment with increasing enthusiasm. If the spring was all they said it was, he would build a hotel near it, and transform the beautiful, unknown locality into a summer resort. There was an ideal situation for a hotel, where the land swept upward into a sort of natural terrace crested with enormous pines. Here the house would be built, and from its front piazza guests rocking in shaker chairs could look over miles of hills and wooded cañons, and far away on clear days could see the mother-of-pearl expanse of the Sacramento Valley.

A few years ago the plan would have been impossible. But now, with the railroad climbing over the Sierra, it would be quite feasible to run a line of stages from Sacramento; or, possibly, Auburn would be shorter. There was even a hope in the back of the Colonel's mind that the railway might be induced to fling forth a spur as far as Placerville. The Colonel had friendships in high places. Things that ordinary mortals who were not rich, unattached pioneers, could not aspire to, were entirely possible for Colonel James Parrish.

But—here came in the "but" which upsets the best laid plans. At this point the squatter had loomed up.

The Colonel had hardly believed in the squatter at first. His claims were so preposterous. He had come shortly after Parrish's last visit, nearly four years ago, and had taken up his residence in the half-ruined cottage which had been built on the land in those days when people had thought Foleys was going to be a great mining center. When Cusack, the drowsy lawyer who "attended to Colonel Parrish's business interests in Foleys," as he expressed it, let his client know there was a squatter—a married man with two children—on the land, the Colonel's reply had been "let him squat." And so the matter had rested.

Now, when the Colonel wanted to take possession of his own, build his hotel and develop his mineral spring, he had received the intelligence that the squatter refused to go—that in fact he claimed the land on a three and a half years' tenancy undisturbed by notice to leave, and on various and sundry "improvements" he had made.

It took the Colonel's breath away. That little clause in the lawyer's letter about the wife and children had induced him to give his permission for the squatter to occupy his cottage. Having no wife or child of his own, he had a secret feeling of friendliness to all men, who, even in poverty and unsuccess, had tasted of this supreme happiness. And he had let the man remain there, undisturbed, throughout the three and a half years, had forgotten him—in fact, did not even know his name.

And then to be suddenly faced by the amazing insolence of the claim! He with his flawless title, his record of scrupulously paid taxes! He wrote to the Foleys lawyer, as to what "the improvements" were, and received the reply that they consisted in "a garden planted out and tended by the squatter's daughters, and a bit of vineyard land that the girls had pruned and cultivated into bearing condition. There were repairs on the house, mending the roof and the porch which was falling down. Allen had made these himself."

Allen! It was the first time Colonel Parrish had heard the squatter's name. It sent a gush of painful memories out from his heart, and for a space he sat silent with drooped head. Why was not the world wide enough for him, and all who bore this name, to pass one another without encounter!

Now, as he rode on the last stage of his journey, and over the hilltops saw the smoke of the Foleys chimneys, his mind had once again fallen on the squatter's name. Strange coincidence that after twenty-one years this name—a common one—should rise up uncomfortably in his path. He smiled bitterly to himself. Fate played strange tricks, and he felt, with a sense of shamed meanness, that he would have regarded the squatter with more leniency if he had borne any other name than Allen.

CHAPTER II
THE GRACEY BOYS

The smell of wood smoke and supper was in the air as the Colonel rode down the main street of Foleys. Under the projecting roof that jutted from the second-story windows and made a species of rude arcade, men were sitting in the negligée of shirt sleeves, smoking and spitting in the cool of the evening. They hailed the new-comer with a word of greeting or a hand raised in salute to the side of a head where a hat brim should have been.

The Colonel returned the salutations, and as Kit Carson paced through the red dust to where the drooping fringe of locust trees hid the façade of the hotel, looked curiously about him, noticing a slight stir of life, an appearance of reviving vitality in the once moribund camp. Foleys was not as dead as it had been four years ago. Fewer of the shop doors were boarded up; there were even new stores open.

He was speculating on this when he threw himself off his horse in front of the hotel. The loungers on the piazza, dustered and shirt-sleeved men, let their tilted chairs drop to the front legs, and rose to greet him to a man. Anybody was an acquisition at Foleys, but Colonel Jim Parrish, with the rumor of bringing a lawsuit into their midst, was welcomed as the harbinger of a new era.

They were all around him shaking hands when Forsythe, the proprietor, armed with a large feather duster, emerged from the front door. He cut the new arrival out from their midst and drew him into the hall. Here, dusting him vigorously, he shouted to Mrs. Forsythe to prepare a room, and between sweeps of the duster, inquired of him on the burning question of the squatter.

"Come to fire old man Allen, eh?" he queried. "Got your work cut out for you with him."

"He'll find he's barked up the wrong tree this time," said the Colonel grimly, "bringing me up from San Francisco on such a fool's errand."

"It's about the galliest proposition I've ever heard. But he's that kind, drunk a lot of the time, and the rest of it tellin' the boys round here what a great man he used to be. He was glad enough to get twenty-five dollars a month holdin' down a small job in the assay office."

At this moment a door to the right opened, yielding a glimpse of a large bare dining-room set forth with neatly laid tables and decorated with hanging strands of colored paper.

"Say," said a female voice, "ain't that Colonel Jim Parrish that just come down the street?"

"That's just who it is," answered the Colonel, "and isn't that Mitty Bruce's voice?"

This question called to the doorway a female vision in brilliant pink calico. It was a buxom, high-colored country girl of some twenty-one years, coarse featured but not uncomely, her face almost as pink as her dress, her figure of the mature proportions of the early-ripening Californian.

"Well, well, is this Mitty?" said the new-comer, holding out his hand. "You have to come up to the foot-hills to see a handsome girl. I'd never have known you, you've grown up so and got so good-looking."

Mitty sidled up giggling and placed a big, red paw in his.

"Oh, get out!" she said, "ain't you just awful!"

"I won't get out and I'm not a bit awful. You've got to take care of me at supper and tell me everything that's happened in Foleys since I was here last."

"Let her alone to do that," said Forsythe. "There ain't anything that goes on in Eldorado and Amador Counties that Mitty don't know. She's the best newspaper we got round here."

Mrs. Forsythe here put her head over the stair-rail and informed the Colonel that his room was ready. He ran up stairs to "wash up" while the other two repaired to the dining-room.

A few minutes later he reappeared and entered the low-ceilinged room that smelled of fresh paint and cooking. It was past the supper hour at Foleys and only a few men lingered over the end of their meal. By a table at the window, cleanly spread and set, Mitty was standing. When she saw him she pulled out a chair and, with its back resting against her waist, pointed to the seat.

"Set right down here," she said, "everything's ready for you."

Then as he obeyed she pushed him in, saying over his shoulder:

"It's real nice to see you again, Colonel. It seems awful long since you was here last."

The Colonel looked up at her with an eye of twinkling friendliness. She was gazing at him with childish pleasure and affection. He had known Mitty since her tenth year when Forsythe and his wife had adopted her, the only child of a dying woman whose husband had been killed in a mine.

"Good girl, Mitt," he said. "Have you got all the gossip of the last four years saved up for me?"

"I guess I can tell you as much as most," she answered, not without pride, and then flourished off to the hole in the dining-room which communicated with the kitchen.

When she had set his supper before him she sat down opposite, her elbows on the table, comfortably settled for the gossip the traveler had requested.

"Foleys seems to be livening up," he said. "I noticed several new stores. What's happening?"

"Foleys!" exclaimed Mitty, with the Californian's loyalty to his native burg, "Foleys is the liveliest town along the mother lode. There ain't nothing the matter with Foleys! It's the Gracey boys' strike up at the Buckeye Belle mine that's whooping things up."

"Oh, that's it, of course," said the Colonel. "They say the Gracey boys have really struck it this time. I heard some talk of it before I came up. The report down below was that it was a pretty good thing."

"You bet," said the young woman with a knowing air. "Nearly a year ago one of the gentlemen connected with it said to me, 'We've got a mine there; bed-rock's pitchin' and there's two bits to the pan.' So I wasn't surprised when I heard they'd struck it. They're goin' to build a twenty-stamp mill next thing you know."

"Good for them!" said the Colonel. "The Gracey boys have been mining for years all over this country and in Mexico and Nevada, and this is the first good thing they've got. How far is it from here?"

"About twelve miles up in that direction—" she gave a jerk of her hand to the right—"up on the other side of the South Fork. They have to come here for everything. Barney Sullivan, the superintendent, does most of their buying."

She looked at the Colonel with a wide-eyed, stolid gaze as she gave this insignificant piece of information. The look suggested to her vis-à-vis that the information was not insignificant to her.

"Barney Sullivan," he said, "I remember him. He's been with them for some years, was in Virginia City when they were there. He's a good-looking fellow with red hair."

"Good-lookin', did you say?" exclaimed Mitty, in a high key of scornful disbelief. "Well, that's more'n I can see. Just a red-headed Irish tarrier, with the freckles on him as big as dimes. It's a good thing all the world don't like the same kind of face."

Her scorn was tinctured with the complacence of one who knows herself exempt from similar charges. Mitty, secure in the knowledge that her own patronymic was Bruce, affected a high disdain of the Irish. She also possessed a natural pride on the score of her Christian name, which in its unique unabbreviated completeness, was Summit, in commemoration of the fact that upon that lofty elevation of the Sierra she had first seen the light.

"You'll be able to see all the Buckeye Belle crowd to-night," she continued; "they'll be in now any time. There's going to be a party here."

The Colonel looked up from his plate with the thrust-out lips and raised brows of inquiring astonishment.

"The devil you say!" he ejaculated. "I arrived just at the right moment, didn't I? I suppose I'll have to stand round looking at the men knifing each other for a chance to dance with Miss Mitty Bruce."

Mitty wriggled with delight and grew as pink as her dress.

"Well, not quite's bad as that," she said with bridling modesty, "but I can have my pick."

Her friend had finished the first part of his supper, and placing his knife and fork together, leaned back, looking at her and smiling to himself. She saw the empty plate, and rising, bent across the table and swept it and the other dishes on to her tray with an air of professional expertness. As she came back with the dessert the last diner thumped across the wooden floor in noisy exit.

The plate that she set before the Colonel displayed a large slab of pie. A breakfast cup of coffee went with it. He looked at them with an undismayed eye, remarking:

"Who's coming to the party? I'll bet a new hat Barney Sullivan will be here—the first man on deck, and the last to quit the pumps. But I don't suppose the Gracey boys will show up."

"Yes, they will—both of 'em."

"What, Black Dan? Black Dan Gracey doesn't go to parties."

"Well, he don't generally. But he's goin' to this one. His daughter, Mercedes, is here, that sort er spidery Spanish girl, and he's goin' for her."

Mitty, having seen that her guest had all that in Foleys made up the last course of a complete and satisfactory supper, went round and took her seat at the opposite side of the table. As she spoke he noticed a change in her voice. Now, as he saw her face, he noticed a change in it, too. There was a withdrawal of joy and sparkle. She looked sullen, almost mournful.

"Black Dan Gracey's daughter here?" he queried. "What's she doing so far afield? The last I heard of her she was in school in San Francisco."

"So she was until two days ago. Then some kind er sickness broke out in the school, and her paw went down to bring her up here. She was so precious she couldn't come up from San Francisco alone. She had to be brung all the way like she was made of gold and people was tryin' to steal her. They stopped here for dinner on their way up. I seen her."

"She promises to be very pretty," said the Colonel absently. "They say Gracey worships her."

"Pretty!" echoed Mitty in a very flat voice. "I don't see what makes her so dreadful pretty. Little black thing! And anybody'd be pretty all togged up that way. She'd diamond ear-rings on, real ones, big diamonds like that."

She held out the tip of her little finger, nipped between her third and thumb.

"I guess that makes a difference," she said emphatically, looking at him with a pair of eyes which tried to be defiant, but were really full of forlorn appeal.

"Of course it makes a difference," said the Colonel cheeringly, without knowing in the least what he meant, "a great difference."

"They was all staring at her here at dinner. There was four men in the kitchen trying to get a squint through the door, until the Chinaman threw 'em out. And she knew jest as well as any one, and liked it. But you oughter have seen her pretend she didn't notice it. Jest eat her dinner sort er slow and careless as if they was no one round more important than a yaller dog. Only now and then she'd throw back her head so's her curls 'ud fall back and the diamond ear-rings 'ud show. I said to paw flat-footed, 'Go and wait on her yourself, since you think she's so dreadful handsome. I don't do no waiting on that stuck-up thing.'"

Mitty turned away to the window. Her recital of the sensation created by the proud Miss Gracey seemed to affect her. There was a tremulous undernote in her voice; her bosom, under its tight-drawn pink calico covering, heaved as if she were about to weep.

The Colonel noted with surprise these signs of storm, and was wondering what would be best to say to divert the conversation into less disturbing channels, when Mitty, looking out of the window, craned her neck and evidently followed with her eyes a passing figure.

"There goes June Allen," she said; "don't she look shabby?"

The name caused the Colonel to stop eating. He raised his eyes to his companion. She was looking at him with reviving animation in her glance.

"That's the daughter of old man Allen what's squatted on your land," she explained. "You ain't ever seen the girls, have you?"

The Colonel, who had finished, laid his napkin on the table.

"No," he answered, "are they children?"

"Children!" echoed Mitty, "I guess not. June's twenty and Rosamund's nineteen. I know 'em real well. They're friends of mine."

He raised his eyebrows, surprised and relieved at the information. It would be less hard to oust the squatter if his children were of this age than if they were helpless infants.

"What sort of girls are they?" he asked.

"Oh they're real lovely girls. And they've got a wonderful education. They know lots. They're learned. Their mother learned it to them—"

Mitty stopped, a sound outside striking her ear. The Colonel was looking at her with quizzical inquiry. The picture of the squatter's children, as educated, much less "learned," filled him with amused astonishment. He was just about to ask his informant for a fuller explanation, when she rose to her feet, her face suffused with color, her eyes fastened in a sudden concentration of attention on something outside the window.

"Here they are," she said in a low, hurried voice. "Get up and look at them."

He obeyed, not knowing whom she meant. In the bright light of the after-glow he saw four figures on horseback—three men and a girl—approaching down the deserted street. Behind them a pack burro, his back laden with bags and valises, plodded meekly through the dust. The Colonel recognized the men as the Gracey brothers and their superintendent, Barney Sullivan. The girl he had not seen for a year or two, and she was at the age when a year or two makes vast changes. He knew, however, that she was Black Dan Gracey's daughter, Mercedes, who was expected at the dance.

The cavalcade came to a stop outside the window. From the piazza the front legs of the loungers' chairs striking the floor produced a series of thuds, and the thuds were followed by a series of hails such as had greeted the Colonel. But the loungers made no attempt to go forward, as they had done in his case. An access of bashfulness in the presence of beauty held them sheepishly spellbound. It remained for Forsythe to dash out with his duster and welcome the new arrivals with the effusion of a mining camp Boniface.

The Colonel, unseen, looked at them with perhaps not as avid a curiosity as Mitty, but with undisguised interest. He had long known the Gracey boys, as they were called, though Dan was forty-three and Rion twelve years younger. He had often heard of their mining vicissitudes, not only from men similarly engaged, but from themselves on their occasional visits to San Francisco. The society of that city had not yet expanded to the size when it fell apart into separate sets. Its members not only had a bowing acquaintance, but were, for the most part, intimate. The Gracey boys had, as the newspapers say, "the entrée everywhere," though they did not, it is true, profit by it to the extent that San Francisco would have liked.

They were not only educated men, who had come from Michigan in their boyhood, but Black Dan Gracey was a figure distinguished—at any rate, to the feminine imagination—by an unusual flavor of romance. Seventeen years before the present date he had met, while mining in Mexico, a young Spanish girl of fourteen, had fallen madly in love with her, and when her parents placed her in a convent to remove her for ever from the hated Gringo, with six of his men, had broken into the convent and carried her off.

It was part of the romance that a year later his child-wife, as passionately loving as he, should have died, leaving him a baby. It was said that Black Dan Gracey had never recovered this sudden severing of the dearest tie of his life. He certainly was proof against the wiles that many sirens in San Francisco and elsewhere had displayed for his subjugation. It was after this, anyway, that the adjective Black had been prefixed to his name. Most people said it had arisen because of his swarthy coloring—he was of an almost Indian darkness of tint—but there were those who declared it was a tribute to his moody taciturnity, for Black Dan Gracey was a man of few words and rare smiles.

Now, standing in the brilliant evening light, the watcher could not but be impressed by the appearance of the two brothers. A fine pair of men, the Gracey boys, muscular, broad-shouldered, and tall; out-door men whose eyes were far-seeing and quiet, who felt cramped in cities, and returned from them with a freshened zest to the stream-bed and the cañon. Rion was obviously many years his brother's junior. He was a more normal-looking person, not so darkly bearded and heavily browed, more full of the joys and interests of life.

As he slid from his saddle to the ground he was laughing, while his elder, the lower part of his face clothed in a piratical growth of black hair, lowered somberly from under a gray sombrero. In their rough and dust-grimed clothes, they still showed the indefinable air of the well-born and educated man, which curiously distinguished them from Barney Sullivan, their companion. Barney was as tall and well set up as either of them, but beyond a doubt he was what Mitty had called a "tarrier," in other words an Irish laborer. He, too, was laughing, a laugh that showed strong white teeth under a short red mustache. His hat, pushed back from his forehead, revealed the same colored hair, thick and wiry. He had a broad, turned-up nose, plenteously freckled as were his hands, raised now to assist Miss Gracey from her horse.

Upon the one feminine member of the party the Colonel's eyes had been fixed, as were those of every man in the vicinity. He calculated that she was nearly sixteen. For a girl with Spanish blood that would mean a young woman, full-grown and marriageable. She still, however, retained a look of childhood that was extremely charming, and in some vague, indistinct way, pathetic, he thought. Perhaps the pathos lay in the fact that she had never had a mother, and that the best care an adoring father could lavish upon her was to hire expensive nurses in her childhood, and send her to still more expensive boarding-schools when she grew older.

She was undoubtedly fulfilling the promise she had always given of being pretty. She sat sidewise on her saddle, looking down at Barney's raised hands. Her hair, which was as black as her father's, was arranged in loosely flowing curls that fell over her shoulders and brushed her chest. In this position, her chin down, her eyelashes on her cheeks, her lips curved in a slow, coquettish smile, she presented a truly bewitching appearance. Under her childish demeanor, the woman, conscious of unusual charms, was already awake. The Colonel felt as Mitty had, that though her entire attention seemed concentrated on Barney, she was acutely aware of the staring men on the piazza, and was rejoicing in their bashful admiration. He could not help smiling, her indifference was so coolly complete. His smile died when he felt Mitty give him a vicious dig in the back.

"Did you see the ear-rings?" she said in a hissing undertone.

"Yes, I think I did."

"Do you suppose they're real diamonds?"

"Why, of course. Black Dan wouldn't give his daughter anything else."

Mitty gave forth a sound that seemed a cross between a snort and a groan.

"And a pack burro!" she exclaimed with fuming scorn. "Did you get on to the pack burro, all loaded up with bags? She has to have her party rig brought along on a pack burro!"

"Well, what's wrong with that?" he said soothingly. "She couldn't go to the party in her riding habit all grimed up with dust. Nobody ever saw a girl at a party in a riding habit."

"Well, the Phillips girl can go all right in a pink flannel skirt and miners' boots," declared his companion with combative heat, overlooking the fact that the festal array of the Phillips girl had been a subject of her special derision. "I guess she don't have to have a pack burro to carry her duds."

The Colonel realized that the moment for gentle reasoning was over. Only the girl's burning curiosity kept down the wrathful tears evoked by a newly stirred jealousy. When she saw Black Dan's daughter slide from her saddle into Barney Sullivan's arms, an ejaculation of mingled pain and rage escaped her that had a note of suffering in it.

The Colonel, in his time, had known such pangs, a thousand times deeper and more terrible than Mitty had ever experienced. He turned to her smiling, not teasingly, but almost tenderly, and saw her face blighted like a rose dashed by rain, pitiful and a little ludicrous. The pitiful side of it was all that struck him.

"Did you see how mighty easy Barney is with her?" she stammered, making a desperate feminine attempt to speak lightly.

"A gentleman has to help a lady off her horse; he can't let her climb down all by herself. Barney's not that kind of a chump. You run along now and get ready. You haven't got such a lot of time, for you've got to help set the tables for supper. And don't you fret. I just feel that you're going to look as nice as any girl in the place. That dress of yours is going to be just about right. Hurry up! Here they are."

Mitty heard the advancing footfalls in the passage and the sound of approaching voices. As the tail of her pink calico skirt disappeared through the kitchen door, the Gracey party entered through the one that led to the office. There were greetings with the Colonel, and he sat down at their table to exchange the latest San Francisco gossip with the mining news of the district, and especially to hear the details of the strike in the Buckeye Belle.

CHAPTER III
THE NAME OF ALLEN

An hour later as the Colonel was leaving his room, the voices of Forsythe and a new-comer ascending the stairs struck on his ear. He leaned over the baluster and looked down at the tops of their approaching heads. Forsythe's bald pate was followed by another, evidently a younger one, by the curly brown hair that covered it. A pair of shoulders in a dusty coat was beneath the head, and, as they mounted, the Colonel heard a voice of that cultured intonation which the far West scornfully regards as an outgrowth of effete civilizations. In short, the owner of the voice spoke like an Easterner who has had a college education.

The Colonel, if he was doubtful about the top of the head, knew the voice directly.

"Jerry Barclay, by thunder!" he exclaimed over the railing. "What the devil are you doing up here?"

The new-comer started and lifted a handsome face, which, in clean-cut distinction of feature, seemed to match the voice. He cleared the last steps at a bound and stretched out a sinewy brown hand to the older man. There was something delightfully frank and boyish in his manner.

"Well, old son," he said, "that comes well from you! About the last person in California I expected to see at Foleys. What's up?"

In the light of the kerosene lamps which illumined the hallway he was shown to be some thirty years of age, tall, slender, upright, with upon him and about him that indescribable air of the man of clubs and cities. His loose sack-coat and flannel shirt set upon his frame with a suggestion of conscious masquerade. He did not belong to the present rough setting, albeit he was so easy of manner and movement that it could not be said of him he was awkwardly out of place anywhere. The genial frankness of his address was the western touch about him, which made him acceptable in a society where his manner of speech might have been resented as a personal reflection. It even outweighed the impression produced by the seal ring he wore. That it was not the outward and visible expression of a mellow friendliness of nature did not matter. What did matter was that it made life much simpler and more agreeable for Jerry Barclay.

"What am I doing up here?" he said in answer to the older man's question. "Looking after my interests. What else would bring a man into these trails? There's an old claim of my father's out Thompson's Flat way, that they've been getting up a fairy tale about. Ever since the Buckeye Belle's panned out so well they keep inventing yarns down below that sound like forty-nine. But the Buckeye Belle *has* made a strike, Forsythe tells me."

"The Gracey boys are here to-night. They'll tell you all about it. Black Dan won't have anything else to do."

The younger man pursed his lips for a whistle of surprise.

"That's luck," he said. "What's Black Dan Gracey doing in a center of civilization like this?"

"Bringing his daughter in for a dance. We've got a party on here to-night. Go into your room and primp up the best you know how. Dancing men are short."

The young man laughed, a deep, jolly laugh.

"Timed it just right, didn't I? Do you suppose the belles of Foleys will take me this way, travel-stained and weary? I'd like to see Black Dan's daughter. They say she promises to be a beauty."

"Promises!" echoed the Colonel; "she kept that promise some time ago. She's sixteen years old, my boy, and she can take your pelt and nail it to the barn door whenever she's a mind to."

The other turned away to the open door of the room Forsythe had lit up for him.

"Sixteen!" he said. "Oh, that's too young! No, Colonel, I've not got to the age when sixteen attracts. But you ought to be just about there. So long! You'll see me later looking on at your gambols with the sixteen-year-older."

His boyish laugh issued from the room, and as the Colonel went down stairs he could hear it above the swishing of water and the sound of smitten crockery.

From below the first tentative whinings of the violins rose, and as he reached the lower hall he heard the rattling of vehicles and the sound of voices as the earlier guests began to arrive. To the right of the hall he discovered Black Dan, secluded in a small room reserved by Forsythe for honored patrons, smoking tranquilly as he tilted back in a wooden arm-chair. The Colonel joined him, and for an hour the smoke of their cigars mingled amicably as they talked over the mining prospects of the district, and the Colonel's scheme for the development of his mineral spring.

It was near nine and the dance had passed its initial stage of bashful gaiety, when they strolled down the balcony to where the windows of the dining-room cast elongated squares of light into the darkness. This room, built on the angle of the house, had a door in the front, flanked by two windows, and down the long side a line of four more windows. Before each aperture there was a gathering of shadowy shapes, the light gilding staring faces.

At the first window the two men stopped and looked in. The dining-room, with its wooden walls, low ceiling and board floor, framed like an echoing shell the simple revel. Its bareness had been decorated with long strands of colored paper, depending from points in the ceiling and caught up in the corners. At intervals along the walls kerosene lamps, backed by large tin reflectors, diffused a raw, bright light, each concave tin throwing a shadow like a stream of ink down the boards below it. In a corner the three musicians worked with furious energy, one blowing a cornet and two scraping violins. A square dance was in progress, and at intervals the man who played the larger violin, his chin dug pertinaciously into the end of his instrument, yelled in strident tones:

"Swing your pardners! Ladies to the right. Shassay all."

Black Dan, satisfied by the first glance that his daughter was provided with a partner, retraced his steps and took a seat at the deserted end of the balcony, whence the red tip of his cigar came and went against a screen of darkness. The Colonel, much interested, remained looking in.

It was an innocently spirited scene, every participant seeming bent on exacting his full share of enjoyment from the fleeting hour. There were girls who had driven in fifteen and twenty miles from the camps and ranches scattered through the district, and who, flushed and excited, were bounding through the measure with an energy which made the floor vibrate. Their partners, also drawn from a radius of twenty miles about Foleys, were of many varieties, from the few mining superintendents of the neighborhood to some of the underground workers on the Buckeye Belle.

Mitty, clad in maidenly white muslin confined by a blue sash, was evidently much in demand. Her dancing, which was marked by a romping vigor, had loosened her hair, and a half-looped brown braid sent a scattering of hair-pins along the floor. Her partner, the proprietor of the local livery stable, was conducting her through the mazes of the dance with many fancy steps. An occasional haughty glance, a loudly defiant quality in her laugh, and the pert air with which she flounced through the figures, indicated to the watcher that she was acutely conscious of Barney Sullivan, leaning against the wall opposite and eying her with jealous, hang-dog adoration.

In this assemblage of rustic beauty, red, over-heated, and somewhat blowsy, Mercedes Gracey looked smaller, finer and more delicately finished than she had in the afternoon glow, with nature for a background. That she should be participating with obvious pleasure in such an humble entertainment did not surprise the Colonel, used to the democratic leveling of ranks that obtained in foot-hill California. It did not strike him as any more remarkable than that she should be enjoying the society of Joe Mosely, who kept the Sunset Saloon at Thompson's Flat, and twenty years before, in the days of his own and the state's uncontrolled youth, had "killed his man" and narrowly escaped lynching in Hangtown.

The watcher's eye left her with reluctance, for a man at any age, even with a heart cold to the appeal of woman, will linger on the spectacle of youthful beauty. Then his glance swept the wall behind her, where the opened windows were filled with men's heads, and along the upper end of which a bench ran. On this bench sat a young woman, alone, her head, in profile toward him, thrown out like a painting against the wooden background.

The Colonel's gaze stopped with a suddenness which suggested the snapping of an internal spring. A fixed, rigid gravity of observation swept all humor from his face, leaving it staring, absorbed, marked with lines. There was nothing about the girl to warrant this access of motionless interest. No better proof could be given of the fact that she was not in any way beautiful or pretty than that, at the very height of the dance, she was evidently partnerless.

Dejection marked her attitude and the youthful profile which she presented to the watcher. Her body had settled back against the wall in a pose of apathetic acquiescence, her hands in her lap, her small feet, which her short skirt revealed, limply crossed. Her dress, of a soft yellowish material, spotted at intervals with a crimson flower, set with some degree of grace and accuracy over the lines of her slightly developed, childish figure. Her feet and hands, the latter showing red against the white forearm that her half-sleeve left bare, were in keeping with the air of fragile smallness which seemed to add a touch of extra pathos to her neglected condition. She did not look like the country girls about her. The Colonel noticed that her hair was cut short as a boy's. Round the ear and temple that he could see, longer hairs curled slightly.

His immovable scrutiny lasted for some minutes. Then he threw his cigar into the darkness, and, pushing by the loungers at the door, entered the room and threaded his way through the dancers to where she sat. In the noise about her she did not hear his approach or know that any one was near, till he sat down on the bench beside her and said,

"You don't seem to be dancing?"

She started and turned a face upon him, the surprise of which was partly dispersed by hope of cheer. It was a charming face, if not a pretty one; the skin of a soft, warm pallor, the chin pointed, the mouth small, the middle of the upper lip drooping in a slight point on the lower. Her eyes of a clear, greenish-brown, showed an unusually straight line of under lid. A smile born of relief and the desire to be ingratiating hovered on her lips, and brought into being a dimple in one cheek.

In the first moment of encounter the Colonel saw all these details. The profile had struck him into a trance-like fixity of observation. Now at the full face, the smile with which he had accompanied his words died away. He stared at her for a moment speechless and motionless. And then, with a muttered ejaculation, he half turned from her and looked at the dancers.

The girl was amazed, for she had never seen him before. Her hopes of a partner were forgotten in her alarmed surprise at the demeanor of the person she thought had come to succor her in a dreary hour. She sat looking at him, wondering what to say and nervously rolling the wad of handkerchief she held from hand to hand.

The next moment he had turned back to her, commanding his features into the conventional smile of young acquaintance.

"I must beg your pardon," he said, "for speaking to you without an introduction, but I thought you'd let an old fellow like me come over here and have a few moments' talk. I don't dance, you see, and so I was having a pretty lonely time out there on the piazza."

His eyes roamed over her face, their eagerness of inspection curiously at variance with his careless words. Her surprise vanished instantly; she turned herself a little that she might more directly face him. She was evidently delighted to have any companion. Looking at him, she smiled with pleased relief and said in a singularly sweet voice,

"Oh, I'm so glad you came! I've been sitting here just this way for ever so long. I haven't danced for three dances. Joe Mosely asked me and then nobody has since. I thought I'd go home, it was so lonesome."

At the sound of her voice, marked not only by a natural sweetness of tone, but by a refinement of pronunciation very rare among the inhabitants of the country districts, the Colonel was again thrown into numbed, staring silence. He felt that he should have liked to rise and walk back and forth for a moment and shake himself, in order to awake from the strange and poignant memories this girl's face and voice brought up. He was recalled to himself by seeing the smile slowly freezing on her lips, and the confidence of her eyes becoming clouded with alarm.

"The child will think I'm mad," he thought, and said aloud: "You've startled me and I guess I've done the same to you. But you look very like—extraordinarily like—some one, some one, I once knew."

She was immediately at her ease again.

"I look like my mother," she said. "Every one says that."

"Where is your mother?" he asked absently, surveying her with a renewed, wary intentness.

"Here," she answered.

"Here?" he queried, looking round the room—"where?"

"Oh, not here to-night"—she looked away from him and gave a quick, short sigh—"home, I mean. Mother's quite sick. Sometimes I think she's very sick."

Her face, which was one of the most flexible mobility, lost all its brightness. Her eyes looked mournfully at him, pleading for a contradiction.

"Perhaps," he said with the rush of pity that he felt for all small feeble things, especially feminine feeble things, "she's not as sick as you think. When you live with a person who is sick you're apt to think them worse than outsiders do."

"Well, perhaps so," she acquiesced, immediately showing symptoms of brightening. "It probably seems queer to you that I should be here to-night when mother's sick. But she and father and Rosamund insisted on my coming. They wanted me to go to a party for once anyway, and have a good time. But I haven't had a good time at all. Just before you came I thought I'd go home, I felt so miserable sitting here alone. Only two people have asked me to dance."

"You've not been in Foleys very long?" the Colonel suggested, in order to account for this strange lack of gallantry on the part of the country swains.

"Three years; nearly four now," she said, looking at him with raised eyebrows. "Of course, I don't know as many people as Mitty Bruce does. And then there are some of the men round here mother never liked us to know. They——"

She paused, evidently considering that she had better not reveal the reasons why she had been cautioned against certain of the local beaux. But her spirit was weak, and her companion not making any comment, she moved a little nearer to him on the bench and said in a lowered key,

"Some of them occasionally get drunk!"

"Occasionally," agreed the Colonel, nodding darkly.

"So I don't know so very many. But I thought I'd know enough to have partners. But you never can tell. And then my hair makes me look such a fright. I might have had more partners if it had been longer."

She passed a small hand, which he noticed was rough and red, over her cropped crown, ruffling the short locks on her forehead.

"How—how did it come to be so?" he asked, looking at it with admiration tinged with curiosity.

"I've been sick. I was very sick last winter with a fever, and so in April when I was getting better they cut it all off. We had a bad winter up here, it was so terribly wet. I never saw anything worse; our house leaked all over."

"It was a wet winter," he assented. "And I heard it was a good deal worse up here than it was down below."

"It was dreadful. The rains were so heavy even in March that a big piece of land near where we live slid down. Where it used to be just a slope it's now like a precipice. And with mother sick and all the trouble to keep things warm and dry, I got the fever. That's why they made me come to-night—just to have a little amusement, mother said, because I'd had such a hard winter. And we made this dress—" she touched the skirt with a hand that betrayed a conscious feminine satisfaction in her apparel—"it's some stuff mother had, very good stuff. We couldn't have afforded to buy anything like it, and I don't think you could here at Foleys. But we did spend something. These flowers—" she indicated two bunches of artificial red roses at her neck and belt—"we bought them. They were a dollar; fifty cents each bunch."

She touched the bunch at her waist with a light, arranging hand, saw something which made her brows contract and her fingers seize on the flowers and drag them hurriedly away from their resting place. Where they had been a red stain—dye from the cheap leaves—disfigured her dress.

She stared at it for a moment, and then looked up at the Colonel in blank, heart-stricken dismay.

"Why, look what they've done," she faltered.

The Colonel for a moment was nonplussed. He had no consolation for such a catastrophe. The girl seized her handkerchief and rubbed the mark with dainty energy. The red dye was imparted to the handkerchief but the stain was only enlarged.

"Mother's dress!" she moaned, rubbing distractedly. "Why, she kept it for years in the trunk, waiting for some such time as this to come. And now look at it!"

She raised tragic eyes to the Colonel's face. He would have delighted in offering her another dress—anything she had chosen to buy. But she was a lady and this he could not do. So he sat looking sympathetically at her, inwardly swearing at the social conventions which made it impossible for him to repair the damage. He felt a man's pity for the meanness of the disaster that had such a power to darken and blight one poor little girl's horizon.

"Don't rub any more," was all he could say, "I'm afraid it's only making it worse. Maybe your mother will know of some way of cleaning it."

The girl made no reply for the moment. He could see that the mishap had completely dashed her spirits. She unpinned the other bunch, which had left an even uglier mark at her throat, and laid them down beside her on the bench.

"What an unlucky evening!" she exclaimed, looking down at them with an air of utter dejection. "Only two people ask me to dance, and the flowers we paid a dollar for spoil my dress, my first party dress. And they all wanted me to come because I was going to have such a good time!"

She looked from her flowers to her stained dress, shaking her head slowly as though words were inadequate to express the direness of the catastrophe. The Colonel was afraid she was going to cry, but she showed no symptom of tears. She seemed a strayed member of the class which is taught to control its lachrymal glands in public and keep its violent emotions out of sight. But her face showed a distress that was to him extremely pitiful.

"Cheer up," he said. "As far as the dancing goes the evening's only half over. And partners—you don't want to dance with these country bumpkins."

He lowered his voice at the words, which were indeed rank heresy in the democratic purlieus of Foleys, and made a surreptitious gesture which swept the room.

"Who else is there?" said the girl, who did not show any tendency to combat his low opinion of Foleys' *jeunesse dorée*. "And when you come to a party you expect to dance."

"I'll get something better for you than that," said the Colonel, rising. "Wait here for a minute or two. I won't be gone long and I'll bring you back somebody worth having for a partner."

She smiled faintly at him, and he turned, passed through the circling whirl of dancers, and stepped out on the balcony again.

She Smiled Faintly at Him

By an adjacent window he saw two masculine figures and smelt the pungent odor of the superior tobacco with which they were beguiling the passing hour. Rion Gracey's face, gilded by the light of the window, was toward him. The well-shaped back which the other presented to his gaze he recognized as that of Jerry Barclay. He bore down upon them, clapping one hand upon Barclay's shoulder, with the words,

"Look here, you fellows, I want partners for a girl in there."

Gracey frowned and said demurringly,

"Now, Jim, what's the use of coming down on me? Don't you know I'm no dancing man?"

The other answered,

"Let's see the girl first. Where is she?"—looking in through the window—"the one over there in pink? Oh, we don't deserve that. What's the matter with your being the Good Samaritan and dancing with her yourself?"

"It's not the one in pink, and you've got to come. The poor little thing hasn't had but two partners this evening and it's most broken her heart. Here, come along! I'm going to see that she has some fun before this metropolitan orgy ends."

Gracey threw away his cigar with a suppressed groan of acquiescence. The other man, shaking his coat into shape, said,

"Lead on. Beauty in distress always appeals to me. Having rounded us up you may as well lose no time in taking us to the sacrifice."

The Colonel with his prizes at his heels reëntered the room. The two men looked very different in the light of the kerosene lamps. Gracey having resolved to do what he had been asked, hid his unwillingness under a demeanor of stiff gravity. Barclay was evidently amused and not averse to following out the adventure. His look of a different world was more marked than ever by contrast with the clumsy country-men about him, but his capacity to adjust himself to all environments made him cross the room with an easy grace, when his companion was obviously out of his element.

The Colonel, flanked by his reinforcements, came to a stand before the young girl. She looked up, smiling, her eye lighting on one man and then on the other. She was surprised, delighted, a trifle embarrassed, as the men could see by a sudden access of color in her cheeks.

"Here," said the Colonel, "are two gentlemen who have been outside watching us and dying to come in and have a dance. Will you take pity on them, Miss—Miss—" he paused, suddenly realizing that he did not know her name.

"Miss," he stammered for the third time, and then bent down toward her and said in a lowered voice,

"My dear young lady, forgive me, but you know I don't know what your name is."

"My name?" she said, smiling. "Why, how funny! My name is Allen, June Allen. My father is Beauregard Allen and we live on the Parrish tract."

The Colonel straightened himself suddenly, almost flinching. The two men were looking at the girl and the girl at them, so that none of the trio noticed his expression. He cleared his throat before he spoke.

"Allen," he said, "Miss Allen, let me introduce Mr. Rion Gracey and Mr. Barclay."

The introductions were acknowledged and as the men sat down on either side of the no longer lonely young woman the Colonel, with a short "Good night," turned and left them.

He passed quickly through the dancing-room on to the balcony, his body erect, his eyes staring straight before him. The name of Allen was loud in his ears. It had struck like a dagger thrust through the trained indifference of years and torn open an old wound.

CHAPTER IV
O, MINE ENEMY!

In his room he lit the lamp and flung the window wide. It opened on the upper balcony, and through the foliage of the locusts he could see the lights of the town, and farther up, between the interstices of the branches, pieces of the night sky sown with stars. The scent of the drooping blossoms was heavy on the air. From below the music came softened, and the house vibrated with the rhythmic swing of the dance. He stood for a moment staring upward and absently listening, then went back into his room, and sat down by the table, his head propped on his hand.

The old wound, so suddenly torn open, was bleeding. The lonely man seemed to feel the slow drops falling from it. Passion and despair, dulled by time, were suddenly endowed with the force they had had twenty-one years ago. They had the vitality of a deathless tragedy.

The time of his courtship and engagement to Alice Joyce had been that period when he had held happiness in his arms and thought that she would stay for ever. Alice had been a school-teacher in Sacramento, an orphan girl sent out from Boston in forty-nine to join relatives already settled in California. Her parents had been people of means and she had been highly educated. But her father had lost his money and then died, and Alice had been forced to earn her living. She was young, gentle-mannered and very pretty. Her daughter—that girl down stairs—was surprisingly, appallingly like her, only Alice had been prettier. Her face in its soft youth rose before him. It was the face of the girl down stairs touched with a clearer bloom, the lips redder, the cheeks more delicately rounded. But the eyes with the straight lower lid and the greenish-brown iris were the same, and so was the pointed chin and the one dimple.

He had been a miner, doing his work with the others in the great days on the American River, when he met her on a trip to Sacramento. He was thirty-four and had cared little for women till then, but he loved her from the first without hesitation or uncertainty. She was his mate, the other half of him who would round out and perfect his life. That he had nothing was of no matter. There was always a living for the man who worked in those uncrowded days, and Jim Parrish was a worker, a mighty man with the pick, who could stand knee deep in the water all day, and at night sleep the sleep of the just on the dry grass under the stars.

Those had been Jim Parrish's great days, "the butt and sea-mark of his sail." Life had unrolled before him like a map, all pleasant rivers and smiling plains. At intervals he went to Sacramento to see Alice. She had other suitors, but she was his from the first, and nestled inside the protection of this strong man's love with the tender trust of her soft and dependent nature.

Parrish had one friend and confidant, John Beauregard Allen. They had crossed the Isthmus together in forty-eight, had roomed together in the sprawling town scattered about the curve of San Francisco Bay, had rushed to the foot-hills when the mill race at Sutter's Creek startled the world with its sediment of yellow dust. Once in a gambling-house in Sonora, Parrish had struck up the revolver which threatened his friend's life, the bullet ripping its way across his own shoulder in a red furrow he would carry to his death.

Allen was a Southerner, a South Carolinian of birth and education, a man of daring and adventurous character, possessed of unusual good looks and personal charm. To Parrish, a simpler nature, born and reared in poverty in a small town in western New York, the brilliant Southerner was all that was generous, brave and chivalrous. The friendship between the two men was of a strength that neither thought could ever be broken. The one subject of friction between them was slavery, already beginning to burn in the thoughts and speech of men. Allen's father was a wealthy slave-owner, and the son was in California to satisfy his spirit of adventure and to conquer fortune on his own account. He was one of that large colony of Southerners, in some cases blatant and pretentious, in others brilliant and large-hearted, which in later years gave tone to the city, formed its manners, established its code of morals, and tried to direct its political life.

The rude environment of the mines was distasteful to him, and he returned to San Francisco where, backed by his father, he started in business. Letters passed between the friends, and as Parrish's courtship progressed he poured out his heart to Allen in pages that, in after years, he remembered with impotent fury. All the hopes and aspirations of his new life, when a woman should be beside him and a woman's hand should be clasped in his, were told to his absent friend. At length, after an engagement of some weeks, the date for the marriage was set. Before this took place Alice wished to visit her relatives, who lived in San Francisco, and there buy the trousseau for which she had been saving her salary. Parrish reluctantly consented to her departure. While she was gone he would build for his bride a cottage in Hangtown where his mining operations were then conducted. Before she left he wrote a letter to Beauregard Allen giving him her address and asking him to call on her.

Alice's visit of a month lengthened to two. Her letters, which at first had been full of Allen's name, toward the middle of the second month contained little or no mention of him. Her excuse for the postponing of her return was that the work of dressmakers had been slower than she had expected. Also her relatives had urged upon her to prolong her stay, as they did not know when they might see her again.

A less blind lover might have seen matter for uneasiness in the more reserved tone, the growing brevity of these letters. A suspicious lover might have wondered why Allen had not only ceased to praise the charm and beauty of his friend's betrothed, but had almost entirely stopped writing. Jim Parrish was disturbed by neither uneasiness nor suspicion. That sweetheart and friend could combine to deal him the deadly blow in store for him was beyond his power of imagination.

Finally a date was set for Alice's return. Her clothes were all bought, packed and paid for. Her last letter, the tone of which for the first time struck him as constrained and cold, told him the steamer on which she would arrive and the hour it was due. Before this Parrish had written to Allen, urging his attendance at his wedding and suggesting that he act as Alice's escort on the trip to Sacramento. To this his friend had replied that he would do so if possible, but the demands of his business were engrossing. The cottage at Hangtown was finished and furnished as well as the bridegroom's scanty means would permit. In a dream of joy he left it, went down to Sacramento, bought the few clothes that went to the making of his wedding outfit, and then waited for the steamer with the high, exalted happiness of the man who is about to be united to the woman he honestly loves.

When the steamer arrived neither Allen nor Alice was on board. He was stunned at first, not having had the least anticipation of such a catastrophe. Then a fear that she might be sick seized upon him and he sought the captain for any information he might have. Contrary to his expectation, the captain was full of information. The lady and gentleman had boarded the steamer at San Francisco, holding through tickets for Sacramento. After they had passed Contra Costa, however, the gentleman had come to him, telling him of a sudden change in their plans and urging him to put them ashore at the first stopping place. This he had done at Benecia. He had heard one of them say something about going to San José. The lady, however, would explain it more satisfactorily in the letter she had left, and he handed Parrish a letter addressed in Alice's writing.

The listener had been dazed during the first part of the captain's recital. He could not understand what had happened, only an icy premonition of evil clutched his heart. Alice's letter cleared up all uncertainty.

In a few blotted, incoherent lines she told him of her intention to leave the steamer with Allen, cross to San José, and there marry him. Her love for her fiancé had been shriveled to ashes before the flame of the Southerner's fiery wooing. But she averred that she had in the beginning repulsed his attentions, fully intending to return to Sacramento and fulfill her engagement with Parrish. She had not known Allen intended accompanying her on the trip to Sacramento. Had she known, she never would have permitted it. It was on the steamer that he had finally prevailed over her conscience and beaten down her scruples, till she had agreed to elope with him.

Jim Parrish never knew how he reached his hotel room that evening. He sat there a long time—a day and a night he thought—staring at his wedding clothes spread on the bed. What roused him from his benumbed condition was a newspaper from San José bearing a marked announcement of the marriage. A letter from Allen followed this. It was short but characteristically grandiloquent. In it he stated that he had broken the sacred obligations of friendship, but that his passion for the woman had overborne every other sentiment. He was from henceforward an outcast from honest men, a fitting punishment for one who had held his honor as his dearest possession, and who had brought a blot upon a heretofore stainless name.

The letter roused Parrish like a hand on his neck. It was so like the writer, with its theatrical pose and its high talk of his honor and his name. A flood of fury rose in the betrayed man, and he walked the streets of the city with murder in his heart. Had he met his one-time friend he would have rushed upon him and stamped and beaten his life out. Feelings of hatred he had never known he could harbor burned in him. At night he walked for miles, his hands clenched as he struggled with these unfamiliar demons that seemed tearing the ligaments of his life apart.

For Alice his love neither changed nor ceased. He believed her to have been overborne by Allen, carried off her feet by the reckless impetuosity he himself had once thought so dazzling. If Allen had left her alone, if when he felt love rise in him, he had withdrawn from her, Parrish knew that the girl would have remained true to him and now would be his wife, nestled in his arms, asking no better resting place. At times, in the lonely watches of the night, he thought that, but for the false friend, she would have been beside him, her head against his shoulder, her light breath touching his cheek as she slept. It goaded him up and out into the darkness torn by the rage that drives men to murder.

Then, his first fury spent, he tried to rearrange his life—to begin again. He gave the cottage at Hangtown to his partner and moved his mining operations to Sonora. Soon after he began to meet with his first small successes. Now that he had no need for money it came to him. By the time the Civil War broke out he was a man of means and mark.

Once or twice in these years he heard of John Beauregard Allen and his wife. They had prospered for a time, then bad luck had fallen upon them. Allen's father, reputed a rich man, died insolvent, leaving nothing but debts. Allen's own business in San Francisco had failed and they had left there in the fifties. Once, just before the war, stopping for a day or two at Downieville, Parrish had accidentally heard that they had been living there and that Mrs. Allen had lost a little boy, her only son. He had left by the first stage, his heart gripped by the thought of Alice, a mother, mourning for her dead child.

In sixty he had returned to the East to fight for the Union. Five years later he came back as Colonel Parrish, a title earned by distinguished services to his country. It was said by his friends that Jim Parrish would have been a millionaire if he had stayed by his mines and his investments as other men had. But Parrish had cared more for the Union than for money. And, after all, what good was money to him! Often in the four years of battle and bloodshed he had wondered if he ever would meet Beauregard Allen face to face in the smoke, and whether, if he did, the thought of a woman and children would hold his hand. But he never did. He learned afterward that Allen had remained in California.

After his return from the war he heard of them only once. This was in a club in San Francisco, where a mining superintendent, recently back from Virginia City, casually mentioned the fact that Beauregard Allen, a prominent figure in early San Francisco, was holding a small position in the assay office there. In the succeeding four or five years they dropped completely out of sight. It seemed to him that what had long been an open wound was now a scar. Peace, the gray peace of a heart that neither hopes nor desires, was his.

And suddenly without warning or expectation, his old enemy was standing in his path. Allen the squatter, the man who was claiming *his* land, the man whose children had been improving it, was John Beauregard Allen! It was Alice's daughter who had been sitting on the bench in her poor dress with her coarsened hands. It was Alice who was the "mother" that was sick.

He rose from his seat with a groan, and going to the window pushed aside the curtain and looked out. The lamp behind him sputtered and, sending a rank smell into the air, went out. The day was dawning. A pale gray light mounted the sky behind the locust trees quivering each moment into a warmer brightness.

By its searching clearness the Colonel's face looked old and worn. It was a face of a leathern brownness of skin, against which the white hair and gray mustache stood out in curious contrast. The brows were bushy, the eyes they shadowed clear gray, deep-set and steady, with an under-look of melancholy always showing through their twinkle of humor. There was no humor in them now. They were old and sad, the lines round them deep as were those that marked the forehead under its rough white hair.

Through the branches of the trees he could see the slopes of his own land, the thick dark growth of chaparral muffling the hillside, and on its crest the glow of the east barred by the trunks of pines. As he remembered, the cottage was somewhere below them, on the edge of the cleared stretch which ran along the road. They were there—Alice and her children, beggars on the land Beauregard Allen was trying to steal from him.

CHAPTER V
THE SUMMONS

Later on in the morning the Colonel waked from a few hours of uneasy slumber. He had thrown himself dressed on his bed and dropped into a sleep from which he had been roused by the morning sounds of Foleys. The lethargy and depression of the night of memories clung heavily to him, and as he dressed he decided that he would leave the camp that morning, sending word to Cusack the lawyer that he would let the matter of the squatter rest for a few days.

As he left the dining-room after breakfast, he was accosted by a stable-man, who informed him that Kit Carson was inclined to "go tender" on one of his front feet. The man did not know when the Colonel intended leaving, but if it was that day he would advise him to "wait over a spell" and let Kit "rest up." Nearly a hundred and forty miles in thirty-six hours—especially with the sun so hot at midday, was a pretty serious proposition even for Kit Carson.

The Colonel stood silent for a moment looking at the man from under frowning brows. It would be possible for him to take one of Forsythe's horses, ride to Milton, and there get the Stockton stage. Forsythe's boy could ride Kit back to Sacramento when his front foot ceased to be tender. But after all, what was the use of running from the situation? There it was, to be thought out and dealt with. It was Fate that had lamed the never tired or disabled Kit just at this juncture.

With a word to the man that he would stay over till the horse was in proper condition, he passed through the hall and along the balcony to the side which flanked the dining-room. Its boarded length was deserted, with, before each window, a social gathering of chairs as they had been arranged by on-lookers during last night's revel. A long line of locust trees, their foliage motionless in the warm air, grew between the hotel fence and the road, throwing the balcony in a scented shade.

Between their trunks the Colonel could survey the main street of Foleys, already wrapped in its morning state of somnolence, its unstirred dust beaten upon by a relentless blaze of sun. Under the covered sidewalk a shirt-sleeved figure now and then passed with loitering step, or a sun-bonneted woman picked her way through the dust. The male population of the camp was, for the most part, gathered in detached groups which marked the doorways of saloons. Each member of a group occupied a wooden arm-chair, had his heels raised high on a hitching bar, his hat well down on his nose, while a spiral of smoke issued from beneath the brim. Now and then some one spoke and the Colonel could see the heads under the tilted hats slowly turning to survey the speaker. At intervals, however, a word was passed of sudden, energizing import. It roused the group which rose as a man and filed into the saloon. When they emerged, they seated themselves, the silence resettled, and all appeared to drowse. The one being who defied the soporific effect of the hour was an unseen player on the French horn who beguiled the morning stillness with variations of the melody, *When this Cruel War is Over*.

The Colonel, smoking his morning cigar, surveyed the outlook with the unseeing eyes of extreme preoccupation. He did not even notice the presence of the saddled horse which a stable-man had led up to the gate just below where he sat. Some louder admonition of the man's to the fretting animal finally caught his ear and his fixed eyes fell on it.

It was a stately creature, satin-flanked and slender-legged, stamping and shaking its long mane in its impatience. The neat pack of the traveler was tied behind the saddle.

"Whose horse is that, Tom?" said the Colonel, knowing its type strange to Foleys. "Didn't the Gracey boys go back last night?"

"Yes. The whole Buckeye Belle outfit rode back at three. This is Jerry Barclay's horse. He's goin' on this morning to Thompson's Flat. Barclay rid him up from Stockton—won't take no livery horse. Has this one sent up on the boat."

As the man spoke the Colonel heard a quick step on the balcony behind him, and the owner of the horse came around the corner, smiling, handsome, debonair in his loose-fitting clothes, long riding boots and wide-brimmed hat.

"Morning, Colonel," he said; "I see the tropical calm of Foleys is affecting you. Take example by me—off for twenty miles across country to Thompson's Flat."

He ran down the steps and out into the road. There, standing in the dust putting on his gloves, he let a quick, investigating eye run over his horse.

"I intended starting at sun-up," he said, "and then they went and forgot to wake me. Now I have to ride twenty miles over roads a foot deep in dust and under a sun as hot as a smelting furnace."

"Shouldn't have been so dissipated last night," said the Colonel. "What time did you get to bed?"

The young man, who was adjusting his stirrup, turned round.

"Oh, that was the dearest little girl last night. Where'd you find her? And how did a girl like that ever grow up in a God-forsaken spot like Foleys?"

He vaulted into the saddle not waiting for an answer. Then as his horse, curvetting and backing in a last ecstasy of impatience, churned up a cloud of dust, he called,

"I'm quite fascinated. Going to stop over on my way back. Give May or April or June or whatever her name is, my love. *Hasta mañana*, old man!"

The horse, at length liberated, plunged forward and dashed up the road, the soft diminishing thud of its hoofs for a moment filling the silence. The stable-man slouched lazily off, and the Colonel was once more left to his cigar and his meditations.

These were soon as deeply engrossing as ever. With his eyes looking down the sun-steeped street he was not aware of a blue-clothed feminine figure which came into view along the highway upon which the balcony fronted. At first she walked quickly in a blaze of sun, then crossed the road, charily holding up her skirt, and approached in the shadow of the locusts. She wore a blue-and-white cotton dress, a sun-burnt straw hat, trimmed with a blue ribbon, and as she drew near was revealed to be a young girl in the end of her teens, large, finely-shaped, and erect.

Walking on the outside of the fence she eyed the Colonel for a scrutinizing moment, then stopping at the gate, opened it with a slight click, and stood hesitating. He heard the sound, looked up, and met her eyes—blue and inquiring—fixed gravely on him. She had a firmly-modeled, handsome face, full of rich, youthful tints and mellow curves. Her straw hat sent a clean wash of shade to just below her nose. Under this, in the blinding steadiness of the sunlight, her mouth and chin, the former large and with strongly curved lips, looked as smooth and fresh as portions of a ripe fruit. There was hesitation but no embarrassment in her attitude. Even at this first glance one might guess that this was a young woman devoid of self-consciousness and not readily embarrassed.

"Are you Colonel Parrish?" she said in a rather loud, clear voice.

He rose, throwing away his cigar, and replied with an affirmative that he tried not to make astonished.

She ascended the steps, again hesitated, and then held out a sun-burnt hand.

"I'm glad I found you," she said, as he released it. "I thought perhaps you might have gone on to the Buckeye Belle. Everybody goes there now. My name is Allen, Rosamund Allen. You met my sister June last night."

"Oh," murmured the Colonel, and then he gave a weak, "Of course. Sit down."

He was glad of the moment's respite that getting her a chair and placing it gave him. She was the second daughter. In that first glance of startled investigation he had seen no particular likeness to either parent. This girl would not tear his heart by looking at him with her mother's eyes.

"I—I—enjoyed meeting your sister last night," he said as they found themselves seated facing each other. "She—she—" He did not know what to say. He wondered why the girl had come. Had some one sent her?

She looked at him with her clear, calm eyes, cool and interested. She was unquestionably handsomer than her sister. A year or two younger he guessed, though much larger, a typical Californian in her downy bloom of skin and fullness of contour. Her simple dress had been designed with taste and set with a grace that was imparted more by the beautiful lines of the body it covered than any particular skill in its fashioning. There was the same neatness and care of detail in her humble adornments that he had noticed in her sister's—the ineradicable daintiness of the woman whose forebears have lived delicately.

"June had such a good time last night," she said with an air of volubility. "At first she said it was dreadful. Hardly any one asked her to dance, and she didn't see how she could wait for father, who was going to call for her at twelve. And then you came and introduced those gentlemen to her. After that she had the loveliest time. She didn't want to go at all when father came. She made him wait till two!"

"I'm glad she enjoyed it. It was pretty dull for her at first. She didn't want to dance with the kind of men that were there. I was glad to introduce Rion Gracey to her. He's more or less of a neighbor of yours, according to foot-hill distances."

The Colonel was fencing, watching the girl and wondering why she had come. She had the air of settling down to a leisurely, enjoyable gossip.

"Yes. We never met him before. It's funny, because they've been here over a year; up at the Buckeye Belle, of course. But then, they ride in here all the time. I've often seen both the Graceys riding past our place. The road in from there goes by our land. You know where that is?—the long strip back there—" waving her hand in the direction of the Colonel's disputed acres—"where the tall pines are, and—"

She stopped, crimsoning to her hair. She had evidently suddenly realized to whom she was so glibly talking. There was no question but that she was embarrassed now. She bent her burning face down and began to make little pleats in her dress with her sun-burnt fingers.

"I know, I know," said the Colonel, exceedingly embarrassed himself, "right back there. Yes, of course. On the road that goes to Thompson's Flat. By the way, I hope your sister's dress wasn't seriously damaged last night. The dye coming off the flowers, I mean."

The girl heaved a breath of relief and tilted her head to one side regarding the pleats she had made from a different view point. For her age and environment her aplomb was remarkable.

"Yes, I'm afraid it's very badly marked. They were such cheap flowers. Mother thinks we can arrange something with rosettes."

She ceased her pleating, raised her head fully, and looked at him.

"Mother was so pleased and so astonished when she heard from June about meeting you. She used to know you well, she said—a long time ago, before she was married."

Her eyes looked innocently and gravely into his. There was no concealment in them. She was speaking frankly and honestly. Now the Colonel knew she had been sent. He braced himself for her coming words.

"Yes, I knew your mother," he said, hearing his voice sound husky. "But, as you say, it was a long time ago."

"Mother got quite excited when she heard it was you. You know she's not well and the least thing upsets her. She couldn't believe it at first. Then she wondered if you wouldn't come up and see her and sent me down to ask you."

Alice had sent her. After twenty-one years Alice had sent this message for him! And it was all so natural and simple—a moment that sometimes, in hours of melancholy brooding, he had thought of, and always seen fraught with tragic passion. He bent to pick up a locust blossom that a wandering zephyr had wafted along the balcony floor. For a moment he made no answer. He could not trust his voice. The girl continued, not noticing his silence.

"She doesn't see many people. She's sick, you know; June said she told you. And then there's not many people round here for her to see. I suppose you'll find her changed if you haven't seen her since she was married. She's changed a good deal lately, poor mother!"

She gave a sigh and looked away from him. The Colonel answered quickly:

"Oh, yes, I'll come, I'll come."

His visitor did not seem to notice anything unusual in his manner of accepting the invitation of an old friend. The trouble of her mother's changed condition was uppermost in her mind.

"I dare say you won't know it's the same person. But don't let her see that. We want her to be bright and cheerful, and if people look surprised when they see her it makes her think she's worse—" She looked anxiously at him, but his face was averted. There was a slight pause and then she said in a low voice:

"Mother has consumption, Colonel Parrish."

This time he turned and stared straight at her. Her eyes, full of sad meaning, were fixed on him. The other daughter's remarks had led him to suppose that Alice was suffering from some temporary illness. Now he knew that she was dying.

"It was Virginia City that did it," the girl continued. "She wasn't strong for years. A long time ago in Downieville our brother, younger than we were, died, and father always thought she never got over that. But in Virginia there were such hard winters and those awful winds blew so! We were there for two years before we came here; and she had pneumonia and after that she didn't get well. But we stayed on there, for father had some work in the assay office, and though everything cost a terrible price, it was better than what he got in the mines over here."

The Colonel was half turned from her in his chair. She could see his profile with the shaggy brows drawn over his eyes.

"She doctored there for a long time, and everything cost so much money! Then one day, one of the doctors told father she'd never get well if she stayed in that climate. 'Take her to California, to the foot-hills where the air's hot and dry,' he said, 'that's the only chance you've got.' So we sold everything and left Virginia and came over here. We tried several places, but some of them didn't seem to suit her, and in others they asked too high rents. We had hardly anything left. And then we just came here and settled on that—on our—on your—" She came to a stammering stop and then ended desperately—"in that empty cottage over there."

The Colonel rose and walked to the balcony rail. He stood for a moment with his back toward her, then slowly wheeled and approached her. She had risen and was looking at him with a perplexed expression.

"That's all right," he said, taking her hand. "I'll be up this afternoon. Will between four and five do?"

She considered as a town lady might whose day was full of engagements. She was, in fact, speculating as to whether she and her sister would be free from the domestic tasks which filled their waking hours.

"Yes," she said, nodding, "that'll be a very good time. Mother rests and we—we are busy in the early part of the afternoon."

She held out her hand to him, and as he walked down the steps beside her to the gate, again expressed her pleasure at having found him.

"June told me what you looked like," she said over the gate, eying him thoughtfully as if she intended giving June her opinion of the stranger's appearance. "So I knew if you were anywhere round I'd find you."

She smiled a last good-by and turned away to the walk under the locusts. The Colonel went back to his seat on the balcony. He lit a fresh cigar and sat there smoking till Mitty came to summon him to the midday dinner.

CHAPTER VI
THE OLD LOVE

At half-past four he was walking through the dust toward the cottage. The main feeling in his heart was dread. But he could not disregard Alice's summons—Alice's dying summons, he felt them to be. He tried to prepare himself by thinking that nearly a quarter of a century had passed, and what havoc it must have wrought. But he saw only the face of the girl he had loved, fresh and sweet, as it had been when he had bidden her good-by on the steamer on a morning full of sun and hope, twenty-one years ago.

He had left the town's main street behind and was now walking on a narrow footpath beside the road which, on one side, skirted his own land. A still, scorching warmth had possession of the hour. The landscape, glazed with heat, seemed to faint under the unwinking glare of sun. From the parched grassland and the thickets of chaparral, pungent scents arose—the ardent odors that the woods of foot-hill California exhale in the hot, breathless quiescence of summer afternoons.

His unseeing eye passed over the rise and fall of the rich tract he had held so negligently. The broken fence beside him divided an ocher-colored expanse of uncultivated land from the road. The air came over it in glassy waves, carrying its dry, aromatic perfume to his nostrils. On its burnt expanse a few huge live-oaks rose dark and dome-like, their shadows, black and irregular, staining the ground beneath them. Beyond the chaparral swept up the hillside, a close growing wall of variegated green where the manzanita glittered amid duller foliage. A splintered edge of rock broke slantingly through the thicket, rose and passed like a bristling crest over the top of the hill, where the pines lifted their plumy heads. It was the "outcrop" of the ledge—that inconsistent and ill-regulated ledge, the promises of which had made a town of Foleys and then, being unfulfilled, had left the town to ruin.

But the Colonel saw none of these things. His eyes were fixed on the turn of the road just beyond. As he remembered, you could see the cottage from there. And as he gained and passed it, the low bulk of the little house broke upon his sight. It was shrouded in vines, carefully trained over the projecting roof of its balcony so that they hung from its edge in a fringe of waving tendrils. Around and beyond it, the juicy, violent green of a vineyard ran into the dryness of the untilled land, and the even emerald rows and dark, loamy stripes of a garden lay like a piece of carpeting between the vineyard and the house. Its look of thrifty habitation came like a shock upon his memory of its ruinous neglect when he had last seen it. Even the gate, that he remembered hung dejected from one hinge, had been mended; the rose bushes that had thrown long festoons across the path had been clipped and tied to restraining poles. These were "the improvements" upon which the squatter based part of his claim.

The Colonel's hand, trembling, raised the gate latch with a click. As he did so he heard a sound from the balcony, and the younger girl, who had introduced herself to him as Rosamund Allen, ran down the steps that led from it and advanced along the path to meet him. Her hat was off and he saw that she had thick, fair hair, its ashen blondness streaked with strands of a coarse, bright gold.

"Here you are," she cried with her easy, friendly manner. "We had just begun to expect you. Isn't it hot?"

She fell into step beside him and they walked slowly up the little path. The cottage at first presented to his gaze only one end cut into by a single window. As they drew nearer he saw the length of its balcony, and that the vine he had noticed was a grape, its thick-twisted stalk running up to the roof like a pillar, its leafage engarlanding the balustrade. A few steps led to the balcony from the walk. He saw the black square of an open doorway and near this, sitting close to the leaf-trimmed balustrade, a shawled female figure in a lounging chair.

His eye fell on it and he involuntarily stopped. The girl beside him suddenly jerked his sleeve.

"That's mother," she said in a hurried whisper. "Take care. She can see us. Now don't look surprised—" then raising her voice a little she said:

"Mother dear, here's Colonel Parrish."

The Colonel, as he mounted the stairs, took off his hat and held it. The woman in the chair was facing him. From the descending folds of the many loose wrappings that hung about her emaciated figure, her head rose, the face looking at him with still, eager interest. She gave a little smile and a waxen hand of skeleton thinness emerged from the folds of her shawls.

"Jim Parrish!" she said in a sweet, husky voice, then looking into his face with eyes of mild, unconscious friendliness, she said softly, "Jim."

He would never have known her till he heard the voice and saw the smile. They were the same. The old dimple had disappeared and a wrinkle had taken its place. The eyes, the clear, greenish-brown eyes, were sunken into dark caverns, the satiny skin grown loose and sallow. Yet it was Alice, Alice old before her time, Alice sick, Alice dying.

He turned round and found a chair, for the moment not daring to speak. He was conscious of the figure of Rosamund walking toward the garden dragging a serpent-like length of hose behind her. Then he placed the chair close to the sick woman and sat down. To him it was a moment that he had thought of in dark reveries, and even in thought found too painful. Now he was conscious that there was a tranquillity about it, an absence of tension, which was due to Alice. Her manner suggested nothing but a peaceful recollection of old friendship. Was it that the near approach of death was wiping out all the disturbing and cruel emotions, all the biting memories, that belonged to life?

She looked at him with her little affectionate smile as a sick sister might.

"It's so queer it being you," she said. "When June told me I couldn't believe it. After—after—how long is it, Jim?"

"Twenty-one years," he said.

"Yes, twenty-one years," she repeated. "How time flies! And what a lot has happened in those twenty-one years. You're rich, they say. And your hair's quite white, but I'd have known you anywhere. You're not much changed."

She continued to look at him with the same gentle, softly exploring air. He had had an idea that even in death he would see shame and remorse in her eyes, but they were as devoid of either as though he had never been other than a girlhood friend.

"It was so odd your just happening on June that way. She says you were so kind to her, she felt immediately you were her friend. Poor little June! It was such an amusement for her that evening. She's not had much pleasure of that kind. And she's twenty now, just the age when a girl longs for a little of the good times of life."

"She's very like you," he answered, "it—it—" he was going to say "shocked me," but he had a feeling she would not understand him. "It surprised me," he said instead.

"Oh, she's very like me. Every one sees it. Her father says she is just a *replica* of what I was when he first knew me. And she's such a sweet, loving little thing. You don't know how they work here—and with me to take care of. God has blessed me in my children, Jim."

She turned her large, sunken eyes on him, their somberness lit by the fire of her maternal passion.

"They are the best girls in the world," she said.

"Then you've been happy, Alice?" he suddenly asked.

"Happy!" she echoed. "Oh, yes, always happy except when our boy died. That was our sorrow. I don't know whether you ever heard of it. He was just a baby, but he was our only son. A beautiful boy. He was John Beauregard Allen, too."

The Colonel made no comment, but she did not notice it, engrossed in her own recital.

"Of course we've not been very successful, especially of late years. But poverty's not so bad when you've got those you love around you. And we've been like a little company, close together, always marching shoulder to shoulder—'a close corporation,' Beau calls it. We've had bad luck of all kinds, but you can bear bad luck when you're all together."

The past, the bitter, terrible past was dead to her. She had probably never understood what it had been to him. Now twenty years of love and struggle had almost obliterated it from her memory, and the coming of death had wiped away its last faint traces.

"You *have* been blessed, Alice," he said in a low voice. "Life has fulfilled all your expectations."

"Not all," she answered. "What doesn't matter for yourself matters for your children. It's hard for me to see them living here, and this way—" she made a gesture which swept the garden and the vineyard. "That's hard for a mother, a mother who was bred differently and bred them for something different. I educated them myself, Jim. They're not like the country girls around us. They're—" she paused a moment and then said with an air of sad solemnity—"the children of a lady and a gentleman."

"Any one can see that," he murmured, "and they're happy too."

He did not know what else to say. He could not condole with her. In her poverty and sickness she had fulfilled the purposes of her life, lived it with a passionate completeness as he had never done. The fullness of it, compared to the barren emptiness of his, augmented the sense of bleak loneliness that lay heavy at his heart.

"They're young," she continued, "they've not known much better. Our bad times began when they were still little. But I—well, before I was sick it was different. I helped them and I was a companion, not a care. Virginia City, too, was a place where, as they grew older there would have been more amusement for them. They'd have had a better chance."

She paused, her lids drooping, an air of musing melancholy on her face. Then she raised her eyes and looked at him.

"Who is there for them to marry here?" she asked.

"Marry!"—the Colonel had not thought of that. "They're very young for that yet, aren't they?" he stammered.

"Young? Yes, perhaps. But June is twenty now."

She let her head drop back on the cushions behind it, and turned it slightly away from him so that he could see her in profile. Her hair was dressed in the fashion of her youth, parted and drawn down sleekly over the tips of her ears. Seen thus, the emaciation of her cheeks partly concealed, her face caught him with its sudden look of familiarity. For a moment the veil of years was jerked back and he saw his old sweetheart. He gave a murmured exclamation and leaned nearer to her, a word of tenderness trembling on his lips. Simultaneously she turned toward him, absorbed in her own thoughts.

"I was twenty-four when I married," she said. "People then thought that was quite old."

He turned away his head, unable to reply, and she went on in her unconscious egotism.

"I want them to marry. It's the only life for a woman. And I have been so happy in my married life, always, from the first till now."

A slight smile touched her lips as her eyes, softened with memories, looked back over a life that love had ennobled.

Suddenly she turned to him. For the first time in the conversation she seemed to transfer her interest from her own affairs to his.

"You never married?" she said. "That was a pity. Life's only half lived without those ties."

"Oh, Alice!" he answered with a groan, and rising he moved to the top of the steps.

"I was mean to you that time, long ago," she said behind him. "But that was all in the past. That's all forgotten now—forgotten and forgiven, isn't it?"

For the moment he made no reply and she repeated in what seemed an absent tone,

"Forgotten and forgiven. It's all so far away now; such years ago. So much has happened in between. It's like another life, looking back on it."

"Yes, all forgiven," he said, "there's no anger with real love."

"Of course not," she agreed, "and time smooths away everything. Isn't it pretty now, with the shadows lengthening out that way?"

They looked over the expanse where the low sun's rays were painting the already brilliant-hued landscape with a wild flare of color. The darkness of the oaks was overlaid with a golden gilding, the dry grass looked orange.

"Have you seen the girls' garden?" she asked. "They did it all themselves and they raise enough vegetables for us and some to sell. They sell the grapes, too. Last summer they made fifty dollars with their grapes."

So "the improvements" were of some practical good. The Colonel saw the word dancing in the air before him.

"But it's hard to see them working so. In summer they're up and out at six. It doesn't seem right to me—their father's daughters. Their grandmother—Beau's mother—had six house-slaves for her own private use, and I, before my father's death, had a French governess."

A step on the path prevented him from replying. Rosamund came around the corner of the house, her face flushed, a hoe in her hand, which he now saw to be earthy. She had an anxious air.

"Mother, are you tired, dear?" she said, mounting the steps. Then turning to the visitor:

"Mother goes in before the sun sets. It gets cool so suddenly. Just the moment the edge of the sun gets down behind the hill, the night comes up, and it's bad for her to breathe that air."

The Colonel assured her he was just about to take his leave. The invalid made no demand for him to stay. Sitting huddled among her shawls she looked wan and shrunken. He felt that the calm interest of her attitude toward him had now, from fatigue, turned suddenly into indifference. He faltered some words of farewell to her, his hand out. Hers, feeling in his warm, strong grasp like a bundle of twigs, was extended and then limply withdrawn.

"Good-by," she said, turning to follow her daughter's movements with a waiting, dependent eye, "won't you come again before you go?"

He murmured an assent from the top steps, but he would leave in a day or two at the longest.

"The girls like seeing you so much;" now she looked at him with some animation. "And they have so little pleasure."

"Why, mother," said Rosamund in half-laughing protest, "that sounds as if Colonel Parrish was a sort of circus, just here to amuse us."

The Colonel was nearly at the bottom of the steps. With some last conventional sentences of farewell, he raised his hat and turned toward mother and daughter for a final glance. They were smiling at Rosamund's words, both looking at him to return his bow with perfunctory politeness. When he turned from them he could hear their voices, low and full of a close and different form of interest, speaking of the adjustment of the invalid's shawls, the window by which her chair should be placed.

He was half-way down the path to the gate when a sound of suppressed singing caught his ear. Turning in its direction he saw coming down through a narrow path in the chaparral a fine red and white cow, and following it, June Allen. She was singing in a crooning, absent-minded way, at intervals flicking the flanks of the cow with a long alder branch she carried, stripped of all its leaves save two at the top. As she approached him she stopped singing, struck the cow with the branch, and began in a thoughtful way to talk to herself.

The attraction she had exercised over him fell on him again the moment he saw her. The very way she appeared to be conversing to herself seemed to him to be imbued with a quaint, unconscious charm, such as a child possesses. With his mind full of the gloom and pain of his interview with Alice, he yet paused, eying the approaching figure. As he stood watching her, she looked up and saw him.

She gave a loud exclamation and her face became illumined with pleasure. Administering to the cow a smart stroke with her switch, she crowded by it and ran forward over the dry grass into which the verdure of the garden intruded.

"Oh, how lovely for me to meet you!" she cried as she came up to him with an extended hand. "I never thought I'd have such luck."

Her hand nestled into his; her face smiling at him was charged with an almost fond delight.

"I'm afraid you're a flatterer, young woman," he said, again noting the astonishing likeness that had so shaken him the evening before. "I don't think you're really glad to see me, or why should you, when you knew I was coming, go off with the cow?"

"That was a bargain," she said, "I wanted to stay and see you just as much as Rosamund did. But as I had the party last night we agreed that it was only fair I should go after Bloss this evening, and Rosamund should stay and take care of mother and see you."

If any commentary was needed on the deadly monotony of their existence, the Colonel felt that it was now given. That two young and attractive girls should regard him as a matter of such deep interest was proof to him of the unrelieved dreariness of their lives.

"So you went for Bloss," he said, looking at the cow which had now passed them and was moving forward with a lurching swing toward a shed in the background.

"Yes, we go for her alternate nights. She wanders all over the tract by day and in the evening we've sometimes a hunt before we can get her."

They were both looking at Bloss, who suddenly stopped, stepped heavily on the garden border, and began to bite a hole in a row of neat, green leaves.

"Bloss!" his companion almost shrieked, "you impudent, desperate cow! Did you ever see such an impertinent thing?"

And she ran toward Bloss, who, feeling the switch suddenly on her flanks gave up the happy dream of an evening feast of young lettuce and directed her course once more toward the shed. June followed her, calling imploringly over her shoulder,

"Please don't go yet, oh, *please* don't! I do want to see you for a moment, but I've got to put this miserable animal in her stable, or she'll spoil the garden. *Please* wait."

To which he called back:

"All right. Don't hurry. I'll stroll down to the gate."

And he moved slowly down the path between the pinioned rose bushes, looking through the barring of the old gate at the dusty road.

He had not to wait long. He was standing there gazing down the road when he heard her light step and hurried breathing as she ran toward him.

"It was too bad," she said as she came to a panting stand beside him, her alder switch still in her hand, "but I couldn't let her eat those lettuces. We've had a lot of trouble with them and when they're good we can sell them as far as Sonora."

She said this with an air of pride, as one who vaunts an admired accomplishment.

"Do you like gardening?" he asked, and then stopped. From the house came a sudden sound of coughing, a heavy, racking paroxysm. The girl's eyes slanted sidewise as she stood motionless, listening. She remained thus, in a trance-like quietude of attention till the sound grew fitful and then ceased.

"How did mother strike you?" she asked in a low voice.

"I—she—" he blundered, and then said desperately: "Well, she's changed, of course, but after a long period of illness—"

He stopped. Unfinished sentences save more occasions than the world wots of.

"Yes, of course," she said eagerly, seizing on even such feeble encouragement. "And she's been sick for such a dreadfully long time, ever since Virginia, more than four years now. She's thin, though, isn't she?"

She looked anxiously at him.

"Long illnesses are apt to make people thin," he said, turning away his head.

"Yes, I suppose so, especially—" She too left her sentence unfinished. For a moment she stood looking down, flicking at an adjacent rose-tree with her switch.

"Tell me about the gardening," he said, seizing on the subject as the one uppermost in his mind. "How do you get your things as far afield as Sonora?"

"I'll tell you about that later;" she suddenly seemed to shake off her anxieties as a child might. Her clouded face turned on him sparkling with new animation, "I'll tell you all about that another time. Now—"

He interrupted her:

"But there may not be another time. You know I'll be leaving soon."

She looked amazed, quite aghast.

"Leaving?" she exclaimed—"leaving Foleys?"

"Yes, I must be back in San Francisco in a few days. And it takes a day to ride from here to Sacramento."

"But—" she stopped, looking thoroughly dashed. The Colonel wondered what was in her mind.

"But not to-morrow?" she asked, drawing near to him and speaking urgently, "you'll be here to-morrow?"

"Yes, I'll be here to-morrow. My horse won't be able to take the ride till the day after. He's gone tender on his forefoot."

She was silent, looking down on the path and absently trailing the leaf-decked tip of her switch in the dust. He regarded her with tender amusement.

"You haven't seen the spring yet," she said abruptly without raising her eyes.

The remark was startling. It was the discovery of this spring which had led to the unpleasantness with the squatter. The Colonel would probably have gone on paying the taxes and letting the squatter live on his premises till the end of things, if the spring had not waked him to the possibilities of ownership. He colored a little. For the first time it seemed to him the young girl had shown bad taste.

"No," he answered, "I haven't seen it. I didn't see that it was necessary. I've had the water analyzed. That was enough."

"But you ought to see it," she continued, still looking at the end of the switch. "It's a wonderful spring. Everybody says so. I discovered it."

Her face, as she began speaking, flushed faintly and then deeper. When she had finished the color was spread over it in a clear transparent blush.

"I doubt whether I'll be able to get there," he replied with just a trace of stiffness in his manner. "It's quite a walk, I understand, and it's so hot—"

She suddenly raised her eyes and moved toward him, her look one of flushed embarrassment, but her manner urgent and determined.

"I'll take you there," she said hurriedly. "I know a way that's quite shady, a path hardly anybody knows of. I found it, the spring and the path both, and I would so like to show it to you."

Her voice fell to the key of coaxing, which was belied by her countenance, full of a keen, waiting anxiousness. She seemed to the man to be tremulously hanging on his word of consent.

"I guess I'll have to go," he said, looking down at her with eyes from which all disapproval had gone. "I'll come up here for you—let's see! The late afternoon's the best time because it's cooler. Say five. How's that?"

"Here?" she said, looking away uneasily. "No, don't come here. You know—" she drew closer to him, and resting her finger-tips on the lapel of his coat pressed them gently against his chest, half whispering—"this is to be a secret expedition. No one must know about it but us two."

The Colonel backed away, eying her with tragical gravity from under his down-drawn brows.

"Look here, young woman," he said, "what are you up to? Are you trying to kidnap the Colonel?"

Her dimple came, but no further indication of amusement disturbed the fluttered uneasiness of her countenance.

"No, no," she said quickly; then tilting her head to one side and looking at him cajolingly, "but how I would like to!"

"I don't think it's safe for me to go," he answered. "I've a suspicion you're some kind of wood nymph or fairy who steals good-looking young men like me and keeps them in the woods for playmates. Can you give me any guaranty that I'll reappear?"

"I'll lead you back myself. And you will go? That's settled. Well, listen:—down the road before you come to the turn there's a break in the fence. It's near the large oak that throws a limb over the road. I'll be there waiting for you at half-past four. Five's too late. And the path I spoke of goes up right behind the oak and is ever so much shorter than the one everybody takes. That's this way, back of the cow-shed and the garden."

She indicated it, and both turned to follow the direction of her pointing finger. As they stood with their backs to the road they heard a heavy, regular footfall padding through the dust. The girl turned first, and her quick, half-frightened ejaculation, "It's father!" made the Colonel swerve round like a weathercock. It was too late for him to escape. Beauregard Allen was close to the gate and was looking at him with a somber, unmoving gaze.

He would have known his old enemy in a minute. But yet there was a change, subtile and demolishing as that which had made Alice a stranger to him. The debonair arrogance that he had once taken for a proud self-respect was gone. A destruction of the upholding sense of position and responsibility had bowed the upright shoulders and made the haughty hawk-eye heavy and evasive. John Beauregard Allen had failed in life, gone down step by step; not in one cataclysmic rush, but gradually, with a woman and children striving desperately to hold him back.

His drinking had been a habit of recent years, a weakness grown of ill-luck and despondency. It showed in a coarsened heaviness of feature, a reddened weight of eyelid. He wore a pair of loose, dusty trousers, thick, unbrushed boots, the blue-and-white cotton shirt of the country-man, and an unbuttoned sack-coat that sagged from his bent shoulders. A grizzled brown beard straggled over his breast, and the hat pushed back from his forehead showed hair of the same color. Yet there still lingered about him the suggestion of the man of breeding and education, and once again upright with the hope of life restored to him, he would have been a fine looking man.

He knew who the Colonel was before he turned, but he too realized there was no possibility of escape. In that one moment before his eye challenged that of his old adversary, he had recognized the situation and decided on his course. He thrust his hands into the pockets of his coat and tried to square his shoulders into their old proud poise. As his glance met the Colonel's he withdrew one of his hands from his pocket and raised his hat.

"How d'ye do," he said in a deep, easy voice; "how d'ye do, Parrish? I heard you were here."

The *savoir faire* of his address was remarkable. His eyes, however, conscious and ashamed, showed his discomfort in the meeting. The Colonel returned the salute and the two men stood facing each other, the gate between them.

"Colonel Parrish," said June in an embarrassed voice, "came to see mother. She had such a nice talk with him. He says he doesn't think she's so much changed."

"I have to thank you," said the father with a faint reminiscence of his old grand manner, "for your kindness to my little girl last evening. June tells me you introduced Rion Gracey and young Barclay to her. That's the son of Simeon Barclay, I suppose?"

The Colonel said that it was. He was extremely uncomfortable, and after the manner of his sex, wanted to escape from this unpleasant position with the utmost speed. He opened the gate and stepped into the road. The squatter slowly passed through the aperture into the disputed domain.

"It was very kind of you, Parrish," he said. "We appreciated it. June would have had a pretty dull time if it hadn't been for you."

The Colonel deprecated all thanks. He was now in the road, his hat raised in farewell. He had noticed that Allen made no allusion to his wife and thanked Heaven that the man who had shown himself so dead to other decencies had enough left in him for that. A backward glance of final adieu showed him the father and daughter side by side by the gateway. The girl was smiling at him. The man stood with his ragged hat ceremoniously lifted over his heavy, hang-dog face.

CHAPTER VII
UNCLE JIM

An hour before the time set by June Allen to go to the spring the Colonel was sitting in his room before a table littered with papers. They were the title deeds and the tax certificates of the Parrish tract. They represented an unmarred record of purchase and possession from the date of acquisition to the present time. As he looked them over he wondered again at the astounding boldness of Allen. Had he relied upon the rightful owner's leniency when he should discover that the claimant's wife had once been Alice Joyce? The thought called forth an angry sentence of pain and disgust. Perhaps so. It was of a piece with Allen's behavior. But—

The Colonel rose to his feet. He had made up his mind what he intended to do. Allen's baseness had no bearing on the matter. Alice and her children were all that concerned him. He threw the papers into the table drawer, looked at his watch, and picking up his hat, left the room.

There were many breaks in the fence—lengths of it were entirely down—but the one June had selected as the place of rendezvous was easy of discovery because of the live-oak that grew near it. The great tree cast a heavy, twisted limb across the road, making an arch of foliage almost as impervious to sunbeams as a roof. A narrow path made a pale, meandering line through the grass beyond it, and then came and went, red as a scar, through the shrubbery of the hillside. As the Colonel drew near he saw June sitting on the ground under the tree. Her figure, clothed in a dress of dull blue, made a harmonious note of color in the gold, bronze, and olive of the landscape.

She caught a glimpse of his head over the fence and jumped up with a gesture of welcome. Then as he stepped through the gap she met him with extended hand.

Viewed at close range, her appearance was an illuminating commentary on a poverty which could never be degraded or ignoble. Nothing could have been cheaper or poorer than her scanty cotton gown or her straw hat. But she had taken pains that the ribbon on her hat should match the tint of her dress, and the old-fashioned turn-over collar of lace which encircled her throat was arranged with a dainty preciseness. She had even put on her one and only pair of corsets—a treasured article of dress reserved for parties and the Sabbath—so unusual was the occasion. The Colonel did not notice these delicacies of detail. He only saw, as any other man would have seen, that a rare distinguishing fineness marked her despite her poor apparel and coarsened hands. It would have taken a woman's deeper insight to see that this was a girl in whom a taste for all that was luxurious, costly and elegant was innate and ready to wake at the first call.

They followed the path across the open land and then began ascending through the chaparral, the girl leading. The shrubs, which were low-growing, offered no shade, and the sun, though slanting to the west, followed them with scorching beams. It was by no means a gentle climb and they spoke little. At intervals a lizard flicked across the path, and an occasional stirring of the underbrush told of the stealthy passage of a snake. From the whole hillside aromatic odors, that seemed to be ascending in swimming undulations, rose into the heat, not sweet and delicate as is the breath of gardens, but coarse, pungent, almost rank, in their triumphant, wild vitality.

In an opening under the pines they paused for a rest. The Colonel noticed that his companion was not as talkative as she had been on the two former occasions. There was an air of troubled abstraction about her. She indicated notable points in the landscape like a dutiful cicerone, but the intensity of interest she had displayed in arranging the trip seemed gone. He wondered if she had revealed to some member of her family her design of showing him the spring and had been reproved for it.

The last portion of the walk was again through thickets, up a hill where the poison oak grew close and high, and then among larger growths of bay and alder, with the Digger pines raising their dim bluish shapes among the more juicy greens. Here they began to follow a faint rill, a tiny thread that broke into a shower of drops over roots and splinters of stone. Finally, pushing aside intruding boughs, she led him into an opening ringed by tall pine trunks, and cried triumphantly:

"Here it is! Do you wonder no one ever found it?"

There was a hollowing out of the bank under the eaves of a large pine root, and here the spring had been bubbling unnoticed for centuries. A delicate fringing of fern hung from the moist earth motionless over its reflection in the small, quivering mirror. Near by there was an outcropping of rock, and broken bits had been used to pave the edge where the crystal lip of water trembled, and to make a little channel for it to slip down. A rusty tin cup hung on a dead bough, and the girl rinsed it, and dipping it in the clear depths, handed it to him.

"Try it," she said. "It tastes quite different here among the pine roots with the smell of the woods all round."

He drank it, marveling at the sharp, acrid tang. She hung the cup back on the twig, and taking off her hat, sat down on a bent root that the pine above it seemed to have thrown out in a kindly desire to be hospitable. The Colonel subsided on to a flat shoulder of rock, rusted with lichen.

"Hasn't it hidden itself in a pretty spot?" she said. "And didn't it hide itself well? Coming on it from the other side you never would have suspected a spring was here among the roots of the trees."

"And you discovered it?"

She nodded, looking down into the tiny basin.

"Here it is! Do You Wonder no one Ever Found it?"

"I traced it up from the little stream that runs away from it. I found it in March, one day when I was prowling."

"Prowling! What's prowling?"

"Prowling?" she smiled, but pensively, her eyes on the water. "It's just wandering about, generally alone, and not going to any particular place.

I've prowled all over here. I can lead you straight to the two old shafts and show you the dumps and the remains of the old windlass. They're almost entirely hidden by wild grapes and things. People who don't know could easily fall in the shafts; one of them's quite deep."

It was now her companion's turn to look pensive. He had sunk the two shafts, and in them, as in the property, how many thousands of dollars he did not like to think.

"Those shafts were made," he said, "fifteen years ago when we all thought you had only to turn over a few shovelfuls of earth and find your fortune." He struck the rock with his hand and said laughingly: "What an old fraud you've been!"

She looked at him without returning his smile.

"Colonel Parrish," she said anxiously, "did you sink those two shafts?"

He nodded, once more surprised at her indirect reference to his ownership of the land. She made no reply, but, plucking a fern growing out of the earth near her, began slowly to shred its leaves from its stalk and sprinkle them on the surface of the water.

"And," she said suddenly, "you intend now, quite soon, to build a hotel back here, under the pines, at the top of the hill, don't you?"

That she should disappoint him with these persistent and almost indecent inquiries, considering the situation, hurt and irritated him. It was so out of keeping with her general suggestion of something sensitive and girlishly naïve.

"I *had* intended building a hotel; came here with that intention. But—" He rose to his feet and said coldly, "Don't you think we'd better be going back again? It's quite a long walk."

"But?"—she echoed, unheeding his last sentences—"but what?"

She made no movement save to clasp her hands on the broken fern. Her face, raised to him, suddenly was pale and set in a curious tenseness of inquiry. It moved the Colonel strangely.

"But what?" she repeated insistently. "You were going to say something else."

"My dear little girl," he answered, "don't trouble your head about these things. It's—it's—a man's dispute and for men to settle. But rest assured of one thing, you'll not suffer by it."

"I!" she exclaimed; "it's not I that matters. But, Colonel Parrish, our mother."

She stopped, her voice quivering like a taut string.

"Your mother?" said the Colonel, with a rising inflection.

"You see how it is with her. Let us stay. Let us stay a little while longer."

"Did you bring me up here to ask me this?" he said, looking steadily at her.

"Yes. I wanted to see you somewhere away from the house, and I thought the spring would be a good excuse. Talking of these things makes me"—the tears rose to her eyes and stood thick in them—"makes me do like this."

They ran over and she brushed them away with her hand.

"You can see; you understand about mother," she went on, struggling to speak clearly. "It's only a question of time. It's nearly the end of everything. And I brought you up here to-day to ask you to let us stay—right or wrong—let us stay till then."

Her voice broke and she held her head down, trying to suppress her sobs. The Colonel turned away, walked to where the tin cup hung, took it off its twig, and looked into it.

"Don't do that," he said, his voice rough; "for Heaven's sake, stop. I'd be angry with you for asking me such a thing if you weren't so—so—I don't know what. Of course you're going to stay."

"What?" he was not looking at her, but was conscious that she had stiffened both in mental and physical fiber at the word—"you're going to let us stay?"

"Of course. As long as you want, always. Don't talk any more about it."

A quick sound came from her, and he heard the rustle of her dress as she rose, her footsteps on the stone near him, and then felt her beside him. She seized the hand hanging at his side, pressed it against the softness of her bosom and against her cheek, then dropped it with a murmur of broken words.

He turned on her bruskly. Her face was shining with tears, but she was smiling. She tried to speak to him, but he laid a finger on her lips and looked at her, shaking his head.

"Don't say any more about it," he said after a moment's pause. "I can't stand this sort of thing. I'm not used to it."

She gently laid her hand on his and drawing it away unsealed her lips. She was smiling radiantly, her dimple deep. And for a moment she enveloped him in a beaming look of affection and gratitude.

"There's lots I want to say, but I suppose I must be obedient," she murmured.

"Of course you must. Come, we ought to be going. Put your hat on or you'll get all freckled."

She went back to the spring and picked up her hat. As she pulled the elastic down over her cropped locks she said gaily:

"I feel so different from what I did when I came up—at least twenty years younger and fifty pounds lighter."

"You'd better not forget how to accomplish that miracle," said her companion. "Thirty years from now you'll probably find it a great deal more to the point than you do to-day."

They started down the path, laughing. The red eye of the sun, a flaming ball, stared at them between the trunks of the pines, and shot long pencils of flushed light into the rustling depths of the thickets. June led the way as before, but she was a different guide. She seemed as light-hearted going down as she had been oppressed coming up. The Colonel was to realize later how ready her optimism was to respond to the first glimmer of cheer, how quick and far was the swing of the pendulum.

Coming to a grassed plateau under the pines they paused for a moment's rest. From the high crest of ground they could see the cottage with the cultivation of its garden cutting into the unfilled land, like an island of green floating in a yellow sea. It looked meaner and more insignificant than ever in the midst of the lazily out-flung landscape now swimming in a bath of colored light.

The Colonel saw in imagination a house he owned in San Francisco on Folsom Street. He had bought it as a favor from a pioneer friend whose fortunes were declining. It was the stateliest house of what was then a street of stately houses, with wide windows, vine-draped balconies, and scrolled iron gates shutting out the turmoil of the street. The thought had been in his mind when it came into his possession that it was the sort of house he would have given Alice, and the still more sacred thought had followed, that his children's laughter might have echoed through its halls. Now he looked down on a hovel, also his property, where Alice had been glad to find a shelter, and in which her daughter had prayed that she might be left to die! Life and its mysteries! How inscrutable, how awful, it all was!

The voice of June at his side roused him.

"Mother's gone in," she said, evidently making these small domestic comments more to herself than to him, "and Rosamund's getting supper."

"How do you know that?" he asked, glad to be shaken from his thoughts. "Have you got second sight? You're such a little witch I shouldn't be a bit surprised if you had."

"You don't have to be a witch to see the smoke coming out of the chimney."

A faint reek of smoke curled up from the cottage roof into the evening air. The Colonel looked at her with a sheepish side-glance. She returned it, smiling in mischievous triumph.

"I'm afraid we're not both witches," she said saucily.

The rest over, they continued their descent by a wider path in parts of which they walked side by side, talking together sometimes, or June talking, for she was very loquacious now, while her companion listened. At the end of a description of their life in Virginia City he said,

"How long is it since you've been in San Francisco? Years, isn't it?"

"Oh, years and years. I was born there, but we left when I was a child."

"It must have been a prodigious length of time ago—in the glacial period, you might say. Sometime you and Rosamund must come down there and visit me. I'll find a place for you to stay, and take good care of you. Would you like it?"

"Oh, Colonel Parrish!" Words failed her. The path was wide and she was walking beside him. He saw her eyes shine.

"I'd see to it that you'd have a good time. Lots of parties and first-rate partners. You'd never sit along the wall there. The fellows would be just breaking their necks to dance with you. And theaters—you like theaters, don't you?"

"Theaters!" she fairly gasped. "I saw *Mazeppa* in Virginia, and it was—oh, I haven't got the words! It was something wonderful."

"Well, we'll see 'em all. Better forty times than you saw in Virginia, and every night if you want. It'll be just as good a time as San Francisco and the Colonel can give two girls like you and Rosamund."

He looked down at her, smiling. She returned the look and said:

"Why are you so good to us? I don't understand it!"

"Don't try to. Never exert your brain in needless ways. That's a fundamental law for the preservation of health. In this particular case I'd be good to myself. You don't know what it would be for me to have two nice girls to take around. I'm a lonely old devil, you know."

"Are you?" she said with a note of somewhat pensive incredulity. "You've never been married, have you?"

"Nup," said the Colonel.

"You'll have to look upon us as your daughters," she continued, "or perhaps your nieces." The path was narrow and she looked into his face with the glance of demure coquetry he was beginning to know and watch for. "Which would you prefer?"

"Daughters," he said gruffly, looking into the bushes.

"But we're already provided with a father," she replied. "And it would be such a pity to waste you. Wouldn't you care to take the position of uncle? That's vacant."

"All right, uncle—Uncle Jim."

"Uncle Jim," she repeated thoughtfully. "It seems funny to come into possession of your first uncle when you're twenty years old."

There was a bend in the path and the bushes grew almost across it. She suddenly quickened her speed, passed him, and ran on before.

"Come on," she called over her shoulder. "I'm just hitting the trail again."

He followed her, turned the bend, and pushing the branches aside, saw her a few feet ahead of him, standing on a flat stone about a foot high, which directly intercepted the path.

"What are you mounted on that for?" he said, laughing. "You look as if you were going to make a speech."

"That's what I'd like to do," she answered, "but I was told not to, and I'm very obedient. Come nearer—quite close."

He approached, a little puzzled, for he saw that she was suddenly grave. The stone raised her a few inches above him, and as he drew near she leaned down, took him by the lapels of his coat, and drawing him close, bent and kissed him softly on the forehead. Then she drew back, and still holding him, looked with tender eyes into his.

"Uncle Jim," she said, "that's your christening."

The next moment she was down and flitting on ahead of him.

"The path's very narrow," she called. "You must be content to follow the oldest living inhabitant."

At the gap in the fence he bade her good-by. To his great delight she caught at his hesitating suggestion that she should occasionally write to him and tell him of their life and her mother's health. He told her he would be up again, he thought, some time during the summer. The date was uncertain. Then, with her hand in his, she said with a wilful shake of her head:

"No, not *á Dios*. It's *hasta mañana,* Uncle Jim. I won't have it anything but *hasta mañana*."

"Well, then, *hasta mañana,*" he answered. "And God bless you, little girl!"

That evening Colonel Parrish went to see Cusack. He brought with him the title deeds and tax certificates of the Parrish tract. They lay scattered on the office table on which the Colonel as he talked leaned a supporting elbow. The interview was short, and there were moments when it was heated, till Cusack realized, as he afterwards expressed it to a friend, "there are certain kinds of fools there's no good bucking up against." The Colonel had determined to recognize the squatter's claim, and to end all further litigation by making a legal transfer of the property to Allen by means of a quit-claim deed. He talked down argument and protest.

"Why the devil should I keep the place?" he vociferated. "I'm sick of paying taxes on it and never getting a cent. I've sunk thousands in it and not got a dollar back. It's been a white elephant from the first. Allen's welcome to it. I'm glad to get it off my hands."

"But the spring," Cusack almost wailed in the acuteness of his disappointment, "the spring and the hotel! They were going to raise Foleys from the dead."

"Spring!" said the Colonel, rising and taking from his pocket a fresh cigar—"damned little picayune tea-cup! That spring hasn't power to raise a mosquito from the dead."

"Did you expect to find a geyser?" the irritated lawyer retorted.

"I didn't expect to find what I did find, you can bet on that," said his client, as he bent forward to apply the tip of his cigar to the lamp chimney.

CHAPTER VIII
PRIZES OF ACCIDENT

It was half-past five the next morning when Kit Carson paced away from the hotel stables into the rosy daylight. With the freshness of the hour on his face the Colonel passed along the hushed street and then out into the red road between its clumps of dusty foliage.

As he skirted what yesterday had been his own land he looked on it with a new eye. It could be made to support them well. No matter how low Allen might sink they need never want again. The hilly part, where the spring was, could be sold or leased to some of the enterprising city hotel men. Or, if they objected to that, they could increase their market gardening to the dimensions of a large agricultural enterprise. They could rent to a rancher a portion of the rich, uncultivated land now lying idle, and thus gain an income sufficient for them to develop their own particular domain. To people of thrift and energy the possibilities of the tract were large. Alice could die in peace. Her girls were provided for.

As the cottage came into view the rider reined up and gazed at it. No smoke issued from the chimney. They all still slept. In the crystal stillness of the morning it looked peacefully picturesque, half veiled in its greenery of shrubs and vines. The air about it was impregnated with the delicate breath of the roses that lined the path from the gate to the balcony.

He gave a slight shake to his rein, and Kit Carson, who had been impatiently pawing with a proud forefoot, moved forward. The rider's glance wandered to a window under the sloping roof, veiled by a blue curtain. Was that the girls' room? The girls! The two faces rose before his mental vision and he turned his eyes from the window and let them pierce, far-seeing and steady—into the distance, into the future. Before he came to Foleys he had not cared, he had not dared, to look into the future. He had cowered before its emptiness. Now the faces of the sisters rose softly bright in its melancholy obscurity, the faces of Alice's daughters—daughters that should have been his.

A week after he reached San Francisco he had a letter from June, a childish, incoherent letter, full of impassioned terms of gratitude, broken into by distressed comments on her mother's health. Then, in more sprightly vein, she told him of how Mr. Barclay was stopping over at Foleys for a few days and came nearly every day and helped them in the garden, and Mr. Rion Gracey, riding back from Foleys to the Buckeye Belle one evening, had dropped in for a visit, and stayed to supper.

The Colonel seemed to see her as she wrote, laughing at one moment and then stopping to dash the tears off her cheek as she had done at the spring. He heard from no one else. Beauregard Allen had accepted the transfer of the property as a business transaction, the manner in which his adversary had desired him to accept it. To his friends in San Francisco the Colonel explained his speedy return and the dropping of the case as he had done to Cusack. It was not worth the time and trouble. The land was remote, the spring a disappointment; he was glad to be rid of it all.

Three weeks after this, sitting alone in his office, he received by the afternoon mail a newspaper. It was the *Daily Clarion*, an organ which molded public opinion and supported a precarious existence in Foleys. Unfolding the flimsy sheet he found a marked paragraph, and turning to it he saw it to be Alice's death notice. She had died three days before "at the residence of her husband, John Beauregard Allen." The paper slipped from his hand to the floor and his head sank. He sat thus till the twilight fell, alone in the dim office where the golden letters that spelled his name—the name of the successful man—shone faintly on the window.

That same afternoon the dead woman's husband and children returned to the cottage after having committed all that remained of her to the grave. Rosamund had succumbed to the strain and sorrow of the last few days, and gone to bed prostrated with a headache. Allen, morose and speechless, had flung himself in a chair in the living-room and there sat, a heavy, inert figure. He had drunk heavily during the last few days of his wife's illness, for he had always loved her, and in his weakness of heart had fled from the sight of her suffering, and tried to find surcease for his own.

It was left to June to prepare their supper and accomplish the toilsome domestic tasks that Rosamund shared with her. With a dead heart she set out the meal, watered the garden, and finally set forth in a flare of sunset to find Bloss and drive her home.

The cow had evidently strayed far. June's search led her to the spots which Bloss was known to frequent, but she could find no trace of her. Sometimes the girl's voice, broken and hoarse with weeping, rose on the rich stillness of the hour, calling to the truant. She became irritable, exasperated against the animal, who, on such a night as this, while her heart was bursting with sorrow, ended the bitterness of the day with so wearisome a hunt. Finally, exhausted by long hours of watching and the fatigue of grief, she burst into unrestrained sobs. With her face shining with tears, her breast convulsed, she tore her way through thickets and scrambled over rocky spurs, every now and then sending up a quavering cry for the strayed cow. At length, brushing through a copse of bay and alder, she came on the torn face of the hill where the landslide had taken place. The ground was covered with a debris of stones and dead trees. Nature, to repair the damage, was already hiding the rawness of the lacerated expanse under a veil of small sprouting vegetation. Here, through a screen of leaves, she at last caught sight of Bloss' red and white side.

She cried to the cow, who gave a lazy flip of her tail but no other sign of movement. June's irritated misery gave way to a spasm of rage, and stooping, she picked up a handful of the loose pieces of stone strewn about her, and threw one at the runaway. It struck with a thud. Bloss gave a surprised snort, and, wheeling, brushed through the thicket. June followed her, the stones pressed in a clutching hand against her breast, one now and then launched in the direction of the cow. These missiles, combined with the thought of home, appeared to animate Bloss' leisurely movements, and she hastened forward through brush and over rock at a lolloping, uncouth trot.

The dusk was settling into night when they reached the shed. June's tears had ceased, but the abstraction of grief held her. She fastened the shed door on the cow, and still absently clasping three or four pieces of stone, entered the house. The door from the balcony gave directly into the living-room. Here, just as she had left him, she found her father.

The daughters of Beauregard Allen did not love him with the same fond blindness to his faults that had marked his wife. In the grinding poverty of their later years they could not but see his apathy, the selfishness of his heavy discouragement, the weakness of his tendency to drink. Though the filial sense was strong in them and the example of their mother's uncomplaining devotion one that they obediently followed, they realized that their father was more a tottering pillar to support than a staff upon which to lean.

Now, a vague, dark bulk in the deserted room, so filled with memories of the dead woman, he was a figure of heart-piercing desolation. His daughter moved to the table and said gently:

"Why, father dear, are you still sitting in the dark? Why didn't you light the lamp?"

He answered with an inarticulate sound and did not move. Setting the stones on the table June drew the lamp toward her and lit it. The sudden flood of light seemed to rouse him. The chair creaked under his weight as he turned. His haggard eyes absently traveled over the lamp and the table near it and finally rested on the scattered fragments of rock. June had bent down to look at the wick which she was carefully adjusting, when she heard him give a suppressed exclamation, and his long brown hand entered the circle of lamplight and gathered up the stones. The wick satisfactorily arranged, she settled the shade and turned away. Her father drew his chair closer to the slanting torrent of light, and holding the stones directly under it, leaned forward, scrutinizing them as he turned them about.

"Where did you get these?" he said without looking up.

She told him, turning again toward the table, absently watching him.

"Near the hillside? Just there where the piece of the hill came down?" he queried.

"Yes, along the ground there. It's all strewed with stones and earth and roots. There's quite a wall of rock left bare and these bits of it are all over. New weeds are sprouting everywhere. I suppose that's what took Bloss there."

He rose and going to a book-case took out a hand magnifying glass, and returning to the light, studied the fragments through it. Something in his face as he bent over them, struck through the lethargy of her dejection.

"Father," she said, drawing near, "what are they? What's odd about them?"

He lifted a face transfigured with excitement, and leaning forward, laid a trembling hand on hers.

"It's float," he said, "undeniable float! If I'm not mistaken we've got the ledge at last."

BOOK II
THE TOWN

CHAPTER I
DOWN IN THE CITY

In the darkness of the early November night Colonel Parrish rattled across town in a hired carriage. It was half-past eight when he left his rooms (they were a fine suite on a sunny corner of Kearney Street), and now as he turned into Folsom Street he calculated that if the girls were ready they could be *en route* by nine o'clock. In the autumn of 1870 the hours for evening entertainments were still early, and the particular entertainment to which the Colonel intended taking June and Rosamund Allen was one of the regular receptions which united the aristocracy of San Francisco at the house of Mrs. Ira Davenport.

The great detached bulks of the buildings that the carriage passed gleamed with lights, for Folsom Street was still the home of the elect. From the arch of lofty porches hall lamps cast a faint gleam into the outer darkness of shrubberies and lawns. Through the scroll-work of high iron gates the imbedded flags of the marble paths shone white between darkly grassed borders. Here and there a black façade was cut into by rows of long, lighted windows, uncurtained and unshuttered. The street suggested seclusion, wealth and dignity. The fortunes, which were later to erect huge piles on San Francisco's wind-swept hill-crests, had not yet arisen to blight the picturesqueness of the gray, sea-girdled city.

His own house was one of the largest in the street. Now, in the darkness, it loomed an irregular black mass, cut into with squares and slits of light. Just a month before the lease of his tenants had expired, and he was able to see one, at least, of his dreams realized—Alice's daughters quartered under his roof.

The revolution of Fortune's wheel had been, where the Allens were concerned, sudden and dizzying. The ledge, that man for years had fruitlessly sought, in one night had been laid bare. Even for the time and the country it was a startling reversal of conditions. In the spring Beauregard Allen had been a beggar. In the summer he saw himself a man of wealth. Experts pronounced the discovery one of moment. The mine, called the Barranca, was regarded as richer in promise than the Buckeye Belle. Distant portions of the tract, which had come into his possession in so unlooked for a manner, were sold for large sums. The whole region was shaken into astonished animation and Foleys was more effectually wakened from the dead than it would have been by the Colonel's original scheme.

Allen's sloth and despondency fell from him like a garment. With the ready money from the land sales he at once began the development of the prospect hole. In July a square tunnel mouth and a board shed intruded on the sylvan landscape near the landslide. In September a fair-sized hoisting works housed the throb of engines and the roll of cars. The noise of Beauregard Allen's strike went abroad through foot-hill California and its echo rolled to San Francisco, where men who had known him in the early days suddenly remembered him as "Beau" Allen, the handsome Southerner, who had come to grief and dropped out of sight in the fifties.

In September he came down to San Francisco and saw the Colonel. The meeting at first was constrained, but as Allen spoke of his daughters and the plans for their happiness and welfare that he had in view the constraint wore away and the two men talked as beings united by a mutual interest. The Colonel had recognized the fact that the breach must be healed. He had had to struggle against his old repugnance, but there was nothing else for it. No wrong, however deep, should stand between him and Alice's daughters, and he could not know the daughters without accepting the father. And how he did want to know them! They had already brought brightness and purpose into his life. In an effort to treat the matter lightly he told himself that the harboring of old resentments, when they blocked the way to the forming of new ties, was too much like cutting off your nose to spite your face. Deep in his heart lay the feeling that, apart from his affection for them, they might need him. He knew Allen of old, and Alice was dead.

It was their father's intention to have them make San Francisco their home. In the larger city they would have the advantages of society and chances to marry well. One of the objects of his visit was to look about for a house whence they could be launched into the little world in which he once had played his part. It was thus that the Colonel, the lease of his old tenant having just expired, was able to offer them his own house for as long a period of years as they might wish.

But Allen, swollen with the pride of his new fortunes, would rent no house. He would buy one, a fitting home for two such girls as his. When it came to that, the Colonel was as willing to sell as to rent. The price of thirty thousand dollars was put upon the Folsom Street mansion, and Allen, being much impressed by its size and old-fashioned splendor, purchased it, paying down the sum of ten thousand dollars, while the Colonel held a mortgage maturing in three years for the other twenty thousand. Allen, despite his sudden accession to wealth, claimed that his expenses just now were of the heaviest. In October he contemplated the building of a twenty-stamp mill at the mine, and the shaft house was to be enlarged. The winter outfits for his daughters would be costly. It was his intention that June and Rosamund should be as richly and modishly clad as any of the young women who cast a glamour over the society of the city.

To-night they were to make their entrance into that society. Mrs. Davenport was an old friend of the Colonel's and he had asked for the invitations, assuring her that she would find his protégées two of the prettiest and sweetest girls in the world. Now as he sprang from the carriage and pushed open the tall gate of scrolled iron-work he smiled to himself, cheerfully confident that he had not overstated the charms of the Misses Allen.

His ring brought one of the new Chinese servants to the door, a quiet man, soft-footed as a cat, and clothed in freshly-laundered white. Standing in the hall under the light he watched this spectral figure flit noiselessly up the stairway. The hall, papered in a deep reddish-purple on which here and there the gleam of gold arabesques was faintly visible, was wide and dim. It would require a galaxy of lamps thoroughly to dispel the gloom that lurked in its dusky corners. A stately staircase, thickly carpeted and with a darkly-polished hand-rail, ran up in front of him. There was a light again at the top of this throwing faint glimmerings on receding stretches of wall, also somberly papered.

Through the wide arch on his right he could look into a half-lighted parlor, where a globe or two in the chandelier shone a translucent yellow. To his left the doors into the reception-room were open, and here by a table, a reading lamp at his elbow, sat Beauregard Allen smoking a cigar. He was in evening dress, but a button or two of unloosened waist-coat, and the air of sprawling ease that marked his attitude, did not suggest the trim alertness of one garbed and tuned for festival.

"Good evening, Parrish," he said. "The girls will be down in a minute. I'm going to beg off. Can't drag me away from a good cigar and comfortable chair on such a damned cold night."

His face was flushed; he had evidently been drinking more than was consistent with a strictly temperate standard, a condition which often marked him after dinner. But the old tendency toward an open and unabashed inebriety had been conquered. Well-dressed, his beard trimmed, the sense of degradation and failure lifted from him, he looked a stalwart, personable man, in whom the joy of life was still buoyantly and coarsely alive.

The Colonel, leaning against the door frame, was about to launch into the desultory conversation that fills gaps, when the rustle of skirts on the stairs caught his ear. June and Rosamund were descending, their cloaks on their arms that they might show themselves in their new finery. Their mourning for their mother took the form of transparent black gauze, through which the delicate whiteness of their youthful arms and shoulders gleamed. They laughed as they met the Colonel's eye, both slightly abashed by the unwonted splendor of their attire.

Their sudden rise from poverty, their translation to the city, and their short stay in its sophisticated atmosphere, had already worked a marked change in them. Their air of naïvely blushing rusticity was gone. They looked finer, more *mondaine*, than they had only six weeks before. Rosamund, who was of an ample, gracious build, had already, by the aid of the admirable dressmaker who had fashioned her gown, achieved a figure of small-waisted, full-busted elegance, which, combined with her naturally fine carriage, gave her an appearance of metropolitan poise and distinction. She had that bounteous and blooming type of looks which is peculiar to the women of California, and which (as is the case with the character that accompanies it) is curiously lacking in feminine subtility and romantic suggestion. By far the handsomer of the two sisters she was not destined to cast the spell over the hearts of men which was the prerogative of June.

She too had improved, but neither skilful dressmakers nor luxurious surroundings would ever make her a radiantly good-looking or particularly noticeable person. Her hair, which had been so unsightly six months before, was now her one beauty. It hung round her head in a drooping mass of brown curls, the longest just brushing the nape of her neck. Through them was wound a ribbon of black velvet in the manner of adornment sometimes seen in eighteenth century miniatures.

The girls grumbled a little at their father's defection, but the truth was that they were so excited by the evening's prospect that their regrets had a perfunctory tone. In the carriage they plied the Colonel with questions as to the nature of the entertainment and the people they were likely to meet. It amused and somewhat puzzled him to see that the anticipation of what he had supposed would be a beguiling and cheerful amusement was throwing them into nervous tremors. As the large outline of the Davenport house rose before them, all attempt at conversation died, and they sat, stiff and speechless, on the seat opposite him.

The Davenport house, as all old Californians know, was at that time and had been for ten years, the focus of the city's social life. Mrs. Davenport was a Southerner and had been a beauty, facts which had weighed with the San Franciscans since the days when "the water came up to Montgomery Street." The Southern tradition still retained much of its original power. The war had not broken it, and the overwhelming eruption of money, which the Comstock was to disgorge, had not yet submerged the once dominant "set." At its head Mrs. Davenport ruled with tact and determination. She appeared to the Allens as a graciously cordial lady of more than middle age, whose sweeping robe of gray satin matched the hair she wore parted on her forehead and drawn primly down over the tips of her ears.

To the sisters it was the entrance into a new world, the world their parents had strayed from and often described to them. Seated in arm-chairs of yellow brocade they surveyed the length of the parlor, a spacious, high-ceilinged apartment, of a prevailing paleness of tint and overhung by crystal chandeliers. The black shoulders of men were thrown out against the white walls delicately touched with a design in gilding. Long mirrors reproduced the figures of women rising from the curving sweep of bright-colored, beruffled trains. A Chinaman, carrying a wide tray of plates and glasses, moved from group to group.

Soon several of the black coats had gathered round the chairs of June and Rosamund. The Colonel had to give up his seat, and June could see him talking to men in the doorways or dropping into vacant places beside older women. He kept his eye on them, however. It delighted him to see that their charm was so quickly recognized. Round about him their name buzzed from a knot in a corner, or a group on a sofa. Many of those present had known Beauregard Allen in his short heyday. Almost everybody in the room had heard of his strike near Foleys and sudden translation from poverty to riches.

When at length the Colonel saw the chair beside June vacant he crossed the room and dropped into it. He was anxious to hear from her how she was enjoying herself.

"Well," he said, "the old man's been frozen out for nearly an hour. Didn't it make you feel conscience-stricken to see me hanging round the doorway looking hungrily at this chair?"

"I was dying for that man to go," she answered. "I did everything but ask him."

"Oh, you sinner!" he said, looking into her dancing eyes. "Where will you go to when you die?"

"Where do you think you will?" she asked, grave, but with her dimple faintly suggested. "I'd like to know, because then I can arrange to have just about the same sort of record, and we could go together."

He could not restrain his laughter, and she added in her most caressing tone,

"It would be so dreary for you to go to one place and me to be in another."

Before he could answer she had raised her eyes, glanced at the door, and then suddenly flushed, her face disclosing a sort of sudden quick snap into focused attention.

"Mr. Barclay," she said in a low voice. "I didn't expect to see him to-night."

The Colonel turned his head and saw Jerry Barclay entering the room in the company of a lady and gentleman. Many other people looked at them as they moved to where Mrs. Davenport stood, for they were unquestionably a noticeable trio.

The woman was in the middle, and between the proud and distinguished figure of Barclay and the small, insignificant one of her other escort, she presented a striking appearance. She was of a large, full build, verging on embonpoint, but still showing a restrained luxuriance of outline. A dress of white lace clothed her tightly and swept in creamy billows over the carpet behind her. It was cut in a square at her neck, and the sleeves ended at her elbows, revealing a throat and forearms of milky whiteness. This ivory purity of skin was noticeable in her face, which was firmly modeled, rather heavy in feature, and crowned with a coronet of lusterless black hair. She was hardly handsome, but there was something sensational, arresting, slightly repelling, in the sleepy and yet vivid vitality that seemed to emanate from her.

"Who is it?" said June in a low voice. "What a curious looking woman!"

The Colonel, who had been surveying the new-comers, looked at his companion with eyes in which there was a slight veiled coldness. The same quality was noticeable in his voice:

"Her name's Newbury, Mrs. William Newbury. Her husband's a banker here."

"Is that her husband with her, that little man?"

"Yes."

"But he's so old! He looks like her father. What did she marry him for?"

"I don't know. I'm not her father-confessor. He's got a good deal of money, I believe."

The Colonel did not seem interested in the subject. He picked up June's fan and said,

"How did you like the young fellow who had this chair just now, Stanley Davenport? He's the last unmarried child my old friend has left."

The girl's eyes, however, had followed the new-comers with avid, staring curiosity, and she said,

"Very much. Are Mrs. Newbury and her husband great friends of Mr. Barclay's?"

"I believe they are. I don't know much about her. I know her husband in business. He's a little dried up, but he's a first-rate fellow in the main."

"Is she an American? She looks so queer and foreign."

"Spanish, Spanish-Californian. She and her sister were two celebrated beauties here about twelve years ago. Their name was Romero—Carmen and Guadalupé Romero—and they were very poor. Their grandfather had been a sort of a Shepherd King, owned a Spanish grant about as big as a European principality, and when the Gringo came traded off big chunks of it for lengths of calico and old firearms and books he couldn't read. The girls were friends of Mrs. Davenport's only daughter Annie, and she gave them a start. Carmen—she was the elder of the two—married an Englishman, a man of position and means that she met in this house. She lives over in England. This one—Lupé—married Newbury about ten years ago."

"Do you think she's pretty?" asked June, anxious to have her uncertainty on this point settled by what she regarded as expert opinion.

"No. I don't admire her at all. She was handsome when she married. Those Spanish women all get too fat. You saw something of Barclay at Foleys after I left, didn't you?"

She dropped her eyes to the hands folded in her lap and said with a nonchalant air,

"Yes, he was at Foleys for over a week. He came back from Thompson's Flat just after you left, and he used to come and see us every afternoon. We had lots of fun. He helped us with the garden, and he didn't know how to do anything, and we had to teach him."

"You saw a lot of Rion Gracey too, I suppose," said her companion, with a sidelong eye on her.

It pleased him to note that at this remark she looked suddenly conscious.

The Colonel had for some time cherished a secret hope. It was one of the subjects of mutual agreement which had made it easier for him and Allen to bury the hatchet. The latter had told him of Rion Gracey's continued visits to the cottage throughout the summer, and both men had agreed that no woman could find a better husband than the younger of the Gracey boys.

June's conscious air was encouraging, but her words were aggravatingly non-committal.

"Oh, yes," she said, "we saw Mr. Gracey often. He was always coming into Foleys to buy supplies for the Buckeye Belle."

At that moment Barclay, who had turned away from his companions, saw her, and with a start of recognition followed by a smile of undisguised pleasure, hurried toward her. The Colonel rose with some reluctance. He was surprised and not entirely pleased at the open delight of the young man's countenance, the confident friendliness of his greeting. He gave up his chair, however, and as he crossed the room to one of his elderly cronies, he saw that Mrs. Newbury was watching Jerry Barclay and June with a slight, lazy smile and attentive eyes.

"I came here to-night solely to see you," said the young man, as soon as the Colonel was out of earshot.

"But how did you know I was here?" asked the innocent June. "I never told you."

"No, you naughty girl, you never did. But I heard it."

"Little birds?" she queried, tilting up her chin and looking at him out of the ends of her eyes.

"Little birds," he acquiesced. "And why didn't you let me know? Don't I remember your making me a solemn promise at Foleys to tell me the first thing if you ever came to San Francisco? You were doubtful then if you ever would."

"Yes, I think you do," she agreed. "That is, if you've got a good memory."

"You evidently haven't."

"I remembered it perfectly and was waiting until we got settled in our new house before I wrote you. I was going to give you a surprise."

"Well, you've surprised me enough already." He leaned a little nearer to her, and looking at her with eyes that were at once soft and bold said: "You've changed so; you've changed immensely since I saw you last."

She dropped her eyes and said demurely,

"I hope it's for the better," then looked up at him and their laughter broke out in happy duet.

The Colonel heard it across the room, and glancing at them felt annoyed that June should look so suddenly flushed and radiant. Evidently she and Jerry Barclay, in the ten days he had spent at Foleys, had become very good friends.

An hour later the Misses Allen were standing at the top of the steps that led from the porch to the street. Guests were departing in all directions, and the lanterns of carriages were sending tubes of opaque, yellow light through the fog. The Colonel had gone in quest of theirs, cautioning his charges to wait in the shelter of the porch for him. Here they stood, close-wrapped against the damp, and peering into the churning white currents. Just below them two men, the collars of their coats up, paused to light their cigars. One accomplished the feat without difficulty; the other stood with his hand curved round the match, which many times flamed and went out.

Suddenly June heard his companion say between puffs,

"Queer, Mrs. Newbury being here!"

"Oh, I don't know," said the other, drawing a new match from his pocket, "Mrs. Davenport knew the Romero girls long before they were married. They were friends of Annie Davenport's. Nobody'd ever breathed a word against either of them then. She wouldn't throw Lupé down on a rumored scandal. I don't see how she could."

"Lots of people have. And you call it a 'rumored scandal' all you want; everybody believes it. She owns him body and soul."

The other man had at last induced the tip of his cigar to catch. He threw back his head and drew a few quick inspirations.

"That's the story. But a woman like Mrs. Davenport is not going to damn her daughter's friend on hearsay. Women have got a creed of their own; they believe what they want to and they disbelieve what they want to. She wants to believe that the affair's purely platonic, and she does it."

"But Barclay! To hang round her that way in public—what a fool!"

"Oh, Barclay!"—a shrug went with the words—"he does what he's told!"

The man turned as he spoke and saw the two girls above him on the step. He threw a low-toned phrase at his companion, and without more words they started out and were absorbed in the darkness. Almost simultaneously a carriage rattled up and the Colonel's voice bade June and Rosamund descend.

A half-hour later, as they were mounting the stairs to their rooms, June said suddenly,

"Did you hear what those men were saying on the steps as we stood there waiting?"

They had both heard the entire conversation, and though they did not understand the true purport of the ambiguous phrases, they realized that they contained a veiled censure of Mrs. Newbury and Jerry Barclay. Their secluded bringing up in an impoverished home where the coarseness of the world never entered had kept them ignorant of the winked-at sins of society. Yet the crude frankness of mining camps had paraded before their eyes many things that girls brought up in the respectable areas of large cities never see.

"Yes, I heard them," said Rosamund.

"What did they mean? I didn't understand them. They seemed to think there was something wrong about Mrs. Newbury."

"I don't know what they meant. But I didn't like her looks at all. I wouldn't want her for a friend."

"They said something of Mr. Barclay too, didn't they?"

"Yes; they said he was a fool and did as he was told."

"Well," said June, bristling, "those are just the two particular things about him I should think were not true. But there was some one that they said she—I suppose *that* meant Mrs. Newbury—owned body and soul. Whom do you suppose they meant?"

"Her husband," said Rosamund promptly. "Whom else could they mean?"

June had felt depressed on the way home. At these words her depression suddenly vanished and she became wreathed in smiles. Thrusting her hand through Rosamund's arm she gave it an affectionate squeeze, exclaiming with a sudden sputter of laughter,

"Well, if his soul isn't a better specimen than his body I don't think it's much to own."

Rosamund was shocked; she refused even to smile, as June, drooping against her shoulder, filled the silence of the sleeping house with the sound of her laughter.

CHAPTER II
FEMININE LOGIC

Social life in San Francisco at this period had a distinction, a half-foreign, bizarre picturesqueness, which it soon after lost and has never regained. Separated from the rest of the country by a sweep of unconquered desert, ringed on its farther side by a girdle of sea, the pioneer city developed, undisturbed by outside influences, along its own lines.

The adventures of forty-nine had infused into it some of the breadth and breeziness of their wild spirit. The bonanza period of the Comstock lode had not yet arisen to place huge fortunes in the hands of the coarsely ambitious and frankly illiterate, and to infect the populace with a lust of money that has never been conquered. There were few millionaires, and the passionate desire to become one had not yet been planted in the bosom of every simple male, who, under ordinary conditions, would have been content to wield a pick or sweep down the office stairs. The volcano of silver that was to belch forth precious streams over the far West, and from thence over the world, was beginning to stir and mutter, but its muttering was still too low to be caught by any but the sharpest ears.

The society which welcomed June and Rosamund was probably the best the city ever had to offer. After the manner of all flourishing communities it aspired to renew itself by the infusion of new blood, and the young girls were graciously greeted. Carriages rolled up to the high iron gates, and ladies whose names were of weight trailed their silk skirts over the flagged walk. Coming in late in the wintry dusk it was very exciting always to find cards on the hall table.

There were often men's cards among them. A good many moths had begun to flutter round the flames of youth and beauty and wealth that burnt in the Colonel's house on Folsom Street. In his constant visits he had formed a habit of looking over these cards as he stood in the hall taking off his overcoat. The frequency with which the card of Mr. Jerome Barclay lay freshly and conspicuously on top of the pile struck him unpleasantly and caused him to remark upon the fact to June.

"Yes, Mr. Barclay comes quite often," she said, "but so does Mr. Davenport and Mr. Brooks and Mr. Pierce, and several others."

She had changed color and looked embarrassed at the mention of his name, and the Colonel had spoken to Rosamund about it. The Colonel had begun to rely upon Rosamund, as everybody did, and, like everybody, he had come to regard her as much the elder of the two sisters, the one to be consulted and to seek advice of. Rosamund admitted that Mr. Barclay did come rather often, but not indeed, as June had said, oftener than several others.

"Does he come to see June, or you, or both of you?" the Colonel had asked bluntly, looking at the last slip of pasteboard left by the young man.

"Oh, June, of course," said Rosamund, with a little quickness of impatience. "They nearly all come to see June."

"I don't see what the devil business he has doing that," said the Colonel, throwing down the card with angry contempt. "What's he come round here for, anyway?"

"Why shouldn't he?" asked Rosamund, surprised at his sudden annoyance.

"Well, he shouldn't," said the Colonel shortly. "That's one sure thing. He shouldn't."

And so that conversation ended, but the memory of it lingered uneasily in Rosamund's mind, and she found herself counting Jerry Barclay's calls and watching June while he was there and after he had gone.

The visits of the young man were not indeed sufficiently frequent to warrant uneasiness on sentimental scores. He sometimes dropped in on Sunday afternoon, and now and then on week-day evenings. What neither Rosamund nor the Colonel knew was that he had formed a habit of meeting June on walks she took along the fine new promenade of Van Ness Avenue, and on several occasions had spent a friendly hour with her, sitting on one of the benches in the little plaza on Turk Street.

The first and second times this had happened June had mentioned the fact to her sister, and that a gentleman should accidentally meet a lady in an afternoon stroll had seemed a matter of so little importance that Rosamund had quickly forgotten it. The subsequent meetings, also apparently accidental, June, for some reason known to herself, had not mentioned to any one. Now it was hard for her to persuade herself that she met Jerry Barclay by anything but prearranged design; and June did not like to think that she met him, or any other man, by prearrangement. So she let him elicit from her by skilful questioning, her itinerary for her afternoon walks when she had no engagements, and took some trouble to make herself believe that the meetings still had at least an air of the accidental.

But why did she not tell her sister of these walks? Why, in fact, had she once or twice lately almost misled Rosamund in her efforts to evade her queries as to how she had passed the afternoon?

If June happened to be looking in the mirror when she asked herself these questions she noticed that she reddened and looked guilty. There was nothing wrong in meeting Mr. Barclay and walking with him or sitting on one of the benches in the quiet little plaza. Their conversation had never contained a word with which the strictest duenna could have found fault. Why, then, did June not tell? She hardly knew herself. Some delicate fiber of feminine instinct told her that what was becoming a secretly tremulous pleasure would be questioned, interfered with, probably stopped. She knew she was not one who could fight and defy. They would overwhelm her, and she would submit, baffled and miserable.

If Jerry Barclay liked to talk to her that way in the open air, or on the park bench better than in the gloomy grandeur of the parlor in Folsom Street, why should he not? And yet she felt that if she had said this to Rosamund with all the defiant confidence with which she said it to herself, Rosamund would in some unexpected way sweep aside her argument, show it worthless, and make her feel that if Jerry did not want to see her in her own house he ought not to see her at all. So June used the weapons of the weak, one of the most valuable of which is the maintaining of silence on matters of dispute.

It was in February that their father suggested that they should return the numerous hospitalities offered them by giving a dance. It would not be a ball. They were still too inexperienced in the art of entertainment, and their mourning was yet too deep to permit of their venturing on so ambitious a beginning. "Just a house-warming," Allen said when he saw that they were rather alarmed by the magnitude of the undertaking. There was much talking and consulting of the Colonel. Every night after dinner the girls sat long over the coffee and fruit, discussing such vital points as to whether there should be two salads at the supper and would they have four musicians or five. Allen called them "little misers," and told them they "never would be tracked through life by the quarters they dropped." It was interesting to the Colonel to notice that Rosamund's habits of economy clung to her, while June had assimilated the tastes and extravagances of the women about her with a sudden, transforming completeness.

It was at one of these after-dinner consultations that he was presented with the list of guests written out neatly in Rosamund's clear hand. Was it all right, or did Uncle Jim think they had left out anybody?

As he ran his eye over it Allen said suddenly:

"They've got Mrs. Newbury down there. What do you think about her?"

The Colonel, who was reading through his glasses, looked up with a sharp glance of surprise and again down at the list, where his eyes stopped at the questioned name.

"Oh, strike her off," he said. "What do you want her for?"

"She's been here to see us," Rosamund demurred, "and she asked us once to her house to hear somebody sing."

"Why shouldn't she come?" said June. "What is there about her you don't like?"

"I didn't say there was anything," he answered in a tone of irritated impatience. "But she's a good deal older than you, and—and—well, I guess it wouldn't amuse her. She doesn't dance. You don't want to waste any invitations on people who may not come."

Apparently this piece of masculine logic was to him conclusive, for he took his pencil and made a mark through the name.

The evening of the dance arrived, and long before midnight its success was assured. It was undoubtedly one of the most brilliant affairs of the winter. It seemed the last touch on the ascending fortunes of June and Rosamund. They had never looked so well. In her dress of shimmering white, which showed her polished shoulders, Rosamund was beautiful, and June, similarly garbed, looked, as some of the women guests remarked, "actually pretty." As a hostess she danced little. Three times, however, Rosamund noticed her floating about the room encircled by the arm of Jerry Barclay. Other people noticed it too. But June, carried away by the excitement of the evening, was indifferent to the comment she might create. So was Barclay. He had drunk much champagne and felt defiant of the world. She felt defiant too, because she was so confidently happy.

By three the last guests had gone. Allen, hardly waiting for the door to slam on them, stumbled sleepily to bed, and June followed, a wearied sprite, bits of torn gauze trailing from her skirt, the wreath of jasmine blossoms she wore faded and broken, the starry flowers caught in her curls.

"Rosie, I'm too tired to stay up a minute longer," she called from the stairs, catching a glimpse of the dismantled parlor with Rosamund, followed by a yawning Chinaman, turning out lights and locking windows.

"Go up, dear," answered Rosamund in her most maternal tone. "I'll be up in a minute. Sing's so sleepy I know he'll go to bed and leave everything open if I don't stay till he's done."

The sisters occupied two large rooms, broad-windowed and spacious, in the front of the house. The door of connection was never shut. They talked together as they dressed, walking from room to room. The tie between them, that had never been broken by a week's separation, was unusually close even for sisters so near of an age, so united by mutual cares and past sorrows.

June's room shone bright in the lights from the two ground-glass globes which protruded on gilded supports from either side of the bureau mirror. It was furnished in the heavily gorgeous manner of the period and place. Long curtains of coarse lace fell over the windows, which above were garnished with pale blue satin lambrequins elaborately draped. The deeply tufted and upholstered furniture was covered with a blue-and-white cretonne festooned with woolen tassels and fringes. Over the foot of the huge bed lay a satin eiderdown quilt of the same shade as the lambrequins.

June, completely exhausted, was soon in bed, and lying peacefully curled on her side waited for her sister's footsteps. As she heard the creak of Rosamund's opening door she called softly:

"Come in here. I want to talk. I've millions of things to say to you."

Rosamund swept rustling into the room and sat down on the side of the bed. Her dress was neither crushed nor torn and the bloom of her countenance was unimpaired by fatigue.

"Dear Rosie, you look so lovely," said June, curling her little body under the clothes comfortably round her sister. "There was nobody here to-night half as good-looking as you were."

She lightly touched. Rosamund's arm with the tips of her fingers, murmuring to herself,

"Lovely, marbly arms like a statue!"

Her sister, indifferent to these compliments, which she did not appear to hear, sat looking at the toe of her slipper.

"I think it was a great success," she said. "Everybody seemed to enjoy it."

"Of course they did. I know I did. I never had such a beautiful, galumptious time in my life."

Rosamund gave her a gravely inspecting side-glance.

"You tore your dress round the bottom, I saw. There was quite a large piece trailing on the floor."

"Yes, it was dreadful," said June, nestling closer about the sitting figure and smiling in dreamy delight. "Somebody trod on it while I was dancing, and then they danced away with it round them, and it tore off me in yards, as if I was a top and it was my string."

"Were you dancing with Jerry Barclay?" asked Rosamund.

"I don't think so." She turned her head in profile on the pillow and looked at her sister out of the corner of her eye. Meeting Rosamund's sober glance she broke into suppressed laughter.

"What's the matter with you, Rosie?" she said, giving her a little kick through the bed-clothes; "you look as solemn as an undertaker."

"I don't think you ought to have danced so often with Jerry Barclay. It—it—doesn't look well. It—" she stopped.

"'It'—well, go on. Tell me all about it. A child could play with me to-night. You couldn't make me angry if you tried."

"June," said Rosamund, turning toward her with annoyed seriousness, "I don't think you ought to be friends with Jerry Barclay."

"What do you say that for?"

Despite her previous remark as to the difficulty of making her angry, there was a distinct, cold edge on June's voice as she spoke.

"I found out to-night. Ever since we heard those men talk that evening at Mrs. Davenport's I had a feeling that something wasn't right. And then Uncle Jim being so positive about not asking Mrs. Newbury here this evening."

"What's Mrs. Newbury got to do with it?"

"Everything. It's all Mrs. Newbury. To-night in the dressing-room some girls were talking about her and Mr. Barclay; I asked them what they meant, and I heard it all. It's a horrid story. I don't like to tell it to you."

"What is it?" said June. She had turned her head on the pillow and stared full face at her sister. She was tensely, frowningly grave.

"Well, they say—every one says—they're lovers."

"Lovers!" exclaimed June. "What do you mean by that? She's married."

"That's just the dreadful part of it. They're that kind of lovers—the wrong kind. They've been for years, and she loves him desperately and won't let him have anything to do with anybody else. And Mr. Newbury loves her, and doesn't know, and thinks Jerry Barclay is his friend."

There was a silence in the room. Rosamund had found it difficult to tell this base and ignoble piece of scandal to her sister. Now she did not look at June because she loved her too much to witness the shame and pain that she knew would be hers.

"It's too horrible," she continued, June uttering no sound. "I wouldn't have told you, but—well, we don't want him coming here if he's that sort of man. And Mrs. Newbury—" she made a gesture of angry disgust—"what right had *she* to come here and call on us?"

June still said nothing. Her hand was lying on the counterpane and Rosamund, placing hers on it, felt that it trembled and was cold. This, with the continued silence, alarmed her and she said, trying to palliate the blow,

"It seems so hard to believe it. He was so kind and natural and jolly up at Foleys, as if he was our brother."

"*Believe* it!" exclaimed June loudly. "You don't suppose *I believe* it?"

Her tone was high, almost violent. She jerked away her hand and drew herself up in the bed in a sitting posture.

"You don't suppose I'd believe a shameful, wicked story like that, Rosamund Allen?"

"But they all said so," stammered Rosamund, taken aback, almost converted by the conviction opposing her.

"Well, then, they say what's not true, that's all! They're liars. Don't lots of people tell lies? Haven't you found out that down here in the city most of the things you hear aren't true? They just like to spread stories like that so that people will listen to them. Everybody wants to talk here and nobody wants to listen. It's a lie—just a mean, cowardly lie."

Her face was burning and bore an expression of quivering intensity. Rosamund, astonished by her vehemence, stared at her disquieted.

"But—but—everybody thinks so," was all she could repeat.

"Then they think what's not so. Do *you* think so?" with eager challenge.

The other looked down, her brows drawn together in worried indecision.

"I don't know what to think," she said. "When he comes up in my mind, especially as he was at Foleys, it seems as if I couldn't believe it either."

"There!" exclaimed June triumphantly. "Of course you can't. Nobody who has any sense could. It's just degraded, low-minded people who have nothing better to do than spread scandals that could believe such a story about such a man."

"But Mrs. Newbury," demurred her sister. "Why did Uncle Jim not want us to ask her to-night?"

"What's Mrs. Newbury got to do with it? I don't know. I don't care anything about her. I don't like her. She looks like a large white seal, walking on the tip of its tail. I think she's common and fat and ugly. But what does she matter? If Mr. Newbury loves her he's got very bad taste, that's all I've got to say. And as to Jerry Barclay loving her? Why, Rosamund—" she suddenly dropped to her most persuasive softness of tone and expression—"you know he couldn't."

"I don't know," said Rosamund. "I don't feel as if I knew anything about men, or what they like, or what they don't like. You might think Mrs. Newbury ugly and they might think her beautiful. You never can tell. And then those men on the steps that night at Mrs. Davenport's"—she shot an uneasy glance at her sister—"that was what they meant."

"Rosie," said June, leaning toward her and speaking with pleading emphasis, "you don't believe it?"

"I don't want to, that's certain."

"Well, then, say you don't."

"I can't say that positively. I wish I could."

She rose from her seat and moved away, absently drawing the hair-pins from her coiled hair. June fell back on the pillow.

"Well, I can," she said. "I never felt more positive about anything in my life."

Her sister turned back to the bedside and stood there looking frowningly down.

"I hope you're right," she said. "I'd hate to think any man like that had ever come here to see us or been a friend of yours."

"So would I," said June promptly. "So would any girl."

"Well, good night. You're tired to death. I'll put the gas out."

June saw the tall white figure move to the bureau and then darkness fell, and she heard its rustling withdrawal.

She lay still for a time staring at the square of light that fell from her sister's room through the open door. Presently this disappeared and she moved her eyes to the faint luminous line which showed the separation of the window curtains. She was still staring at it wide-eyed and motionless when it grew paler, whiter and then warmer with the new day.

She had spoken the truth when she said she did not believe the ugly story. There are many women who have the faculty of quietly shutting a door on obvious facts and refusing them admittance into the prim sanctuary of their acceptance. How much more might a young girl, loving, inexperienced and tender, refuse to believe a blasting rumor that had touched a figure already shrined in her heart!

But the shock she suffered was severe. That such a story should be coupled with his name was revolting to her. And far down in the inner places of her being, where nature has placed in women a chord that thrills to danger, a creeping sense of dread and fear stirred. But she smothered its warning vibration and, with her eyes fixed on the crack of light, repeated over and over:

"Lies! lies! Miserable, cowardly lies!"

CHAPTER III
ONE OF EVE'S FAMILY

It was a few weeks after the ball that the Colonel heard of the expected arrival in town of Rion Gracey and Barney Sullivan *en route* to Virginia City.

From the great camp across the mountain wall in the Nevada desert, an electric current had begun to thrill and extend its vibrations wherever men congregated. The autumn rumors that Virginia was not dead persisted. The mutterings of the silver volcano had grown louder and caught the ear of the hurrying throng. The reports of a strike in Crown Point rose and fell like an uneasy tide. The price of the stock that in the spring of seventy had sold for seventy-five cents had risen to two, and then to three, dollars. Men watched it disquieted, loath to be credulous where they had so often been the dupes of manager and manipulator, yet tempted by the oft-repeated prophecy that the great bonanzas of Virginia were yet to be discovered. Throughout California and Nevada the miners that three years before had left the dying camp as rats leave a sinking ship, began to bind up their packs and turn their faces that way. It was like the first concentrating movement of a stealthily gathering army. The call of money had gone thrilling along the lines of secret communication which connect man with man.

The Graceys had large holdings in Virginia. The group of unprofitable claims consolidated under the name of the Cresta Plata was theirs, and Rion and his superintendent were going up "to take a look around." This was what the Colonel heard down town. It was a piece of intelligence that was reported as of weight. Mining men watched the movements of the Gracey boys as those about great rulers follow their actions in an effort to read their unexpressed intentions. When the Graceys moved into camps or out of camps, operators, managers and financiers noted the fact. That Rion and Sullivan should take a detour to San Francisco instead of going straight up from Sacramento argued that their need was not pressing.

The Colonel thought he knew why Rion had taken such a roundabout route. He and Allen had had many conversations on the subject of the match they wished to promote and had not the least idea of how to set about promoting. The Colonel had also tried to have talks with June about it. It seemed to him that a good way to further the matter and elicit some illuminating remark from her was to tell her at intervals that Rion Gracey was a man of sterling worth in whose love any woman would find happiness. To all of which June invariably agreed with an air of polite acquiescence which the Colonel found very baffling. His pet was to him the sweetest of living women, but he had to admit it was not always easy for him to understand or manage her.

On the afternoon of the day he had heard of Rion's expected arrival he had gone to see the new house a friend had just completed on Van Ness Avenue. The visit over he stood at the top of the flight of stone steps, looking up and down the great street, and wondering, as he tapped on his shoe with his cane, whether he would go across to Folsom Street for dinner or down to his club.

Suddenly his idle glance fell on a pair of figures on the block above, walking with the loitering step which betokens engrossing conversation. Their backs were toward him, but one at least he thought he recognized. He ran down the steps and in a few minutes had gained on them and was drawing quickly nearer. He had not been mistaken. The black silk skirt, held up to reveal a pair of small feet in high-heeled shoes, the sealskin jacket, the close-fitting black turban hat, below which hung an uneven shock of short, brown curls, were too familiar to him to permit of any uncertainty. The man he was not sure of, but as he drew closer he saw his face in profile, and with a start of surprised annoyance recognized Jerome Barclay.

At the corner they turned up the cross street. A short distance farther, on the angle of a small plaza, intruded into the gray city vista a green stretch of grass and shrubbery. The Colonel wondered if it was the objective point of their walk, and this thought added to the disquietude he already felt at the sight of Barclay, for when people went into parks they sat on benches and talked, sometimes for hours.

He was close at their heels before they heard his hail and turned. A momentary expression of annoyance, gone almost as soon as it came, passed over Barclay's face. June looked confused and, for the first instant, the Colonel saw, did not know what to say.

"Well," he said, trying to speak with genial unconsciousness, "what are you doing up here so far from your native haunts?"

"I met Miss Allen on the avenue just below there," said Jerry quickly, "walking up this way to make a call on some friends of hers."

He spoke with glib ease, but his eye, which lighted for an instant on June's, was imperious with a command. June was taken aback by his smooth readiness. She did not like what he said, but she obeyed the commanding eye and answered with stammering reluctance:

"Yes, the Nesbits. I was going there this afternoon. They're just a block beyond here."

It was not exactly a lie, June thought, for had Barclay not appeared she would doubtless have gone to the Nesbits, wondering all the time what had happened to him. But Barclay had appeared, as he always did now at the time and place he so carelessly yet so scrupulously designated, and June would not have seen the Nesbits that afternoon.

"Suppose you take a little *pasear* with me instead of going to the Nesbits," said the Colonel. "I'm not conceited, but I think I'm just as interesting as they are."

"And what are *you* doing up here?" she said, her presence of mind, and with it her natural gaiety of manner, returning. "You're as far from your native haunts as I am."

"I was calling, too," he answered, "on the Barkers. But *I* didn't meet any one sufficiently interesting to keep me from fulfilling my duties, and I have seen the new house from the skylight to the coal-bin."

"Never mind," she said consolingly, "you've met me. That's your reward for good conduct."

They had arrived at the upper corner of the plaza where only the breadth of a street divided them from the green, tree-dotted sward, cut with walks and set forth in benches. Barclay, raising his hat and murmuring some conventional words of farewell, turned and left them, and the Colonel and his companion strolled across the road and over the grass toward a bench, behind which a clump of laurels grew shelteringly, a screen against the wind and fog.

"This is the most comfortable of all the benches," said June artlessly as they sat down. "The laurels keep the wind off like a wall. Even on cold days, when the fog comes in, it's a warm little corner."

"You've been here before," said the Colonel, looking at her out of the sides of his eyes.

A telltale color came into her cheeks, but the city and its ways were training her, and she managed to exclude confusion and consciousness from her face.

"Oh, yes," she answered, "several times. I sometimes rest here after I've been taking a long walk."

"That must be dull," said her companion. "I can't see anything cheerful in sitting on a park bench by yourself."

He looked at her again. But his bungling masculine line of procedure was not of the kind to entrap even so untried a beginner. It made her smile a little, and then she looked down to hide the smile.

"Wasn't it jolly that we met?" she said, stroking the satiny surface of her new jacket and presenting to his glance a non-committal profile. The Colonel knew her well enough by this time to realize that she intended neither to confess nor to be trapped into revelations of past occupancy of the bench. He returned to less intricate lines of converse.

"Who do you think's to be here to-morrow?"

"A friend?"

"A friend from Foleys,—Rion Gracey, and Barney Sullivan with him."

"Rion Gracey!" She looked pleased and slightly embarrassed. "Really—really!" She paused, her face full of smiles, that in some way or other showed disquietude beneath them.

"They're down from Foleys and going on to Virginia in a day or two. Queer they came around this way, wasn't it?"

Again the Colonel could not keep from attempts to plumb hidden depths. Again his inspecting eye noticed a fluctuation of color. June was unquestionably surprised by the news, but he could not be sure whether she was pleased.

"You'll have to have them up to dinner," he continued. "You saw so much of them last summer before you left that you'll have to offer them some kind of hospitality."

"Of course," she said hastily, flashing an almost indignant look at him. "They'll take dinner with us, or breakfast, or lunch, or anything they like. I'd love to see them and hear about everything up there. I want to hear how Barney Sullivan's getting on with Mitty. I thought they'd be engaged by this time."

"Perhaps they are"—it must be confessed that the Colonel's interest in the love affairs of his friend Mitty sounded perfunctory—"I wish Rion was, too."

"Yes," in a small, precise voice, "wouldn't it be nice?"

"It would make me very happy," said the Colonel gravely, "very happy, June. You know that."

"Would it?" with a bright air of innocent surprise. "Why?"

The Colonel turned and looked at her squarely, almost sternly.

"You know why, June Allen," he said.

She had taken off her gloves and now suddenly slipped her hand into his and nestled nearer to him.

"Don't talk solemnly," she said, in a coaxing voice. "Don't make me feel as if I was in church."

He cast a side-glance at her, caught her twinkling eye, and they both laughed.

"You aggravating girl!" he said. "It's all for your own good that I'm talking solemnly. I want you to be happy."

"Well, I am happy, very happy. Don't you think I look like a person who's happy?"

He did not look at her, and she raised herself, and taking him by the two ears gently turned his face toward her.

"Excuse me," she said politely, "but as you wouldn't look at me I had to make you. Don't I look happy?"

"Happy enough now," he answered. "I was thinking of the future."

"Oh, the future!"—she made a sweeping gesture of scorn—"the future's so far away no one knows anything about it. It's all secrets. Let's not bother with it. The present's enough."

Her hand, as she held it up in front of her, suddenly caught her eye and fixed her attention.

"Look at my hands," she said. "They're getting quite white and ladylike. They're losing their look of honest toil, aren't they? How I've hated it!"

He held out his big palm and she placed her left hand, which was nearest him, in it. Her hands were small, the skin beautifully fine and delicate, but they showed the hard labor of the past in a blunting and broadening of the finger-tips. The Colonel looked at the little one lying in his.

"I don't see that there's anything the matter with them," he said. "This one only wants one more thing."

"What's that?"

"A ring."

This time June was caught.

"A ring?" she said. "Well, I have several, but they're not very pretty, and I thought I'd wait till father gave me a really handsome one."

"I don't mean a handsome one. I mean a plain, little gold one; just a band and worn on this finger."

He designated the third finger. June understood.

"Oh, Uncle Jim!" she said, trying to pull her hand away, blushing and rebellious.

The Colonel held it tight, feeling the opportunity too valuable to be trifled with.

"And Rion Gracey to put it on," he added.

Her answer came almost angrily as she turned away her face.

"Not for a moment."

"No, for a lifetime."

There was no reply and the Colonel loosed her hand. She pushed it back into her glove saying nothing. As she began to fasten the buttons he said:

"Do you often meet Barclay when you are out walking, as you did this afternoon?"

Women, who are timid by nature, and who, combined with that weakness, have an overmastering desire to be loved and approved of, are of the stuff of which the most proficient liars can be made. Had June, in childhood, been intimidated or roughly treated she would have grown up a fluent and facile perverter of the truth. The tender influences of a home where love and confidence dwelt had never made it necessary for her to wish to conceal her actions or protect herself, and she had grown to womanhood frank, candid and truthful. Now, however, she found herself drawn into a situation where, if she were to continue in the course that gave her the happiness she had spoken of, she must certainly cease to be open, even begin to indulge in small duplicities. It was with a sensation of shamed guilt that she answered carelessly:

"No, not often. Now and then I have."

"Rosamund says he doesn't come to the house as much as he used."

This was in the form of a question, too.

"Doesn't he? I haven't noticed much."

Her heart accelerated its beats and she felt suddenly unhappy, as she realized that she was misleading a person especially dear to her.

"I'm glad of that, Junie dear. I don't like him to be hanging round you. He's not the man to be your friend."

June began to experience a sense of misery.

"What are you down on him for?" she said. "I like him. I like him a great deal."

It seemed to her that by thus openly voicing her predilection for Barclay she, in some way or other, atoned for her previous prevarications.

"Like him a great deal?" repeated the Colonel, staring somberly at her. "What does that mean?"

She was instantly alarmed and sought to obliterate the effect of her words.

"Oh, I like him very much. I think he's interesting and handsome, and—and—and—very nice. Just that way."

Nothing could have sounded more innocently tame. The simple man beside her, who had loved but one woman and known the honest friendship of others as uncomplex as himself, was relieved.

"Barclay's not the man for a good girl to be friends with," he continued with more assurance of tone. "He's all that you say, handsome, and well educated, and a smooth talker and all that. But his record is not the kind a man likes. He's done things that are not what a decent man does. I can't tell you. I can't talk to you about it. But rely on me. I'm right."

"I know all about it," she answered, turning round and looking calmly at him.

"All about it!—about what?"—he stammered, completely taken aback.

"About that hateful story of Mrs. Newbury."

The Colonel's face reddened slightly. He had the traditional masculine idea of the young girl as a being of transparent ignorance, off which the wickedness of the world glanced as bird-shot off the surface of a crystal ball. Now he was pained and shocked, not only that June should have heard the story but that she should thus coolly allude to it.

"Then if you've heard it," he said almost coldly, "you should know without my telling you that Jerry Barclay's no man for you to know, or walk with, or have any acquaintance with."

"You don't suppose I believe it, do you?" she said with the same almost hard composure.

This indeed was a new view of the situation. For six years the Colonel had heard the affair between young Barclay and Mrs. Newbury talked of and speculated upon. It had now passed to the stage of shelved acceptance. People no longer speculated. Their condemnation savored even of the indifference of familiarity. The only thing that nobody did was to doubt. And here was a girl, looking him in the face and calmly assuring him of her disbelief. Had he known more of women he would have realized how dangerous a portent it was.

"But—but—why don't you believe it?" he asked, still in the stage of stammering surprise.

"Because I know Mr. Barclay," she answered triumphantly, fixing him with a kindling eye.

"Well, that may be a reason," said the Colonel, then stopped and drew himself to an upright position on the bench. He did not know what to say. Her belief in the man he knew to be guilty had in it a trustfulness of youth that was to him exceedingly pathetic.

"You can believe just what you like, dear," he said after a moment's pause, "it's the privilege of your sex. But this time you'd better quit believing and be guided by me."

"Why, Uncle Jim," she said leaning eagerly toward him, "I'm not a fool or a child any more. Can't I come to conclusions about people that may be right? I know Mr. Barclay well, not for as long as you have, but I shouldn't be surprised if I knew him a great deal better. We saw him so often and so intimately up at Foleys, and he couldn't be the kind of a man he is and be mixed up in such horrible scandals. It's impossible. He's a gentleman, he's a man of honor."

"Yes," nodded the Colonel, looking at the shrubs in front of him, "that's just what he'd say he was if you asked him."

"And it would be right. He's not capable of doing dishonorable things. He's above it. Rosamund thinks so, too."

"Oh, does she?" said the Colonel.

If he had not been so suddenly stricken with worry and foreboding he could not have forborne a smile at this citing of Rosamund as a court of last resort.

"Yes, Rosamund said she couldn't believe it either. If you knew him as we do you'd understand better. It's all lies. People are always talking scandal in this place—I've heard more since I came here than I heard in the whole of my life before. It's a dreadful thing, I think, to take away a man's character just for the fun of talking."

She had spoken rapidly and now paused with an air of suspended interest, which was intensified by her expression of eager questioning. The Colonel looked at her. In a dim way she was struck, as she had been before, by the intense melancholy of his eyes—sad old eyes—that told of a life unfulfilled, devastated, at its highest point of promise.

"June, dear," he said in a low voice, "you're not in love with this man?"

The color ran over her face to the hair on her forehead. The directness of the question had shocked her young girl's delicacy and pride. She tried to laugh, and then with her eyes down-drooped, said in a voice of hurried embarrassment:

"No, of course not."

He smiled in a sudden expansion of relief. All was well again. In his simplicity of heart it did not occur to him to doubt her.

CHAPTER IV
DANGER SIGNALS

Jerome Barclay lived with his mother in a new house on Taylor Street, near Jackson. They had only been there a short time. Before that South Park had been their home. But within the last year or two the fortunes of South Park had shown symptoms of decline, and when this happened Mrs. Simeon Barclay had felt that she must move.

Since her arrival in San Francisco in the early fifties, Mrs. Barclay had made many moves. These were not undertaken because her habitats had been uncomfortable, but because the fashionable element of the city had shown from the first a migratory tendency which was exceedingly inconvenient for those who followed it. Mrs. Barclay had followed it assiduously from the day she had landed from the steamer, and had in consequence lived in many localities, ranging from what was now Chinatown and in the fifties had been the most perfectly genteel and exclusive region, to the quietly dignified purlieus of Taylor Street.

Simeon Barclay had crossed the plains in an emigrant train in forty-nine, and between that and sixty-four, when he died, had made a fair fortune, first as a contractor and afterward as a speculator in real estate. In St. Louis, his native place, he had begun life as a carpenter, seen but little prosperity, and married a pretty servant girl, whose mind was full of distinctly formed ambitions. When he went to California in the first gold rush he left his wife and son behind him, and when, from the carpentering that he did with his own hands in forty-nine, he passed to the affluent stage of being a contractor in a large way of business, he sent for her to join him. This she did, found him with what to their small experience were flourishing fortunes, and immediately started out on that career of ambulating fashion which she had followed ever since.

Barclay senior's fifteen years of California life were full to the brim. He made fortunes and lost them, lived hard, had his loves and his hates openly and unblushingly, as men did in those wild days, and became a prominent man in the San Francisco of the early sixties. He had but the one child, and in him the ambitions of both parents centered. The Missouri carpenter had never been educated. He was always, even at the end of his life, uncertain in his grammar, and his wife had found it difficult to teach him what she called "table manners."

Father and mother had early resolved that their son should be handicapped by no such deficiencies. They sent him to the best schools there were in San Francisco and later to Harvard. There he was well supplied with money, developed the tastes for luxurious living that were natural to him, forgathered with the richest and fastest men of his class, and left a record of which collegians talked for years. After his graduation he traveled in Europe for a twelve-month, as a coping stone to the education his parents had resolved should be as complete as money could compass.

Shortly after his son's return Simeon Barclay died in the South Park house. When it came to settling up the estate it was found that he had left much less than had been expected. The house and the income of a prudently invested eighty thousand dollars was all the widow and son had to their credit when the outlying debts were paid. It was not a mean fortune for the place and the time, but both were querulous and felt themselves aggrieved by this sudden lightening of what had been for fifteen years a well-filled purse.

Jerry, to whom a pecuniary stringency was one of the greatest of trials, attempted to relieve the situation by speculating in "feet on the lode" in Virginia City, and quickly lost the major part of his inheritance. Even then there was no need for worry, as the son had been taken into the business the father had built up, which still flourished. But Jerry showed none of the devotion to commercial life that had distinguished the elder man. In his hands the fortunes of Barclay and Son, Real Estate Brokers, rapidly declined. He neglected the office, as he did his home, his mother, his friends. A devotion, more urgently engrossing and intoxicating than business could ever be, had monopolized his thoughts, his interests and his time.

He was twenty-four when he returned from Europe, handsome, warm-blooded, soft-tongued, a youth framed for the love of women. It speedily found him. He had not been home six months when his infatuation for the wife of William Newbury was common talk.

She was three years his senior, mismated to a man nearly double her age, dry, hard, and precise. She was a woman of tragedy and passion, suffering in her downfall. She had at first struggled fiercely against it, sunk to her fall in anguish, and after it, known contending conflicts of flesh and spirit, when she had tried to break from its bondage and ever sunk again with bowed head and sickened heart. People had wondered to see the figure of Lupé Newbury bent in prayer before the altars of her church. In her girlhood she had not been noted for her piety. Waking at night, her husband often heard her soft padding footfall as she paced back and forth through the suite of rooms she occupied. He had never understood her, but he loved her in a sober, admiring way, showered money on her, believed in her implicitly. This fond and unquestioning belief was the salt that her conscience rubbed oftenest and most deeply into the wound.

In those first years Jerry had given her his promise never to marry. He told her repeatedly that he regarded her as his wife; if she were ever free it would be his first care to make her so before the eyes of the world. But six years had passed since then, years during which the man's love had slowly cooled, while the woman's burned deeper with an ever-increasing fervid glow. The promise which had been given in the heat of a passion that sought extravagant terms in which to express itself, was now her chief hold upon him. In the scenes of recrimination that constantly took place between them she beat it about his ears and flourished it in his eyes. As she had no cunning to deceive him in the beginning, she had no subtilities to reawake old tenderness, rekindle old fires. She was as tempestuously dark in her despair as she was furious in her upbraidings, melting in her love. He was sorry for her and he was also afraid of her. He tried to please her, to keep her in a good temper, and he refrained from looking into the future where his promise and his fear of her, were writ large across his life.

It was for his protection from scenes of jealousy and tears that he had conducted his friendship with June in a surreptitious manner. He had the caution of selfish natures, and the underhand course that his intrigue necessitated had further developed it. He wanted to please himself always and to hurt no one, because people, when they are hurt, disturb the joyous tenor of life. Now, where June was concerned, he was not doing any harm. He saw the girl in a perfectly open manner except that he did not see her in her own house. He had a right to spare himself the railings to which he knew Lupé would subject him, and which he dreaded as only a man can who hears them from the lips of a woman he has ruined and no longer loves.

That it was unfair to June he would not permit himself to think. He liked seeing her too much to give it up, so he assured himself that it was a harmless pleasure for both of them. Of course he could not marry her. Even if he were free to do so he had no such feeling for her. They were only friends. Their conversation had never passed the nicely designated limits of friendship. He had never touched her hand save in the perfunctory pressure of greeting and farewell. His respect for June was genuine, only it was not as strong as his regard for his own pleasure and amusement.

Yet, despite the assurances of the platonic coolness of his sentiments, his desire for her society grew with what it fed on. When by some engagement, impossible to be evaded, they could not take their accustomed walk together, he was filled with an unreasonable disappointment, and was almost angry with her till she should appear again.

On the last occasion the Colonel had interrupted them only a few minutes after they had met. Jerry, cheated of the hour he had intended spending on the park bench with her, left them in a rage. And so imperative was his wish to see her that the next evening, indifferent to the fact that he would probably find the Colonel there, he made up his mind to go to the house on Folsom Street and pay one of his rare calls.

Rion Gracey and Barney Sullivan were dining with the Allens that night. There was much to talk about and the party sat long over the end of dinner, the smoke of the men's cigars lying in light layers across the glittering expanse of the table. There were champagne glasses beside each plate, the bubbles rising in the slender stems to cluster along the rim. These had appeared midway in the dinner, when, with much stumbling and after repeated promptings and urgings from Rion, Barney Sullivan had announced his engagement to Summit Bruce.

With glasses held aloft the party pledged Mitty and her lover. The encomiums of his fiancée which followed made Barney even redder than the champagne did.

"Oh, there's nothin' the matter with Mitt," he said with a lover's modesty, "I ain't gone it blind choosin' her."

"Mitty Bruce!" the Colonel exclaimed. "Mitty Bruce is the finest girl in the California foot-hills!"

"I guess Barney thinks just about that way," Rion answered, forbearing to stare at the blushing face of his superintendent.

"Oh, Mitt's all there!" Barney repeated, allowing himself a slight access of enthusiasm. "She's just about on top of the heap."

Greatly to his relief the conversation soon left his immediate affairs and branched out to the other members of the little Foleys group. Black Dan was still at the Buckeye Belle. His daughter was at school in New York where she had been sent in the autumn at her own request. The girls asked anxiously after her. The few glimpses they had had of the spoiled beauty had inflamed their imaginations. It seemed part of the elegant unusualness which appertained to her that she should be sent to New York to finish her education, with beyond that a polishing year or two of European travel.

"How wonderful she'll be when she comes back," Rosamund had said with an unenvious sigh. "Perfectly beautiful and knowing everything like the heroine of a novel."

A slight trace of bitterness was noticeable in Rion's answer.

"I think she'd have been a good deal more wonderful if she'd stayed here. She's just the apple of her father's eye, the thing he lives for. And now, unless he goes East, and that's almost impossible with things waking up this way in Virginia, he may not see her for a year or two."

The mention of Virginia broke the spell of gossip and small talk and the conversation settled down to the discussion of the business, which, in different degrees, absorbed the four men. It was curious to notice the change wrought in them by this congenial theme. Sullivan's uncouthness and embarrassment fell from him with the first words. His whole bearing was transformed; it became infused with alertness and gained in poise and weight. The heaviness of his visage gave place to a look of sharpened concentration. His very voice took on different tones, quick, sure and decisive.

But it was to Rion Gracey that the others deferred. June, sitting silent in her chair, noticed that when he spoke they listened, Sullivan with foxlike keenness of face, the Colonel with narrowed eyes, ponderingly attentive over his cigar, her father with a motionless interest showing in knit brows and debating glance. Leaning back in an attitude of careless ease, Rion spoke simply but with a natural dominance, for here he was master. A thrill of surprised admiration passed through the girl. He was a man among men, a leader by weight of authority, to whom the others unconsciously yielded the foremost place.

The room was dim with smoke when they finally rose from the table. The mining discussion was still in progress, but Rion dropped out of it to turn to his hostess and draw back her chair. As he did so he leaned over her shoulder and said in a lowered voice:

"It's too bad I've got to go on to-morrow. I wanted to see you again. I wanted to talk to you."

The words were simple enough. The young girl, however, looking uneasy, turned to glance at him. She met his eyes, keen, deep-set, quiet, the eyes of the out-door man accustomed to range over airy distances. In them she saw a look which caused her to drop her own. Murmuring a word or two of reply she turned and passed through the doorway into the sitting-room just behind Rosamund. That young woman suddenly felt her arm pressed by a small, cold hand, and in her ear heard a whisper:

"Don't leave me alone this evening with Rion Gracey. Please don't."

Rosamund turned and shot an inquiring side-glance at her sister's perturbed face. She strolled toward the sitting-room bay-window and began to arrange the curtains, June at her heels.

"Why not?" she said in a whisper, pulling the heavy folds together.

"I'm afraid of what he's going to say. Oh, please"—with as much urgency as the low tone employed permitted—"if he suggests that we go into the drawing-room to look at photographs or albums or anything, you come along, too."

"But why?"

"Rosie, don't be such a fool!" in an angry whisper.

Rosamund was about to retort with some spirit when the click of the iron gate caught her ear. She drew back the curtains and peeped out. A step sounded on the flagged walk and a tall, masculine figure took shape through the density of the fog-thickened atmosphere. She closed the curtains and looked at June with an unsmiling eye.

"You needn't be afraid of being left alone with anybody," she said. "Here's Jerry Barclay."

June drew back, her eyebrows raised into exclamatory semi-circles, an irrepressible smile on her lips.

"Rosamund," called Allen from the table, "where's the ash receiver? Gracey's got nothing to put his ashes in but the blue satin candy box one of June's young men gave her for Christmas."

The entrance of Jerry Barclay a moment later had a marked effect upon the company. He was known to the four men and not especially liked by any one of them. The Colonel had begun to feel for him a sharp, disquieted repugnance. The one person in the room to whom his entrance afforded pleasure was June, and this she made an effort to hide under a manner of cold politeness.

An immediate constraint fell on the party which the passage of the evening did not dispel. Gracey was angry that the advent of this man whom he mentally characterized as "a damned European dandy" had deprived him of a tête-à-tête with June. He had not intended, as the young girl feared, to ask her to marry him. He had the humility of a true lover and he felt that he dared not broach that subject yet. But he had hoped for an hour's converse with her to take with him on his journey as a sweet, comforting memory. Sullivan detested Jerry, whose manner he found condescending, turned from him, and began talking with an aggressive indifference to his host. But the Colonel was the most disturbed of all. What worried him was the difference between June's manner to Jerry to-day, when others were present, and June's manner to Jerry yesterday, when they had been walking alone on Van Ness Avenue.

By eleven o'clock they had gone and Allen having stolen to bed, the sisters were left together in the sitting-room. They were silent for a space, Rosamund moving about to put out lights, give depressed cushions a restoring pat, and sweep the ashes of the fire into a careful heap beneath the grate, while June idly watched her from the depths of an arm-chair.

"Aren't people funny?" said the younger sister suddenly, turning from her kneeling position on the rug, the hearth-brush in her hand. "They seem to be so different in different places."

"How do you mean?" said June absently. "Who's different in a different place?"

"Well, Barney is. He's all right and looks just as good as anybody up at the mines. And down here he's entirely different, he looks so red, and his feet are so big, and his hands never seem to know where to go unless he's talking about mining things. His clothes never looked so queer up at Foleys, did they? They seemed just like everybody else's clothes up there."

"Oh, Barney's all right," returned the other, evidently taking scant interest in the problem. "I'm glad he and Mitty are going to be married."

"But Rion Gracey's not like that," continued Rosamund, pursuing her own line of thought. "He's just the same everywhere. I think he looks better down here. He looks as if he were somebody, somebody of importance. He even makes other people, that look all right when he's not by, seem sort of small and insignificant."

"Whom did he make look small and insignificant?" said June suddenly in a key of pugnacious interest.

"Jerry Barclay. I thought Jerry Barclay looked quite ordinary and as if he didn't amount to much beside Rion. The things he said seemed snappish and sometimes silly, like what a girl says when she's cross and is trying to pretend she isn't."

"I don't think it very polite, Rosamund," said June in a coldly superior tone, "to criticize people and talk them over when they've hardly got out of the house."

"Well, perhaps it isn't," said Rosamund contritely, returning to her hearth-brushing, "but like lots of other things that aren't just right it's awfully hard not to do it sometimes."

The girls went up stairs and June was silent. Rosamund thought she was still annoyed by the criticism of her friend, and so she was. For deep in her own heart the thought that Rosamund had given voice to had entered, paining and shocking her by its disloyalty, and making her feel a sense of resentment against Rion Gracey.

CHAPTER V
THE GREAT GOD PAN

In the spring in San Francisco the trade winds come and all wise Californians move inland. In the early seventies the exodus to the country was not noticeably large. Rural hotels were still small and primitive. To be able to evade the fog-laden breath of the trades was the luxury of the well-to-do, and the well-to-do evaded them by retiring to country houses which dotted the teeming reaches of the Santa Clara Valley, or sought the shelter of the live-oaks where the golden floor of the valley slopes up into the undulations of the hills.

The Allens moved down early in April. Their father, after an afternoon's excursion in a buggy with a real estate agent, came back one evening and told them he had rented the De Soto house, back of San Mateo, for three years, and they must be ready to move into it in a week.

He was full of business and hurry in these days, and said he could not help them much. Neither would he be with them a great deal, as he would spend most of his summer in town with occasional trips to Virginia City. Crown Point was steadily rising and the rumors of a new bonanza were on every tongue. Rion Gracey had not returned, and Black Dan had ridden over the mountains into the Nevada camp on his own horse, a dislike for modern modes of locomotion being one of his peculiarities. Allen had bought heavily of the rising stock and seen himself on the road to even more dazzling fortune. He had rented the De Soto place for the highest price any real estate agent had yet dared to ask. People who knew of the rate of his expenditure talked of a beggar on horseback. But the Barranca was paying well and the twenty-stamp mill was up and going.

The De Soto estate was part of the princely grant that the Señorita Esperanza de Soto brought as a marriage portion to her husband, Peter Kelley, a sailor from a New England clipper which touched at Yerba Buena in thirty-eight. At the time the Allens rented it, part of the great tract had been parceled out and sold to householders. The central portion, where Peter and the Señora Kelley had built a stately home, was practically as it had been when the Yankee seaman first ranged over it and realized the riches of his bride. Now both sailor and señora were dead, and their only son, Tiburtio Kelley, preferred a life in Paris on the large fortune accumulated by his thrifty father, to the *dolce far niente* of empty, golden days in the Santa Clara Valley.

This central strip of the tract, which ran from the valley up into the first spurs of the hills, was still a virgin wilderness. Huge live-oaks, silvered with a hoar of lichen, stretched their boughs in fantastic frenzies. Gray fringes of moss hung from them, and tangled screens of clematis and wild grape caught the sunlight in their flickering meshes or lay over mounds of foliage like a torn green veil. The silence of an undesecrated nature dreamed over all. Woodland life seldom stirred the dry undergrowth, the rustle of nesting birds was rare in the secret leafy depths of the oaks. Here and there the murmurous dome of the stone pine soared aloft, the clouded dusk of its foliage almost black against the sky.

For nearly two miles the carriage drive wound upward through this sylvan solitude. As it approached the house a background of emerald lawns shone through the interlacing of branches, and brilliant bits of flower beds were set like pieces of mosaic between gray trunks. The drive took a sweep around a circular parterre planted in geraniums—a billowing bank of color under a tent of oak boughs—and ended in a wide, graveled space at the balcony steps.

The house was a spreading, two-story building of wood, each floor surrounded by a deep balcony upon which lines of French windows opened. Flowering vines overhung, climbed and clung about the balcony pillars and balustrades. Roses drooped in heavy-headed cascades from second-story railings; the wide purple flowers of the clematis climbed aloft. On one wall a heliotrope broke in lavender foam and the creamy froth of the bankshur rose dabbled railings and pillars and dripped over on to the ground. It was a big, cool, friendly looking house with a front door that in summer was always open, giving the approaching visitor a hospitable glimpse of an airy, unencumbered hall.

The move completed, June and Rosamund began to taste the charm of the Californian's summer life. There were no hotels near them. No country club had yet risen to bring the atmosphere of the city into the suave silence of the hills. It was a purely rural existence: driving and riding in the morning, reading in the hammock under the trees, receiving callers on the balcony in the warm, scented end of the afternoon, going out to dinner through the dry, dewless twilight and coming home under the light of large, pale stars in a night which looked as transparently dark as the heart of a black diamond.

They were sometimes alone, but, as a rule, the house contained guests. The Colonel at first came down constantly, always from Saturday to Monday and now and then for a week-day evening. But in May the sudden leap of Crown Point to one hundred and eighty upset the tranquillity of even cooler natures than Jim Parrish's, and the stock exchange became the center of men's lives. The long expected bonanza had been struck. The San Franciscans, once more restored to confidence in the great lode, were seized with their old zest of speculation, and all the world bought Crown Point. Allen saw himself on the road to a second fortune, and threw his money about in Virginia with an additional gusto, as it had been the scene of some of his poorest days.

Even the Colonel was attacked by the fever and invested. His financial condition had given him grounds for uneasiness lately, and here was the chance to repair it. A mine in Shasta, in which he had been a large owner, shut down. He owned property in South Park, and the real estate agents were beginning to shake their heads at the mention of South Park property. It surprised him to realize that for the first time in years he was short of ready money. He sold two buildings far out among the sand dunes on upper Market Street, and with the rest of his kind bought Virginia mining stock with Crown Point and Belcher at the head.

Under the live-oaks back of San Mateo the girls only faintly heard the rising rush of the excitement. The current circled away from their peaceful corner, lapped now and then by a belated ripple. The country life they both loved filled them with contentment and health. Rosamund took to gardening again. Her face shaded by a large Mexican hat, she might be seen of a morning in confab with the Irish gardener, astonishing him by her practical knowledge. In the evening she surreptitiously "hosed" the borders, wishing that her visitors would go back to town and leave her to the peaceful pursuit of the work she delighted in and understood.

June was not so energetic. She did not garden or do much of anything, save now and then go for a walk in the wild parts of the grounds.

As might be expected, Mrs. Barclay always moved down to San Mateo in April. She was not rich enough to own a large country place, but she did the best that was in her and rented a pretty cottage outside the village. Here Jerry came from town every Saturday and stayed till Monday morning, and to her surprise not infrequently appeared unannounced on week-day afternoons, saying that business was dull, and there was no necessity waiting about in town. The year before she had complained greatly that her son's visits to San Mateo were rare. This summer she had no such grievance. He kept a horse in her small stable, and as soon as he arrived had it saddled and went out for a ride. Sometimes on Sunday he rode over and called on the Allens, but there were other people to visit in the neighborhood and he did not go to the Allens'—so he told his mother—as often as he would have liked.

The direction he took on the week-day afternoons was always the same. No rain falls during the California summer, there are no dark hours of thunder and cloud; it is a long procession of blue and gold days, steeped in ardent sunshine, cooled by vagrant airs, drowsy with aromatic scents—a summer made for lovers' trysts.

Half-way up the winding drive to the De Soto house Jerry had learned there was a path through the underbrush which led to an opening, deep in the sylvan wilderness, under the thick-leaved roof of an oak. It had been a favorite spot of the late Señora Kelley's, and all the poison oak had been uprooted. With the canopy of the tree above—a ceiling of green mosaic in which the twisted limbs were imbedded—and the screen of lightly hung, flickering leafage encircling it, it was like a woodland room, the bower of some belated dryad.

Sometimes Jerry had to wait for her, and lying prone on the ground, his horse tethered to a tree trunk near by, lay looking up, his senses on the alert to catch her step. Sometimes she was there first, and as he brushed through the covert, he saw her dress gleaming between the leaves in a spattering of white. His heart was beginning to beat hard at the sound of her advancing footfall. While he waited for her he thought of nothing, his whole being held in a hush of expectancy. When she came he found it difficult for the first moment to speak easily.

On an afternoon early in June he sat thus waiting. All the morning the thought of this meeting had filled his mind, coming between him and his business. On the train coming down the anticipation of it held him in a trance-like quietude. He talked little to his mother at lunch. He kept seeing June as she came into sight between the small, delicately leaved branches, dots of sun dancing along her dress, her eyes, shy and full of delight, peeping through the leaves for him. He answered his mother's questions at random and ate but little. The picture of the white-clad girl grew in intensity, striking him into motionless reverie, so that, his eyes fixed, he seemed scarcely to breathe.

It was very warm. Lying on his back on the dried grass, his hands clasped under his head, he gazed straight before him at the long fringes of moss that hung from a gnarled bough. His senses were focused in an effort to disentangle her footstep from the drowsy noises of the afternoon. All scruples, apprehensions of danger, were swept away by the hunger for her presence. His mind had room for no other thought. Every nerve was taut, every sense quiveringly alert, as he lay, still as a statue, waiting for her.

Suddenly he rose on his elbow staring sidewise in the concentration of his attention. The subdued, regular brush of her dress against the leaves came softly through the murmurous quietness. He sprang to his feet, strangely grave, his glance on the path she came by. In a moment her figure speckled the green with white, and she came into view, hurrying, sending sharp, exploring looks before her. She saw him, instantly fell to a slower pace, and tried to suppress the gladness of her expression. But he saw it all, and the quick breath that lifted her breast. Her hand hardly touched his, and moving a little away from him, she sank down on the ground, her white skirts billowing round her. She pressed them into folds with arranging pats, avoiding his eyes, and repeating some commonplaces of greeting.

Jerry returned to his reclining posture, lying on his side, his elbow in the grass, his hand supporting his head. He, at first, made no pretense of moving his eyes from her, and answered her remarks shortly and absently.

Against the background of variegated greens she presented a harmony of clear, thin tints like a water color. Her dress of sheer, white muslin was cut away from the throat in a point, and smoothly covering her arms and neck, let them be seen beneath its crisp transparency, warmly white under the cold white of the material. The heat of the afternoon and the excitement of the meeting had called up a faint pink to her cheeks. In her belt she had thrust a branch of wistaria and the trail of blossoms hung down along her skirt. She wore a wide leghorn hat, and in this she had fastened another bunch, the flowers lying scattered across the broad rim, and one spray hanging over its edge and mingling with the curls that touched her neck.

Jerry had never seen her look as she did this afternoon. Love, that she felt assured was returned, had lent her the fleeting beauty of an hour. She did not seek to penetrate the future. The happiness of the present sufficed her. She said little, plucking at a tuft of small wild flowers that grew beside her, conscious to her inmost fiber of her lover's eyes.

"Why don't you take off your hat?" he said. "There's no sun here."

She obediently took it off and threw it on the ground. The black velvet she wore around her head had become disarranged and she raised her hands to draw it into place and tuck a loosened curl under its restraint. He watched her fixedly.

"Now," he said, reaching out to draw the hat to him and taking one of the wistaria blossoms from it, "put this in."

"I have no glass," she demurred, stretching a hand for the flower.

"That doesn't matter. I'll be your glass. I'll tell you if it isn't all right."

She tucked the stem of the blossom into the velvet band, so that its trail of delicate lavender bells fell downward behind her ear.

"How is that?" she said, facing him, her eyes downcast. Her coquetries of manner had deserted her. With the flush on her face a glowing pink and her lashes on her cheeks, she was a picture of uneasy embarrassment.

"Perfect," he answered. He continued to stare at her for a moment and then said suddenly in a low voice,

"Good heavens, how you've changed! It's a little over a year now that I've known you and you're an entirely different person from the girl with the short hair I met up at Foleys. What have you done to yourself? What is it that has changed you?"

"I think it's because I'm happy," she said, beginning again to pick the wild flowers.

"Why are you happy?"

"I don't know. It's hard to say. I—" she paused and began to arrange her flowers in a careful bunch.

He suddenly dropped his eyes to the ground and there was a silence. The sleepy murmur of insects rose upon it. The sun, in an effort to penetrate the inclosure, scattered itself in intermittent flickerings of brilliant light that shifted in golden spots along the tree trunks or came diluted through the webbing of twigs and vine tendrils. It was still very hot and the balsamic odors of bay-tree and pine seemed to grow more intense with the passing of the hour.

"You were such a quiet little thing up there," Jerry went on, "working like a man in that garden of yours and never wanting to go anywhere. Things down here may have made you happy, but I sometimes wonder if they haven't made you frivolous, too."

When Jerry ceased staring at her and began to talk in this familiar, half-bantering strain, she felt more at ease, less uncomfortable and conscious. She seized the opening with eagerness and said, smiling down at her little bouquet:

"But you know I am frivolous. I love parties and pretty clothes and lots of money to spend, and all the good times going. I was that way at Foleys, only I didn't have any of those things. I can be serious, too, if it's necessary. When I haven't got the things to be frivolous with, I can do without."

He stretched out his hand and plucked a long stalk of feather-headed grass.

"Can you?" he said indolently. "Are you sure you're not telling a little story?"

"No, no, quite sure. I have two sides to my character, a frivolous one and a serious one. You ought to know that by now."

"Which have you shown to me oftenest?" He was peeling the stalk of its shielding blade of grass.

"I don't know. That's for you to say. Perhaps it's been an even division."

He looked up. She was smiling slightly, her dimple faintly in evidence.

"And I suppose the dimple," he said, "belongs to the frivolous side."

"Yes. Even my face has two sides; the frivolous one with the dimple and the serious one without."

"Let me see them," he said. "Let me judge which of the two is the more attractive."

He leaned forward and with the tip of the long spear of grass, touched her lightly on the cheek.

"Turn," he commanded, "turn, till I get a good profile view."

She turned, presenting her face in profile, pure as a cameo against the leafy background.

With the Tip of the Long Spear of Grass, He Touched Her Lightly on the Cheek

"That's the serious side," she said, raising her chin slightly, so that her curls slipped back, disclosing her ear.

"And now for the frivolous," he answered. "I don't seem to know the serious side so well."

She turned her head in the other direction, her eyes down-drooped. He drew himself nearer to her over the ground, the grass spear in his hand.

"And so this is the frivolous. Shouldn't the dimple be here?"

He touched her cheek again with the tip of the grass, and as he did so the dimple trembled into being. She looked at him slantwise, laughing, with something breathless in the laughter.

As she met his glance her laughter died away. His face had changed to something unfamiliar and hard. He was pale, his eyes fierce and unloving. For a moment she looked at him, some phrase of inquiry dying on her lips, then she made an attempt to rise, but he drew close to her and caught her hands. She turned her head away, suddenly white and frightened.

"June," he whispered, "do you know how much I love you?"

It was a whisper unlike anything she had ever heard before. A whisper within herself responded to it. She sat still, trembling and dizzy, and felt his arms close about her, and her consciousness grow blurred as his lips were pressed on hers.

The instant after he had loosed her and they had shrunk from each other in guilty terror, the girl quivering with a rush of half comprehended alarm, the man struggling with contending passions. His face seemed to her full of anger, almost of hatred, as he cried to her,

"Go home. I'm sorry. I shouldn't have touched you. We can't come here again this way. I'm not free to love you. Go home."

He made an imperious gesture for her to go, almost as though driving her from his presence. White as death and dazed by the terrifying strangeness of it all, she scrambled to her feet, and turning from him, set out at a run. She brushed through the bushes, her eyes staring before her, her breast straining with dry sobs. In one hand she still held her little bunch of wild flowers, and with the other she made futile snatches at her skirt, which she had trodden upon and torn.

Gaining the end of the wood, she came into the open garden, glaring with sun, deserted and brilliant. Back of it stood the house, shuttered to the afternoon heat and drowsing among its vines. She was about to continue her course over the grass to the open front door, when a footstep behind her, rapid as her own, fell on her ear. For an instant of alert, lightly poised terror, she paused listening, then shot forward across the grass and on to the drive. But her pursuer was fleeter than she. Close at her shoulder she heard him, his voice full of commanding urgency.

"Stop, I must speak to you."

She obeyed as she must always obey that voice, and wheeled around on him, pallid and panting.

"June, dearest, forgive me. I forgot myself and I've frightened you. But we mustn't meet—that way—any more."

She looked at him without answering. He was as pale as she. The lower part of his face seemed to tremble. He had difficulty in controlling it and speaking quietly.

"It's true what I said," he went on. "I love you. I've done so for months. I was to blame, horribly to blame. You're so young—such a child. I was the one to blame for it all."

"For what?" she said. "What's there to blame anybody for? What has happened all of a sudden?"

He came closer to her and looked her steadily in the eye.

"I am not free," he said in the lowest audible voice. "I can't marry you. I am not free."

She repeated with trembling lips,

"Not free! Why not?"

"No. If I were—oh, June, if I were!" He turned away as if to go, then turned back, and said,

"Oh, June, if I were, we would be so happy! If I could undo the past and take you—!"

His voice broke and he looked down, biting his underlip. She understood everything now, and for the moment speech was impossible. There was a slight pause, and then he said,

"I wouldn't let myself see the way it was going. I lied to myself. I loved you better every day, and I persuaded myself I didn't, and that it was nothing but a friendship to both of us. We mustn't meet this way any more. But we will see each other sometimes at people's houses? We're not to be strangers."

She turned dazedly away from him to go to the house. For a step or two he let her go. Then he followed her, caught her hand with its bunch of limp flowers, and said with urgent desperation:

"I'll see you sometimes. I can't give you up entirely. Perhaps—perhaps—later, when time has passed, we can be friends. June, I can't give it all up like this."

She turned on him a face whose expression pierced through his egotism.

"Let me go into the house," she whispered. "I can't say anything now. Let me go into the house."

He dropped her hand, and turning, walked rapidly toward the driveway. June ran to the house.

It was wrapped in complete silence. Not a sound or movement came from it. She had but one idea, to mount the stairs unseen, gain her room and then lock the door. Noiseless and fleet-footed she sped up the veranda steps, flew through the open door, and then cowered against the wall. Rosamund was on the stairs coming down.

"June," she said sharply, "where did Jerry Barclay come from, and what was he saying to you out there? I've been watching you from the window."

Then she saw her sister's face. Her own changed in a flash. Its severity vanished, and concern, alarm, love, took its place. She ran downward to the figure at the stair-foot, pressed against the wall.

"What's happened? June, what's the matter?"

Her startled whisper broke the sunny stillness with a note of the deadly realism of life amid the sweet unconcern of nature. She tried to clasp June, who made an effort to squeeze past her, crushed against the wall, her head down, like one who fears recognition. When, finding it impossible to escape, she suddenly collapsed at Rosamund's feet, curled up like a person in physical anguish, and cried with smothered violence,

"He's not free, Rosamund. It's all over; everything's over. It's all true, and we've got to end it all. He's not free."

Rosamund realized vaguely what had happened. She was a loving woman, but she was a practical one, too. There were people in the house who must not see June just at this crisis. She was much the larger and stronger of the two girls, and she bent down and attempted to raise the prostrate figure.

"June, listen. We were going out driving at five. Mary Moore may be down at any moment. Come quick; she mustn't see you. She's the worst gossip in San Francisco. Come, I'll help you."

She dragged the girl up with an arm around her, hurried her to the top of the stairs, along the hall, and into her room. There she let her fall into an arm-chair, and, stepping back, locked the door.

In the sweet-scented, airy room, with its thin muslin curtains softening the hot brilliancy of the landscape, June sat in the arm-chair, silent and motionless, her face pinched. Rosamund, who had never seen her sister like this, did not know what to do, and in despair, resorted to the remedies she had been accustomed to using when her mother had been ill. She softly rubbed June's temples with cologne and fanned her. Finally she knelt down by her side and said tenderly,

"What is it, Junie, dear? Tell it to me."

"I have told it to you," said June. "He's not free; that's all. You all said it, but I wouldn't believe it. Now he's said it and I've got to believe it."

She spoke in a high, hard voice, and Rosamund, kneeling on the floor, put her arms round her, and said with ingenuous consolation,

"But now you know it, the worst's over."

"Everything's over," said June dully.

Her eyes fell to her lap, and there, in one hand, she saw the wilted remains of the little bunch of wild flowers. A sudden realization of what her feelings had been when she picked them, how joyous, how shyly happy, how full of an elated pleasure of life, and what they were now, fell upon her with desolating force. She gave a cry, and, turning from her sister, pressed her face against the back of the chair and burst into a storm of tears.

CHAPTER VI
READJUSTMENT

June and July passed, and the life in the De Soto house was very uneventful. As soon as the group of guests left June requested her sister to ask no more visitors for a time, and the mid-summer days filed by, unoccupied in their opulent, sun-bathed splendor.

The blow at first crushed her. Despite the warnings she had received, it had come upon her with the stunning force of the entirely unexpected. The very fact that Jerry had been attacked by scandal had lent an exalted fervor to her belief in him. Even now, had there been a possibility of her continuing in this belief, she would have persisted. Weak, loving women have an extraordinary talent for self-deception, and June combined with weakness and love an irrepressible optimism. She tried to plead for him with herself, argued his case as before a stern judge, attempted in her ignorance to find extenuating circumstances for him, and then came face to face with the damning, incontrovertible fact that he himself had admitted.

It was a blasting experience. Had she known him less well, had their acquaintance been of shorter duration, the blow would probably have killed her love. But the period of acquaintance had been long, the growth of affection gradual. By the time the truth was forced upon her, her passion had struck its roots deep into her heart, and she was not strong enough to tear it out.

In the long summer days, wandering about the deserted, glowing gardens, she began the work of reconstructing her ideal. She told herself that she would always love him, but now it was with no confidence, no proud joy in a noble and uplifting thing. With agonizing throes of rebirth, her feeling for him passed from the soft, self-surrendering worship of a girl to the protective and forgiving passion of a woman. As it changed she changed with it. The suggestion of the child that had lingered in her vanished. The freshness of her youth went for ever. The evanescent beauty that happiness had given her, which on the day of Barclay's declaration had reached its climax, shriveled like a flower in the heat of a fire. She looked pale, pinched, and thin. Eying her image in the glass, she marveled that any man could find her attractive.

In the first period of her wretchedness she was numbed. Then, the house swept of its guests and she and Rosamund once more alone, her silence broke and she poured out her sorrows to her sister. Rosamund heard the story from the first day at Foleys to its fateful termination in the Señora Kelley's woodland bower.

She listened with unfailing sympathy, interrupted by moments of intense surprise. The revelations of the constant meetings with Barclay, which had been so skilfully kept secret, amazed and disconcerted her. She tried to conceal her astonishment, but now and then it broke out in startled queries. It was so hard to connect the unconscious and apparently candid June of the winter with this disclosure of a June who had been so far from candid. It was nearly impossible to include them in the same perspective. The culprit, engrossed in the recital of her griefs, was oblivious of her sister's growing state of shocked amaze, which sometimes took the form of silence, and occasionally expressed itself in gently probing questions.

"But, June," she could not help saying in protest, "didn't you realize something wasn't all right when you saw he'd rather meet you outside than see you at home?"

June turned on her an eye of cold disapproval.

"No. And I don't see now that that's got anything to do with it."

Rosamund subsided meekly, unable to follow the intricacies of her sister's mental processes.

She did not argue with June—it was hopeless in the sufferer's present state of mind—and she made few comments on Barclay's behavior. But she had her opinion of him, and it was that he was one of the darkest of villains. As to her opinion of June's part in the story, she was a loyal soul and had none. All she felt was a flood of sympathy for the shocked and wounded girl, and a worried sense of responsibility in a position with which she felt herself unable to cope. It was with great relief that, toward the end of July, she received a letter from the Colonel, who had been six weeks in Virginia City, telling her he would be with them on the following Sunday.

She drove down to the train to meet him with the intention of preparing him for the change in his favorite. She had written to him that June was not well. Driving back from the station she had ample time to expatiate on this theme and warn him not to exclaim unduly on her changed appearance. The Colonel began to be apprehensive and ask penetrative questions, to which she had no answer. He leaped out of the carriage at the veranda steps and ran up to the top, where June stood.

The change in her, flushed with welcome, was not strikingly apparent at the first glance. It was later that he began to realize it, to be startled and then alarmed. She sat quiet through dinner, nibbling musingly at her food, once or twice not answering him. The empty silence of the house struck chill on him, and when he had commented on the absence of visitors, she had said with sudden gusty irritation,

"There's been nobody here for over a month. I don't want anybody to come. I'll go away if anybody's asked. I like being alone this way."

He looked at Rosamund with an almost terrified inquiry. She surreptitiously raised her brows and gave her head a warning shake.

It was late in the evening before he had a chance to speak to Rosamund alone. Then, June having gone to her room, and he and Rosamund being left alone in the sitting-room, he laid his hand on the young girl's shoulder, and said in a voice of command,

"Now, Rosamund, I've got to hear all about this. What the devil's been going on down here?"

She told him the whole story, greatly relieved to have a listener who could advise her.

The Colonel was staggered by it. He said little, but Rosamund was not half-way through when he began pacing up and down, his hands in his pockets, every now and then a low ejaculation breaking from him. He, too, was astounded by the account of June's underhand behavior. He had thought the two girls as simple as children. That his own particular darling could have consented to, and then so dexterously carried out, a plan of procedure so far from what he had imagined a young girl would do, was painful and shocking to him. But as June's love could not be killed by one sort of disagreeable revelation, so his could suffer no abatement from another kind. Manlike, he immediately began to make excuses for her.

"She was too young to be allowed to go round that way alone," he burst out angrily. "There was nobody to take care of her. What good are two old Silurians like me and your father to look after girls? I told him six months ago he ought to get some kind of an old woman in the house who'd knit in corners and hang round after you."

Rosamund continued her story and he went on with his walk. Now and then, as she alluded to Barclay's part in the affair, suppressed phrases that were of a profane character broke from him. When she had concluded he stood for a moment by the window looking out.

"Well, the mischief's been done. He's made the poor little soul just about as miserable as she can be. I'd like to blow the top of his head off with one of my derringers, but as I can't have that satisfaction there's no good thinking of it. All we can do is to try and brace her up some way or other."

Rosamund made no answer and after a moment of silence, he continued,

"And I suppose it lets poor Rion out?"

"Oh, yes," breathed Rosamund with a melancholy sigh.

The Colonel walked to the other window muttering in his wrath.

"He was coming down here, Rosie, to ask her. They've made a pile of money up there, in this Crown Point business, and they're buying up all the claims that might have clouded the title of the Cresta Plata. They believe there's a bonanza there, and the Gracey boys don't often make mistakes. They'll be millionaires before they're done. But that doesn't count. What does is that Rion Gracey's the finest man in California, bar none. The woman that he married would be loved and taken care of, the way—the way a woman ought to be. Good Lord, what fools we are and how we tear our lives to pieces for nothing!"

"Don't blame her, Uncle Jim. She's just got so fond of that man she hasn't any sense left."

"Blame her! Have I ever blamed her? Why, Rosie, I'd die for her. I'll have to go up to Virginia and put Rion off. What can I say to him?"

"Tell him she doesn't care for him," said the truthful Rosamund.

The Colonel paused by the table, looking down and jingling the loose silver in his pockets.

"No," he said, "I'm not going to tell him that. That would be harder on Rion than on most men. Women, you know, change. June's very young. She's still a child in many things."

"She isn't the same sort of child she was two months ago," said Rosamund sadly.

"No, but she's young in years—only twenty-one. Dear girl, that's a baby. Your mother was older than that when I knew her, and—and—she changed."

"How changed?" Rosamund asked with some curiosity.

"Her heart changed. She—other men cared for her before your father came along. She once cared for one of them."

The Colonel paused and cleared his throat.

"Mother was engaged to some one else before father. She told me so once, but she didn't say who."

"Well, there was no doubt of her second love being deep. In fact, it was the deeper of the two."

"I wish June would care for Rion Gracey. But if you'd hear her talk!"—with hopeless recollection of June's sentimental transports. "It sounds as if she didn't know there was a man in the world but that miserable Barclay. She's just bewitched. What's the matter with women that they're always falling in love with the wrong man?"

There was another pause.

"I'll do my best," said the Colonel at length, "to keep Rion from coming down and trying his luck. He mustn't see her now. She'd refuse him in such a way that he'd never dare to come near her again. And you, Rosie, try and cheer her up and keep her from thinking of Barclay."

On Monday morning the Colonel left for San Francisco, and a few days later was again *en route* for Virginia City.

The rest of the summer slowly passed, idle and eventless. June brightened a little with the passage of the weeks, but was far from her old self. Now and then she saw Barclay at the station, in the house of friends, or met him in the village. At first he merely bowed and passed on. But before the summer was over he had spoken to her; in the beginning with the short and colorless politeness of early acquaintanceship, but later with something of his natural bonhomie.

Once at an afternoon garden fête she suddenly came out on a balcony and found him there alone. For a moment they stood dumb, eye full on eye, then began speaking of indifferent things, their hearts beating hard, their faces pale. It was the first conversation of any length they had had since the meeting in the wood. They parted, feeling for the moment poignantly disturbed and yet eased of the ache of separation. From that on they spoke at greater length, talking with an assumption of naturalness, till finally their fragmentary intercourse assumed a tone of simple friendliness, from which all sentiment was banished. This surface calm was all that each saw of the other's heart, but each knew what the calm concealed.

In October the Allens returned to town. The Colonel had managed to keep Rion Gracey from going to San Francisco "to try his luck" until this late date. It would have been impossible had not Fate been with him. In the growing excitement of the reawakened mining town Rion was continuously occupied, and he was a man to whom work was a paramount duty.

But in October he slipped his leash for a week and ran down to San Francisco. In four days he returned, as quiet as ever, and inclined to be harder with his men. The Colonel knew what had happened, and Black Dan guessed. Outside these two, no one understood why Rion Gracey had become a more silent and less lenient man after a four days' visit to the coast.

CHAPTER VII
BUSINESS AND SENTIMENT

The winter of '71-'72 was a feverish one for San Francisco. The rising excitement in Virginia ran like a tidal wave over the mountains to the city by the sea and there broke in a seething whirl. There was no stock market in the Nevada camp. Pine Street was the scene of the operations of capitalist and speculator—the arena where bull and bear met.

In Virginia men fought against the forces of nature. They matched their strength with the elements of the primeval world. Water and fire were their enemies. Their task was the tearing out from the rock-ribbed flanks of the mountains the treasure that nature had buried with jealous care. They performed prodigies of energy, conquered the unconquerable, rose to the height of their mighty antagonist, giant against giant.

In San Francisco men fought with one another. The treasure once in their hands, the battle lost its dignity and became the ignominious scramble of the swindler and the swindled. The gold and silver—thrown among the crowd—ran this way and that, like spilled quicksilver. Most of it ran the way its manipulators directed, into pockets that were already full, carrying with it the accumulation of gold from other pockets less full, whose owners were less cunning.

Through the winter Crown Point and Belcher—the neighboring mine into which the ore-body extended—continued to rise. Confidence had been restored; everybody was investing. Clerks and servant girls drew their savings out of banks and stocking feet and bought shares. In April the stock had reached its highest point, seven hundred and twenty-five dollars. In May, one month later, it dropped to one hundred and seventy-five. It was the greatest and most rapid decline the San Francisco stock market had ever known.

The city was for the moment stunned by it. The confidence in Virginia—for three years regarded as "petered"—had returned in full force. The sudden drop knocked the breath from the lungs of those who had been vociferating the recrudescence of the Comstock. A quantity of fortunes, great and small, were swept away in the collapse. The brokers' cries for "mud" drew the last nickels from the clerks and the servant girls, the last dollars from their employers. When the wave receded the shore was strewn with wrecks. For the second time this wave had slowly risen to level-brimming flood, broken, swept back and left such a drift of human wreckage.

Throughout the city there was wailing. Nearly everybody had suffered. The last remnant of the fortune left to Jerry Barclay by his father was gone. His mother too had lost, fortunately not heavily. But she bemoaned her few thousands with as much zeal as her cook did the five hundred, which constituted the savings of years.

Among the heaviest losers was Beauregard Allen. Had not the Barranca been behind him he would have been a ruined man. As it was, the second fortune he saw himself possessed of was swept away in a few disastrous days. The Barranca, while its yield had not of late been so large or so rich as during its first year, still gave him what he once would have considered a princely income. But he lived up to and beyond it. His expenditures during the last year had been exceedingly heavy. He had private extravagances of his own, besides the lavish manner of living in which he encouraged his daughters. He had leased the De Soto house for three years at a fancy rent. The Colonel's mortgage on the Folsom Street house would mature in another year. The interest which fell due in January he had neglected to pay. He had had the money and then a jeweler had threatened to bring suit for an unpaid-for diamond bracelet, and the money had gone there, quickly, to keep the jeweler quiet.

Three years ago at Foleys had any one told him that he would own a mine like the Barranca and enjoy an income from it such as still was his, he would have wondered how he could best expend such wealth. Since then the beggar on horseback had ridden fast and far. Now, in morose absorption, he reviewed his expenses and his debts. His petty vanity forbade him to economize in his manner of living. He had raised his head before men and he would not lower it again. Some financiering would be necessary to pay up his brokers, maintain the two fine establishments in which his daughters ruled, and have the necessary cash for the diamond bracelets and suppers after the theater that absorbed so many uncounted hundreds. There was solace in the thought that Parrish held the mortgage on the Folsom Street house. However restive other creditors might grow Parrish could be managed.

The Colonel in these troublous days was also glumly studying his accounts. Crown Point, which was to repair the recent decline in certain of his investments, had swept away in its fall a portion of that comfortable fortune in which its owner had felt so secure. He had had several losses of late. From the day of his relinquishment of the Parrish Tract bad luck seemed to follow him. Owing to an uncontrollable influx of water the mine in Shasta had been shut down indefinitely. The South Park houses were declining in value, the city was growing out toward the property he had sold on upper Market Street, which a year ago had been a bare stretch of sand. The Colonel looked grave as he bent over his books; his riches were something more than a matter of mere personal comfort and convenience.

On a blank sheet of paper he jotted down what his income would be after all these loppings off. Then over against the last line of figures jotted down a second line of his expenditures. For some time he pondered frowningly over these two columns. They presented a disconcerting problem.

For the past six or seven years he had spent some five thousand per annum on himself, the rest on certain charities and what he lumped together under the convenient head of "Sundries." It was a word which covered among other things numerous presents and treats for June and Rosamund. "Sundries" had consumed a great deal of ready money, nearly as much as Allen's diamond bracelets and theater suppers, and the Colonel sighed as he realized they must suffer curtailment. The private charities were represented by a few written words with an affixed line of figures: "Carter's girl at Convent;" "Joe's boy," "G. T.'s widow." When the figures were added up they made a formidable sum.

The Colonel looked at it for another period of frowning cogitation. Then on the edge of the paper he put down the items of his own private account. There was only one which was large—the rent of the sunny suite on the Kearney Street corner. Through that item he drew his pen.

The next time he dined with the Allens he told them that he was going to move. He had found his old rooms too large and he had decided to take a smaller suite in the Traveler's Hotel. The girls stared in blank surprise. Allen looked at him with quick, sidelong curiosity. He wondered at the move. He knew that Parrish had been hard hit, but he still must have enough left to live on comfortably in the style he had maintained since his return from the war. The Traveler's Hotel was a come-down—a place on the built-out land below Montgomery Street, respectable enough, but far different from the luxurious rooms on the Kearney Street corner.

The girls were amazed, distressed, had endless questions as to why Uncle Jim should do such a strange thing. He laughed and parried their queries. Had they forgotten that he was a pioneer, who had slept under the stars on the American River in forty-nine? In those days the Traveler's Hotel would have been regarded as the acme of luxury.

"And why," he said, "should the old man to-day turn up his nose at what would have been magnificence to the young man in forty-nine?"

During this winter of storm and stress June stood on the edge of the excitement looking on. The selfishness of a purely individual sorrow held her back from that vivid interest and participation that would once have been hers. She was tender and loving to the Colonel, and she bore patiently with the moody irritation that often marked her father's manner, but for the most part she gave to the matters that once would have been of paramount interest, only a shadow of her old blithe attention.

Yet she was not entirely unhappy. She had accepted the situation, and, knowing the worst, tried to readjust her life to an altered point of view. Her comfort lay in the thought that Jerry loved her. The enchantment of the days when she had dreamed a maiden's dreams of a life with the one chosen man, was for ever gone. She marveled now at the rainbow radiance of that wonderful time when mere living had been so joyous, and happiness so easy and natural.

But Jerry loved her. In the rending of the fabric of her dreams, the shattering of her ideals, that remained. She hugged it to her heart and it filled the empty present. Of the future she did not think, making no attempt to penetrate its veil. Only her youth whispered hope to her, and her natural buoyancy of temperament repeated the whisper.

Of Jerry's feelings toward her she knew, without being told, but one evening, late in the winter, he again spoke of them. It was at a party at Mrs. Davenport's. For the first time during the season they had danced together. As a rule their intercourse was limited to the few words of casual acquaintanceship, greetings on the stairway, conventional commonplaces at suppers or over dinner-tables. Under this veil of indifference each was acutely conscious of the other's presence, thrilled to the other's voice, heard unexpectedly in a lull of conversation or the passing of couples in a crowded doorway.

At Mrs. Davenport's party Jerry had drunk freely of the champagne and the restraint he kept on himself was loosened. Moreover, Lupé was not present, and he felt reckless and daring. After a few turns among the circling couples they dropped out of the dance, and he drew June from the large room into a small conservatory. Here in the quiet coolness, amid the greenery of leaves and the drip of falling water, he took her two hands in his, and in the sentimental phrases of which he had such a mastery, told her of his love.

She listened with down-drooped eyes, pale as the petals of the lilies round the fountain, the lace on her bosom vibrating with the beating of her heart.

"Say you love me," he had urged, pressing the hands he held, "I want to hear you say it."

"You know I do," she whispered, "I don't need to say it."

"But I want to hear you say those very words."

She said them, her voice just audible above the clear trickling of the falling water.

"And you'll go on loving me, even though we don't see each other except in these crowded places, and I hardly dare to speak to you, or touch your hand?"

"I always will. Separation, or distance, or time will make no difference. It's—it's—for always with me."

She raised her eyes and they rested on his in a deep, exalted look. She was plighting her troth for life. He, too, was pale and moved, and the hands clasped round hers trembled. He cared for her with all the force that was in him. He was neither exaggerated nor untruthful in what he said. When he told a woman he loved her he meant it. There would have been no reason or pleasure to Jerry in making love unless the feeling he expressed was genuine. Now his voice was hoarse, his face tense with emotion, as he said:

"It's for life with me, too. There's no woman in the world for me but you, June. Whatever I've done in the past, in the future I'm yours, for ever, while I'm here to be anybody's. Will you be true?"

"Till I die," she whispered.

Their trembling hands remained locked together, and eye held eye in a trance-like steadiness that seemed to search the soul. To both, the moment had the sacredness of a betrothal.

"Some day perhaps we can be happy," he murmured, not knowing what he meant, but anxious to alleviate the very genuine suffering he experienced. She framed some low words over which her lips quivered, and in his pain he insisted:

"But you will wait for me, no matter what time passes? You won't grow tired of waiting, or cease to care? You'll always feel that you're mine?"

"I'm yours for ever," she answered.

These were the only words of love that passed between them, but at the time they were uttered they were to both as the words of a solemn pact.

For the rest of the winter Jerry avoided her. His passion was at its height. Between it and his fear of Lupé he was more wretched and unhappy than he had ever been in his life.

During the spring, with its tumult of excitement and final catastrophe, and the long summer of dreary recuperation, June walked apart, upheld by the memory of the vows she had plighted. Money was made and lost, the little world about her seethed in angry discouragement while she looked on absently, absorbed in her dream. What delighted or vexed people was of insignificant moment to her. In the midst of surroundings to which she had once given a sparkling and intimate attention she was now a cool, indifferent spectator. Her interest in life was concentrated in the thought that Jerry had pledged himself to her.

CHAPTER VIII
NEW PLANETS

The year after the Crown Point collapse was a sad and chastened one. Money was tight on all sides. Large houses were closed, servants discharged, dressmakers' bills cut down. Many families hitherto prominent dropped out of sight, preferring to hide their poverty in remote corners of the city, whence, in some cases, they never again emerged. The winter, shorn of its accustomed gaieties, was dull and quiet.

With the spring there came a revival of life and energy. The volatile spirit of the Californians began to rise. One of the chief causes of this was a new series of disturbing rumors from Virginia City. In February a strike was reported in the recently consolidated group of claims known as the California and Consolidated Virginia. A vein of ore seven feet wide and assaying sixty dollars to the ton had been uncovered. Talk of the Nevada camp was in the air. The San Franciscans were incredulous, as fearful of mining stock as the singed cat of the fire, but they listened and watched, feeling the first faint unrest of hope and temptation.

Socially too, the city showed signs of returning cheerfulness. This was due not only to the natural rebound after a period of depression, but to two new arrivals of the sort which those small segregated groups known as "society" delight to welcome and entertain.

The first of these was Mercedes Gracey. Glamour of many sorts clung about the name of this favorite of fortune. To her natural attractions were added those supposed to be acquired by a sojourn in older and more sophisticated localities. Mercedes had passed from her New York boarding-school to the finishing influences of a year "abroad." She had traveled in Europe with a chaperone and taken on the polish of accomplishment under the guidance of experienced teachers. Such news of her as had drifted back to San Francisco was eagerly seized upon by the less fortunate home dwellers. From time to time the newspapers printed items about Miss Gracey's triumphant career. Before her arrival San Francisco had already developed a possessive pride in her as a native daughter who would add to the glory of the Golden State.

Mercedes would not, probably, have been the object of such interest had not the fortunes of her father and uncle been for the past three years steadily ascending. The Gracey boys had of late risen from the position of a pair of well-known and capable mining men to that of two of the most prominent figures in the state. Their means were reported large. They had been among the few who had got out of the Crown Point excitement at the right moment, selling their stock at the top price. They were now developing their Cresta Plata property. Should this pan out as they expected there was no knowing where the Gracey boys' successes would end. Mercedes was the only woman relative they possessed. It was no wonder that she was regarded with an almost reverential interest, and her return evoked as much curiosity as though it were that of an errant princess.

Black Dan, who had gone to New York to meet her, brought her back in triumph. His idolatrous love had known no abatement in the two years' separation. To have her finally restored to him, in an even completer state of perfection, was a bewildering happiness to him. His primitive nature strove to show its gratitude and tenderness in extravagant ways. He showered presents on her, ordered the finest suite in the newly-completed Lick House to be prepared for her, offered to rent any country place she might choose. That she should accompany him to the rough life of Virginia, where he spent most of his time, he never expected. It would be enough for him to see her on his frequent visits to the coast.

The other notable visitor who arrived in the city almost simultaneously was a young Englishman, Lionel Harrower. He, too, took up his residence in the Lick House, and it was but natural that some of the interest evoked by the appearance of Black Dan's daughter should be deflected toward him.

Young Harrower was a nephew of that Englishman who fifteen years before had married Mrs. Newbury's sister, Carmen Romero. He was finishing his education by a trip around the world, and had decided to make a stop of some length in California, then a *terra incognita* to the traveling Briton. From his Spanish-Californian aunt he had brought letters to the Newburys, Mrs. Davenport, and other prominent San Franciscans.

The Englishman of Harrower's class was at that time a rarity in the far West. Bonanza heiresses had not yet arisen to be the bait for well-born foreigners of all nations. California, outside its own borders, still enjoyed its original reputation as a land of picturesque gold-diggers and romantic gamblers, and the wandering noble of Anglo-Saxon or Gallic extraction avoided it as an unsafe place, where men were still free with the revolver and the bowie knife.

Harrower was an even more engrossing object of local curiosity than Mercedes. He was a good-looking young man of five and twenty, quiet in manner, non-committal and brief of speech, deeply interested in all he saw, and very shy. He was the heir to a baronetcy and fine country place in Warwickshire. His grandfather, the present baronet, was in his eighty-first year, and, though a hale old man, could not be expected to live much longer. When he died Lionel Harrower would inherit the title and lands, thereby coming into possession of one of the oldest and most beautiful estates in the county. The young man neither looked nor hinted any of these matters. But they were all carefully set down in the letters that Carmen Romero wrote to her sister and her friends, and they passed from mouth to mouth, accumulating material as they progressed. San Francisco had not had enough experience in the visiting patrician to be familiar with all the delicate gradations of rank, and Harrower was regarded as of hardly less distinction than a reigning Grand Duke.

With the appearance of these two interesting strangers the city emerged from its apathy of depression. A desire to impress the new-comers hospitably took possession of it. Both Mercedes and Harrower were caught in the whirl of a round of entertainments, during which they constantly encountered each other. Thrown thus together their acquaintance rapidly grew. Harrower had not been a month in San Francisco when the little world about him was speculating on his interest in the daughter of Black Dan Gracey.

Mercedes was now nearly nineteen years of age. With her Spanish blood to round and ripen her, that corresponded to the Anglo-Saxon woman's twenty-five. For all her American birth and education she was at heart a Latin, subtile, complex, and revengeful. There was little of her father in her. She had none of his simple largeness of temperament, but was made up of feline intricacies of caprice, vanity, and passion. At the present stage in her life her strongest instinct was love of admiration. She had early comprehended the power of her beauty, and to exercise this power was to her a delight which never lost its zest. To throw a spell over men was the thing Mercedes loved best to do, and could do with remarkable proficiency, considering her years and inexperience.

So far she had had few opportunities. Mrs. Campbell, the chaperone to whom her father had intrusted her, was a capable New England woman who had early recognized the responsibilities of her position. Mercedes, rich and beautiful, was a prize for which princes might have sued. But Mrs. Campbell had received instructions from Black Dan that he did not want his daughter taken from him by marriage with a foreigner, and Mercedes, during her year in Europe, was guarded like a princess traveling incognito.

When she returned to San Francisco she had never yet received an offer of marriage, and even her admirers had been restricted in number and kept sternly at bay.

To Mercedes, Lionel Harrower represented all that was most choice in position and rank. Through her travels she knew more of the class he stood for than the admiring San Franciscans, and it was a class in which she ardently desired to install herself. She questioned the young man of his country and his people, prevailed upon him to show her a photograph of the stately Elizabethan manor house which was his home, and to talk to her of the life he led upon his ancestral acres. It was like an English novel, and Mercedes saw herself moving through it, lovely, proud and desired, as its conquering heroine.

In June she left the Lick House for the country place in the Santa Clara Valley that Black Dan had taken for her. This was the estate of Tres Pinos, one of the show places of the great valley, recently thrown upon the market by the death of its owner.

Tres Pinos soon became the focusing point of the region's summer life. The wide balconies were constantly filled with visitors, the velvet turf of the croquet grounds was swept by the crisp flounces of women's dresses, the bedrooms in the big house were always occupied. Mrs. Campbell, precise, darkly clad, and primly well-bred, presided with an all-seeing eye, astonishing the Californians by her rigid observance of the smaller conventionalities. Through all Mercedes flitted, clad in French dresses, more ornate and elegant than any ever seen before in California, a smilingly gracious and finished person, evoking fear and jealousy in her own sex, and eliciting a rather awed admiration from the other.

That Lionel Narrower was a constant visitor at Tres Pinos the gossips were quick to note. When the young man announced his intention of spending the summer in California it seemed to them that there was no more doubt as to the state of his feelings. What they did not know was that his presence at Tres Pinos was evoked by a constant flutter of scented notes from the chatelaine. There were many times when he had refused the invitations with which Miss Gracey showered him. He had found California, its scenery and people, of so much interest, that a single segregated interest in one particular human being had had no time to develop in him. But Mercedes did not think this. She felt quite sure that Lionel Harrower was remaining in California because of an engrossing and unconquerable sentiment for her.

One Sunday, late in June, he made one of the party which was spending the week-end at Tres Pinos. In the warm middle of the Sabbath afternoon, her visitors scattered over the croquet ground or enjoying the siesta in the shuttered gloom of their bed chambers, Mercedes started out to find him. She slipped down the wide staircase, peeped into the dim drawing-room, cooled by closed blinds and filled with the scent of cut flowers, and then slipped out on to the balcony.

A spiral of cigarette smoke rising from a steamer chair betrayed his presence. He was comfortably outstretched in loose-jointed ease, a novel raised before a pair of eyes which looked suspiciously sleepy, his cigarette caught between his lips. At the sound of her voice he sprang up, but she motioned him back into his chair, and sitting down opposite began to rally him on his laziness. He looked at her with drowsy good humor, his lids drooping. Her figure in its pale colored muslin dress was thrown out against a background of velvety lawns and the massed, juicy greens of summer shrubbery. It was the middle of the afternoon, hot and still. From the croquet ground came the soft, occasional striking of balls.

"Just listen to them," said the young man, "they're actually playing croquet!"

"Lots of people play croquet on Sunday," said Mercedes with some haste, as she disliked to have it thought that she was ignorant of any intricacy of etiquette. "I don't see anything wrong in it."

"It's not the Sunday part of it. It's the energy. Fancy standing out in that sun of your own free will!"

"You're horribly lazy," said the young girl. "It's your worst fault. You do nothing all day but lie about on the balcony and drink lemonade."

"I *could* drink beer," said Harrower dreamily, "but I've never seen anything but lemonade."

"Well, I've come to tell you that I'm going to insist on your being more energetic. I want you to take me for a drive."

"A drive! Now? But, my dear Miss Gracey, the sun's simply scorching."

Mercedes flushed slightly. Her cavalier's manner of accepting the suggestion did not please her.

"If you're afraid of your complexion," she said, "you can hold my parasol over your head. I'll drive."

Harrower laughed. When she said things of this kind he thought her what he would have called "great fun." Still he would have much preferred remaining on the balcony with his novel and his cigarette, to braving the heat of the afternoon, even in Miss Gracey's smart new pony phaeton, with

Miss Gracey in the driver's seat. He sat up, rubbing his eyes into a more wakeful brightness and smothering a yawn.

"Where are we to drive to? Menlo Park again?"

"No, I'm going to take you back in the hills to the De Soto place. It was originally an old Spanish grant and part of the place is just the way it used to be. The Allens live there. They moved down early this year, so I don't think you met them in town. Some people think the girls are very pretty."

"Pretty girls!" said Harrower, pricking up his ears. "By all means let's go."

He looked at her laughing, for he thought she would enjoy the humor of his sudden enthusiasm. Instead, for a fleeting second, her face was clouded with annoyance. Then she recovered herself and rose to her feet, moving away from him.

"The horses are ready now," she said. "I'll go up for my hat and parasol and I'll expect to find you at the steps when I come down."

The heat was waning, the live-oak shadows lying dark and irregular over the drive, when the phaeton approached the Allens' balcony. The light dresses of the Allen girls were thrown up by the darker gown of dignified middle age. Mrs. Barclay was sitting in a wicker arm-chair near the balustrade fanning herself with a palm-leaf fan. Mercedes muttered annoyance to her companion, and then her glance was charged with a sudden infusion of interest as it fell on a graceful masculine back bending over a table set with plates and glasses, behind which June Allen was standing.

"That must be Jerry Barclay," she murmured to Harrower, as, with dexterous exactness she brought up the phaeton wheels against the mounting block. "I've not met him yet. He's been in Virginia City, like everybody else."

"Ah—aw! Yes, of course," Harrower murmured vaguely, not knowing or caring in the least about Jerry Barclay, but filled with sudden admiration for the fresh-faced, blonde girl who rose at their approach and came to the top of the steps. Though she had never seen him before she included him in the sweet frank smile and friendly glance with which she greeted Mercedes.

"Rosamund," said Mercedes, throwing the reins around the whip with the easy flourish of the expert, "I've brought over Mr. Harrower. He's making a collection of Californian specimens, and I thought perhaps he'd like to see you. He'll put you down under the head of vertebrate fauna, I suppose."

The stranger, whose face had grown exceedingly red, did not know whether in the free, untrammeled West this constituted an introduction. The young woman, however, solved the difficulty by coming down a step or two and extending a welcoming hand. He looked into a pair of gray eyes, unusually honest and direct, and heard her saying in a voice, not low-keyed, but clear and full,

"I'm glad you came, Mr. Harrower. It was very kind of Mercedes to bring you."

On the balcony above Mrs. Barclay had risen and was looking at the new-comers with avid curiosity. She had already talked them threadbare in every drawing-room from Millbrae to Menlo Park. Her personal acquaintance with both was very slight and this was a good opportunity to improve it and arrive at conclusions, to air which she could once again make a tour of the country houses and be sure of eager attention.

Behind her, at a table laden with a silver pitcher, glasses and plates, June was standing. She was pouring out a glass of lemonade, which Jerry was waiting to take to his mother, when the phaeton drove up. The glass was filled and the pitcher set down, before either of them looked at the new arrivals. Then Jerry turned and his eyes fell on them. He stopped short, the glass in his hand. Mercedes, a smile of greeting on her lips, was just mounting the steps.

"Heavens, what a girl!" he said in a whisper, turning to June.

"Yes," she answered in an equally low voice, "she's very pretty."

"Pretty! pretty!" he ejaculated, mechanically setting the glass down. "Why she's a dream!"

He turned again and looked at Mercedes, who was speaking to his mother. His face was staring with admiration, a slight fixed smile on his lips. It was the look of the male suddenly stricken by the physical charm of the female. June dropped her eyes to the table with a sensation of feeling cold, insignificant and small.

"Your mother's lemonade," she said, pushing the glass toward him. "You were going to take it to her."

He did not appear to hear her. His eyes were fastened on Mercedes, the slight smile still on his lips. Forgetful of the glass with which June had touched his hand, he slowly walked across the balcony to where Mrs. Barclay stood and said gaily,

"Mother, won't you introduce me to Miss Gracey? We came very near meeting at Foleys three years ago and just missed it. I don't want that to happen again."

When June had welcomed her guests she went back to her seat behind the table. Presently Mrs. Barclay drew her chair nearer to her, for Mrs. Barclay began to feel that to be a fifth among four young people so well pleased with one another was not entertaining. So she moved up toward June and talked to her about the dishonesty of the new butcher at San Mateo as compared with that of the old butcher at Menlo Park.

June listened and now and then spoke. She did not seem to know much about either butcher, and Mrs. Barclay made a mental note of the fact that she must be a poor housekeeper. Once or twice she looked at the elder woman with eyes that were disconcertingly empty of attention. When that lady rose to go she remarked that the girl looked pale and tired. She said this to Jerry on the way home.

"Did she?" he answered absently. "Poor little June! She's just the dearest little woman in the world. But isn't that Gracey girl a wonder? I never saw a more beautiful face."

CHAPTER IX
THE CHOICE OF MAIDS

During the months of summer, dwellers along the line of the railway became familiar with the figure of Lionel Harrower. He constantly went down to San Mateo on Sunday afternoons and returned to town on Sunday evening. This, at first, was regarded as the outward and visible sign of his devotion to Miss Gracey, but by and by it was remarked that he did not take the Gracey carriage which so often stood under the live-oaks at the depot, but mounted a hired hack and was driven off in the direction of the De Soto house.

It was a Sunday or two after Mercedes had driven him there that the young Englishman had appeared on the balcony steps, very red and warm from the heat of the afternoon, and paid a long call, which extended so far into the twilight that he was bidden to dinner and did not go back to town till a late evening train.

It had evidently been an enjoyable afternoon, for he repeated it, and then again repeated it, and finally let it develop into a habit. He wrote to his relations in England that he was deeply interested in California and was studying the mining industry of that remarkable state. And it is true that once in the middle of the summer he went to Virginia for a few days and came back with his mind full of excellent material for a letter to his grandfather which should prove how profound had been his study of the American mining and engineering methods.

The first afternoon that Mercedes found him on the Allens' balcony she was openly surprised. The second she was sweet and gracious, but her rose-leaf color deepened at the sight of him, and it was noticeable that, for one who was usually so completely mistress of herself, she was distrait and lacking in repose. On leaving, she had asked him if she could drive him back to the station, as her road lay that way, to which the young man had answered, with the stiff politeness of embarrassment, that he was to stay to dinner—"he always did on Sunday."

This was the inception of a situation that, before the summer was over, had caused more heart-burnings, more wakeful nights and distressed days, than the peaceful valley had known in many years.

For the first time in an existence of triumph and adulation Mercedes knew defeat. She had been certain of her attraction for Harrower, and confident that by her beauty and her wiles she could, before his departure, fan his interest to a warmer flame. Yet July was not spent before she realized that a force more potent than any she could put forth was leading the young man in another direction. His visits to the Allens' grew more and more frequent as those to Tres Pinos became less so. Curiosity in his interest in the occupants of the De Soto house evolved itself into curiosity in his interest in Rosamund Allen. He forgot the tours he had intended to take into the interior, showed no more interest in Virginia City, and gave up his plan of a horseback expedition to the Yosemite. He spent the summer in town, making trips to San Mateo that grew more and more frequent.

It was difficult for Mercedes to believe it, but when she did it kindled sleeping fires in her. She was doubly wounded; heart and pride were hurt. Her overmastering vanity had received its first blow. Not only had she lost the man for whom her feeling was daily growing warmer, but it would be known of all men that he had withdrawn his affections from her to place them on a girl far her inferior in looks, education and feminine charm. That he should have preferred Rosamund was particularly maddening—Rosamund, whom she had regarded as commonplace and countrified. She looked in her glass, and furious tears gathered in her eyes. It was staggering, incomprehensible, but it was true. She was discarded, and people were laughing at her.

Two instincts—strong in women of her type—rose within her. One demanded revenge and the other protection of her pride. She burned with the desire to strike back at those who had hurt her, and at the same to hide the wounds to her self-love. She knew of but one way to do the latter, and it came upon her—not suddenly, but with a gradually uplifting illumination—that it could be successfully combined with the execution of the former.

Mercedes, who liked gossip, had heard the story of Jerry Barclay's complication with Mrs. Newbury, and of how it was popularly supposed to have prevented his marriage to June Allen. The busy scandal-hunters of the city had somehow unearthed the story that Jerry and June would have married had the former been free. Mercedes, with her woman's quickness, guessed that June was the sort of girl who would remain constant in such a situation. But Jerry was a being of another stripe, a man of an unusual attraction for women and of a light and errant fancy. She had not met him half a dozen times when she came to the conclusion that his love for June was on the wane, his roving eye ready to be caught, his ear held, by the first soft glance and flattering tongue he encountered.

Thus the way of protecting herself and of hitting back at one at least of the Allens was put into her hand. She did not care for Jerry, save as he was useful to her, though he had the value of the thing which is highly prized by others. She used every weapon in her armory to attract and subjugate him. Jerry himself, versed in the wiles of women as he was, was deceived by her girlishly open pleasure in his attentions, her fluttered embarrassment when he paid her compliments.

His first feeling toward her was an unbounded admiration for her physical perfections, to which was added a complacent vanity at her obvious predilection for him. But the woman that he regarded as a naïve ingenue was a being of a more complex brain, a more daring initiative, and a cooler head than he had ever possessed. Vain and self-indulgent, the slave of his passions, he was in reality a puppet in the hands of a girl fifteen years his junior, who, under an exterior of flower-like delicacy, had been eaten into by the acids of rage and revenge.

While he still thought himself a trifler in the outer court of sentiment he was already under her dominion. He thought of himself as taking an impersonally admiring interest in her when he was continually haunted by the thought of her, and hastened to spend his spare hours beside her, his eyes drinking in her beauty, his vanity fostered and stimulated by the flattery she so cunningly administered. Like Paris, he felt himself beloved by goddesses. June's image faded. Two years had passed since his confession in the wood. He had seen her only at intervals and then under a perpetual ban of restraint. He was not the man to remain constant to a memory. June hovered on the edges of his consciousness like a sad-eyed shadow, looking at him with a pleading protest that made him feel angry with her. She was a dim, unappealing figure beside the radiant youthfulness, the sophisticated coquetries of Black Dan's daughter.

During the early part of the summer June was in ignorance of the momentous shuffling of the cards of her destiny. She lived quietly, rarely going to the city, and spending most of her time in the gardens or on the balcony. Rosamund, who went about more, marketed in the village and shopped in town, began to hear rumors of Jerry's interest in Miss Gracey. She met them riding together in the hot solitude of the country roads, saw them meet on the trains to the city. Finally the rumors passed to San Francisco and the Colonel heard them. He came down to San Mateo that Saturday to talk things over with Rosamund. They were worried and uneasy, a sense of calamity weighing on them both.

Though June was one of those women who obstinately adhere to the bright side, who cling to hope till it crumbles in their hands, she felt, during the summer, premonitions of ill fortune. Those inexplicable shadows of approaching evil that Nature throws forward over the path of sensitive temperaments had darkened her outlook. She questioned herself as to her heaviness of heart, assuring herself that there was no new cloud on her horizon. In the constancy of her own nature she did not realize, as a more experienced woman would, that her hold on Jerry was a silken thread which would wear very thin in the passage of years, and be ready to snap at the first strain.

But the moods of apprehension and gloom began to be augmented by ripples from the pool of gossip without. She heard that Jerry was oftener in San Mateo than ever before, and she saw him less frequently. One afternoon she met him driving with Mercedes, and the girl's radiant smile of recognition had something of malicious triumph under its beaming sweetness. June drove home silent and pale. In her room she tried to argue herself out of her depression. But it stayed with her, made her preoccupied and quiet all the evening, lay down with her at night, and was heavy and cold at her heart in the morning.

At the end of September they returned to town. They had been back a few weeks when one afternoon she met Jerry on the street and they stopped for a few moments' conversation. It was nothing more than the ordinary interchange of commonplaces between old friends, but when he had passed on, the girl walked forward looking wan and feeling a deadly sense of blankness. He was the same man, gay, handsome, suave, and yet he seemed suddenly far removed from her, to be smiling with the perfunctory politeness of a stranger. The chill exhaled by a dying love penetrated her, pierced her to the core. She did not understand it, him, or herself. All that she knew was that the sense of despondency became suddenly overpowering, and closed like an iron clutch on her heart.

It was an overcast autumn that year, with much gray weather and early fogs. The city had never looked to June so cheerless. She was a great deal alone, Rosamund's time being more and more claimed by Lionel Harrower. He was her first lover, and it was a part of Rosamund's fate that he should have come to her unexpected and unasked for. She was of the order of women who stand where they are placed, doing what comes under their hand, demanding little of life, and to whom life's gifts come as a surprise.

That such a man as the young Briton should prefer her to her sister, whose superior charm she had always acknowledged and been proud of, was to her astonishing. She was sobered and softened in these days of awakening love. One could see the woman, the mother, ripe, soft, full of a quiet devotion, slowly dawning. Sometimes she was irritable, a thing previously unknown. She could not believe that Harrower loved her, and yet as the days passed, and she found the hours spent with him growing ever more disturbingly sweet, she wondered how she could ever support a life in which he did not figure, and the thought filled her with torturing fears.

One gray afternoon, Rosamund having left for a walk in the park with Harrower, June, after wandering about the empty house for a dreary hour, resolved that she too would go out for a stroll. She had felt more cheerful lately. Jerry had come to call two days before, when she was out, and this fact had seemed to her a proof of his unwaned interest. She had written him a brief note, stating her regrets at missing him and her hopes that he would repeat the visit soon. This was only polite and proper, she assured herself.

Her walk took her to Van Ness Avenue and then up the side street toward the little Turk Street plaza. For the past two years it had been a favorite promenade of hers. The present was not sufficiently fraught with pain to render memories of a happier past unbearable. She strolled through the small park and then returned and walked back toward the avenue. As she turned the corner into the great thoroughfare, she stopped, the color dying from her face, the softness of its outlines stiffening.

Walking slowly toward her were Jerry and Mercedes Gracey. They were close together, Mercedes lightly touching with the tips of her fingers the top of the ornamental fence beside her. Her eyes were down-drooped, her whole air one of maidenly modesty, which yet had in it something coyly encouraging. Jerry, close at her shoulder, was looking down at her, with the eyes of a lover.

For the first moment June was too stricken to move. She stood spellbound, poised in mid-flight, hungrily staring. Then the desire for concealment seized her, and she was about to turn and steal back to the corner whence she had come, when Mercedes raised her eyes and saw her. She threw a short, quick phrase at Jerry, and he started and drew himself up. June moved forward, and as she approached them forced her lips into a smile and bowed. She was conscious that Jerry had flushed and looked angry as he raised his hat. But Mercedes enveloped her in a glance of fascinating cordiality, inclining her head in a graceful salutation.

A half-hour later June gained her room and sank into an arm-chair. For some time she sat motionless, gazing at the gray oblongs of the two windows with their shadowy upper draperies. As the look in Jerry's face kept rising upon her mental vision, she experienced a slight sensation of nausea and feebleness. But even in this hour of revelation she kept whispering to herself,

"He couldn't! He couldn't! He couldn't have the heart! He couldn't hurt me so!"

The few poor memories she had of moments of tenderness between them, the meager words of love that she had regarded as binding vows, rose in her mind. It had seemed to her he could no more disregard them than she could. She thought of herself responding to the love of another man—of its impossibility—and sat bowed together in her chair, for the first time catching a revealing gleam of the difference in their attitudes. Then the memory of Mrs. Newbury came to her, and with it a strengthening sense of his unbreakable obligation. Nearly three years ago, when June had first heard of this, it had seemed so degraded and repulsive that she had shrunk from the thought of it. Now, sitting lonely in the twilight, her eyes staring at the gray panes, she recalled it with relief, found it a thing to be glad of, to congratulate herself upon. The city had put its stain upon her. Her maidenly fastidiousness was smirched with its mud.

Plunged in these dark thoughts she did not hear the door open, nor see Rosamund's head gently inserted. It was not till the rustling of her advancing skirts was distinct on the silence that June started and turned. The last light of day fell through the long window on the younger girl's face, rosy with exercise, and shining with a new happiness. She paused by June's chair and stood there, looking down. For the first time in her life the preoccupation of her own affairs prevented her from noticing her sister's sickly appearance.

"It's all arranged, June," she said in a low voice.

"Arranged!" repeated June, looking up quickly, her ear struck by something unusual in her sister's tone. "What's arranged?"

"Everything between Mr. Harrower and me. We're—we're—"

"You're engaged?" said June, almost solemnly.

Rosamund, looking into the upturned face, nodded. There was a sudden pricking of tears under her eyelids, an unexpected quivering of her lips. She bent down and laid her cheek against her sister's, and in the dim room they clung together for a silent moment, one in the first flush of her woman's happiness, the other in the dawning realization of her desertion.

CHAPTER X
THE QUICKENING CURRENT

The last quarter of 1873 was for California and Nevada a period of steadily augmenting excitement. The rumor of new strikes in the California and Con. Virginia grew with each week, seizing upon the minds of men, shaking them from the lethargy of their disbelief, arresting them in the plodding ways of work by the temptation of riches, in vast quantities, easily made, open to the hands of all who dared.

Reports from Virginia by wire, by letter, by word of mouth poured into San Francisco. The news that a southeast drift had run into a rich ore-body in the California and Con. Virginia was two weeks later supplemented by a rumor that a chamber had been cut in the ledge, the ore-surface assaying from ninety-three to six hundred and thirty-two dollars per ton.

The male population of the city surged back and forth across the mountains, seized with the fever for gold. The wild days of mining speculation were not yet fully inaugurated, but with the increasing discoveries shares in all the properties near the new bonanzas began to rise, and the world once more began to buy. From across the mountains truth and rumor flowed in ever-accelerating waves to San Francisco, and stocks began to leap as they had done in the Crown Point and Belcher days.

In the middle of this outer ring of excitement the little group of the Colonel and his friends was shaken by tumults of its own creating. The great wheel outside spun round with fury while the little wheel inside flew with an equal speed. It seemed as if the fever of life around them was communicating itself to them, making their blood flow quicker, their pulses throb harder, lifting them up to planes where the air was charged with dynamic forces, and electric vibrations hummed along the serene currents of life.

Both Allen and the Colonel were smitten by temptation. Like a man suddenly arrested in happy, undisturbed wayfaring by some irresistible call to sin, the Colonel stood irresolute, fighting with his desire once more to "try his luck." His resources had grown smaller again within the last year, and he found it meant financiering to keep up the donations for "Carter's girl" and "G. T.'s widow." Early in the year he had sold one of the South Park houses, almost the only good piece of property he still retained, paid his assessments for the new pumps they were putting up in the mine in Shasta and placed "Joe's boy" in business. "Carter's girl" would not be a care much longer. She was eighteen and engaged to be married. "G. T.'s widow" was the only pensioner that would remain on his hands till either he or she was called to a final account. The Colonel felt that he must live up to her ideal of him, which was that he was as good financially as the Bank of England.

Allen had not a thought to give to such matters as individual pecuniary obligations. He was continually at his mine or in Virginia, returning for brief visits at odd times, when he talked thickly and volubly of the wonderful developments of the Nevada camp. He was deteriorating rapidly. He drank now in the daytime. There were stories going about that ore in the Barranca was very low grade, the ore-body narrowing. In October the Colonel met a mining man from the locality who said it was common talk at Foleys that the Barranca was "pinching out." Whether it was or not Allen was known to be investing in "wildcat" in Virginia. He went about with his pockets full of maps which he was perpetually unrolling and pointing out this or that undeveloped claim which would some day yield a new bonanza and was now a prospect hole in the sage brush.

The engagement of Rosamund filled him with delight. He was a man whose affection was largely founded on pride, and it satisfied him that one of his girls should "capture," as he expressed it, a fiancé so eminently eligible. He made much of Rosamund, of whom he had never before been as fond as he was of June, and treated Harrower with a familiar jocoseness under which that reserved young man winced and was restive.

"He thinks I'm rich," Allen had said one evening to the Colonel as they sat alone over their cigars. "He thinks he's going to get a fortune with Rosamund."

"What put that into your head?" the Colonel had asked in sudden annoyance. "The boy loves her as he ought to. He's a man, that fellow. He's not after money."

"Maybe that's your opinion," the other had returned, "but I happen to have a different one. He takes me for a millionaire mining man and thinks Rosamund's going to get her slice of the millions for a dowry. He's going to get left, but that's not my concern or yours. Rosamund'll have as good a trousseau as any girl, but when you come to dowry—!"

He broke off, laughing. The Colonel found it difficult to respond without a show of temper.

"You're all off," he answered dryly. "When his grandfather dies—and the old fellow's over eighty now—he'll have one of the finest estates in the part of England where he's located. What's he want with your money? Why, he could buy up and put in his pocket a whole bunch of plungers like you, with your wildcat shares. Can't you believe that the boy's honestly in love with a girl like Rosamund?"

"Oh, Jim, you're an old maid!" the other returned with his irritating, lazy laughter. "He's in love with Rosamund all right, but he's also in love with the money he thinks he's going to get with her. But don't you fret. It'll be all right. He's a decent enough fellow, but it's a good thing for us he's not got more sense."

Thus the older men had their anxieties, as the young people had theirs. And all this agglomeration of divers emotions and interests concentrated, even as the pressure in the city without, the year sweeping toward its close with ever-increasing momentum, like a river rushing toward the sea.

October was a month of movement, pressure and stir. While San Francisco waited expectant for its first cleansing rains, Harrower left for England, to return in the spring and claim his bride. In the long gray afternoons June sat much at home, brooding over the sitting-room fire, waiting for a visitor who never came. Mercedes moved up from Tres Pinos and took possession of the city house her father had rented for her. She was blooming and gay after her summer in the country. Her heart was swelled with triumph, for she knew the game was won, and, caught in the eddies of the whirling current, she too was swept forward toward a future that was full of tantalizing secrets.

CHAPTER XI
LUPÉ'S CHAINS ARE BROKEN

One of the most harassed and uneasy men in these stormy days was Jerry Barclay. He had arrived at a point in his career where he stood arrested and uncertain between diverging paths. His infatuation for Mercedes drew him to her like a magnet and sent him from her in troubled distress, not knowing what to do, longing for his freedom and sometimes wondering whether he would marry her if he had his freedom.

He thought she loved him as other women had done, and he often wondered if he really loved her. In the sudden glimpses of clairvoyance which come to souls swayed by passion, he saw life with Mercedes as a coldly splendid waste in which he wandered, lonely and bereft of comfort. Shaken from his bondage by one of these moments of clear sight, he felt a conviction that he did not love her, declared himself free of her enchantments, and at the first glance of invitation in her eyes, the first beckoning gesture of her hand, was back at her side, as much her slave as ever.

He pushed June from his mind in these days, saw her seldom, and then showed that cold constraint of manner which the artless and unsubtile man assumes to the woman toward whom he knows his conduct to be mean and unworthy. June lay heavy on his conscience. The thought of her and what she was enduring made him feel ashamed and guilty. And he was angry that he should feel this way—angry with June, against whom he seemed to have a special grievance.

He argued with himself that he was under no obligation to her. He had never made any binding declaration to her, and he had honestly told her that he was not free to marry. How many men would have done that? If she was so unsophisticated as to take the few sentimental remarks he had made as a serious plighting of vows it was not his fault. He affected to have forgotten the remarks. Even in thinking to himself he assumed the air of one who finds it too trivial a matter for remembrance. But the truth was that every sentence was clear in his mind, and the recollection of the pure and honest feeling of that year stung him with an unfamiliar sense of shame.

In his heart he knew that of the three women who had played so prominent a part in his life, June was the one he had really loved. There were moments now, when, deep in the bottom of his consciousness, he felt that he loved her still. The clairvoyant glimpses of a life with her were very different. But he was not free! Why, he said to himself with a magnanimous air, why waste her life by encouraging her in fruitless hopes? Mercedes was quite a different person. She could take care of herself.

They were certainly troublous times for Jerry. He had a man's hatred of a scene and the interviews he had with Mrs. Newbury were now always scenes. He left her presence sore and enraged with the fury of her taunts, or humiliated by the more intolerable outbursts of tears and pleadings, into which she sometimes broke.

He felt with a sort of aggrieved protest that after nearly ten years of devotion Lupé ought to be more reasonable. Jerry was confidently sure that, as he expressed it, he had "shown himself very much of a gentleman" where Lupé was concerned. He had been gentle and forbearing with her. Long after his affection had died he had been patient with her exactions and borne her upbraidings. He had kept a promise that had been made in the first madness of their infatuation and that many men would have regarded as ridiculous. In his behavior to his mistress Jerry saw himself a knight of chivalry. He did not tell himself that the main ingredient of his chivalry was a secret but acute fear of the violent woman whom his neglect had rendered desperate. She had threatened that she would kill herself. Once or twice of late, in what he called her "tantrums," she had threatened to kill him. After these interviews Jerry went from her presence chilled and sobered. She was in despair and he knew it and knew her. Some day Lupé might keep her word.

One afternoon in October he had stopped in at the Newbury house to pay one of those brief visits which had replaced the long stolen interviews of the past. He had met Newbury down town in the morning and been told that Lupé was not feeling well. She had lately suffered from headaches, an unknown ailment for her. Newbury was worried; he wanted her to have the doctor, for she really looked bad and seemed very much out of spirits.

Jerry found her looking exceedingly white and very quiet. She had evidently been ill and showed the marks of suffering. He was relieved to see that she was in a fairly tranquil state of mind, with no intention of making a scene. In fact, to his secret joy he found that he could keep the conversation on the impersonal, society plane upon which he had often before attempted to maintain it, invariably without success. But Lupé to-day had evidently no spirit to quarrel or to weep. She sat in a large arm-chair in an attitude of listless weariness, her skin looking whiter, her hair and eyes blacker than usual. She had lost in weight and though in her thirty-seventh year was as handsome as she had ever been.

Jerry kept one eye on the clock. If he could get away early enough he was going to see a new horse Black Dan had just given Mercedes. A year of practice had made him very expert in bringing interviews with Lupé to an abrupt end, leaving her too quickly to give her time to change from the serenity of general conversation to the hysterical note of rage and grievance.

"Well, Lupé," he said, rising and going to her side, "I must be going. I'm glad you're so much better. You ought to take more exercise."

He took her hand and smiling down at her pressed it. She looked at him with her somber eyes, large and melancholy in their darkened sockets. The look was tragic and with alarm he attempted to draw his hand away. But she held it, drew it against her bosom, and bowed her face on his arm.

"Oh, Jerry," she almost groaned, "is this you and I?"

"Of course, dear," he said glibly, patting her lightly on the shoulder with his free hand. "You'll be all right soon if you'll take more exercise. You're just a little bit inclined to the lazy—all you Spanish women are."

She made no answer and he could feel her body trembling.

"Come, Lupé," he said with a touch of urgency in his voice, "I must go, my dear girl. I've got something to do at half-past four."

"Are you going to Miss Gracey's?" she said without moving or loosening her hold of his hand.

"Oh, Lupé, dear," he answered impatiently, "don't let's get on those subjects to-day. I've had such a nice time here with you this afternoon, just because you've been pleasant, and quiet and reasonable. Now don't spoil it all by beginning to fight and find fault."

She raised her head but still held his hand pressed against her heart.

"I'm not going to fight," she said in a low tone, "my fighting days are over."

"That's the most sensible thing that I've heard you say for a long time. You've just worn yourself out by the way you've stormed and raged. That's why you've felt so sick. It isn't worth while."

"No, I suppose not." She looked up at him with eyes of gloomy tenderness, and opening her fingers one by one let him draw his hand away.

"You're going to Miss Gracey's?" she said again.

He averted his head with a quick movement of impatience.

"Please tell me," she pleaded, "I'm not bad tempered to-day."

"Well, yes, since you say so, I *am* going there. But there's no necessity to get excited about it. You know, Lupé, we've known each other a long, long time."

He paused, furtively watching her, on the alert to fly if she showed the symptoms of storm he knew so well. But she remained passive, almost apathetic. The thought crossed his mind that she must have been much sicker than Newbury had imagined, and a gust of pity for her stirred in him. He bent down and kissed her heavy hair.

"You know," he said gently, "when years roll by as they have with us changes come. But we'll always be friends, won't we, Lupé?"

"I don't know," she said, "always is a long word. But I'll always love you. That's my punishment for my sins."

The clock chimed the half-hour and Jerry patted her again on the shoulder. It was as bad to have Lupé talk of her sins as it was to have her upbraid him with his.

"I'll see you again soon," he said brightly, "but I must fly now. Take good care of yourself. Try and be more cheerful and go out more. Fresh air's the thing for you."

When he had put on his coat in the hall he appeared at the open doorway and smiled a last good-by at her. She was sitting in the arm-chair in the same listless attitude. She nodded to him without smiling, and he was again struck by her unusual pallor and the darkness of her eyes.

"She's really been sick," he said to himself as he ran down the steps, for he was late. "Poor Lupé! How hard she takes everything!"

The next afternoon he was summoned from his office by a message that a woman wanted to see him in the hall outside. He went out wondering and found Pancha, the Mexican servant maid who had been in Mrs. Newbury's service since her marriage and was in the secret of their liaison. After the fashion of her race the woman wore a black shawl over her head in place of a hat, and her face between its folds was drawn and pale. In a few broken sentences she told him that her mistress was desperately ill; something terrible had happened to her in the night. It was hard to grasp her meaning, for she spoke very poor English and Jerry had no Spanish, but he learned enough to know that Lupé was undoubtedly in a serious state. With the assurance that he would come as soon as he could he sent the woman away and went back into the office.

Half an hour later he started for the Newbury house. He was alarmed and chilled. He could not picture Lupé—a woman of superb physique—stricken down in twenty-four hours. She had been pale and listless but otherwise well yesterday. Pancha, who was not used to sickness, had probably been frightened and had exaggerated. Thus he tried to lift the weight which had suddenly fallen on his heart. He no longer loved Lupé, but he "did not want anything to happen to her," he thought to himself as he approached the door.

Here at the curb he saw two doctors' buggies, and, at the sight, his sense of alarm increased. There was no question about it; something serious was evidently the matter.

He asked for Newbury and after a moment's wait in the hall saw the door into the sitting-room open and that gentleman issue forth, closing the door on a murmur of male voices. Newbury looked an aged man, gray and haggard. Without any greeting, evidently too distraught by sudden calamity to wonder how Jerry had heard the bad news, he said in a low voice:

"They're holding a consultation in there"—his sunken eyes dwelt on the young man's and he shook his head. "No hope, none. She can't possibly get well. They don't think she'll live more than a day or two."

"What—what—is it?" stammered Jerry, horror-stricken. "What's happened to her?"

"A paralytic stroke. She had it early in the evening. Pancha found her lying on the sofa like a person resting, but she was paralyzed and couldn't speak. That was what the headaches meant and we were such fools we didn't think anything of them."

"Is she conscious? Does she know?" Jerry asked, not knowing what to say, his whole being flooded with a sense of repulsion and dread.

"I think so and so does Pancha. The doctors don't. She can't speak or move but her eyes look full of life and intelligence, and once or twice she's tried to smile."

A soft footfall on the stairs above caught their ears and they looked up. The Mexican woman was descending, her eyes on Jerry. Newbury cried at her in Spanish, his voice suddenly hoarse with a muffled agony of fear. She shook her head and answered in the same language, speaking at some length. Newbury translated:

"She's told Lupé that you're here and thinks she wants to see you. She says she's tried to speak, and, as far as she can follow, she's under the impression that Lupé's asked for you."

It was a hateful suggestion to Jerry. He was shocked enough already without having to suffer seeing Lupé in this unfamiliar state. He detested sad things and kept them out of his life with the utmost care. But Newbury and the woman were watching him. He realized that they both expected him to go. Deep down in the inner places of his soul the thought that Lupé could not speak passed with a vibration of relief.

They followed Pancha up the softly carpeted stairs and along the passage. The woman passed through a doorway, making a gesture for them to wait, then put her head out and beckoned them in.

The darkness of evening had fallen and the large room was well-lighted. By the bed two gas jets, burning under ground-glass globes, threw a brilliant light over the sick woman. She was lying straight and stark on her back, the bed-clothes smooth over the undulations of her body and raised into points by her feet. Spreading over the pillow beside her, like the shadow of death waiting to cover her, was her hair, a black, dense mass, crossing the bed and falling over its edge. Her face was as white as the pillow, her eyes staring straight before her with a stern, frowning look. A stillness reigned in the room; death was without the door waiting to get in.

Newbury went toward her. Jerry hung back gazing fearfully at her. She was invested with a strange, alien terror, a being half initiated into awful mysteries. The inflexible sternness of her face did not soften as her husband bent over her and said gently:

"Dearest, Jerry came to see how you were. He's here. Would you like to see him?"

She gave a low sound, undoubtedly an affirmative. Pancha, who was at the foot of the bed, enunciated a quick phrase in Spanish. Newbury stepped aside and beckoned Jerry forward. As her lover came within her line of vision her eyes softened, the stiffened lips expanded with difficulty into a slight smile.

"Of course she knows you," Newbury said in a choked whisper. "Oh, my poor Lupé!"

His voice broke and he turned away convulsed and walked to the window. With the Mexican woman watching him from the foot-board, Jerry bent down and kissed her very softly on the forehead and both eyes. She made an effort to lift her face to his caress like a child, and as he drew back her eyes dwelt on his, full of the somber and unquenchable passion that had killed her. He tried to speak to her but found it impossible. Memories of the old days rushed upon him—of her resistance to his fiery wooing, of the first years of their intimacy and the tortures of her conscience that her love could never deaden, and now this ending amid the ruins of her anguish and his hard coldness.

He turned and groped his way out of the room. On the stairs Newbury joined him, touched beyond measure at the sight of his grief. With assurances that he would be up in the morning to inquire, Jerry escaped from the house and fled into the night, now dark and full of the chill of fog.

He could not sleep, and in the morning walked up to the house before breakfast for news. The servant at the door told him that Mrs. Newbury was dead, having passed away quietly without renewal of consciousness or speech as the day was dawning.

Without a word he turned from the door and walked down the street to where a car line crossed it. Standing on the corner waiting for the car, he was accosted by a boy selling the morning papers, and mechanically, without consciousness of his action, he bought one.

In the same mazed state he opened it and looked at the front page. The first paragraph that met his eye was an announcement that the rumored strike of a great ore-body of astounding richness in the Cresta Plata was confirmed. The excitement in Virginia was intense, the mine being regarded as second only to the Con. Virginia. "This," concluded the paragraph, "will raise the fortunes of the Gracey boys far above the six naught mark, well up on the list of bonanza millionaires."

CHAPTER XII
A MAN AND HIS PRICE

The ball given by Mrs. Davenport, to introduce to San Francisco society the fiancée of her son Stanley, was long remembered as one of the most brilliant entertainments ever given in California.

The exhilaration of prosperity was in the air. Stocks were mounting, everybody was making money. More new dresses were ordered for Mrs. Davenport's ball than ever before for any one function. The jewelers were selling diamonds to men and women who five years before had lived in two-room cabins and worn overalls and calicos. Black Dan Gracey had come down from Virginia to see his daughter and bought her a diamond tiara which it was said eclipsed anything of the kind ever sold in San Francisco or even New York. The bonanza times were beginning, and the fiery wine of life they distilled mounting to the heads of men.

To Rosamund's surprise June announced her intention of going to the ball. She had gone out little lately, since the death of Mrs. Newbury, now six weeks past, not at all. Every evening she had sat in the parlor in Folsom Street, waiting. But the visitor she expected never came. It was typical of her ineradicable optimism that she should still have expected him. Rosamund had heard and seen enough to feel certain that he would never come, that every leisure hour he had was spent with the daughter of Black Dan Gracey. All Mercedes' other charms were now enhanced by the luster of great wealth, and the Colonel had told Rosamund that Jerry's business was practically nil, his private fortune gone. It was necessary to say no more.

June dressed herself for the ball that night as for a crisis. She had ordered a new gown, and sheathed in its glimmering whiteness, with filmy skirts falling from her hips to the floor in vaporous layers, was an ethereally fairy-like figure. Like many women who are not handsome but possess a delicate charm of appearance, she varied singularly in looks. To-night the evanescent beauty, that was now and then hers, revisited her. She was not the blushing, soft-eyed girl that Barclay had kissed in the woods at San Mateo, but a graceful woman in whose fragile elegance there was something spiritual and poetic. She noticed her pallor and accentuated it with powder, rubbing it along her shoulders till they looked like marble. In all this luminous whiteness of skin and raiment her lips were unusually red, her eyes dark and brilliant. She scrutinized herself in the mirror, drew down tendrils of hair from the coil that now crowned her head, studied her profile and coiffure in the hand glass and tried different jeweled pendants round her neck. She was like a general before battle who reviews his resources and tries to display them to the best advantage.

Owing to a delay in the arrival of the carriage they were late. It was half-past ten—an unwonted hour for those days—when they entered the house. At its wide-flung portals currents of revelry and joy seemed to meet them. There was the suggestion of festival in the air; the rhythm of dance music swelled and faded over the hum of voices. Room opened from room with glimpses of polished floors between long trains, reflections of bare shoulders in mirrors, gleams of diamonds, sharp and sudden under the even flood of light from the chandeliers. Over all hung the perfume of flowers, great masses of which stood banked in corners, or hung in thick festoons along the walls.

The Colonel escorted his charges to the end of the drawing-room where Stanley Davenport's fiancée stood beside the hostess receiving guests and congratulations. Their few sentences of greeting accomplished, they moved aside toward the wide door of entrance. From this vantage point their eyes were instantly attracted by the figure of Mercedes Gracey surrounded by a little group of admirers.

In the full panoply of ball dress the young woman was truly magnificent. Black Dan's last gift was a fitting crown for such a head. She was profusely bejeweled, exceedingly bare as to neck and shoulders, and robed in a sparkling splendor of lace traced out and weighted with silver which looked like a symbolic incarnation of the riches she represented. She was brilliantly animated, turning her head this way and that as the members of the little court pressed on her notice. Rosamund, who was very quick to notice significant details, was struck by the fact that there were nearly as many women as men about her.

She was about to mention this to June, when the various young men, who had detached themselves from other groups at the appearance of the Misses Allen, bore down upon them, fluttering programs. A wall of black coats formed about the girls, and the Colonel, seeing the intricate rites of program comparing fairly inaugurated, backed away from them and leaned against the door frame, idly surveying the scene.

A hand on his shoulder made him start and turn, and then break into the broad smile of fellowship he reserved for just a few people.

"Rion, old son!" he exclaimed grasping the hand of his friend, "what brings you here, floundering round among all these trains and frills?"

The other laughed. He had not been in San Francisco for nearly a year. He was a little leaner, harder and tougher than he had been on his last visit, when the Colonel had only seen him once or twice and he had refused an invitation to dine in Folsom Street.

"I'm down to escort my niece. Dan couldn't come, so I was offered up. Mercedes had a notion she had to have the males of her family grouped round her to-night and telegraphed up for one of us. Dan would rather shut down the Cresta Plata than disappoint her, so as he couldn't come I had to."

"You're being broken in early. At my age it's about all a fellow's good for. I take the girls wherever they go, and what's more, I enjoy it. Have you seen them yet?"

Mercedes

He indicated the white-robed figures of June and Rosamund in front of him. Rion nodded. Before he had spoken to the Colonel he had stood just behind him watching June. Her back was toward him but as she turned he caught glimpses of her profile. He had not dared to speak to her. His stop with the Colonel was a half-way halt, a pause to gain courage, cheered by a hope that the older man might break the ice of their meeting.

"How are they?" he said in a matter-of-fact tone, while his heart pounded with mingled hope and dread of June's turning and seeing him.

"Well, very well," said the other briskly. "Rosamund's a perfect picture of health and happiness. And June—well, perhaps she's a little thin and not quite up to her usual spirits. But she looks very pretty to-night."

He waited to see what Rion would say to this. The Colonel had wondered of late if his friend had heard any gossip of June and Barclay. He knew the mining man led a simple life of engrossing work among men, far from the circles where the meaner spirits of the world seek to unveil the hidden wounds of their fellows. Rion's answer struck upon his complacency with an impact of disturbing surprise.

"Do you know if Barclay's here yet? Have you seen him? Mercedes sent me to find out if he'd come. He said he'd be late, and she seems to think it's about time for him to illuminate the place by his presence. But I can't find him."

"Barclay!" exclaimed the older man in a disgusted tone. "What's Mercedes want with him? A handsome girl like that oughtn't to bother her head about a skunk like Barclay."

"Go slow, Jim, go slow now," said Rion, laughing; and placing his big hand on the Colonel's shoulder he pressed it hard. "Mustn't talk that way to me about Jerry any more. He's going to become a member of the family. He and Mercedes are engaged. It's announced to-night. That's why I'm here. That's why Mercedes wanted the men of the family to rally round her, and lend the weight of their approval to something they don't approve of at all."

For the first moment the Colonel was too staggered to speak. He had expected it—as Rosamund had—but not so soon, not so indecently soon. His mind leaped forward to the certainty of June's hearing it suddenly from a partner and something distressing happening.

"Stay here, Rion, for a moment," he said quietly. "I want to speak to Rosamund."

Even as he stepped forward, Rosamund, a few yards in front of them, wheeled suddenly from the two men before her, and came toward him. One glance at her face told him that she too had heard.

"Uncle Jim," she whispered, as they came together and she made a desperate clutch at him, "quick! something dreadful's happened. Mercedes and Jerry are engaged and it's announced to-night. Everybody's talking of it. Jack Griscom's just told me. What'll we do? June may hear it at any moment. We've got to get her away before she does."

June stood just beyond them. Breaking into Rosamund's last words came the little blow of her fan striking the floor. Her program fluttered down beside it.

"Why, Miss Allen," said her companion, a youth who had been the first to impart the news of the evening, "what is it? You're dropping everything."

As he bent on his knees to pick up the fallen properties, the Colonel roughly pushed him aside. June's stricken face appalled him. He drew one of her hands through his arm, and said in a low authoritative voice:

"Come. We're going home. Walk to the door and I'll get the carriage in a minute."

She made an effort and turning moved toward the door. In the passing in and out of laughing people, flushed with exercise and pleasure, no one noticed her except Rion, who suddenly saw her approach and sweep by, her eyes staring before her, her face set like a stone. Rosamund had taken the fan and program from the astonished boy, and with a rapid sentence to the effect that her sister felt faint, followed them. Rion dared to touch her arm as she passed through the doorway.

"What's the matter with June?" he said bruskly. "She looks as if she were dying."

"She's sick. She—she—feels faint. It's—it's—a sort of an attack."

She hurried on down the long flagged hall, at one side of which was the dressing-room. Rion followed and saw the three enter it. He stood outside, irresolute, not liking to look in through the open doorway and unable to go away. Presently the Colonel emerged, saw him, and hurrying toward him, said in quick, low-toned urgency:

"You're just the man I want. June's sick. I'm going to get the carriage and I don't want any of these fools of people round here to see her. You bring her down as soon as she's ready."

"What's the matter with her?" Rion asked again. "Is it serious?"

"It's—it's—the heart," said the Colonel, bent on shielding his darling even to her lover and his own friend. "She's—she's—had attacks before. Yes, it's damned serious."

He was gone with the words, and Rion, standing by the dressing-room door, looked in and caught a glimpse of June standing between Rosamund, who was fastening her cloak, and a white-capped negress who was draping a lace scarf over her head. She looked like a sleep-walker, wide-eyed and pallid under their arranging hands. He did not move away this time, but instead walked to the door and said to Rosamund:

"The Colonel wants me to take you to the carriage."

As they moved toward him he entered, drew June's hand inside his arm and walked down the hall to the door. There were several short flights of marble steps leading from the porch to the street. When he came to these he threw her cloak aside, pushing it out of his way, put his arm around her and half carried her down. Her body in the grasp of his arm seemed pitifully small and frail. She said nothing, but he felt that she trembled like a person in a chill.

At the foot of the steps the carriage stood, the Colonel at the door. The hour was an auspicious one for an unseen exit. It was too late for the most dilatory guest to be arriving, and too early for the most unfestal to be leaving. The street was devoid of pedestrians and vehicles, and lit by the diminishing dots of lamps and the gushes of light from the illuminated house, presented a vista of echoing desertion.

The Colonel opened the carriage door, helped Rosamund in first and lifted June in after her. He was standing with the handle in his hand when a footstep he had vaguely heard advancing through the silence struck loud on his ear. He turned quickly and saw a man come into view from the angle of the side street, walk rapidly toward the house, and then stop with that air of alertly poised hesitancy which suggests a suddenly-caught and concentrated attention. The object of this attention was the Colonel's figure, and as the new-comer stood in that one arrested moment of motionless scrutiny, the Colonel saw by the light of an adjacent lamp that it was Jerry Barclay. They recognized each other, and the advancing man drew back quickly into the shadow of the house.

"Rion," said the Colonel, turning to his friend, "would you mind taking the girls home? I've just remembered something I have to do that will detain me for a few minutes. I'll go round the other way and be at Folsom Street almost as soon as you are."

He waited to see Rion enter and then slammed the door on him, and drew back from the curb.

As the carriage disappeared around the corner he walked forward to the spot where Jerry was concealed. He could see his figure pressed back against the fence, faintly discernible as a darker bulk amid the darkness about it, a pale line of shirt bosom showing between the straight blackness of the loosened coat fronts.

"I knew that was you, Jerry," he said. "It's no good hiding."

Jerry stepped forward into the light of the lamp. He was enraged and chagrined at the encounter.

"Hiding?" he exclaimed haughtily. "Why should I be hiding?"

The Colonel came close to him and said with low-toned emphasis:

"Because you're a liar and a coward, Jerry Barclay; and you were afraid to meet me."

Jerry drew back crying with amazed rage:

"Colonel Parrish!"

"And you tried to hide from me to-night when I know what you are and what you've done. You scrub—you—"

Barclay hit furiously at him, but the older man evaded the blow, and seizing him by the loosened fronts of his coat, with his open hand struck him on both sides of the face and then flung him against the fence. He squared himself to meet an onslaught but Jerry struck heavily and fell, a dark, sprawling mass on the sidewalk. The oath that he shouted as he reeled back was bitten in two by an ejaculation of pain and he lay motionless, groaning in the dark.

"Stay there and howl," said the Colonel. "If I stayed another moment I'd kick you as you lie."

And he turned and ran down the street. The rattle of a carriage struck his ear and a coupé turned the corner, its lamps glaring like two round yellow eyes. He hailed it, thrust a handful of silver into the driver's hand, and gave him the Allen address on Folsom Street.

As the carriage rattled across town he lay back, his blood singing in his ears, his heart racked with rage and pain. He had done no good, probably been very foolish. But as June's face rose on his memory, he wished he had hit harder, and the recollection of Jerry groaning against the fence soothed his pain.

CHAPTER XIII
THE BREAKING POINT

In the middle of the December afternoon the Colonel had come in early to his rooms to change his coat and brush up a bit. He was going to call on the wife of a pioneer friend who had just returned from Europe. The Colonel was punctilious and called in a black coat, which he now stood brushing beside the window and anxiously surveying, for he had been a man who was careful of his dress, and the coat looked shiny.

It was a chill gray day and he looped back the lace curtains to see better. Outside, the fog was beginning to send in long advancing wisps which projected a cold breath into the warmest corners of the city. A mental picture rose on his mind of the sand dunes far out with the fleecy curls and clouds sifting noiselessly over them. The vision was not cheering and he put it out of his mind, and in order to enliven his spirits, which were low, he whistled softly as he brushed.

The room—the bare hotel parlor of that kind of suite which has a small windowless bedroom behind it—looked out on the life of one of the down-town streets. The Traveler's Hotel had not yet quite fallen from grace, though the days of its prosperous prime were past. On the block opposite it a few old sheds of wood and corrugated iron (relics of the early fifties) toppled against one another and sheltered a swarming vagabond life. The hotel itself still preserved its dignity. The shops on its ground floor were respectable and clean. There was a good deal of Spanish and Italian spoken in them, which seemed to accord with their pink and blue door-frames, the Madeira vines growing in their windows, and the smell of garlic that they exhaled at midday.

The Colonel was giving the coat a last inspection when a knock made him start. His visitors were few, and his eyes were expectantly fixed on the door when in answer to his "come in" it slowly opened. A whiff of perfume and a rustle of silks heralded the entrance of June, who stood somewhat timidly on the threshold looking in.

"Junie!" cried the Colonel in delighted surprise. "My girl come to see the old man in his lair!"

And he took her by the hand and drew her in, kissing her as he shut the door, and rolling up his best arm-chair.

She did not sit down at once and he said, still holding her hand by the tips of the fingers and looking her over admiringly:

"Well, aren't you a beautiful sight! And just the best girl in the world to come down here and see me."

She smiled faintly and answered:

"Wasn't I lucky to find you? I've been coming for some days only—only—" she sat down on the arm of the chair, prodding at the carpet with the end of her umbrella and looking down.

"Only you had so many other things to do," he suggested.

"No, not that," still looking down at the tip of the umbrella. "Only I think I hadn't quite enough courage."

She rose from the arm of the chair and walked to the window. As she moved the rustle of her rich dress and the perfume it exhaled filled the room. The Colonel looked at her uneasily. It was three weeks since the Davenport ball. She had kept her room for some days after the ball, saying she was sick. After that she had appeared, looking miserably ill, and in manner cold and uncommunicative. She had spoken of Jerry's engagement to no one, not even to Rosamund. To the Colonel she had been gentle, quiet, and for the first time in their acquaintance indifferent and unresponsive. What her appearance this afternoon portended he could not guess.

"Not enough courage!" he now repeated. "Was there ever any time since I've known you when you wanted courage to come to me?"

"Never before," she answered, standing with her back to him looking out of the window.

Her voice, her attitude, her profile against the pane, were expressive of the completest dejection. She was expensively and beautifully dressed in a crisp silken gown of several shades of blue. Every detail of her appearance was elegant and fastidious. In her years of city life she had developed all the extravagance, the studious consideration of her raiment, of a fashionable woman. Now her costly dress, the jeweled ornaments she wore, her gloves, her hat with its long blue feather that rested on her bright-colored hair, the tip of the shoe that peeped from her skirt, combined to make her a figure of notable feminine finish and distinction. And surrounded by this elaboration of careful daintiness, her heaviness of spirit seemed thrown up into higher relief.

"Come, sit down," said the Colonel, rolling the chair toward her. "I can't talk comfortably to you when you stand there with your back to me looking out of the window as if we'd been quarreling."

She returned to the chair and obediently sank into it. Her hands hung over its arms, one of them languidly holding the umbrella. He had thought his suggestion about quarreling would make her laugh, but she did not seem to have heard it.

"And now," he said, drawing a chair up beside her, "let's hear what it is you hadn't the courage to tell to your Uncle Jim? Have you been robbing or murdering, or what?"

"I've been staying in the house mostly, looking out of the window. I—don't feel much like going out. I—oh, Uncle Jim," she said, suddenly turning her head as it rested on the chair-back and letting her eyes dwell on his, "I've been so miserable!"

He leaned forward and took her hand. He had nothing to say. Her words needed no further commentary than that furnished by her appearance. With the afternoon light shining on her face, she looked a woman of thirty, worn and thin. All the freshness of the young girl was gone.

"That's what I've come to talk about," she said. "I don't feel sometimes as if I could live here any longer, as if I could breathe here. I hate to go out. I hate to meet people. Every corner I turn I'm afraid that I may meet *them*—and—and—then—" her voice suddenly became hoarse and she sat up and cleared her throat.

For a moment a heavy silence held the room. The Colonel broke it.

"How would you like to go up to Foleys for a while?" he suggested. "Your father was telling me the other day that the superintendent of the Barranca had a nice little house and a very decent sort of wife. You could stay there. It would be a change."

"Foleys!" she echoed. "Oh, not Foleys! It's too full of the past before anything had happened. No, I want to go away, far away, away from everything. That's what I came to talk about. I want to go to Europe."

"Europe!" he exclaimed blankly. "But—but—you'd be gone for months."

"Yes, that's just it. That's what I want—to be gone for months, for years even. I want to get away from San Francisco and California and everything I know here."

The Colonel was silent. He felt suddenly depressed and chilled. San Francisco without June! His life without June! The mean little room with its hideous wall paper and cheap furniture came upon him with its true dreary strangeness. The city outside grew suddenly a hollow place of wind and fog. Life, that was always so full for him, grew blank with a sense of cold, nostalgic emptiness. He had never realized before how she illumined every corner of it.

"Well, dearie," he said, trying to speak cheerfully—"that sounds a big undertaking; sort of thing you don't settle up all in a minute. You couldn't go alone and Rosamund couldn't go with you."

"I know all that. I've thought it all out. I haven't slept well lately and I arranged it when I was awake at night. I could take some one with me, a sort of companion person. And then when Rosamund got married and came over there with Lionel, why, then I could stay with them. Perhaps I could live with them for a while. He has such a big house."

She paused, evidently waiting to see how the Colonel would take her suggestions.

"That's all possible enough," he said,—"but—well, there's your father. How about him?"

"Oh, my father!" the note of scorn in her voice was supplemented by a side look at him which showed she had no further illusions as to her father. "My father can get on very well without me."

Even if she had come to know Allen at his just worth, the hardness of her tone hurt the Colonel. It showed him how deep had been the change in her in the last three years.

"It's hard on him just the same," he said, "to lose his two daughters at once."

"Parents have to lose their children," she answered in the same tone. "Suppose I'd married a foreigner like Rosamund?"

The Colonel did not answer. Suddenly she laid the hand near him on his.

"There's only you and Rosamund," she said. "And now Rosamund's going too."

"It's—it's—pretty hard even to think of," he answered.

"But, Uncle Jim," she urged in the egotism of her pain, blind to all else, "I *can't* stay here. It's too much. You must guess how I feel."

"I can guess," he answered, nodding.

"I can't bear it. I can't stand it. If I could die it would be all right, but I can't even die. I've got to go on living, and if I stay here I've got to go on hearing everybody talking about them and saying how happy they are. Every time I go out I run the risk of meeting them, of seeing them together, with Jerry looking at her the way he used to look at me."

She spoke quietly, staring at the window before her with steady eyes.

"June," he said almost roughly, "I want to talk sensibly to you. All the traveling in Europe won't make you feel better if you don't make an effort to shake yourself free of all this. Now listen—Barclay's shown you what he is. He's a blackguard. I told it to you three years ago, and you know it now by your own experience. Why do you love him? Why do you go on caring for a dog like that? I—I—upon my word, dearest, if it was any girl but you I'd be ashamed of her."

"You don't love a man because he's good, or noble, or any of those things. It's not a thing you reason about. It's something that steals into you and takes possession of you. I know what Jerry is. I suppose it's all true what you say. He may be different from what I thought he was. He may be cruel and unkind to me. But that won't make me change."

"But good God, he's treated you like a dog—thrown you over for a girl with money, made surreptitious love to you when he was bound to a woman he'd ruined and whose husband was his friend! Heavens, June, you can't love a dirty scrub like that! You're a good girl—honest and high-minded—you can't go on caring for him when you see now what he is!"

"Oh, Uncle Jim, dear, you can't change me by talking that way. Women don't love men with their reason, they love them with their hearts. The Jerry that I know is not the Jerry that you know. There are two, and they're quite different. The Jerry that I know and used to meet in the plaza on Turk Street, was always kind and sweet to me, and I used to be so happy when I was with him! I know now they're both true. I guess yours is as true as mine. But even if it is, I care just the same. There's no arguing or convincing—only just that fact."

"After he's made a public show of you and engaged himself to Mercedes not two months after Mrs. Newbury's death? Such a dirty record! Such a mean, cold-blooded, calculating cur! Oh, June, where's your pride?"

"Dead," she said bitterly, "dead long ago."

She suddenly sat upright, turned on him, and spoke with somber vehemence:

"There's no pride, there's no question of yourself—sometimes I think there's no honor, with a girl who feels for a man as I do for him. I know him now, all about him. I know in my heart that he's what you say. I think sometimes, deep down under everything, I have a feeling for him that is almost contempt. But I'm his while he's alive and I am. I can't any more change that than I can make myself taller or shorter. If I'd known in the beginning what I do now it would have all been different. It's too late now to ask me where my pride is, and why I don't tear myself free from such a bondage. It's spoiled my life. It's broken my heart. Sometimes I wish Jerry was dead, because then I know I'd be myself again."

He looked at her horrified. Pallid and shrunken in her rich clothes, eaten into by the passion that now, for the first time, he heard her confess, it seemed to him that she could not be the girl he had met at Foleys three and a half years ago. To his strong, self-denying nature, her weakness was terrible. He did not know that that weakness was one of the attributes which made her so lovable.

"I dare say there's something bad about me," she went on. "I can see that other people don't feel this way. I know Rosamund wouldn't. If Lionel had not really cared for her and asked her to marry him she would have gone to work and just uprooted him from her mind like a weed in a garden. She wouldn't have let things that weren't right get such a hold on her. But I—I never tried to stop it. And now the weed's choked out everything else in the garden."

"Don't let it choke out everything. Root it up! Tear it out! Don't be conquered by a weed, June."

"Oh, Uncle Jim," she almost groaned with the eternal cry of the self-indulgent and weak, "if only I had stopped it in the beginning! I wouldn't have grown to love him so if I'd known. It's been such useless suffering. Nobody's gained anything by it. It's all been such a waste!"

There was a silence. The Colonel sat looking down with his heart feeling heavy as a stone. When he came against that wall of acquiescent feminine feebleness, he felt that he could say nothing. She stirred in her chair and said, her voice suddenly low, her words coming slowly:

"They're to be married in January. It's going to be a short engagement. Black Dan's going to give them a house down here with everything new and beautiful. I'll see them all the time, everywhere. I know just the way they'll look, smiling into each other's eyes."

She stopped and then sat up with a rustling of crushed silks.

"How do people bear these things? I haven't hurt anybody or done any harm to have to suffer this way. When I'm alone I keep thinking of them—how happy they are together, not caring for anything in the world but each other. I think of him kissing her. I think that some day they'll have a baby—" her voice trailed away hoarsely and she sank back in the chair, her head on her breast.

The Colonel got up and walked to the window. These same savage pangs had once torn him. In his powerful heyday it had taken all the force of his manhood to crush them. How could she wage that blasting fight? He turned and looked at her as she sat fallen together in the embrace of the chair.

"I think you're right, June, about going away," he said. "It's the best thing for you to do. The old man'll have to get on as well as he can for a while without you."

She did not move and answered in a dull voice:

"It's the only thing for me to do."

"When were you thinking of going?"

"Soon—as soon as I can. Anyway before January. I must go before then. And—and—Uncle Jim, this was what I came to ask you and was afraid. We've been a long time getting to it."

She looked at him with a sort of tentative uneasiness.

"It's asking a good deal," she added, "but you've always been so good to me."

"What is it, dearie?" he said gently. "Don't you know it's my pleasure to do anything for you?"

"I want you to give me the money to go with."

For a moment the Colonel was so surprised that he looked at her without answering. As she spoke the color came faintly into her face.

"It—it—won't be so very much," she went on hurriedly, "perhaps enough for a year. I thought five thousand dollars would do."

"Five thousand dollars," he said, recovering himself, "five thousand dollars? Why of course—"

He paused, looking down on the floor and asking himself where he was to get five thousand dollars.

"I'll get it for you, only you'll have to give me a few days."

She leaned forward with a sudden energy of animation and clasped his hand.

"I knew you'd do it," she said. "I knew if I came to you for help I'd never be disappointed. I asked father for it, and he!—" she completed the sentence with a shrug.

"He hadn't it, perhaps," suggested the Colonel.

"That's what he said. He said he couldn't possibly give it to me, that he was in debt now. And look at the way we live! Look at this dress! He knows how I feel. He has only to look at me, but he said he couldn't give it."

"Will five thousand be enough, do you think?" said the Colonel, who had no comments to make on Allen, of whose mode of life and need of money he knew more than June.

"I don't know. I don't know anything about traveling. I've never been anywhere but in California and Nevada. But it ought to be enough for a while. Anyway, if I had that I could go, I could get away from all this. I could get away from San Francisco and California, and the people and things that torture me."

She rose from the chair and picked up her umbrella. Her languor of dejection had returned. She cast a listless eye toward the pane and said:

"I must go. It'll soon be dark." Then she moved toward the window and for a moment stood looking down on the street.

"It's quite easy for you to give it to me, isn't it?" she asked without turning. "You're not like father, always talking about your wonderful, priceless stocks, and with not a cent to give a person who's just about got to the end of everything."

"Don't talk about that," he answered quickly. "There can't be a better use for my money than to help you when you're in trouble. I'll see you in a few days and arrange then to give it to you."

She turned from the window.

"Well, good-by, then," she said. "I must go. Good-by, Uncle Jim, my own dear, dear Uncle Jim."

She extended her hand to him, and as he took it, looked with wistful eyes into his.

"I feel as if you were really my father," she said. "It's only to a father or mother that a person feels they can come and ask things from as I have from you to-day."

The Colonel kissed her without speaking. At the doorway she turned and he waved his hand in farewell, but again said nothing.

June walked home through the soft gray damp of the late afternoon. As she looked up the lines of the long streets that climbed the hills, then sloped down toward the water front, she saw the fog blotting them out, erasing outlines, stealthily creeping downward till the distance looked like a slate blurred by a wet sponge. She remembered evenings like this in the first year of her San Francisco life, when she walked home briskly with the chill air moist on her face and her imagination stirred by the mystery and strangeness of the dim, many-hilled city, veiled in whorls and eddies of vaporous white. There was no beauty in it to-night, only a sense of desolation, cold and creepingly pervasive as the fog.

CHAPTER XIV
BED-ROCK

It took the Colonel a week to raise the money. He did it by selling the second of his South Park houses. The sale being a hurried one of property already well on the decline, the house realized less than, even in the present state of eclipse, it was worth. Five years before it had been appraised at fifteen thousand dollars. To-day the best offer he could get was nine.

He placed the money in the bank, the five thousand to stay there till June had decided more definitely on her movements. The remainder he would leave on deposit to his own account. June, in Europe, with five thousand dollars to her fortune, was not beyond the circle of his sense of responsibility. Some one must have money to give her when she needed it, as she certainly would. Her habits of economy had long ago been sloughed off with her faded cotton dresses and her country-made boots. Rosamund would be able to give her a home, but there must be some one somewhere upon whom she could make a demand for funds.

There was no need now for the Colonel to study his accounts. He knew them through and through. There was so little to know. The shut-down mine in Shasta and his mortgage on the Folsom Street house were all that was left to him. On the day that the sale of the South Park house was decided upon he wrote to Rion Gracey, asking him for a position, any overground position that the owners of the Cresta Plata thought he would suit. It was a hard letter to write. He was nearly sixty, and he had never, since his youth, asked any one for anything for himself. But one must live, "G. T.'s widow" had to be considered, not to mention June, living in England and having to be dressed as June should always be dressed.

Two days later the details of the sale were completed and the money deposited. Late that afternoon the Colonel, clad carefully in the shiny coat June had caught him brushing, went across town to Folsom Street. He had done what she had asked and all was ready.

The servant told him she was confined to her room with a bad cold, and after a few minutes' wait in the hall, he was conducted up stairs, and found her lying on a sofa in the great front room, with its lofty ceiling and tall, heavily draped windows. The sofa was drawn up before a small fire that sent a fluctuating glow over her face, flushed with a slight fever, and burnished the loose coil of brown hair that crowned her head. She had a heavy cold, her voice was hoarse, her words interrupted at intervals by a cough. She was delighted to see him, sitting up among the cushions on which she reclined to hold out her hand, and rallying him on the length of time since his last visit.

"But I've been busy," he said, drawing a chair up to the foot of the sofa, "busy over your affairs, young woman."

"My affairs," she answered, looking puzzled; then with sudden comprehension, "Oh, the money!"

"That's it," he nodded, "the money. Well, it's all ready and waiting for you in the bank. When you want it we'll open an account for you, or buy a letter of credit with it, or make whatever arrangement seems best. Anyway, there it is whenever you want to go."

"Oh, Uncle Jim!" she breathed. "And now what do you think's happened?"

"What?" he asked with suddenly arrested attention. It was on his mind that startling things might be expected to happen in the Allen household at any moment.

"I'm not going!"

"You're not going? Junie, don't tell me that!"

The joy in his voice and eyes was transfiguring in its sudden radiance.

He left his chair and sat down on the end of the sofa near her feet, leaning toward her, pathetically eager to hear.

"I've changed my mind,"—a gleam of her old coquetry brightened her face. "Isn't that one of the privileges of my sex?"

"What made you change it? Good Lord, dearie, I'm so glad!"

"I'll tell you all about it. There are several threads to this story. In the first place Rosamund didn't like it. She thought it was queer for me to go to Europe alone and leave father, and just before her wedding, too. She wouldn't hear of my not being at the wedding. But the other reason was more the real one."

She sat up, her elbow in the cushions, her head on her hand, the fingers in her loosened hair. Her eyes on the fire were melancholy and contemplative.

"You remember what I said to you about not being able to live here any longer? How I couldn't stand it? Well, father's going to Virginia City."

"What difference does that make? He's been going there for years."

"Yes, but to live I mean. To take us and make our home there. That's the reason I've changed my mind. I needn't go so far as Europe. We're all going to leave California and live in Nevada."

The Colonel was astonished. He was prepared for strange actions on Allen's part, but a bodily family removal to Virginia when his affairs were in so complicated a condition was unlooked for, and incomprehensible. And why had not Allen spoken to him of it? When in town they saw each other almost daily on Pine and Montgomery Streets.

"Isn't it a very sudden decision of your father's?" he asked. "He had no idea of it last week. You didn't know it when you came to see me that day, did you?"

"I didn't know of it till two days ago. It's all happened in a minute. Father himself didn't know it. I was still thinking about going away and arguing with Rosamund about it, when he came and told us he'd decided to move to Nevada, that he had more business there than here, and it would be much cheaper having one house in Virginia than for him to be up there, with us down here in San Francisco. What made it particularly easy and convenient was that some one wants to buy the house."

This was a second shock, but there was illumination in it. The listener felt now that he was getting to the heart of the matter.

"Buy the house!" he ejaculated. "This house?"

"Yes, this house. I've forgotten the man's name. Some one from Sacramento wants to buy it just as it stands, with the furniture and everything. It's not a very good offer, but property's gone down here, as it has all over this side of town, and father says it's not bad, considering that it makes it so much easier for us to go."

He was, for the moment, too astonished to make any comments. She spoke as though the sale was decided on, the move settled. He knew that neither of the sisters was aware of the mortgage he held on the property, and he listened to her in staring silence as she went on:

"So that's why I'm not going to Europe. Virginia's far enough away from San Francisco. I'll—I'll—not see them up there or hear about it as I would down here. And then there was another reason that's made me glad to stay. When I thought of leaving you and Rosamund—it was so hard—too hard! I don't seem to be one of those independent women who can go about the world alone far away from the people they love. I'd leave my roots behind me, deep down in the ground I came from. I don't think I could ever pull them up. And if I tried and pulled too hard they'd break, and then I suppose I'd wither up and die."

She turned her eyes from the fire to him. She was smiling slightly, her face singularly sad under the smile. He looked at her and said softly:

"My girl!"

He sat on with her for a space, discussing the move and making plans. With some embarrassment he told her of the fact that he had written to Rion Gracey, applying for a position. The thought that he would be in Virginia called the first real color of life and pleasure into her face that he had seen there for weeks. He saw that the excitement of the move, the hope of change from the environment in which she had so suffered, had had a bracing and cheering effect on her. It was evident that she had set her heart on going. Despite her cold and general air of sickly fragility she was more like herself, showed more of her old vivacity and interest, than she had done since the night of the Davenport ball.

On his way down the stairs he decided, if Allen was not in, to wait for him in the sitting-room. But as he reached the stair-foot a faint film of cigar smoke and the more pungent reek of whisky floated from the open doorway, and told him that the master of the house was already there.

Allen was sitting by the table, a decanter and glass near his elbow, his cigar poised in a waiting hand, as he listened to the descending footsteps. The Chinaman had told him that Colonel Parrish had called to see June, and Allen stationed himself by the doorway to catch the visitor on his way out.

"That you, Jim?" he called, as the footfall neared the end of the flight. "Glad you came. Drop in here for a minute before you go. I've something I want to talk to you about."

The Colonel entering, noticed that the other was even more flushed than he usually was at this hour, and that his glance was evasive, his manner constrained. He pushed his cigar-case across the table with a hand that was unsteady, and tried to cover his embarrassment by the strident jocularity of his greeting. The Colonel, sitting down on the arm of a heavy leather chair, did not beat about the bush.

"What's this June's been telling me," he said, "about you all moving to Virginia? Since when have you decided on that?"

"Only a day or two ago. I was going around to see you to-morrow, about it, if you hadn't come this afternoon. I've about made up my mind to go. My business is all up there now. There's no sense living in Virginia two-thirds of the time and running a house down here."

"How about Rosamund's wedding?" the Colonel asked.

"Have it up there. You can have a wedding in Virginia just as well as you can in San Francisco. I can rent a house—a first-rate house, furnished and all ready, and give her just as good a send-off as any girl in California. That's what I calculate to do. It'll require money up there or down here, but that's an expense that's got to be."

"June says you've had an offer for this house. Who made it, and what's he offered?"

Allen leaned forward to knock off the ash of his cigar on the tray beside him.

"That's what I wanted to see you about," he said slowly. "Yes, I've had an offer. It's from a man named Spencer from Sacramento. Just come down here to settle. He's got a big family, and wants a good sized house and garden for the kids to play in. Fashionable locality doesn't count for much with him. He's offered twenty-five thousand down for the place as it stands, furniture and all."

There was a slight pause and the speaker added:

"It's what decided me to go to Virginia, get rid of this—and—and—get some ready money. I'm pretty close to the ragged edge, Jim."

"I don't see how it's going to benefit you," said the Colonel. "My mortgage and the interest for two years back, paid in full, doesn't leave you much more than your fares to Virginia."

Allen got up, walked a few steps away, then came back and stood by the Colonel's chair. His face was deeply flushed, but it had lost its embarrassed air. He looked resolute and determined.

"Jim," he said doggedly, "I've got to have that money."

"Beau Allen," said the Colonel in the same tone, "by what right do you dare to say that to me?"

For a silent moment they eyed each other, then the elder man went on:

"Twenty-five years ago you stole my sweetheart. Four years ago you tried to steal my land and I gave it to you, because you had a wife and two helpless children; and now you're trying to steal my house."

"I've got the same right as I had before," said the other, "I've still got two helpless children."

"Am I to be robbed to provide for your children?"

"You're using pretty strong words, Jim, but you've had provocation. You've met bad usage at my hands and you've given back good. Give it back once more, for the last time. Give it back for the sake of my two girls. They're as helpless now as they ever were, and God knows I'm as unable to help them."

"Why should I keep on providing for your children? You're their father, younger than I, and as able-bodied. Four years ago I put you on your feet when I gave you the Parrish Tract. You've had your chances, the best I could give you. I'm on the ragged edge too. I'm sixty years old and I've had to apply for a position."

"Listen to me, Jim," with desperate urgence. "Let me have this money till after Rosamund's marriage. Let me have fifteen thousand dollars of it. So help me God, I'll invest the rest in your name in any securities you mention. Don't you see I've got to have money till after that? I can't let Harrower know we're bust. *You* think he doesn't care. But I tell you he does. What's going to happen to Rosamund if he throws her over at the last moment?"

The Colonel was silent, looking at the ash tray from beneath down-drawn, bushy brows. Allen close at his elbow continued with fevered intensity:

"Rosamund's wrapped up, body and soul, in that man. What's she going to do if he backs out? And you know him; you've seen the kind he is, daft about his family and his ancient, honorable name. Even if he doesn't want money with her do you think he, with his ancestors' portraits hanging on the walls, wants to marry a girl whose father's a busted mining speculator—in debt all round, who hasn't got the means to buy his daughter a decent dress to get married in? Look at June! Are the futures of both my daughters going to be ruined because I'm broke? Good God, Parrish, you care for them! You can't now, when you see what June's been brought to, stand in the way of Rosamund's happiness."

The Colonel sat looking at the ash tray for a frowning moment, then he said:

"What have you done with the spring? If there had been no mineral on the land the spring would have brought you an income for years."

"I sold the land with the spring on it, after the Crown Point collapse. Blake, the hotel man in San José, bought it, and is building a hotel up there now. That's the past. I'm not defending it, nor my life between then and now. I'm talking of my children. Put me, and what I am, out of the question. It's my two girls that count just now."

The Colonel rose, and walking to the fireplace, stood there with his elbow on the mantel-piece, looking down at the small fire that glowed in the grate. Allen by the table watched him with anxious, waiting eyes.

"I've got chances in Virginia," he said. "Living on the spot there's a different proposition from running back and forth like this. The Maybough properties that I'm interested in are looking pretty promising. Inside of a year, if they turn out as we expect, I may be able to pay you the whole sum back."

The Colonel gave a suppressed sound, short and scornful, but did not raise his head. The other went on.

"Fifteen thousand will carry us to Virginia and over the wedding. Harrower's to be back in the spring and they'll be married as soon as he comes. Spencer wants the house in January or February. That will just about fit in. We can go to Virginia as soon as the sale's completed and have everything ready and in shape by the time Harrower gets here. And it will be better for June, too, better to get her out of all this. She feels pretty bad, poor little girl! One of the reasons that makes me so keen about selling the place and leaving is to get her away from all this talk about Barclay and that Gracey girl."

The Colonel, without raising his eyes, said:

"You'll want the whole twenty-five thousand."

"No—no—" said Allen with undisguised eagerness, hope illuminating his face, "fifteen will do, though of course twenty would be better. Fifteen ought to carry us well along into the summer, and by that time the Maybough should be paying. There'll be the wedding and the trousseau. Of course twenty would be better, but if you'll let me have the fifteen I can do it. I'll invest the other ten any way you may say and—"

He stopped as the Colonel turned from the fire with a short laugh.

"Sell the house," he said, "and take it all."

"What?—" Allen did not quite dare to believe it.

"Sell the house. See Spencer as soon as you can, and I'll give you satisfaction of the mortgage."

"Jim!" the other ejaculated, and held out a shaking hand.

But the Colonel brushed by it and passed into the hall, where his hat and coat hung. Allen followed him, trying to talk, but he stopped the feeble words of gratitude. Standing under the hall lamp, the light falling on his white hair, he said,

"There's no thanks between you and me. If it wasn't for your daughters I'd see you standing on the corner begging for nickels and not drop one in your tin cup. And you know it. You know, too, what I feel about them, and why I feel it. You know I'd do it again if I had the money. But I haven't. There's not much more to be got out of me. You've about sucked me dry."

The night was clear and he walked home, slowly and lingeringly by a circuitous route of cross-streets. At first he paced onward in an absorbed reverie, his eyes down, striking the cracks in the pavement with the tip of his cane. Presently he looked up above the housetops, at the widths of sky sown with great, calm stars. It was early night; only the larger stars were visible. Once or twice as he walked on looking up, he laughed, a short, dry laugh, at himself and the follies he had committed.

When he reached his own room in the Traveler's Hotel he found Rion's answer to his letter. Standing under the feeble light that fell from the sitting-room chandelier he read it. It was short, for Rion was but a poor correspondent. The position of assistant secretary of the Cresta Plata would be vacant on January first. The Gracey boys would be flattered if one of James Parrish's reputation and position would care to fill it. The salary would be five hundred dollars a month.

The Colonel turned the letter over, eying it. The heaviness of his spirit was lightened. Through the few lines he seemed to feel the strong grip of the mining man's hand, to meet the searching look of his keen, honest eyes. They would all be together in Virginia—not such a bad beginning for a new life at sixty.

BOOK III
THE DESERT

CHAPTER I
NEVADA

The mountain wall of the Sierra bounds California on its eastern side. It is a rampart, towering and impregnable, between the garden and the desert. From its crest, brooded over by cloud, glittering with crusted snows, the traveler can look over crag and precipice, mounting files of pines and ravines swimming in unfathomable shadow, to where, vast, pale, far-flung in its dreamy adolescence, lies California, the garden. On the other side—gaunt, hostile, gray—is Nevada, the desert.

In other lands nature and man have ended their struggle for supremacy. Man has conquered and nature, after long years of service, is glad to work for him, to quicken the seed he sows, to swell the fruit on the branch, and ripen the heads of grain. She laps him round with comfort, whispers her secrets to him, reveals herself in sweet, sylvan intercourse. And he, cosily content, knows her as his loving slave, no more rebellious, happy to serve.

But in Nevada, nature is still unconquered, savage and supreme. It is the primordial world, with man a shivering stranger amid its grim aloofness. When the voice of God went out into the darkness and said, "Let there be light," the startled life, cowering in caves and beneath rocks, may have looked out on such a land—an unwatered waste, treeless, flowerless, held in an immemorial silence.

Man as we know him has no place here. He is a speck moving between the dome of sky and the floor of earth. Nature scorns him, has watched him die and whitened his bones in a few blazing weeks. The seed he plants withers in its kernel, the earth he turns up, frosted with alkali, drops apart in livid flakes. The rare rivers by which he pitches his tent are sucked into the soil, as though grudging him the few drops with which he cools his burning throat. An outcast from a later age he is an intruder here. These solemn wastes and eternal hills have not yet learned to call him master.

When the pioneers trailed across it, Nevada was to them only "the desert," a place where the horrors of heat and thirst culminated. They knew it as a sterile, gray expanse, breaking here and there into parched bareness, and with lines of lilac-blue or reddish-purple hills seeming to march with them as they moved. From high places they saw it outspread like a map, its surface stippled with sage and the long green ribbon of a tree-fringed river looping across its grim aridity. At evening it took on limpid, gem-like colors. The hills turned transparent sapphire and amethyst, the sky burned a thin, clear red. An unbroken stillness lay upon it and struck chill on the hearts of the little bands who, oppressed by its vast indifference, cowered beneath its remote, unfamiliar stars.

As they passed across it they mined a little; here and there they scraped the surface, clustered round a stream-bed for a day or two and sent the water circling in their pans. But California, the land of promise, was their goal. With the western sun in their eyes they looked at the mountain wall and spoke of the Eldorado beyond where the gold lay yellow in the sluice box, and flecked with glittering flakes the prospector's pan.

That was in forty-nine. Ten years later they were hurrying backward over the mountains to the streams that drain Mount Davidson. Nevada had its wealth too, a hidden, rock-ribbed wealth, jealously buried. They tore it out, built a city of tents and shacks as they delved, and in ten years more were gone again, dispersed over the far West like the embers of a fire which a wind scatters.

Then once again the barren state drew them back. Deep in the roots of Mount Davidson one of the greatest ore-bodies in the world lay buried. This time they gathered in their might. Miner, engineer, assayer, stock-jobber, manipulator, manager and millionaire poured over the mountain wall, bringing in their train the birds of prey that follow in the wake of the mining army. The city of tents and cabins grew into a city of streets and buildings and spread, climbing the mountain side in terraces. A railroad crawled perilously to it, looping over the mountain flanks. In a cleared nook by a river the smoke of its mills blackened the sky.

Isolated from the rest of the world, encircled by desolation, the town seethed and boiled with an abnormal activity, a volcano of life in the midst of a dead land. About it the desert brooded, pressing in upon it, watching and waiting. To it the little city was an outside thing, hostile, alien, unwelcome. It scorned the pigmy passions of its men and women, had no sympathy with the extravagances of their money madness. When they had been brushed away like an ant-hill by a passing foot, it would sweep over their town, obliterate their traces, reclaim its own. And once again the silence of a landscape where there is neither ripple of water nor murmur of leaf would resettle in crystal quietude.

Confined within their own walls, with no outlet for the pressure under which they lived, the inhabitants of Virginia burned with a wild activity and energy. The conditions of life were so unusual, so fiercely stimulating to effort and achievement, that average human beings were lifted from their places and became creatures of dauntless initiative. They conquered the unconquerable, accomplished triumphs of daring and ingenuity where under ordinary circumstances they would have recoiled before insuperable obstacles. They were outside themselves, larger for good or evil than they had ever been before or would be again. Nature had dared them to her vanquishing and they had risen to the challenge.

In the spring of 1874 the ferment incident to the opening of the great ore-body that has gone down in history as the "Big Bonanza," began to bubble toward boiling point. Month by month stocks had steadily risen, and month by month the huge treasure chamber, filled with silver as a nut is with kernel, developed in ever-increasing richness. The city was packed close as a hive with bees with twenty-five thousand souls all quivering to the increasing momentum of the excitement. The mines were a dynamo whence electric vibrations spread into the world outside. The dwellers in huts among the sage were shaken by them. They thrilled along the Pacific slope. In New York and London men felt them and their pulses quickened. The Bonanza times were nearly at the flood.

The city grew with astonishing rapidity, breathlessly climbed the side of Mount Davidson in ascending tiers of streets. There was no time for grading or paving. Two stories in the front meant four in the back, the kitchens of B Street looked over the shingled roofs of the shops on C Street. It was a gray town, clinging to a desolate mountain side, in a gray country. At its base, appearing to force it up the slope, were the hoisting works of the mines, dotted so close along the lode they nearly touched. Every mine in this line was a mighty name in the world of finance. New York, London and Paris waited each morning to hear news from the town in the wilderness. And as the ant-hill swarmed and trembled with the fury of its concentrated life, the desert looked on, serene, incurious, still.

CHAPTER II
OLD FRIENDS WITH NEW FACES

The Allen girls moved to Virginia City in April. Their father had gone there early in the year and taken a house which would be a proper and fitting place from which to marry Rosamund. He had found what he thought suitable in the mansion, as they called it in Virginia, of one Murchison, a mining superintendent, who, in the heyday of sudden riches, had built him a comfortable home and then died.

The Murchison mansion had come on the market just at the right moment, Allen told people. Men wondered where his money came from, as the current talk among his kind was that "the bottom had fallen out of the Barranca, and Allen was bust." He himself spread the story that successful speculations had once again set him on his feet. That something had done so was proved by his renting of the Murchison mansion, a furnished house in the Virginia City of that period being an expensive luxury.

It stood at the south end of B Street, perched high on the top of two sloping terraces which were bulkheaded by a wooden wall, surmounted by an ornamental balustrade. Small fruit trees and flowering shrubs clothed the terraces in a thin, flickering foliage, just showing its first, faint tips of green when the girls arrived. A long flight of steps ran up to a balcony which rounded out about the front door, and upon which one seemed to be mounted high in the air, looking down over a dropping series of flat and peaked roofs to where the dark red walls and tall chimneys of the hoisting works clustered about the city's feet. Beyond this unrolled the wild, bare landscape, undulating line of mountain beyond mountain, cut clear as cameos against the blue Nevada sky.

The vivid green streak made by the Carson River gleamed to the right. At the limit of sight, fitted into a gap between the hills, was the Carson desert, a patch of stark, yellow sand.

The girls were not surprised at the style of the house. They knew vaguely that their father's affairs were not as satisfactory as they had been, but of their truly desperate nature they had no suspicion. There were delays in the sale of the Folsom Street property, and it was not till March that the new tenant appeared from Sacramento to take possession. In response to their father's orders they obediently gathered together their belongings, closed the house, and made the move to Virginia without assistance from him.

Events had fallen together in an unexpected way, but one that in the end spared June those glimpses of her lover's happiness that she had told the Colonel would be unbearable. It is true that she had to see the carriages drive to Jerry's marriage and hear the sound of his wedding bells. But before that event circumstances had developed which made radical changes in the plans of bride and groom. Black Dan had discovered that Jerry's business had dwindled to nothing, his private fortune vanished in the Crown Point collapse. The bonanza king, with his rapidly accumulating millions, had a sturdy, American objection to an idle man, especially when that man was to be the husband of his only child, and was known to be of a light and pleasure-loving temperament. A position was made for Jerry on the Cresta Plata, with duties sufficiently exacting to keep him continually occupied, and with the added attraction of an exceedingly generous salary.

Mercedes sulked when she heard it. She did not want to live in Virginia. She had thought she might go there from time to time, flit through it, a disturbing vision of beauty to miners and millionaires, but to take up her residence there was a different matter. She wanted to occupy the fine house her father had given her in San Francisco, entertain royally and be a queen of society, with Jerry as a necessary satellite circling about. She complained to Black Dan, even cried a little, and for the first time in her life found him obdurate.

The doting father was troubled about the future of his child. He disliked the marriage she was making, but knew that to protest against it was hopeless. He mistrusted Jerry, whose record he had often heard canvassed, and whose style, as a charmer of women, he despised. He wanted the pair under his eye. He wanted to keep his hand tight on his son-in-law. He did not believe that the man loved Mercedes, and he took a bitter satisfaction in bringing him to Virginia and setting him to work.

"Rion and I can watch him," he thought to himself. "We'll keep his nose to the grindstone, and if he shows any symptoms of lifting it we'll hold it closer."

Black Dan said little of his uneasiness to any one save his brother. The two men had the same opinion of Jerry, and though neither expressed it to the other, each felt cold doubts as to the happiness of the marriage.

Early in January, after a honeymoon of less than a week, Jerry was summoned to his new duties. He and Mercedes were installed in a house on B Street which had been hired and hastily refitted for them. Here in the heart of a biting Nevada winter their married life began. Neither bride nor groom guessed that it was being surreptitiously watched by three pairs of interested eyes. To the observation of the suspicious and inimical Graceys that of Colonel Parrish was added. He too had come to Virginia on the first of January to assume his position as assistant secretary of the Cresta Plata. He and Rion had settled themselves in comfortable quarters on the floor over Caswell's drug store, where their rooms gave on a balustraded wooden veranda which looked out on the turmoil of C Street.

It was not from Jerry, but from Mercedes that the first signs of discontent came. She had hated Virginia from the first glimpse of it. The cold, bleak town, buffeted by furious winds, clinging to its bare mountain side, revolted her. Her little soul shrank before the loneliness of the silent desert. She was essentially a Southron, a lover of sunshine, bright colors, and gaiety. Moreover, for the first time in her life, she felt neglected. In Virginia City in 1874 there were more engrossing interests than the allurement of women. It was a man's town, where the softer sex was in the background, save as a diversion and spectacular luxury. Mercedes was often lonely. Jerry had flung himself into the speculative fever of the time with fury. Even Black Dan was preoccupied and abrupt. Making millions is, after all, the most absorbing pastime that man may know.

Finally a delicacy of the throat developed, and Mercedes looked pale and thin, and began to cough. It was April, she had been married four months, and she wanted to go; she wanted San Francisco and sunshine, and the amusements for which she lived.

Jerry did not protest. The dream of passion was at an end. The Mercedes he had come to know in the intimacy of married life was so different a being from the Mercedes who had beguiled him in the summer, that he was not sorry to have her leave him. His pride was hurt and he felt angry and bitter against her, but he had no poignant regrets. Neither had loved. The ignoble instincts that had drawn them together were satiated. Her woman's spite had worked itself out. His lust for her wealth, his desire for her possession, were satisfied. They were willing to part.

She left in April, it being understood that Jerry was to "go below" to see her every two weeks. The story that her health had been impaired by a climate which had proved too severe for many before her, was given out as the reason for her departure. Black Dan even was made to believe it. He also believed her assurances that she would return in the summer. He thought the few tears she shed were grief at parting with a husband whom he supposed she loved. He determined to watch Jerry closer than ever, and for this purpose moved into the house on B Street, where the husband was now left alone.

Thus it fell out for June that she was spared the sight of Jerry as a joyous bridegroom. Almost simultaneously with the Allens' move to Virginia, Mercedes left it. June and Rosamund were arranging the Murchison mansion on B Street when Mrs. Jerome Barclay was beginning those extensive purchases in San Francisco which were to render her home on Van Ness Avenue a truly "palatial residence."

June saw her old lover often. The contracted size of the town made it impossible for her to avoid him. More than once they encountered each other in the houses of friends, and were forced to interchange the little dead phrases of society. Both were shaken by these accidental meetings. June dreaded and shrank from the sight of his face and the sound of his voice; but Jerry went away from her presence, stirred and uplifted, his mind full of the thought of her, his sense of her charm reawakened.

His life, crowded with the strenuous business of men, was empty of what had been for years its main interest and preoccupation. The vain man, confident of his attractions, had been played with and scornfully cast aside. The bitterness of his marriage was as wormwood to him. He felt sore toward Mercedes, whose indifference toward him had roused in him the angry amaze that a spoiled child feels toward the stranger who is proof against its blandishments. He felt himself wronged, and in a way, trapped. They made him work like a day laborer for his salary, and his wife had left him. That was what he'd got by marrying! Lupé, poor, dead Lupé, would not have treated him so! And June—what a fool he'd been! He forgot that June had no money, and for that reason he had put her resolutely aside. He forgot that last year he had avoided her and tried to banish all thought of her. In his longing for the adulation and tenderness upon which he had lived her image came nearer and nearer, grew more and more disturbing and sweet.

Early in May Rosamund left for a week's visit to San Francisco to accomplish the major part of her trousseau-buying. June, left in the Murchison mansion to "keep house"—a duty which she performed but ill—found many empty hours on her hands. She had made few friends in the new town. The apathy which had fallen on her at the time of Jerry's engagement had not lifted, and the coming loss of Rosamund weighed heavier every day. In the tumult around her her life was quiet and colorless. She told the Colonel that he was the only constant visitor she had.

"If you've another as regular as I am," he had answered, "I'll have to look into it."

Then he had added, in what he fondly thought was a light, unmeaning tone, "Don't even see much of Rion?"

"Rion?" June had replied with the arched eyebrows of surprised query. "I don't see him at all."

After that there was nothing more to be said, except of course for the Colonel to go to Rion and ask him why he had not called on Miss Allen, and for Rion, red and embarrassed, to answer that he did not suppose Miss Allen would care to see him, but if she did he would go.

There was one house to which she did pay constant visits. This was Mitty Sullivan's, on the north side of town, near the Cresta Plata hoisting works.

These were booming days for Mitty. Her husband's fortune was mounting in leaps too vast and rapid to be easily calculated. The Gracey boys' belief in their superintendent had not been misplaced. The brawny, half-educated Irishman had risen to a commanding position, and was respectfully alluded to as having "the best nose for ore in the two states." He was already very rich, having for the past four years successfully speculated on "inside information." His great gains made even the princely salary he received on the Cresta Plata seem small. He was in the thick of the whirlpool now and Mitty was with him. She had a baby, a girl, and she saw it, backed by the fortune that she and Barney were making, going to Europe and marrying "a lord." For Mitty's horizon had widened with astonishing rapidity since the days when she waited on table at the Foleys hotel.

On one of the afternoons of Rosamund's absence June walked across town for a chat and a cup of tea with her old-time friend. From B Street and its neat house-fronts and gardens she descended to the never-ending movement of the street below. This—the main stem of the mining city—for ever seething with a turbulent current of life, was the once famous C Street, a thoroughfare unique in the history of American towns.

The day shift would not be up for hours yet. When its time was up the mines would vomit forth thousands of men, who, penned all day in the dark, stifling heat of the underground city, would pour into the garish brilliancy of the overground one for the diversions of the night. Here, in the gusto of their liberation, they would range till daylight, restless eddies of life, passing up one street and down the other, never silent, never still, pressing vaguely on through the noise and glare, with the encircling blackness hanging round their little piece of the animated, outside world, like an inky curtain.

At all hours the street was crowded. Now it stretched up its mile or two of uneven length like a gray cañon, filled to both walls with a human river. Under the arcade formed by a continuous line of roofs that jutted from the second-story windows across the sidewalk, an endless throng passed up and down. They collected in groups before shop windows, overflowed the sidewalk and encroached on the middle of the roadway, congested in a close packed, swaying mass of heads in front of the bulletin boards where the stock quotations were pasted up, gathered in talkative knots at corners.

The street, in the mud of which playing cards, bits of orange peel, fragments of theatrical posters, scraps of silk and ribbon were imbedded like the pattern in a carpet, was as full as the sidewalk. The day of the overland freighters was past, but ore wagons still drove sixteen-mule teams, the driver guiding by a single rope, the mules bending their necks under the picturesque arches of their bells. Between these, busy managers flashed by in their buggies, stopping here and there to lean from their seats for a moment's converse with a knot of men. In more fashionable equipages, brought up from San Francisco and drawn by sleek-skinned, long-tailed horses, the wives of suddenly enriched superintendents lolled back gorgeously, their beruffled silk skirts floating out over the wheel, the light flashing on their diamonds.

Over all this movement of life there was an unceasing swell of sound, a combination of many notes and keys, more noticeable by reason of the outlying rim of silence. Thousands of voices blended into a single sonorous hum, through which broke the jingling of pianos from the open doors of saloons, the click of billiard balls, the cries of the drivers to their mules, the raucous voices of street hawkers selling wares at populous corners, and the sweet, broken melody of the bells. Beneath this—a continuous level undertone—was the murmur of machinery, with the faint throb of the engines beating through it like the sound of the steady, unagitated pulse-beats of a laboring Titan.

June pressed through the throng, walking rapidly toward the upper end of C Street. Here, looking down on the dark red walls and tall chimneys of the Cresta Plata, stood the pretty, one-story cottage where Mitty Sullivan lived. It was surrounded by a square of garden, in which lilacs were budding and apple-trees showed a delicate hoar of young blossom. Mitty's prosperity revealed itself in many ways. She had a nurse for the baby as well as a "hired girl." She was exceedingly anxious to spend money and very ignorant of how to do it. She had passed the stage—a recognized station in the ascending career of the western wife—where her husband had presented her with diamond ear-rings. The silver, crystal, and Britannia metal in the superintendent's cottage were astonishing; only to be rivaled in extravagance by the dresses which hung in Mitty's own wardrobe and which had been ordered—regardless of cost—from the best dressmakers in San Francisco.

She greeted June with affection and drew her into the parlor, recently furnished with a set of blue and gold brocade furniture, the windows draped with lambrequins to match. There was a brilliant moquette carpet on the floor and the walls were hung with oil paintings, which Barney had bought on a recent visit to the coast. A quantity of growing plants in the windows added a touch of beauty to the glaring, over-furnished room.

Mitty herself had grown into a blooming matron, a trifle coarse, for she was fond of "a good table" and saw to it that her hired girl knew how to produce one, and already menaced by the embonpoint which is so deadly a foe to Californian beauty. The baby girl on her arm was a rosily healthy infant, with Barney's red hair and her mother's freshness of color. Twenty years later she would bring her share of the Bonanza fortune, which her father was then accumulating, to the restoration of the old New York family into which she was to marry. Her sister—yet unborn—was to do the same charitable act by the castle and estates of an English earl, who in return would make her a countess.

The greetings over, the baby was placed by the table in her high chair and given a string of spools and a rubber rabbit to play with, while Mitty, comfortably settling herself in an arm-chair, inquired if June had noticed the stock quotations on her way down. The hired girl, who was setting down the tea tray, listened with open attention for the answer. Both mistress and maid were "plunging" according to their means, and when June confessed that she had passed the bulletins without reading the figures, the two speculators looked at each other in open dismay.

"It's so long to wait till Barney comes home," Mitty complained. "I thought of course you'd read them as you passed."

June was contrite, but could remember nothing.

"And I wanted to know so much! They say that Peruvian's getting soft. They were saying so this morning anyway. You didn't even hear anything as you came along? I believe you're the only woman in Virginia who doesn't speculate."

June had not even heard. The knowing volubility of Mitty on the fluctuations of stocks in which she was as well versed as Barney himself, seemed little short of miraculous to the only woman in Virginia who didn't speculate.

The servant, who had been eagerly listening to the conversation, now broke in.

"I'll run up and have a squint round, Mrs. Sullivan. Maybe I can pick up more than Miss Allen."

Mitty tried to be dignified and give the proposition a deliberate consideration. But her consent came with a promptitude it was difficult to suppress. As the woman whisked out through the kitchen door she said in a tone intended to excuse her lack of discipline:

"That girl's got all her money in Peruvian, and hearing it was 'soft' has sort of upset her. Last week she told me she was thirty thousand dollars ahead. She only came to live with us because Barney being one of the big superintendents, she thought she'd get points, and as she's an A 1 girl I've got to humor her."

They chatted over their tea, Mitty regaling her guest with the gossip of the day, of which she was full. They had been talking some time when the conversation turned on Mercedes and Jerry. It was the first time the subject had come up between them. Mitty knew part at least of her friend's story, and she had tried to spare her, but she hated Mercedes, who had treated her with scornful indifference, and she hated Jerry because Barney did. She was glad now to give her candid opinion to the woman they had combined to hurt.

"They said it was her health that was bad, and that was why she had to quit and go below. Health!" with a compressing of the corners of her mouth and a glance of sidelong meaning. "Her health's all right; it was her temper."

"Temper!" said June faintly. "Uncle Jim said her throat was delicate and she had a cough."

"Cough!" snorted Mitty. "We all have coughs, but we don't leave our husbands and go cavorting down to San Francisco to throw round money and pick up some other man. She didn't care for him. That was all that was the matter. It's a simple disease and a lot of 'em get it."

June silently stirred her tea. Every word pierced her, but she wanted to hear them. She had heard nothing of the separation, except the generally accepted story of Mercedes' delicate health. Instinct told her that Mitty, the woman, had looked deeper and would know more of what had really been the case. Without speaking she raised her eyes from the cup and fixed them on the baby, who in an excess of affection was licking the face of the rubber rabbit. Mitty went on with complacent volubility:

"Barney thought maybe it was a baby. He's a simple, innocent sort of man, Barney Sullivan. But I said to him, 'Don't you fear, there won't be any babies in that house! The Lord ain't goin' to make such a break as to give that woman a baby.' I guess not," said Mitty, folding her arms and looking grimly round the room as if challenging an unseen audience to contradict her.

June returned to the stirring of her tea while her hostess continued,

"No. She just hated Virginia. Nobody was standing round here to kiss her boots and do the doormat act. And she didn't like Jerry well enough for him to make her stand it. You have to like a man a good deal to stay here in winter,"—in the tone of one who is forced to admit a melancholy fact. "If you don't, you're liable to pretend to get sick and have to go below for a spell. I've seen many of 'em go that way."

"Didn't Jerry try to stop her?" said June in a low voice.

"Try to stop her?"—with angry contempt—"not much! He didn't *care*. Why, June Allen, he was glad, downright *glad*, I believe, to have her go. He don't care for anything under the canopy but Jerry Barclay."

"He cared when he married her." June's voice was lower still and shook. Her friend noticed it and determined to sow seed, now she had the opportunity.

"Next to himself Jerry Barclay cares for money. That's what he was after, and he didn't get it the way he expected. He's got the smoothest tongue any man ever had in his head, and he's used it right along to get money with. How long was Mrs. Newbury dead when he got engaged to Mercedes Gracey? And do you suppose he'd have ever asked her if they hadn't struck one of the biggest ore-bodies in Virginia on the fifteen-hundred-foot level of the Cresta Plata? But they've got him by the leg up here now,"—with an exultant laugh—"the whole three of 'em's on to him. They give him a big salary and don't they make him work for it—oh, my! There ain't no drones in the Gracey boys' hive, you can bet, and Jerry Barclay's got to hustle for every cent he earns. No San Francisco and good times for him! If Mercedes was to cry and do the loving wife act to Black Dan and say she couldn't live without her husband I wouldn't bet but what she'd get him. But she ain't done it. She don't want him, Junie. That's what's the matter in that shebang. Neither one of 'em wants the other."

"Why did she marry him?" said June. "Why did she—"

The baby here interrupted by giving vent to a loud exclamation, and at the same time disdainfully casting her rubber rabbit on the floor. Then she leaned over the arm of her high chair, staring with motionless intentness at the discarded rabbit, as if expecting to see it get up and walk away.

"That's the thing that gets me," said Mitty thoughtfully. "Why *did* she marry him? She could have got a better man than Jerry, though I suppose he was about the best in sight at the time. But she's like the baby here—always cryin' and stretchin' out for toys she can't reach. Then you give her the toy and she looks it all over and suddenly gives a sort er disgusted snort, and throws it on the floor. She ain't got no more use for it, and the first thing you know she'll be stretchin' out for another one."

June made no answer to this and Mitty, big with her subject, for her dislike of Mercedes was an absorbing sentiment, went on:

"She treated him like dirt. Barney was up there one night while they were at dinner. He was just in the room in front with the curtains down between and they didn't know he was there. He said he could hear her pickin' at Jerry because he'd been half an hour late for dinner. He said she kep' on pickin' and pickin' and Jerry not saying a word. Barney says to me when he got home, 'Jerry's paid high for his position.' And I says to him when he told me, 'That woman's goin' to make every one pay high for anything they get out er her. She's not givin' things away free gratis.'"

The baby's contemplation of the fallen rabbit had by this time lost its charm. She threw herself back in her chair and raised her voice in a wail distinctly suggestive of weariness of spirit and *ennui*. Mitty lifted her, a formless, weeping bundle, from her chair, and June's offer of the rabbit was met by an angrily repulsing hand and a writhing movement of irritated disgust.

"She's tired, poor lamb!" said Mitty, rocking her gently to and fro and slapping on her back with a comforting, maternal hand. "We try to keep her awake till Barney gets in. He just thinks there's nothing in the world like his baby."

The dusk was beginning to subdue the brilliancy of sunset, and June, buttoning herself into her jacket, bade mother and child good night. Mitty's cheerful good-bys followed her down the passageway, the baby's now lusty cries drowning the last messages which usually delay feminine farewells.

Once outside, she walked rapidly toward home, avoiding the crowds on C Street, and flitting, a small, dark figure, through less frequented byways. Tumult was in her heart, also the sense of dread that had been with her ever since she came to Virginia and knew her old lover was so near.

Since his marriage she had tried with desperate persistence to uproot him from her thoughts. She not only had begun to realize his baseness of character, but the realization was becoming not a matter of words, but a living force which was beginning to chill the feeling that for so long had held her in its grasp. The first symptom of a decline in love, the comprehension and dislike of the faults of the being loved, had begun to stir in her.

Now Mitty's unexpected revelation had upset this more normal and serener frame of mind. She felt herself suddenly swept backward toward a point that she had hoped was far behind. An elation rose in her that frightened her and filled her with shame. Jerry sordid, throwing her from him for the lust of money, was a bearable thought. It was Jerry loving and beloved that had been too bitter to be borne. And Mitty had said there was no love on either side—he was glad to have his wife go.

A turmoil of many feelings battled in her and the two strongest and most violently opposed were fear and joy. As she stole homeward through the darkening streets fear became stronger than joy. The future loomed suddenly sinister. Her loneliness stretched darkly menacing before her. Rosamund would soon be gone—gone so far, never again to be reached with an outstretched hand or a calling voice. And Jerry would be there, close to her, Jerry who did not love his wife, and was glad to have her go.

CHAPTER III
SMOLDERING EMBERS

Rosamund's marriage was set for the end of May. There had been great preparations for the event, which was to be the most brilliant one of its kind that had ever taken place in the town or state. A costly trousseau had been ordered from San Francisco. It was understood that the wedding breakfast was to come from the same place and be the most sumptuous and elaborate ever given in Virginia. Men heard these rumors with surprise and once more wondered where Allen was getting the money "to splurge with." Even the astute Graceys were puzzled. Only the Colonel was non-committal and looked on quietly.

"Rosamund's going to have the finest send-off I can give her," Allen said to him a week before the wedding. "It's the best I can do for her. It's a good thing Harrower's only here for a few days."

The Colonel felt like adding it was an extremely good thing, as otherwise Harrower might be called upon to pay for the splendor of his own nuptials. Twenty-five thousand dollars would not go far with a man, who, with debts pressing on every side, was spending money as Allen was in giving Rosamund a fine "send-off."

A week before the day set Harrower arrived and took up his residence at the International Hotel. It was a feverish, over-crowded week, full of bustle and fussy excitement. There were people constantly at the Murchison mansion and Allen was constantly out of it. Had Harrower been more versed in the ways of the American parent he would have realized that his future father-in-law was avoiding him. But the young man, who thought everything in the place curious and more or less incomprehensible, regarded his behavior as merely another evidence of the American father's habit of letting his children manage their own affairs. He did not like Allen and wanted as quickly as possible to get through the spectacular marriage, and take Rosamund away to the peace of his ancestral acres and the simple country life they both loved.

To June this last week was a whirl of days and nights, reeling by over a dragging, ceaseless sense of pain. To both girls the separation was bitter, but Rosamund, passing into the arms of an adored husband, for the first time in a life of unselfishness, did not enter into her sister's feelings. She spoke often of the visit June was to pay them next winter. Lionel was as anxious as Rosamund for her to come. The bride and groom were to travel on the continent for part of the summer and then visit his people, introducing Rosamund to her new relations. But by November they would be settled in Monk's Court—that was Lionel's home—and then June was to come. Rosamund even hinted at a cousin of Lionel's, a "very decent chap" Lionel had said, who was rich and single and "just the right sort for June."

There were six months between now and then, six short months to Rosamund beginning a brilliant new life with her lover; and six long months to June alone in the mining city, surrounded by the gray desert.

The wedding day came and the excitement quieted down to the sudden hush of that solemn moment when the voice of a priest proclaims a man and a woman one. The ceremony was performed in the house, Lionel, after some qualms, having agreed to it. June stood beside her sister in the alcove of the bay-window and listened to the words which pledged her to a man of another country and to a life in a distant land. Rosamund was pale as she turned from the clergyman to greet the guests that pressed round her. It was a sacred moment to her, the giving of herself in its fullest and deepest significance to the man she loved, till death should part them.

It was beyond doubt a very brilliant wedding. The house, hung with flowers—every blossom sent up from San Francisco wrapped in cotton wool—lost its bare, half-furnished look and became a bower. The costumes of the women—many imported from Paris—were in all cases costly and in some beautiful. The men, who squeezed past one another on the stairway and drank champagne in corners, stood for more wealth than the whole of the far West had known till the discovery of the Cresta Plata and the Big Bonanza. The millions that the arid state was pouring out in a silver stream were well represented in the Murchison mansion that afternoon.

Rosamund

The breakfast seemed to June a never-ending procession of raised champagne glasses and toasts. She had a vision of the Colonel's white head bent toward Rosamund over the low-bowled, thin-stemmed glass in which the golden bubbles rose, and of the husky note in his voice as he wished her joy. She saw her father, with reddened face and bloodshot eyes, rise to his feet, and with the southern fervency of phrase, which he had never lost, bid his daughter God-speed and farewell, the glass shaking in his hand. Harrower stood up beside his bride, her listening face fair and spiritual between the drooping folds of her veil, and said a few words of thanks, halting and simple, but a man's words nevertheless.

Then the time came for the bride to go up stairs for the change of dress. The guests made a path for her, and June followed the tall figure with its long, glimmering train.

They said little as Rosamund took off her wedding finery and donned her traveling dress. But at the door of the room they clasped each other in a dumb embrace, neither daring to speak. As she descended Rosamund drew her veil down to hide her tears. Her lips were quivering, her heart was rent with the pain of the parting. June came behind her, calm and dry-eyed, the bleak sense of depression that she had felt for weeks closing round her black and heavy. Part of herself—the strong, brave part—seemed to be torn away from her with the going of the sister, upon whom she had always leaned.

She stood on the balcony and waved her hand as the carriages drove away toward the station. Most of the guests went with them to see the bride and groom off. A stream of people poured down the stairs, laughing, chattering, calling back good-bys to June, as she stood by the door, pale but resolutely smiling. She noticed the three tall figures of the Colonel and the Gracey brothers as they crossed the street together, the Colonel turning to wave his hand to her. Her father had gone before them. Finally everybody had left, and she turned slowly back into the deserted house.

How empty is was! Her footsteps echoed in it. She passed into the parlor, into which, from the broad bay-window the afternoon light poured coldly. Linen had been stretched over the carpet, and on this white and shining expanse the broken heads of roses and torn leaves lay here and there. The flowers in the recess where the bride and groom had stood were already fading, and the air was heavy with their dying sweetness.

She looked into the dining-room at the expanse of the rifled table, where the mounds of fruit had been broken down by eager hands and the champagne bubbles rose languidly in the half-filled glasses. There were no servants about and the perfect silence of the house was more noticeable in this scene of domestic disorder. She had ascended the stairs and was looking out of a back window when she saw its explanation. From the kitchen entrance the servants, headed by the chef brought up from San Francisco for the wedding, stealthily emerged. Struggling into their coats and hastily jamming on their hats they ran in straggling line in the direction of the depot, intent, as the rest of the world, on seeing the bride depart. Last of all the Chinaman issued forth, and setting his soft felt wide-awake on his carefully uprolled queue, stole with soft-footed haste after them.

Nothing can be more full of the note of human desolation than an occupied house suddenly vacated. June passed from room to room feeling the silence as part of the depression that weighed on her. Through the windows she could see the wild, morose landscape, beginning to take on the hectic strangeness of tint that marked its sunset aspect. Its weird hostility was suddenly intensified. It combined with the silence to augment her sense of loneliness to the point of the unendurable. She ran down the stairs and out on to the curve of balcony which extended from the front door.

Some children were playing in the street below, and their voices came to her with a note of cheer. Leaning listlessly against the balustrade she looked up the street, wondering when her father would be back. She had ceased to note his comings and goings, but this evening she watched for his return as she might have done in her childhood. There was no sign of him, and might not be for hours. After the train left he would probably range about the town, whose night aspect he loved.

She turned her head in the opposite direction, and her eyes became suddenly fixed and her body stiffened. A man was coming down the street, swinging lightly forward, looking over the tops of the houses toward the reddening peak of the Sugar Loaf. There was only one man in Virginia with that natural elegance of form, that carriage full of distinction and grace.

For the first moment he did not see her, and in that moment June felt none of the secret elation that had been hers in the past at sudden sight of him. Instead, a thrill of repugnance passed through her, to be followed by a shrinking dread. She moved softly back from the balustrade, intending to slip into the hallway, when he turned his head and saw her.

The old pleasure leaped into his face. She saw that he pronounced her name. He flung a cautious look about him and then crossed the road. With his hand on the gate he gazed up and said, with something of secrecy in his air and voice:

"Have they all gone?"

June's affirmative was low. Her repugnance had vanished. Her desire to retreat had been paralyzed by the first sound of his voice.

"And they've left you all alone?"

The tone was soft with the caressing quality that to Jerry was second nature when an attractive woman listened.

"Yes, they went to the station to see them off. I didn't want to go, so I stayed," she returned stammeringly.

Jerry opened the gate.

"Can I come up?" he said in the lowest tone that would reach her ear. "I hate to think of you all by yourself up there, and Rosamund gone."

June looked at him and murmured an affirmative that he could not have heard, but he put his foot on the lowest step. She dropped her eyes to her hands resting on the balustrade, while the beating of her heart increased with his ascending footfall. When he had reached her side she was trembling. In those few sentences from the bottom of the stairs he seemed suddenly to have obliterated the past year. The words were ordinary enough, but his eyes, his tone, his manner as he now stood beside her, were those of the old Jerry, before Mercedes had stolen him away.

She raised her eyes to his and immediately dropped them. The soft scrutiny of his gaze—the privileged gaze that travels over and dwells on a loved face, with no one to challenge its right—increased her flushed distress. Jerry, too, was moved. For both of them the moment was fraught with danger, and he knew it better than she.

"You're all tired out," he said, with his tender tone slightly hoarse. "Let's go in and sit down."

She led the way through the hall, now beginning to grow dim with the first evening shadows, into the long, bare parlor. There was a sofa drawn up against the wall and on this she sat, while Jerry placed a small gilded chair close in front of her.

"How deserted it looks!" he said, gazing about the room. "I suppose everybody was here? I saw a perfect mob of people going down to the station."

"Yes, everybody went, even the servants. They stole away without telling me. They didn't even wait to clear the things off the table. That's why it's so quiet."

Both spoke rapidly to hide their agitation. The woman's was more apparent than the man's. She kept her eyes down and Jerry watched her as she spoke. It was the first time for over a year that he had had a chance to scrutinize her at will. She had changed greatly. Her freshness was gone, her face looked smaller than ever and to-day was almost haggard. But Jerry had had his fill of beauty. She loved him still, and she was the one woman of the three he had loved. Ever since Mercedes had left him he had been telling himself this, and the thought had been taking fiery possession of him, growing more dominant each day.

"Rosamund's made a fine marriage, hasn't she?" he went on, with more fluency. "Some day she'll be Lady Rosamund, and won't she be a stunning Lady Rosamund? She's made for it. Do you remember the time when I was up at Foleys and you had the garden there? What a lot has happened in these last four years."

"Yes, a lot," June assented. A broken rose-bud lay on the sofa beside her. She picked it up and began to open its leaves.

"And who'd have supposed then that Rosamund was going to live in England, and some day be Lady Rosamund?" There was a slight pause, and he added in a lower voice, as if speaking to himself: "Who'd have supposed any of the things were going to happen that did?"

June pressed apart the rose petals in silence.

"Who'd have supposed I would have done the things that I have done?" he said, speaking in the same low voice, but now it was suddenly full of significance.

He was looking directly at her. His eyes called hers, and with the rosebud still in her hand, she looked into them for a long motionless moment. It was a look of revelation. He saw her will, like a trapped bird, fluttering and struggling in his grasp.

"You're just the same, June," he said on a rising breath.

"No, no," she faltered, "I've changed in every way. You don't know how I've changed. I'm quite a different person."

"But you haven't lost faith in me?" he said, leaning nearer to her.

She drew back, pressing her shoulders against the sofa, and gazing at him with a sort of suspended apprehension. He did not seem to notice her shrinking and went on impetuously:

"You understand if there were mistakes and errors and—and—and—miserable misunderstandings, that I was led into them. I was a blind fool. Mercedes never cared for me. She told me so three months after we were married. She left me of her own free will. She was glad to go, and I—well, I'll tell *you* the truth, June—I wasn't sorry."

His face was full of angry confession. He had had no intention of talking to her in this way, but now he suddenly wanted to reinstate himself in her good opinion and be soothed by her sympathy. She stopped him.

"Don't talk about it. It's done. If you made a mistake, it's done, and that's the end. Oh, Jerry, don't talk about it."

She rose to her feet; the room was getting dim. Outside the royal dyes of sunset had faded from the sky and the twilight was softly settling.

"I'll have to light the gas," she stammered. "The servants haven't come in yet. This half-light makes me blue."

Jerry stood aside as she went to the mantel and from among the embanked flowers drew the matchbox. The chandelier hung just above his head draped with garlands of smilax. It was high and as June came forward with the lighted match, he stretched out his hand to take it from her. They were close together under the chandelier as their hands touched. Each felt the tremulous cold of the other's fingers and the match dropped, a red spark, between them.

With suddenly-caught breath Jerry stretched his arms out to clasp her but she drew back, her hands outspread before her, crying,

"Don't, Jerry, don't! Oh, please don't!"

She backed away from him and he followed her, not speaking, his face set, his arms ready to enfold her. She was stopped in her recoil by the sofa, and standing against it she looked at him, with agonized pleading, whispering,

"Don't, Jerry. Oh, please go. Please go and leave me! You loved me once."

He stopped, stood looking at her for a moment of stricken irresolution, then turned without a word and left the room.

June fell on the sofa, her face in her hands. She heard his step in the passage, then sharp on every stair as he ran down to the street. In the darkening room she sat trembling, her face hidden, alone in the empty house.

CHAPTER IV
A WOMAN'S "NO"

Rion Gracey called on June as the Colonel had suggested, called again the week after, and in a short time formed a habit of dropping in every Sunday evening. He generally found the Colonel there, and in the first stages of reopening the friendship the elder man had been very convenient in relieving the meetings of the constraint which was bound to hover over them. But as the spring Sundays passed and the constraint wore away, Rion did not so thoroughly appreciate the presence of his friend. With surprise at his own subtility—for the mining man was of those who go forcefully over obstacles, not around them—he discovered what evenings the Colonel did not dine with June and began to make his appearance then.

He generally found her alone. She had made no effort to enlarge her acquaintance, and after the wedding her father was constantly in San Francisco or at more congenial haunts in the town. It raised agitating hopes in Rion to see that she was openly and unaffectedly glad to see him. There was a confidence, a something of trust and reliance in her manner that—for him—had not been there before. He thought she had never been so winning as she was on these lonely evenings, when her face lighted at the sight of him, and her smile was full of a soft welcome, touched with girlish shyness.

Women like to think that the beloved member of their sex plays so filling and absorbing a part in the life of the enslaved man, that all other matters are crowded from his mind. The interests of business dwindle to the vanishing point, the claims of friendship have no place in a heart out of which all else has been pushed. Love, while it lasts, holds him in a spell, and then, if only then, the woman is a reigning goddess.

Rion Gracey was not of this order of man. He had loved June since his meeting with her at Foleys, but he had led a life so full of work and business, so preoccupied with a man's large affairs, that there were periods of weeks when he never thought of her. Yet she had been and was the only woman he had ever truly cared for and ardently desired. Before his meeting with her women had been merely incidents in his onward career. When, during the summer at Foleys, he had come to know her, he had realized how different was the place she would have taken in his life from the transitory interests which were all he had so far known. Then, for the first time, he understood what a genuine passion means to a genuine man.

When she had refused to marry him he had left her sore and angry. But the crowded life in which he was so prominent a figure soon filled with vital interests every moment of his days. His wound was not healed, but he forgot its ache. He rigorously pushed the thought of her from his mind. She was not for him, and to think of her was weakness. Then he heard a rumor that Barclay was an admirer of hers, and he shut his mouth and tried harder than ever not to think.

But time passed and June did not marry. Jerry, given his freedom, married Mercedes. Rion, a man to whom small gossip was dull, a thing to give no heed to as one walked forward, heard none of the talk of Jerry's change of heart. It filtered slowly into Virginia, which was across the mountains in another state, and occupied in a big way with big matters. Even Barney Sullivan, who was well primed with San Francisco gossip after Mitty's return from visits, "down below," did not mention to his chief anything of Miss Allen and Jerry Barclay.

When he heard she was coming to Virginia the love-obsession that the woman likes to believe in, came near taking possession of him. For a day or two he was shaken out of the current of his every-day life and found it hard to attend to his work. The thought of seeing her again filled this self-contained and masterful man with tremors such as a girl might feel at the coming of her lover. The first time he saw her on C Street he found it difficult to collect his thoughts for hours afterward.

The change in her, the loss of what good looks she had once possessed, did not diminish or alter his feeling. If he had been asked if he thought her pretty he would have honestly said he did not know, he had never thought about it. He did not know how old she was, nor could he cite any special points of beauty that his eye, as a lover, had noted. Her only physical attribute that had impressed him was her smallness, and this he had noticed because in walking with her, her head only came to a little above his shoulder, and he was sometimes forced to bend down to hear her.

He had been wondering what to do when the Colonel asked him to call. Unless the suggestion had come from some one in authority he never would have dared to go, for he was a lover at once proud and shy, not of the kind who batter and browbeat a woman into acquiescence. Her first meeting with him, dominated as it was by mutual embarrassment, at least showed him that she was not displeased to see him. Since then the meetings had been frequent, her pleasure at his coming open for any one to see, and Rion's hopes, in the beginning but faint, had waxed high and exultant.

To June, he and the Colonel were the only two figures of an intimate interest in her life. He seemed to fill its emptiness, to cheer its isolation. She looked forward to his coming, hardly knowing why, except that a sense of comfort and strength came with him. He was often in her thoughts, and she found herself storing up small incidents in her daily life to tell him, for no reason but that his unspoken sympathy was pleasant. She felt the consciousness—so sweet to women—that all which concerned her was of moment to him. Now and then the Colonel's past assertions that the girl who married Rion Gracey would be happy, rose in her mind. She began to understand that it might be so, and what it would mean, this strong man's love and protection guarding a woman against the storm and struggle of the world, with which she personally was so unfitted to cope.

One evening, a month after the wedding, he found her sitting on the balcony reading. It had been warm weather for a day or two and the windows and doors of the lower floor were thrown open, showing the receding vista of dimly-lighted rooms and passages. She was dressed in white and had a book he had given her lying open across her knees. As the gate clicked to his opening hand she started and looked down, then leaned forward, her face flushing, her lips parting with a smile of greeting. It was a look that might have planted hope in any man's heart.

"I'm so glad you've come," she said, gazing down on him as he ascended. "I was just wondering if you would. When you want a thing very much it never seems to happen. But now you've happened, so I never can say that again."

"Yes, I've happened," he answered with the phlegmatic air with which he hid his shyness. "Are you all alone again?"

"Yes, quite alone. But I've been reading the book you gave me and it's made me forget all about it. I've nearly finished it. It's a splendid book."

"I'll get you another to-morrow," he said, leaning with his back against the railing and looking at her with a fond intentness of which he was unconscious. She was pretty to-night in her white dress and with her cheeks flushed with pleasure at his coming. Rion, who did not notice looks, noticed this, and it stirred his heart.

"Let's go in," he said. "There's a sort of chill in the air. You mustn't catch cold. If you got sick you'd have to be sent down to San Francisco. There's no proper person here to take care of you."

She rose and stood in front of him, half turned to go.

"Wouldn't that be dreadful!" she said with careless lightness. "I wouldn't go. Uncle Jim would have to give up his work on the Cresta Plata and take care of me."

"We wouldn't want you to go," he answered, as he followed her into the hall. "Anyway, I'd want to keep you here."

She did not appear to notice the change of pronoun, nor the fact that his voice had dropped on the last sentence. With her white dress sweeping spectrally before him he followed her into the dim parlor.

Something in the intimacy of the still, soft dusk, and the sudden wakening into imperious dominance of his feeling for her, made him move away from her and about the room. Through the open door of the dining-room he saw the white square of the table glimmering in the twilight, with one place set, the crumpled napkin on the cloth, the single wine glass, its lower half dark with wine, a scattering of crimson cherries dotting the glaze of a plate.

"Did you dine alone, too?" he asked.

"Yes, father's dining in town to-night and you or Black Dan sent the Colonel into Empire till to-morrow."

She looked round at him over her shoulder, the lighted match in her hand sending a glow over her face, which was half-plaintive, half-laughing.

"It's very mean of you to send the Colonel away on nights when he dines with me."

"Well, honestly, I never thought about it," stammered Rion, trying to look contrite, but glad in his heart that the Colonel was, for this evening at least, well out of the way. "And, anyway, it was Dan who sent him. He thinks there are certain things nobody can do as well as Parrish."

"Of course he's right about that," she answered. "But he ought to remember that one of the things the Colonel does best is to be company for me."

The gas was lit and she was adjusting the shade of a lamp on a side table. As she spoke she looked over the bright chimney at him, with the smile that held in it so much of melancholy.

"It's pretty dreary for you here, isn't it?" he said.

Her lips suddenly trembled and she bit the under one. For a moment her control was shaken, and to hide it she bent over the lamp, pretending to arrange the wick. The pause was heavy till she said in her usual tone:

"Well, lately it *has* been rather lonely. It's hard to get used to Rosamund's not being here."

She crossed the room to the sofa and sat down in the corner of it, Rion taking a chair near her. As she patted her skirt into satisfactory folds, she said, her eyes fixed on her arranging hand,

"It takes a person a long time to get used to some one they care for going so far off. I sometimes wonder if they ever do."

He looked at her, murmuring some casual response, his mind not on his words. Against the sheer white of her dress a locket she wore suspended round her neck by a narrow black velvet, caught and lost the light as her breast rose and fell. He was conscious of its regular gleam, of the darkness of her hand against the white folds of her skirt, of the slim smallness of her figure reclining in the angle of the sofa.

Another pause fell between them, this time uncomfortable with a sense of extreme constraint; June's hand ceased moving and joined its companion in her lap. She raised her eyes timidly and met his, intent, motionless, fixed deeply upon her. The locket rose brightly into the light on a sharply caught breath.

"Why did Black Dan send the Colonel into Empire?" she faltered.

"Do you remember what I asked you more than two years ago in San Francisco?" was his answer.

She tried to temporize and said nervously,

"Two years back is a long way to remember."

"I asked you to marry me, and you said no. Do you remember?"

She nodded.

"I'm going to ask you the same thing again."

"Oh, Rion!" she murmured in an imploring undertone.

"I can only say the same things I said then. I'm not a smooth talker, like some of the men you've known. I want you for my wife, and I'll do everything I can to make you happy. That's about the whole thing."

She rose with some broken words he did not catch and passed round behind the sofa, where she stood, her hand resting on the back, her face averted. He rose, too, but made no attempt to approach her.

"I don't know much about women," he continued. "I don't know how to talk to them. You're the only one of them I've ever felt this way to; and

I'm pretty sure I'll never feel so to any other. I love you. I've tried to stop it and I can't. It's stronger than I am."

She made no reply, and after waiting a moment, he said, his voice slightly hoarse:

"Well, say something to me."

"I don't know what to say," she murmured, her face turned away.

He made a step toward the sofa, and as she heard him, she drew back as if frightened. He stopped instantly, regarding her with a sudden frowning fixity of suspicion and anger.

"Don't you care for me, June?" he said.

"Yes, yes, of course—so much, so much more than I used to. But, Rion—"

She turned and looked at him, one of her hands raised as if to ward him off. He started forward to seize the hand, but she quickly drew it back and clasped it round the locket.

"Not that way," she faltered, "not the way you want."

"Are you going to say no to me again?"

"Oh, Rion!" she pleaded.

"Do you care for me? Answer. Don't beat about the bush."

"I care for you immensely. I've always cared for you, but lately it's been something quite different, something much deeper. You've been so kind to me."

"Never mind about my kindness, do you love me?"

"I—but—no—not—" she stammered a series of disconnected words, and came to a stop.

He took a step nearer to her and said in an authoritative voice, "Answer me. Will you be my wife?"

"I can't," she said, in the lowest tone he could hear.

"You can't? Then it's no again?"

"It's not exactly no. Or if it is, it's not the same kind of no it was before."

"What do you mean by that? There's only one kind of no in a matter like this."

"Well, this is a different kind. It must be a different kind. It mustn't be a no that makes us strangers as it did before."

He gave a suppressed exclamation, angry and violent, and turned to the table for his hat.

"A man's not a fool or a child," he said, "to be spoken to like that."

She followed his movements, saw him stretch his hand for the hat, and cried,

"Oh, don't go—don't go this way—don't be angry with me—let me explain."

He turned and looked at her with a face grown cold and hard.

"What is there to explain? I want you to be my wife. You don't want to. That's the whole matter."

"Oh, no it isn't. It's not like it was the other time. I didn't care then, but I do now, more than you think, much more. Everything's different. I can't bear to have you go. I can't bear to lose you."

"Is that the reason you've looked so pleased whenever I came? Was that the reason you told me just now that you wanted me to come so much you didn't think I would? I've been a fool, no doubt, but it seems to me that a smarter man than I might have thought you meant it."

She flushed deeply, up to her hair.

"I did mean it," she said in a low voice.

Hope sprang to his face and he came close to her:

"Then if you meant it, say you love me, say you'll marry me. That's the only thing I want you to say to me."

She shrank away again and without waiting for her answer, he turned—the light gone from his face—and reached for his hat.

"Don't go; don't go," she begged. "There are things I want to say to you,"—but this time he did not let false hopes beguile him.

"Good-by," he said gruffly, and walked to the door.

As he passed her she slipped round the sofa and came after him:

"It mustn't be good-by. Say good night. I won't let you say good-by."

"It's good-by this time, young woman," he said grimly. "Good-by for keeps."

She laid her hand on his arm and that stopped him. With an air of enforced patience he stood, his face turned from her, waiting. For a moment she did not speak, and he said:

"Come, what is it? If it's that I'm to dangle round as I've been doing for the past two months, let's not waste time over that; I'm not that kind of a man. There's too much for me to do to waste my time and thoughts hanging round a girl who's only fooling with me."

"I was not fooling," she said humbly; "I meant it all."

"Evidently we didn't both mean the same thing."

"No, but now that we understand, don't go off this way saying it's to be good-by for keeps. I shall be so lonely without you. I trust in you so. I lean on you—"

"Lean on the Colonel," he interrupted, almost brutally. "He's a more reliable staff than I am."

"But we can still be friends," she urged, not appearing to notice his harshness.

"No, we'll not be friends."

Looking down at her he forgot his sternness and his voice grew suddenly roughened with feelings he could not disguise.

"I can't be your friend, June Allen. There may be men who can be the friend of the women they feel to as I do to you, but I'm not that kind. I can be your husband, only that. There's to be no play at friendship where I'm concerned, no taking your hand to shake when I want to take you in my arms and keep you there, where no other man in the world can lay his finger on you or think of you as something he can try to win. You must belong to me, want to belong to me, come to me of your own free will, or else we must be strangers."

He took her hand, lifted it from his arm and with a short "Good-by" turned and left the room.

June stood under the chandelier listening to his retreating footsteps as they passed along the hall and then down the outside stairs. She remained motionless, looking down, her ear strained to catch the diminishing footfalls as they reached the end of the steps and were deadened in the dust of the street. He was leaving her never to come back, disappearing from her life and the place he had of late taken in it, into the night and the distance. As she listened her heart momently grew heavier, the sense of empty desertion about her became suddenly overwhelming.

"Everybody I care for is going away from me," she whispered to herself. "Soon there won't be anybody left."

CHAPTER V
"HER FEET GO DOWN TO DEATH"

Jerry was in a bad temper. For some days he had been disturbed by rumors of Rion Gracey's attentions to June. In the long twilights of the summer evenings Rion had been constantly seen mounting the steps of the Murchison mansion. The single state of the Gracey boys had long been a matter of comment, and, as their riches grew it was regarded with increasing wonderment. Black Dan's heart may have been buried in the grave of his child-wife, but Rion had never paid any attention to any woman. Therefore, when it was known of men that he was a frequent visitor at the Allens', the little world in which he was a marked man began to whisper.

Jerry did not at first hear these rumors. He was not only kept busy from morning till night but he was entirely preoccupied in his own affairs. His feminine love of intrigue for its own sake was overpowered by such respect and honest tenderness as he still possessed for June. After his interview with her he determined not to see her again. June was not like Lupé Newbury and his feeling for her was different. He said to himself with a sense of magnanimity that no unhappiness should ever come to her from him, and in order to be on the safe side he would keep away from her.

As had been the case with Jerry all his life, there was method in his morality. He had gained at least one thing by his marriage and that was his connection with the all-powerful Graceys. Though he disliked both men, who, he knew, regarded him with secret contempt, their patronage was too valuable to be jeopardized. June's happiness and honor were precious things, but no more so than his own connection with the owners of the Cresta Plata. So he stayed away from her, feeling himself a paladin of virtue, and sentimentally thinking of her alone in the Murchison mansion, dreaming of him.

This agreeable arrangement of the situation was suddenly disrupted by the stories of Rion's attentions. Jerry's high thoughts of renunciation were swept away in a flood of jealous indignation. At first he refused to believe it. He was absolutely confident of June's constant and long-suffering affection for him. That she should marry some one else he had deemed impossible.

But one of the Gracey boys—it did not much matter which—the owners of one of the richest mines on the Comstock, was a very different matter. Money loomed the largest thing on Jerry's horizon. He did not believe it could take a less prominent place on that of other people—of June especially, whose father he knew to be financially embarrassed. The thought of her—his own especial property—triumphantly marrying a millionaire, leaving him, as it were, stranded, having lost everything and been "done" on every side, infuriated him. The jealousy that had possession of him was fierce, the jealousy of the man whose love is of the destructive, demolishing kind.

On the day he had risen up in a bad temper he had heard what amounted to confirmation of the rumor. One of the office clerks in the Cresta Plata had told him that Rion's infatuation for the young woman was leading him into lovers' extravagances. A man who had always been indifferent to his dress, he was now getting all his clothes from San Francisco. He had books, flowers, and candies sent up for her all the time. He was with her constantly.

"Rion Gracey's never looked at a woman before," was the young man's final comment, "and that's the kind that it takes most hold on. He's got it bad and can't hide it. It's out on him for any one to see, like the measles."

Jerry's jealousy and alarm boiled past the point of prudence. He made up his mind to get off early that afternoon and go to see June, and, as he expressed it in his own thoughts, "have it out with her." He had no idea what he intended to say, but he was going to find out what her attitude was to Rion, and, if need be, accuse her of her perfidy.

He had perfected his plan of escape from the office when Black Dan informed him that he was considering the purchase of a new horse and would be obliged if Jerry—a notable judge of horseflesh—would take it for a spin along the grade road and report his opinion of it. Black Dan's requests in this way were exceedingly like commands. But no one, from Barney Sullivan, the smartest superintendent in Virginia, to the youngest miner working on the ore-breasts, had ever dared to question them. With his face red with rage Jerry bowed his head in acquiescence, and that afternoon at the hour when he had hoped to be confronting June in her own parlor he was flying along the road toward Carson, cursing to himself as he held the reins over the back of Black Dan's new horse.

The afternoon was magnificent, held in a diamond-like transparence and blazing with sun. The mountain air tempered its heat. As Jerry flew along that remarkable road which curves, like an aërial terrace, round the out-flung buttresses of Mount Davidson, the Sierra, a lingering enameling of snow on its summits, spread before him. Rising high in tumbled majesty, mosaics of snow set in between ravines of swimming shadow, it looked unsubstantially enormous and unreal like scenery in dreams. Between it and Mount Davidson vast, airy gulfs of space fell away that seemed filled, as a glass might be with water, with a crystal stillness. The whole panorama, clarified by thin air, and with clear washes of shade laid upon it, was like a picture in its still, impersonal serenity.

Jerry, in his rage, let the horse have its head and they sped forward, past the outlying cabins that made a scattering along the approach to the town, past the timbered openings of the lone prospector's tunnels, to where the ledge of road rimmed the barren mountain flank. They were flying forward at an exhilarating pace when he noticed a woman's figure some distance in front walking on the narrow edge of path and moving forward at a brisk rate of speed. As he overhauled it his glance began to fasten on it with growing eagerness. The woman heard the thud of the flying hoofs behind her, and drew aside, as close to the outer edge as she dared, looking with eyes that blinked in the sunlight at the approaching buggy. Jerry's face flushed with a sudden realizing of the completely unexpected. It was June.

She did not recognize him at first, and drew back, as the horse, in a swirl of dust and spume flakes, came to a stop beside her. Then she saw who it was and with a low-toned "Jerry!" stood staring at him.

"Yes, it's I," he said hurriedly, leaning forward. "Get in and I'll take you for a spin."

She drew away, shaking her head. The spirited horse, excited by its run, began to bite at the bit, arch its neck and back prancingly. Jerry had to withdraw his attention from the girl, and, swearing in a soft undertone, bestow it on the animal.

"Come, June," he said, trying to speak coaxingly, "there's no harm in driving for half an hour with me. This is a new horse I'm trying for Black Dan and it's a perfect stunner."

She murmured a refusal, backing away from the wheels. The horse paused for a moment in its curvetings and Jerry had an opportunity to look at her and say in his most compelling tone:

"I only want you to drive up a mile or two with me. It's a glorious afternoon, and it's worth something to ride behind a horse like this. I'm not going to say anything to you you won't like to hear. You needn't be afraid. You and I are too old friends not to trust each other."

She wavered.

"Come, get in," he said, his voice soft and making an urgent upward movement with his chin, that seemed to draw her into the buggy as his hand might. She put her foot on the step and the next moment was beside him. The horse leaped forward and the road began to flash by like a yellow ribbon.

For some moments they were silent, Jerry with his eyes on the road ahead. They whirled round one of the projecting spurs of the mountain and, seeing the long curve before them clear of vehicles, he turned and looked at her. His eyes as they met hers were hard and angry.

"I've been hearing things about you!" he said.

"Things! What things?"

"I fancy you know."

"I don't know what you mean," she answered uneasily. "What sort of things?"

"The last sort of things in the world I want to hear."

She looked away making no answer and he said:

"I've heard that Rion Gracey is in love with you."

"Oh, is that it?" she commented in a low voice.

Her manner irritated him. She did not seem to realize the seriousness of the charge.

"Yes—that's it," he replied, continuing to regard her with a look of pugnacious ill-humor.

She again made no reply and he persisted angrily:

"Is he?"

"I don't want to talk about it. It's not fair. You've no right to ask."

"No right to ask!" he exclaimed in enraged amazement. "No right to ask! My God, that's a remark for you to make to me!"

He turned his face to the horse, his mouth set, his lips compressing words that he dared not utter. It was evidently all true. The thought that she might be already engaged to Rion entered his mind, carrying with it a sensation of appalling blankness. With a flash of revealing truth he saw that his life, with June completely gone from it, would be for ever savorless and without meaning. He had not realized before how much he cared for her.

For a space there was silence. They sped round another buttress and saw an unobstructed semicircle of road before them. Without looking at her he said abruptly:

"Are you going to marry him?"

"No," she answered.

"No?" he almost shouted, this time turning to stare at her.

She turned her face away repeating the negative.

"Why not?"

"I—I—don't—oh, Jerry, don't question me this way. It's not fair."

"But he *has* asked you?"

"Yes."

"And you've refused him?"

"Yes."

"Why?"

"I haven't got that sort of feeling for him. I admire him. I respect him above all men. I can't tell you how much he was to me, how I leaned on him, depended on him, but—"

She stopped, looking down. Jerry, holding the reins in his loosely gloved hand, leaning toward her, and into her ear whispered:

"But you don't love him."

He turned back to the horse with his face alight with triumph. The relief that she was still his, that love of him had made her refuse such an offer, intoxicated him. He could have sung and shouted. He was silent, however, his eyes on the horse, conscious in every fiber of the proximity of the woman who, he now knew, had not the power to break from his influence.

Neither spoke again, till the buggy, cresting the last rise, came out on the shoulder of the mountain, whence the road loops downward through the sage to Washoe Lake. Below them, at the base of the Sierra, the lake lay, a sheet of pure blue, its banks shading from the gray of the surroundings to a vivid green where the water moistened them. There was something human in this evidence of the land's readiness to bloom and beautify itself when the means were given it. It was a touch of coquetry in this austere, unsmiling landscape that seemed so indifferent.

Silent, the man and woman looked down, neither thinking of what they saw. The spirited horse was now willing to rest for a space, and stood, an equine statue against the sky, eagerly sniffing the keen air, his head motionless in a trance of alert attention, his ears pricking back and forth. A gulf of silence encircled them, pin-points of life in an elemental world.

June sat with relaxed muscles, her hands in her lap, her eyes on the lake. The stormy, troubled joy, so far from happiness, that was hers when with Jerry, held her. She had no desire to speak or move. The consciousness of his presence was like a drug to her energies, her reason, and her conscience. Sitting beside him, in this sun-steeped, serene solitude, the sense of wrong in his companionship became less and less acute, the wall of reserve between them seemed to evaporate. Sin and virtue, honor and dishonor, seemed the feeble inventions of timid man, oppressed and overwhelmed by this primordial nature which only sympathized with a pagan return to itself.

From an absent contemplation of the landscape Jerry turned and looked at his companion. He surveyed her with tender scrutiny, noting points in her appearance he had loved—the slight point with which her upper lip, just in the middle, drooped on her under one, the depression of her dimple, the fineness of her skin.

"No one else in the world has got the same sort of face as you," he said at length.

"That's not to be regretted," she murmured foolishly.

"You've the dearest little mouth, the way your upper lip comes down in a point on your lower one! I don't believe there's another woman in the world with such a queer little fascinating mouth."

He continued to gaze at her, half-smiling, but with intent eyes. Both felt the desire to talk leaving them. The silence of the landscape seemed to take possession of them, to make speech seem trivial and unnecessary.

"Why did you refuse Rion Gracey?" he said suddenly in a lowered voice.

She did not reply and he repeated the question.

"I didn't care for him," she said so low he could hardly hear the words.

He laid his hand on hers, gathering up her small fingers in his large grasp.

"Why?" he repeated, pressing them.

She turned away in evident distress and he whispered:

"Was it because you loved me?"

Her head drooped and he put his lips almost against her cheek as he whispered again:

"It was. I know it."

They were silent once more, neither looking at the other now. Both trembled, guilt and fear strong in their hearts.

At this moment a rabbit sprang from a sage bush across the path, and the horse, curling backward in a spasm of fear, rose to its hind legs and then leaped forward along the road. It took Jerry a full five minutes to control him and turn his head toward home.

"I'll take you back now," he said, throwing the words sidewise at her as they flew onward. "I'll stop at the mouth of Crazy Saunders' Tunnel. You can walk in from there. If I drove you into town some idiot would see us and make talk. I never saw anything like this place. If Saint Cecilia and Jephthah's daughter settled here for a week they'd cook up some gossip about them."

There was no more speech between them till they saw the timbered opening of Crazy Saunders' Tunnel loom in sight. Beyond, the first cottages of the town edged the road.

At the tunnel's mouth Jerry drew up. June put her foot forward for the step, and as she did so he leaned toward her and said:

"I'm coming to see you soon."

She looked quickly at him, protest and alarm in her face.

"No, don't do that," she said almost sharply. "I don't want you to. You mustn't."

"Why not?" he answered in a tone of cool defiance. "Why shouldn't I? We're old friends. I see no reason why I shouldn't come up to see you now and then."

The fretting horse, capering and prancing with impatience, cut off further conversation. June scrambled out, reiterating:

"No, don't come. I don't want you to."

As the horse sprang forward Jerry called over his shoulder:

"*Hasta mañana*, Señorita. I'm not going to say good-by."

June walked home with her eyes down-drooped, her head hanging. She took no heed of the brilliant colors that were lending beauty to the crumpled skyline of the mountains. She did not see the people who passed her, some of whom knew her and wondered at her absorption. Her thoughts went back to the days at Foleys when she and Rosamund had made money with the garden and had been so full of work and healthy, innocent happiness. Then she thought of the life in San Francisco, with its growth of lower ambitions, its passion and its suffering. And now this—so dark, so menacing, so full of sudden, unfamiliar dread!

A phrase she had heard in church the Sunday before rose to her recollection: "Her feet go down to death." As her thoughts roamed somberly back over the three epochs of her life the phrase kept recurring to her, welling continually to the surface of her mind, with sinister persistence—

"Her feet go down to death."

CHAPTER VI
THE EDGE OF THE PRECIPICE

Since his connection with the Graceys Jerry had been buying stock in the numerous undeveloped and unpaying mines which had cropped up like mushrooms round the edges of the town. In the end of July a new strike in the two-thousand-foot level of the Cresta Plata sent the stock of the mines in the vicinity suddenly up. As the vein was opened it developed into a discovery of great importance. The shares Jerry held doubled in value and continued to advance. August was not half over when he realized that, on paper at least, he was again a rich man.

The realization brought with it a pulsing sense of exhilaration. It meant not only the joys of independent wealth, which were to him among the dearest on earth, but the liberty to do with his life what he pleased. It was not only freedom from the Graceys, with whom his work had become a detested servitude, but an escape from the bonds his marriage had cast round him. Escape from it all—the scorn of his employers, the drudgery of his position, the meaningless tie that held him to an unloved wife and denied him the woman he craved.

The fever of the time and his own mounting fortunes was in his blood. Actions that under normal conditions would have seemed to him base he now contemplated with a sense of headstrong defiance. He was on fire with the lust of money and the desire of woman. The two passions carried him off his feet, swept away his judgment and reason. But the instinctive deceptiveness of the lover of intrigue did not desert him. While he was inwardly contemplating desperate steps, on the surface he appeared to be merely full of boyish animation and high spirits.

To June alone he was different, a man of almost terrifying moods, before whom at one moment she shrank and the next melted. He had brushed aside her request not to see her, as he would later on brush aside all her requests, her reticences and modesties, and be the master of a broken and abject slave.

Despite his desire to be with her he saw her seldom. The mining town offered few opportunities for meetings, which, however innocent they might be, were more agreeable if they took place in the seclusion of parks and quiet byways than on the crowded sidewalks of the populous streets. There were no wooded lanes for man and maid to loiter in, no plazas with benches in sheltered corners. In its hand-to-hand fight against elemental forces the town had no time to make concessions to the delicately debatable diversions of social life. It only recognized a love that was honestly licit or frankly illicit.

A few hurried visits at the Murchison mansion in the late afternoon when the Colonel was known to be busy at the office and Allen was still down town, were the only times that Jerry had been able to have speech with her. These interviews had at first been presided over by an outward seeming of that coolly polite friendship of which Jerry liked to talk. The conversation avoided all questions of sentiment as the man and woman seemed to avoid the proximity one of the other, sitting drawn apart with averted eyes, talking of impersonal matters.

But as his holdings advanced in value, as he saw himself day by day loosening the bonds that bound him to his employers, his wife, a society of which he was weary, his restraint was relaxed. His words grew less fluent, his pose of friend changed to that of the man on whose conversation moments of silence fall while he looks with ardent eyes on a down-drooped face. June made a last desperate stand, tried with despairing struggles to draw back from the fate closing around her. Even now she did not realize how close she was to the edge of the precipice. But Jerry did. He knew they were standing on its brink.

One evening, early in September, June and the Colonel were sitting together at dinner in the dining-room of the Murchison mansion. Allen had gone to San Francisco for a week, and the Colonel was to dine with June every evening till his return. He spent as much of his time as possible with the young girl in these lonely days. Even Mitty Sullivan and the baby were away, having gone to Lake Tahoe for two months. Thus the one house to which June could constantly go and be cheered by the society of a woman friend was closed to her.

Since Rosamund's wedding the Colonel had seen a distinct change in his darling. He set it down to grief at her sister's departure. She was pale and listless. The joy of youth had gone completely from her. Of late he had noticed that she was often absent-minded, not answering him if he spoke to her. He worried over her with a man's helplessness in situations of complicated feminine tribulation. Allen, drunk half of the time, absent the other half, was no guardian for her. Yet the Colonel could not take her away from him. He was her father. Sometimes when he let himself build air castles over his after-dinner cigar, he thought that perhaps Allen might die or marry again and then June would come to him and be his daughter. He would watch over her and lap her round with love and tenderness, and far off, in a rosy future, he would see her giving her hand to Rion, the man, he told himself, that Providence had made for her.

Her appearance to-night shocked him. She was pallid, the delicate blue blur of veins showing on her temples, her eyes heavy and darkly shadowed. He noticed that she ate little, crumbling her bread with a nervous hand, and only touching her lips to the rim of the wine glass. She was unusually distraught, often not answering the remarks he made to her, but sitting with her lids down, her eyes on her restlessly moving fingers.

Toward the end of dinner a sense of apprehension began to pervade him. If she continued to droop this way she might contract some ailment and die. Her mother had died of consumption and consumption often descended from parent to child. He knew now that her likeness to Alice went deeper than mere outward form into the secret springs of thought and action. It was one of those careful and perfect reproductions of type to which Nature is now and then subject. June was her mother in looks, in character, in temperament. It was so singularly close a resemblance that it seemed but natural to dread for her the disease that had killed the elder woman.

"You feel perfectly well, Junie?" he inquired, trying to speak easily but with anxious eyes on her.

"Well?" she repeated. "Oh, quite well! I've never been better. What makes you ask?"

"I thought you looked pale, paler than usual, and seemed out of spirits. *Are* you out of spirits, dearie?"

"I've not been very cheerful since—since—Rosamund left."

She concluded the sentence with an effort. The half-truth stuck in her throat. She had been in a state of confused misery for days, but the pain of her deception pierced through it.

"I hate to leave you looking like this," he continued. "I'm sure you're not well."

"Leave me!" she exclaimed with a startled emphasis. "You're not going to *leave* me?"

Her face, full of alarmed protest, astonished him.

"Of course I'm not going to *leave* you. I'm going down to San Francisco on Monday for two weeks, that's all. Business of Black Dan's."

She sat upright, bracing her hands against the edge of the table and said, almost with violence:

"Don't go. I don't want you to go. You *mustn't* go."

"But, my dear little girl, it's only for two weeks, perhaps less. I expect to be back Friday evening. I know it's lonely for you, but you know we have to put up with a good deal on our way through this world. You've found that out, honey. We've got to have our philosophy pretty handy sometimes."

"Oh, philosophy! I haven't got any. I only seem to have feelings."

She rose from her chair, the Colonel watching her with anxiously knit brows. Her distress at the thought of his leaving her filled him with uneasy surprise. It seemed so disproportioned to the cause. She passed round the table and came to a halt beside him.

"Can't you put it off?" she said, trying to speak in her old coaxing way. "Put it off till I go to England to visit Rosamund."

"Oh, June!" he exclaimed, hardly able to forbear laughing. "What a thing for a girl who's lived among mining men almost all her life to suggest! You won't go for over two months yet, and this is important. It's about the new pumps for the two-thousand-foot level. I leave on Monday."

"Monday!" she repeated with the same air of startled alarm. "*Next* Monday?"

"Yes. If all goes well I won't be gone two weeks. I'll be back Friday night. I'll bring you up some new books, and anything else you can think of. You know this is business, and there's no fooling with Black Dan. If you were sick in bed it would be a different matter. But as it is I must go."

Without more words she turned away and went slowly back to her seat. The Colonel, worried and baffled, watched her apprehensively. He thought to prick her pride into life and said rallyingly:

"I'm beginning to think you're just a little bit spoiled. The old man's making a baby of you. You're just as much of a child as ever."

He looked at her with a twinkling eye, hoping to see her laugh. But she was grave, leaning languidly against the back of the chair.

"I'm not as much of a child as you think," was her answer.

On the following Monday, *en route* to the depot, the Colonel paused on the outskirts of the crowd round the stock bulletins pasted up in a broker's window. He did not see that Jerry was on the other side of the crowd. But Jerry saw him, and through the openings between the swaying heads, eyed him warily.

As the elder man turned away in the direction of the depot, Jerry backed from the edges of the crowd to watch the retreating figure. His handsome face only showed a still curiosity, but there was malevolence in his eyes. He had quietly hated the Colonel since the night of the Davenport ball and awaited his opportunity to return that blow.

"Old blackguard!" he thought to himself, "I'll be even with you soon, now!"

The month of September advanced with early darkening evenings and the clear sharpening of outlines which marks the first breath of autumn. It was easier for Jerry now to see June. In the late afternoons the twilight came quickly and he could mount the long stairs to the Murchison mansion without fear of detection. The Colonel was away. Allen had returned but was much out, and when at home was closeted in a small room of his own that he called his office. The way was clear for Jerry, but he still advanced with slow and cautious steps.

The Colonel had been gone over a week when one evening June entered the office to consult with her father about an unpaid household bill for which a tradesman had been dunning her. The shortness of money from which Allen had been suffering since Rosamund's marriage, was beginning to react upon June. Several times of late the holders of accounts against her father had paid personal visits to the Murchison mansion. She had not yet grasped the hopeless nature of their situation. Even in the town Allen's insolvency was not known. It was simply rumored that he was "hard-up."

As she opened the door in answer to his "Come in" she smelt the sharp odor of burning paper, and saw that the grate was full of charred fragments. Portions of a man's wardrobe were scattered about on the various pieces of furniture, and on a sofa against the wall two half-packed valises stood open. Allen sat at his desk, amid a litter of papers, some of which he had been tearing up, others burning. As his eye fell on his daughter he laid his hand over an open letter before him.

She came in, holding the bill out toward him, and timidly explaining her entrance and its cause, for of late he had been fiercely irascible. To-night, however, he greeted her with unusual gentleness, and taking the paper from her hand looked at it and laid it aside.

"Thompson," he said; "tell him his account will be settled in a few days. And any of the others that send in bills like this, tell them the same thing."

"Are you going again?" she asked, looking at the valises.

"Yes, to-morrow. You can just casually let these fellows know that I've gone down to San Francisco to sell some stock, and everything will be satisfactorily settled up when I get back."

"When will you get back?" she asked, not from desire for his presence, but to know what to say to the uneasy tradesmen.

"You tell them next week," he said, "that'll quiet them. But I may be longer. It may be two or even three weeks. I've lots of things to arrange, so don't you worry if I don't show up next week or even later."

He tore the letter he had been covering with his hand into small pieces and, rising, threw them into the grate on the smoldering remnants of the others.

"Uncle Jim's down below now," she said, "you'll probably see him."

"But he'll be back in a few days, won't he?" he queried, looking at her with sudden, sharp inquiry. "If—if—I should be delayed, as I told you I might be, he'll be here and he'll look after you. You see more of him now than you do of me. He seems to be more your father than I."

"He's here oftener," she said apologetically, "you're away so much."

"Maybe that's it. I'm not kicking about it. He's the Graceys' right hand man now. He's on top of the heap. He'll always look out for you, and he'll be able to do it."

He turned to throw some more papers on the burning pile, missing her look of surprise.

"Always look out for me!" she repeated. "There's no need for him to do that. You'll be back soon."

"You needn't take me so literally. But you ought to know by this time that the future's a pretty uncertain thing. If anything should happen to me, it's just as I say, he'd be here on the spot ready and willing to take care of you. You can't look for much from me. If I died to-morrow I wouldn't leave you a cent. The Barranca's petered."

"But the stocks you're going to San Francisco to sell? They must be worth a good deal. Everybody's stocks seem to be worth something now. Mitty Sullivan's cook says she's thirty thousand ahead."

"Oh, yes, they'll bring something." He spoke absently, took up Thompson's bill and thrust it on a spike with others of its kind. "There they are, all the tradesmen. Don't let them bother you. You'd better run along now and let me finish up."

"Can I help you pack?" she suggested with timid politeness.

He shook his head, his eye traveling down a new letter he had picked up from the desk.

"Good night," she said, moving toward the door.

He dropped the letter and, following her, put his arm around her and kissed her. It was an unexpected caress. He and his daughter had grown very far apart in this last year.

"Good-by," he said gently, and turning from her went back to his papers.

"Run along," he said without looking up. "I'll be busy here for some hours yet."

When she came down to breakfast the next morning he had already gone. The Chinaman told her he had left early, driving into Reno by private conveyance in order to catch the first morning train to the coast.

That evening Jerry beat out the last spark of her resistance. He held her close in his arms, his cheek against hers, and revealed to her his plan of elopement. Trembling and sobbing she clung to him, under his kisses the words of denial dying on her lips. He paid no heed to her feeble pleadings, hushing her protests with caresses, whispering of their happiness, murmuring the lovers' sentences that, since Eve, have been the undoing of impassioned women.

When he stole down the steps in the darkness of the early night, triumph was in his heart. She was his when he chose to take her, her will as water, her resistance only words. A new world of love, liberty and riches lay before him. The bleak town and its bitter memories would soon be far behind, and June and he in a strange country and a new life would begin their dream of love.

CHAPTER VII
THE COLONEL COMES BACK

Jerry's plans had been laid with the utmost secrecy and care. It behooved him to be wary, for he knew that detection would mean death. Neither the Colonel nor Black Dan would have hesitated to shoot him like a dog if they had known what he contemplated, and working day by day in an office with these men, in a town the smallness and isolation of which rendered every human figure a segregated and important unit, it required all the shrewdness of which he was master to mature his design and arouse no suspicion.

The time had now come when everything was suddenly propitious. Had the Prince of Darkness been giving Jerry's affairs his particular attention, circumstances could not have fallen together more conveniently for the furthering of his purpose.

In the office of the Cresta Plata it was arranged that every two weeks he should be given three or four days off to go to San Francisco and visit his wife. These holidays, which were grudgingly doled out by Black Dan, always included the Sunday, as the older man was determined his son-in-law should have as little immunity from work as possible. In the middle of the week Jerry was informed that he could leave for San Francisco on the following Saturday morning to report again at the office on Wednesday.

The granting of this five days' leave of absence made the elopement easy of accomplishment, robbing it of the danger of detection that Jerry realized and shrank from. He and June could leave on Friday night and take the overland train eastward. They would have five days' start before discovery was made, and in five days they would be so far on their journey that it would be easy for them to conceal themselves in some of the larger towns along the route. Mercedes, who was a bad correspondent, could be trusted not to write to her father, and Allen, according to June's artless revelations, was gone for a much longer time than he wanted known. Finally the last and most serious obstacle was removed in the shape of the Colonel. Jerry being in the office knew that his enemy would not be back before Tuesday or Wednesday, as the work of inspecting the pumps had been slower than was anticipated.

Months of waiting and planning could not have arranged matters more satisfactorily. Luck, once again, was on his side, as it had been so often in the past.

Early on the Friday morning he went to the livery stable that he always patronized, and where he knew the finest team of roadsters in Nevada was for hire. Mining men of that day were particular about their horses. There were animals in the Virginia stables whose superiors could not be found west of New York. The especial pair that Jerry wanted were only leased to certain patrons of the stable, but Jerry, an expert on horseflesh, besides being Black Dan Gracey's son-in-law, had no difficulty in securing them for that evening.

He had had some idea of driving into Reno himself and letting June come in on the train, but he had a fear that, left alone, she might weaken. To be sure of her he must be with her. Moreover, there was little risk in driving in together. They would not start until after dark and their place of rendezvous would be a ruined cabin some distance beyond the Utah hoisting works on the Geiger grade. The spot would be deserted at that hour, and even if it were not, the spectacle of a buggy and pair of horses was so common that it would be taken for that of some overworked superintendent driving into Reno on a sudden business call.

From the stable he returned to the office and alone there wrote a hasty letter to June. He had told her the outline of his plan, and that Friday would be the day, but he had given her no details of what their movements would be. Now he wrote telling her minutely of the time and place of departure and impressing upon her not to be late. He would, of course, be there before her, waiting in the buggy. There was a party of Eastern visitors to be taken over the mine in the afternoon, and it would be easy for him to get away from them, leaving them with Marsden, the foreman, change his clothes, and be at the place indicated before she was. He was still fearful that she might fail him. Now, as the hour approached, he was so haunted by the thought that he asked her to send at least a few words of answer by his messenger.

Half an hour later Black Dan entered the office and paused by his son-in-law's desk to give him some instructions as to the Eastern visitors and the parts of the mine they were to be shown. They were people of importance from New York, the men being heavy shareholders in the Cresta Plata and the Con. Virginia. The ladies of the party were to be relegated to the care of Jerry and Marsden the foreman, and not to be taken below the thousand-foot level. Black Dan and Barney Sullivan would take the men farther down. Jerry was to be ready in the hoisting works at four o'clock.

As Black Dan was concluding his instructions Jerry's messenger reëntered the office and handed the young man a small, pale gray envelope. It was obviously a feminine communication, and its recipient, under the darkly scrutinizing eye of his father-in-law, flushed slightly, but he gave no other sign of consciousness, and as Black Dan passed on to the inner office, he sat down and opened the letter.

It was only a few lines in June's delicate hand-writing:

"I will be there. I go to my ruin, Jerry, for you. Will there be anything in our life together that will make me forget that? June."

Jerry read it over several times. It certainly did not breathe an exalted gladness. Away from him she always seemed in this condition of fear and doubt. It was his presence, his hand upon her, that made her tremulously, submissively his. He would not be sure of her till she was beside him to-night in the buggy.

Would that hour ever come? He looked at the clock ticking on the wall. With every passing moment his exaltation seemed to grow stronger. It was difficult for him to be quiet, not to stop and talk to everybody that he encountered with a feverish loquacity. The slowly gathering pressure of the last month seemed to culminate on this day of mad rebellion. Within the past two weeks his stocks had increased largely in value. He was a rich man, and to-night with the woman he loved beside him he would be free. He and she, free in the great outside world, free to love and to live as they would. Would the day never pass and the night never come?

In San Francisco the Colonel was completing the business of the pumps as quickly as he could. He felt that he was getting to be a foolish old man, but he could not shake off his worry about June. Her words and appearance at their last interview kept recurring to him. Many times in the past year he had seen her looking pitifully fragile and known her to be unhappy, but he had never before felt the poignant anxiety about her that he now experienced.

Despite his desire to get back with as much speed as possible, unforeseen delays occurred, and instead of returning on Friday, as he had hoped, he saw that he would not be back before Wednesday. He wrote this to June in a letter full of the anxious solicitude he felt. To this he received no answer, and, his worry increasing, he was about to telegraph her when he received a piece of information that swept all minor matters from his mind.

On Thursday at midday he was lunching with a friend at the club, when, in the course of conversation, his companion asked him if he knew the whereabouts of Beauregard Allen. The words were accompanied with a searchingly significant look. The Colonel, answering that Allen was in Virginia, paused in his meal and became quietly attentive. He knew more than others of Allen's situation. Of late he had scented catastrophe ahead of his one-time comrade. The man's face opposite him struck an arrow of suspicion through his mind. He put down his wine glass and sat listening, his expression one of frowning concentration.

His friend was a merchant with a large shipping business between San Francisco and Australia. That morning he had been to the docks to see a ship about to sail, which carried a cargo of his own. The ship took few passengers, only two or three, he thought. While conversing with the captain he had seen distinctly in the doorway of an open cabin Beauregard Allen unpacking a valise. In answer to his question the captain had said it was one of his passengers taken on that morning. He had brought no trunks, only two valises, and given his name as John Montgomery.

"It was Beauregard Allen," the Colonel's informant continued. "The man's no friend of mine, but I've seen him round here for years. He looked up and saw me and drew back quick, as if he did not want to be recognized."

"He'd taken passage this morning, you say?" asked the Colonel.

"Yes, to Melbourne. There was only one other passenger, a drunken boy being sent on a long sea voyage by his parents. They'll make a nice, interesting pair."

The Colonel looked at his plate silently. He was sending his thoughts back over the last year, trying to collect data that might throw some light on what he had just heard.

"You're certain it was Allen, not a chance likeness?" he said slowly.

"I'll take my oath of it. Why, I've seen the man for the past four years dangling around here. I know his face as well as I know yours, and I had a good look at it before he saw me and jumped back. He's got in too deep and skipped. Everybody has been wondering how he kept on his feet so long."

"He's in pretty deep, sure enough," said the Colonel absently. "You said Melbourne was the port? When do they sail?"

"Midday to-day. They're off by now. They'll be outside the heads already with this breeze."

The Colonel asked a few more questions and then rose and excused himself. His business was pressing.

His first action was to send a telegram to Rion Gracey, asking him if Allen had left Virginia and where June was. The answer was to be sent to the club. Then he went forth. His intention was to inquire at the hotels patronized by Allen on his frequent visits to the city. As he went from place to place the conviction that the man seen by his friend had been June's father, and that he had fled, strengthened with every moment.

A feverish anxiety about June took possession of him. If her father had decamped leaving her alone, she would have to face his angry creditors. He thought of her as he had last seen her, exposed to such an experience, and his heart swelled with pity and rage. Possibly she knew, had guessed what was coming and had begged him to stay with her to protect and care for her in a position for which she was so little fitted. And he had left her—left her to face it alone!

He returned to the club, having heard no word of Allen, and found Rion's answer to his telegram. It ran:

"Allen left for coast Wednesday morning. June here. What's amiss?"

It seemed to the Colonel complete confirmation of his fears. Allen leaving Wednesday morning would reach San Francisco some time that night. Evidently his plans had been made beforehand, for the ship he had taken was one of the fastest merchantmen on the Pacific and was scheduled to leave at midday Thursday.

Nothing was suspected at Virginia yet, and June was there alone. At any moment now, the information being in the hands of more than one person, Allen's flight might be made public, and she, his only representative, would become the victim of the rage of the petty creditors who would swarm about her. He was the one human being upon whom she could call. No duty or business would hold him from her. A thrill of something like joy passed through him when he realized that now, at last, he could stand between her and all trouble—a lion with its cub behind it.

He took the evening train for Virginia, hoping to reach Reno the next morning and catch the branch line into the mining town. But luck was against him. A snow-shed was down near the summit. Though it was only the latter half of September, a premature blizzard wrapped the mountain heights in a white mist. For eight hours the train lay blocked on an exposed ridge, and it was late afternoon when it finally set the Colonel down at Reno.

The delays had only accelerated his desire to be with June. During the long hours of waiting his imagination had been active, picturing her in various distressing positions, besieged by importunate creditors. He hired the fastest saddle horse in the Reno stables and rode the twenty-one miles into Virginia in an hour. It was dark when he reached there. The swift ride through the sharp autumnal air had braced his nerves. He was as anxious as ever to see her, but he thought that before he did so he would stop for a few moments at the Cresta Plata and see Rion, explain his early return, and learn if anything was known in Virginia of Allen's flight.

The office was already lighted up and behind it the great bulk of hoisting works loomed into the night, its walls cut with the squares of illumined windows, its chimneys rising black and towering against the stars. A man who came forward to take his horse told him that the gentlemen were all in the mine with a party of visitors. The Colonel, hearing this, turned his steps from the office to the door of the hoisting works a few yards beyond.

The building, full of shadows despite the lanterns and gas jets ranged along its walls, looked vacant and enormous in its lofty spaciousness. The noise of machinery echoed through it, the vibration shaking it as if it were a shell built about the intricacies of wheels, bands, and sheaves that whirred and slid in complicated, humming swiftness against the ceiling. The light struck gleams from the car tracks that radiated from the black hole of the shaft mouth where it opened in the middle of the floor. It was divided into four compartments, and from these a thin column of steam arose and floated up to the roof. Here and there a few men were moving about, and aloft behind their engines were the four engineers. They were mute as statues, their eyes fixed on the dials in front of them which registered the movements of the cages underground; their ears on the alert to catch the notes of their bells, to them intelligible as the words of a spoken language. Near the shaft mouth sitting on an overturned box was Rion Gracey.

He saw the Colonel and rose to his feet with an exclamation of surprise and pleasure. The elder man, drawing him aside, told him the reason of his return and asked him news of June. Moving toward the door they conversed together in lowered voices. The Colonel, now convinced that no suspicion of the nature of Allen's absence had yet reached Virginia, felt his anxieties diminished. He said that he might attend the dinner which Black Dan was giving that evening to the Easterners. Rion was now waiting for them to come up. Barclay and the women ought to be up at any moment; they had been underground nearly two hours, an unusual length of time, for even on the thousand-foot level the heat was intense.

His anxieties soothed, the Colonel left the building, his heart feeling lighter than it had felt for two weeks.

With a step of youthful buoyancy he mounted the steep cross-streets which connected by a series of stairs and terraces the few long thoroughfares of the town. He was out of breath when he saw the dark shape of the

Murchison mansion standing high on its crest of ground against a deep blue, star-dotted sky. His approach was from the side, and that no lights appeared in any of the windows in that part of the house did not strike him as unusual. But when he reached the foot of the long stairway and looking up saw that there was not a gleam of light to be seen on the entire façade, his joy suddenly died, and in its place a dread, sharp and disturbing, seized him.

For a moment he stood motionless, staring up. The shrubs that grew along the sloping banks of the garden rustled dryly in the autumn night. There was something sinister in the high form of the house, mounted aloft on its terrace, no friendly pane gleaming with welcoming light, no sound near it but the low, occasional whispering of dying vegetation. As he ran up the steps, his footfall sounded singularly loud and seemed to be buffeted back from empty walls.

His first and second pull of the bell brought no response. Between them he listened and his ear caught nothing but the stillness of desertion. His third furious peal was answered by a distant footstep. He heard it come shuffling along the hall, pause, and then a light broke out through the glass fanlight above the portal. The door was opened a crack, and through this aperture a section of the Chinaman's visage was revealed, lit by a warily inspecting eye.

The Colonel pushed the door violently in, sending the servant back with it against the wall. Kicking it to behind him he demanded between his panting breaths:

"Where's Miss Allen?"

"She's gone," said the Chinaman, exceedingly startled by this violent entry. "All gone."

"All gone! All gone where?"

"I no savvy. The boss he gone two, thlee days. Gone San Francisco. Miss Allen she go just now."

"She's only just gone? You mean she has just gone down town to buy something or see some one?"

"No. She go 'way. She say, 'Sing, I go 'way.' She take a bag."

"She's gone with a bag. Where the devil has she gone to? Don't be such a damned fool! Where'd she go?"

"No savvy. She no tell me. She take bag and go just now. She give me letter for you. I get him. He tell you."

"You've got a letter for me? Why didn't you say that before? Go get it, and go quick."

The Chinaman shuffled up the hall and turned into the dining-room. The Colonel, having caught his breath, leaned against the wall under the hall gas. He thought probably June had gone to Lake Tahoe to visit Mitty Sullivan. Considering the situation it was the best thing she could have done. As the servant reappeared with a letter in his hand he said:

"When did she leave this?"

"Now," answered the laconic Oriental. "She give him to me and say, 'Give him Colonel Pallish. He come back Tuesday, Wednesday mebbe. You give him letter sure; no forget.' You come back before, I give him now."

The Colonel had not listened to the last phrases. He moved closer to the gas and tore open the letter. To his surprise he saw that it was several pages in length, covered closely with June's fine writing. His eye fell on the first sentence, and he uttered a sudden suppressed sound and his body stiffened. The words were:

"Dear, darling, Uncle Jim. I who love you more than anybody in the world am going to hurt you so much. Oh, so terribly! Will you ever forgive me? Will you ever again think of June without sorrow and pain?"

He stood motionless as a thing of stone, while his glance devoured the page. He did not read every word, but from the closely written lines sentences seemed to start out and strike his eyes. He turned the sheet and saw farther down a paragraph that told him everything:

"The future is all dark and terrible, but I am going. I am going with Jerry. I am going wherever he wants, I am what he wants to make me. It's only death that can break the spell. Good-by, dearest, darlingest Uncle Jim. Oh, good-by! If I could only see you again for one minute! Even when you read this and realize what I have done I know that you will love me and make excuses for me, I who will be no longer worthy your love or your pity."

The Colonel's hand with the letter crushed in it dropped to his side. For a moment he stood rigid, his face gray in the gas light. It was too unexpected a blow to be grasped in the first paralyzing second. Then he turned furiously on the servant, shouting:

"Where did she go? Where did she go?"

The man cowered terrified against the wall, stammering in broken phrases,

"I no savvy! How I savvy? She go with a bag. She say, 'Give him the letter' and I give him. You read him. I no savvy any more."

The Colonel's hand on his chest forcing him back against the door-post cut short his words:

"When did she go? How long ago? Answer honestly, or, by God, I'll kill you!"

His face added to the man's terror, but it also steadied his shaking nerves:

"She go not one hour; thlee-quarters. She come to me with bag and say, 'Good-by, Sing, I go for long time.' She give me the letter and say give him to you Tuesday, Wednesday. Then she go."

"Which way?"

"I don't see. I don't look. I go down stairs. I go sleep on my bed. I hear bell and wake. That's all."

The Colonel released him and turned to the door. The man evidently knew no more than he said. She had been gone less than an hour. That was all there was to tell.

As he ran down the long stairs he had no definite idea in his mind. She had left to run away with Jerry three-quarters of an hour earlier. That was all he thought of for the moment. Then the frosty sharpness of the night air began to act with tonic force upon him. His brain cleared and he remembered Rion's words. Half an hour ago Barclay was still in the mine. There had evidently been some delay in his coming up. No trains left the town as late as that. June had gone somewhere to meet him, to some place of rendezvous whence they would probably drive into Reno. If Barclay had not yet left the mine he could be caught, and then——

With wild speed he ran along the streets, leaping down the short flights of steps that broke the ascending sidewalks. He thrust people aside and rushed on, gray-faced and fiery-eyed. For the second time in his life there was murder in his heart.

Through the darkness of his mind memories of her passed like slides across a magic lantern. A sudden picture of her that day long ago at the spring, when she had asked him to let her mother stay in his cottage, rose up clear and detached on his mental vision. He heard again the broken tones of her voice and saw her face with the tears on it, childish and trustful, as it had been before the influence of Jerry had blighted its youth and marred its innocence.

The fury that possessed him rose up in his throat. He could not have spoken. He could only run on, tearing his way through the crowds on C Street, across it to a smaller thoroughfare and down that to where the dark mass of the Cresta Plata buildings stood out against the night. He heard the distant hum of the machinery, and then, unexpected and startling, the roar of men. It was like the noise when the day shift came up and every ascending cage was packed solid with miners.

As he approached the door the men began to come out, streams of them, some running, others gathering in knots. Hundreds of men poured into the night, gesticulating, shouting, congesting in black groups, whence a broken clamor of voices rose. He realized the strangeness of it, that something was the matter, but it was all dim and of no importance to him. His mind held only one thought. Rushing past them he cried:

"Barclay! Is Barclay up yet? Do you know where Barclay is?"

An Irishman, who stumbled against him in the dark, paused long enough to shout to him:

"It's Barclay that's hurt. Hurry up, Colonel, they'll be wanting you inside. It's a doctor I'm after. God knows if he is where they say he is, there's no life in him now."

CHAPTER VIII
THE AROUSED LION

Black Dan, as he walked to the office that Friday morning, had been giving serious thought to the situation of his son-in-law. Mercedes had not spent the summer in Virginia as her father had hoped and expected. When he saw her in San Francisco, as he did every few weeks, she talked of her delicate throat and expressed a fear of the climate. It was evident that she could not or would not live there.

That his daughter loved her husband Black Dan had no doubt. And as he walked to the mine that morning he was pondering a scheme he had lately been considering of sending Jerry to San Francisco, to be placed in charge of his large property interests. Though he regarded his son-in-law with contemptuous dislike, he could not deny that the young man had worked hard and faithfully all summer. Moreover, the stealthy watch kept upon him had revealed no irregularities in his conduct. In a place and at a time when men led wild lives with wilder associates, Jerry's behavior had been exemplary. His life had been given to work and business; women had no place in it.

With these thoughts in his mind Black Dan entered the office and paused by his son-in-law's desk. As he stood there a boy walked in and handed the young man a small gray envelope that bore a superscription in a delicate feminine hand. Black Dan also saw that Jerry, under his unshakable *sang-froid*, was disconcerted. That the receipt of the letter was disturbing to its recipient was as plain to the older man as that the letter was from a woman.

He passed on to his own office with his mind in an entirely different condition from what it had been when he entered the building. After all their watchfulness, was Jerry playing at his old game? The thought made Black Dan breathe curses into his beard. He saw Rion, himself and the Colonel out-witted, and Jerry laughing at them in his sleeve. And deeper than this went the enraging thought of Mercedes supplanted by one of the women that flourish in mining camps, birds of prey that batten on the passions of men.

He had work to do, however, and, for to-day, at least, would have to put the matter out of his mind. Time enough when the Easterners were gone. Black Dan, like many men of his day and kind, was particularly anxious to impress the Easterners, and to make their three days' stay in the town a revel of barbaric luxury. The dinner he was to give them that evening was to be a feast of unrivaled splendor, every course ordered from San Francisco, the wine as choice as any to be bought in the country, the china, glass, and silver imported at extravagant cost from the greatest factories of Europe, the cigars of a costly rarity, a brand especially sent from Havana for the bonanza king and his associates.

Now from among the specimens of ore that stood along the top of his desk he selected one of unusual form and value to give to the most distinguished of the strangers. It was a small square of blackish mineral on which a fine, wire-like formation of native silver had coiled itself into a shape that resembled a rose. It had the appearance of a cunning piece of the silversmith's art, a flower of silver wire delicately poised on a tiny fragment of quartz rock. Thrusting it into his coat pocket, he left the office, on his way out passing Jerry, who was bending studiously over his desk.

He walked rapidly up through the town, to the same livery stable to which his son-in-law had already paid a visit. One of the diversions to which the visitors were treated was the drive along the mountain road to Washoe Lake. This, Black Dan had arranged, would be the entertainment for the following morning. He with his own Kentucky thoroughbreds, would drive the men, while the women of the party would follow in a hired trap, drawn by the horses Jerry had ordered, and driven by the expert whip of the stable, known as Spanish George. Such a division of the party suited Black Dan admirably, for he disliked women, shunning their society, and when forced into it, becoming more somber and taciturn than ever.

His plan, however, received an unexpected check. He was told that the horses were engaged by Mr. Barclay for that evening. Frowning and annoyed, he demanded why that should prevent him from having them the next morning, and received the information that Mr. Barclay was to drive into Reno that night with them, sending them back in the morning, when they would be too tired by the twenty-one miles over the grade, to go out again immediately.

Black Dan stood in the doorway of the stable looking with attentive eyes at his informant. As the man amplified his explanation with excuses, the bonanza king said nothing. For the moment his own thoughts were too engrossing to permit of words. A puppy that was playing near by in the sunlight trotted toward him and bit playfully at his toe. He turned it over with his foot, following its charmingly awkward gambols with a pondering gaze.

"Then I suppose I can't have Spanish George either?" he said. "Mr. Barclay'll take him in to drive the horses back, and he'll take his time about it."

"Oh, you can have Spanish George all right," said the stable-man, relieved that he could give his powerful patron something he wanted. "Mr. Barclay's driving some one in with him. He'll have one of the Reno men bring the horses back."

Black Dan looked up, his broad, dark eyes charged with almost fierce attention.

"Who's he driving in?" he asked.

"Don't know, sir. He didn't say. All he said was that he couldn't take a driver, as he had some one with him and he'd send the team back in the morning with a man from Reno."

The other looked down at the puppy, rolling it gently back and forth with his large foot.

"When did you say he was going?" he asked.

"Six-thirty. His valises have come up already. They're in the office now."

He pointed backward with his thumb toward the small, partitioned-off box called the office. But Black Dan did not seem particularly interested in the valises.

"Well," he said, taking his foot off the puppy and pushing it carefully aside, "send along the best you have with Spanish George to drive. Be at the International at eleven sharp. I don't want to start later than that."

He left the stable and walked slowly down the street toward the Cresta Plata. His eyes were downcast, his face set in lines of absorbed thought. Whom was Jerry driving into Reno that night?

As he walked he pieced together what he had just heard with what he knew already. One hour before the dinner to the Easterners—at which he was expected—Jerry had arranged to leave the town, driving into Reno with some companion. The companion and the gray note instantly connected themselves in Black Dan's mind. He felt as certain as a man could be without absolute confirmation that Jerry was driving in with a woman. The daring insolence of it made the blood, which moved slowly in the morose and powerful man, rise to his head. Could it be possible that Jerry, on the way to see his wife, was going to stop over in Reno with some woman of the Virginia streets?

Black Dan's swarthy skin was slightly flushed when he reached the office. He said nothing to Jerry as he passed his desk. In his own private office he sat still, staring in front of him at the geological map hanging on the wall. He was slow to wrath, but his wrath, like his love, once roused was of a primitive intensity. As he sat staring at the map his anger gathered and grew.

At four o'clock the eastern party and their guides were due to meet in the hoisting works for their excursion down the mine. It was nearly a half-hour later, however, when the two ladies, who made up the feminine portion of the party, slunk out of the spacious dressing-rooms, giggling and blushing in their male attire. Jerry, Marsden the foreman, and one of the shift bosses, were lounging about the mouth of the shaft waiting for them. There were greetings and laughter, the women hugging themselves close in the long overcoats they wore against the chill of the downward passage, and pulling over their hair the shapeless cloth caps they had been given for head-gear.

Through the wide opening that led to the dumps the figure of Black Dan, dark against the brilliance of the afternoon, could be seen walking on the car tracks with the rest of the party. In the muddy overalls, long boots and soft felt hat which was the regulation underground dress of the men, he presented the appearance of some black-browed, heavily bearded pirate in the garb of a tramp. As the cage slid up to the shaft mouth, he entered the building, gave the embarrassed women an encouraging nod, and selected a lantern from a collection of them standing in a corner.

With little cries of apprehension the women stepped on the flat square of flooring, their three escorts ranged closely round them, the signal to descend, was given, and the cage dropped quickly out of sight into the steaming depths. Black Dan, Barney Sullivan and the strangers were to descend on the cage in the next compartment, and while they waited for it to come up, stood talking of the formations of the mineral, how it had been found and of the varying richness of the ore-bodies. Suddenly Black Dan thought of his specimen, which had come from a part of the mine they were to visit first, and turning went into the men's dressing-room, where he had left it in his coat pocket.

His clothes had been hung on the last of a line of pegs along the wall. To this he went, and, ignorant of the fact that Jerry had undressed after him, thrust his hand into the pocket of what he thought was his own coat. Instead of the stone his fingers encountered a letter. He drew it out and saw that it was the one he had seen handed to his son-in-law a few hours before.

At once he drew the paper from the envelope. No qualm of conscience deterred him; instead he experienced a sense of satisfaction that his uncertainty should be thus simply brought to an end. His eye traveled over the few lines, instantly grasping their meaning. He knew the signature. Jerry was not intriguing with a common woman of the town; he was deserting his wife with a girl, hitherto of unspotted reputation, and for years beloved by Rion. It meant ruin and misery for the two human beings nearest to the bonanza king's heart.

For a moment he stood motionless, the letter in his hand, and before his eyes he saw red. Then it cleared away. He put the paper back in its envelope and thrust it in his pocket. When he came out into the shaft house Barney Sullivan noticed that his face was reddened and that the whites of his eyes were slightly bloodshot. One of the strangers rallied him on his absence, which had been of some minutes' duration, and he made no answer, simply motioning them to get on the cage with an imperious movement of his head.

The shaft of the Cresta Plata was over two thousand feet in depth, and the heat of the lower levels was terrific. Here the miners, naked, save for a cap, breechclout, and canvas shoes, worked twenty-minute shifts, unable to stand the fiery atmosphere for longer. Cold air was pumped down to them from the surface, the pipes that carried it following the roofs of the long, dark tunnels, their mouths blowing life-giving coolness into stopes where the men could not touch their metal candlesticks, and the iron of the picks grew hot. There were places where the drops that fell from the roof raised blisters on the backs they touched. On most of these lower levels there was much water, its temperature sometimes boiling. The miners of the Cresta Plata had a saying that no man had ever fallen into water that reached to his hips and lived. At the bottom of the shaft—the "sump" in mining parlance—was a well of varying depths which perpetually exhaled a scalding steam.

Black Dan took his guests to the fifteen-hundred-foot level, whence the greatest riches of the mine had been taken. He was more than usually silent as they walked from tunnel to tunnel and drift to drift. Barney Sullivan was the cicerone of the party, explaining the formation, talking learnedly of the dip of the vein, holding up his lantern to let its gleam fall on the dark bluish "breast" into which the miners drove their picks with a gasp of expelled breath. Nearly an hour had passed when Black Dan, suddenly drawing him back, whispered to him that he was going up to the eight-hundred-foot level to see Jerry, to whom he wished to give some instructions about the dinner that evening. Barney, nodding his comprehension, moved on with the guests, and Black Dan walked back to the station.

As he went up in the cage he passed level after level, like the floors of a great underground building. Yellow lights gleamed through the darkness on the circular forms of west timbers, hollowed caves trickling with moisture, car tracks running into blackness. Each floor was peopled with wild, naked shapes, delving ferociously in this torrid inferno. At the eight-hundred-foot level he got off, the bell rang, and the empty cage went sliding up. The landing on to which he stepped was deserted, and he walked up one of the tunnels that branched from it, called to a pick-boy, whom he saw in the distance, that he wanted Mr. Barclay found and sent to him at once. The figure of the boy scudded away into the darkness, and Black Dan went back to the landing.

It was an open space, a small, subterranean room, the lanterns fastened on its walls gilding with their luster the pools of water on the muddy floor. There were boxes used for seats standing about, and on pegs in the timbers the miners' coats hung. Where the shaft passed down there were several square openings—larger than ordinary doorways, iron-framed and with plates of iron set into the moist ground—which gave egress to the cages. Now there was only a black void there, the long shaft stretching hundreds of feet upward and downward.

Black Dan sat on a box, waiting. Afar off from some unseen tunnel he could hear the faint sound of voices. Near by, sharply clear in the stifling quiet, came the drip of water from the roof. It was still very hot, a moist, suffocating heat, regarded by the miners as cool after the fiery depths below. He pushed back his hat and wiped the sweat from his face. His eyes, as he waited, kept watch on the openings of the three tunnels that diverged from this central point.

One of them was an inky arch in a frame of timbers. In the distance of the others lights gleamed. Now and then a bare body, streaming with perspiration, came into view pushing an ore car. With an increasing rattle it was rolled to the shaft opening and on to a waiting cage which slid up. The miner slouched back into the gloom, the noise of the empty car he propelled before him gradually dying away. Black Dan could hear again the voices and then, muffled by earth and timbers, the thud of the picks. Sitting on an upturned box—the king of this world of subterranean labor—he sat waiting, motionless, save for his moving eyes.

Suddenly from the undefined noises, the beat of an advancing footfall detached itself. He gave a low, inarticulate sound, and drew himself upright, a hand falling on either knee, his dark face full of a grim fixity of attention. Down one of the tunnels the figure of Jerry came into view, walking rapidly.

He was smiling, for this summons made his escape from the mine easier than it would otherwise have been. A word or two from Black Dan and then up on the cage, and then—away into the night where love and a woman were waiting. The culminating excitement of the day made his eye brilliant and deepened the color of his face. Full of the joys and juices of life, triumphantly handsome even in his rough clothes, he was a man made for the seduction of women. Black Dan felt it and it deepened his hate.

"Did you want me?" he called as he drew near. "One of the pick-boys said you sent for me."

"Yes, I want to see you for a moment. I want to ask you about something."

The elder man rose slowly from his box. His eyes were burning under the shadow of his hat brim.

"Come over here near the light," he said. "I've something I want to show you."

Near the entrance to the shaft there was a large lantern, backed by a tin reflector. It cast a powerful light on the muddy ground and the plates of iron that made a smooth flooring round the landing. Black Dan walked to it and stood there waiting. As Jerry approached he drew June's letter from his pocket and handed it to him.

Jerry was taken completely off his guard, and for a moment was speechless. He took the letter and turned it over.

"What's this? Where—where'd you get it?" he faltered, his tongue suddenly dry.

For answer a terrible burst of profanity broke from the older man. He fell on Jerry like a lion. In the grip of his mighty muscles the other was borne back toward the opening of the shaft, helpless and struggling. He clutched at the iron supports, for a moment caught one and clung, while the cry of his agony rang out shrill as a woman's. In the next his hands were torn away and the slippery iron plates slid beneath his feet. For one instant of horror he reeled on the edge of the abyss, then went backward and down. A cry rose that passed like a note of death through the upper levels of the mine.

Black Dan ran back toward the nearest tunnel mouth. The thud of the picks had stopped. The miners, men who work with death at their elbow, came pouring down and out, scrambling from stopes, running from the ends of drifts, swarming up ladders from places of remote, steaming darkness. White-faced, wild-eyed, not knowing what horror of sudden death awaited them, they came rushing toward the place where their chief stood, a grim-visaged figure at the mouth of the tunnel.

He checked them with a raised hand, even at such a moment able to assert his command over them.

"Keep cool, boys. You're all right. There's been an accident. It's Barclay. For God's sake, tell Marsden to keep those women back."

In the shaft house above, Rion, tired of waiting, was lounging up and down when the bell of one of the compartments gave an imperious summons for the cage to descend.

"They're coming up at last," said Rion, moving to the edge of the shaft and stretching himself in yawning relief. "I never knew Easterners to stand the heat so long."

CHAPTER IX
HOME

On the Friday morning June rose with an oppression of death-like dread weighing on her. Jerry had only told her to hold herself in readiness for that day; she knew nothing further. But the morning was not half spent when a letter came from him, naming the time and place of their departure. As she read her dread deepened. The ardent words of love with which the letter began and ended had no power to overcome her sickened reluctance. She was moving onward toward an action which she contemplated with despair and yet toward which she continued inevitably to advance.

There are many women like June, who, without the force to resist the importunities of conquering lovers, never lose their sense of sin. In the arms of the man they have surrendered to it is heavy at their hearts. The years do not lift it, and the men who have brought them to ruin grow to feel its chill and despise the woman who has not been strong enough to resist or completely give herself up.

During the rest of the morning she remained in her room trying to sort her clothes and pack her bag. Her mind was in a state of stupefied confusion. She could find nothing, could not remember where anything had been placed. At times a sensation of nausea and feebleness swept over her, and she was forced to stop in the work she was doing, and sit down. When at midday the servant summoned her to lunch, the gathered possessions and souvenirs of years were scattered over the furniture and about the floor.

In the afternoon she wrote the letter to the Colonel. She wrote rapidly, not letting herself pause to think, the pen flying over the paper. When it was finished, she sealed it without reading it over.

The rest of the day passed with lightning swiftness. As she roamed from room to room, or sat motionless with drawn brows and rigidly clasped hands, the chiming of the hours from clocks in various parts of the house struck loud on her listening ear. The clear, ringing notes of three seemed hardly to have sounded when four chimed softly. The hours were rushing by. With their headlong flight her misery increased. There was now no sitting quiet, spellbound in waiting immobility. She moved restlessly from window to window looking out on the desolation that hemmed her in. It had no pity for her. Her little passion, a bubble on the whirlpool of the mining town, was of that world of ephemera that the desert passed over and forgot.

At sunset the landscape flushed into magical beauty and then twilight came, and suddenly, on its heels, darkness. The night was a crystalline, deep blue, the stars singularly large and lustrous. As she put on her hat and jacket she felt that her mouth was dry, and if called upon to speak she would have had difficulty in articulating. Over her face she draped a thin, dark veil sufficient at this hour to obscure her features entirely. On the way out she called the Chinaman and gave him the letter for the Colonel, whom she did not expect back before Wednesday.

She made her way to the end of the town through the upper residence streets. They were quite dark at this hour and she slipped by, a slim shadowy shape, touched now and then into momentary distinctness by the gleam of a street lamp. Outside the clustering lights of the city, she turned downward toward where the Geiger grade, looping over the shoulder of the mountain, enters the town. Once on the road itself she walked with breathless speed, the beating of her heart loud in her own ears. She passed the last of the hoisting works, the sentinel of the great line that was stirring the world, and saw the road stretch gray and bare before her.

Her light footfall made no sound in the dust. Straining to penetrate the darkness with a forward gaze she advanced, less rapidly. The dim form of the deserted cabin loomed up, and then, just beyond it, gradually taking shape out of the surrounding blackness, a buggy with a muffled figure in the seat.

For a moment she stopped, feeling faint, her clearness of reason and vision becoming blurred. But in an instant the weakness passed and she walked on hesitatingly and softly, staring at the indistinct figure and drawn irresistibly forward. As she approached, she saw that the man sat motionless, his back toward her. She was close to the buggy when the soft padding of her footsteps in the dust caught his ear. He turned with a start, revealing by the faint starlight that section of a coarse, strange face to be seen between the peak of a woolen cap and the edge of an upturned coat collar.

"Pardon, lady," he said in a hoarse voice, "Mr. Barclay hasn't come yet."

June came to an abrupt halt by the side of the carriage. She stood without movement or sound, paralyzed by the unexpectedness of the unknown voice and face. For the first dazed moment following on the shock there was a complete suspension of all her faculties.

There had been much surreptitious speculation in the livery stable as to whom Jerry Barclay was driving into Reno. The man now in the buggy had been sure it was a woman. Seeing his suspicions verified he tried to distinguish her features through the darkness and the veil she wore. He leaned forward, eying her keenly, but making out nothing beyond a slender shape, the face concealed by a film of gauze.

"He's probably been detained at the mine," he said cheeringly. "They've that gang of Easterners goin' down this afternoon."

The girl made no answer, but drew back a step or two from the carriage.

"If you'll get in I'll drive you up and down for a spell," he said. "It's cold work standin' round on a night like this."

"No," she answered in a muffled voice; "no."

"Put your bag in, anyway," he suggested, stretching a hand for it.

She drew back another step and moved the hand holding the bag behind her.

"Just as you like," he returned, the familiarity of his manner suddenly chilled by annoyance. "It's for you to say."

She retreated still farther until stopped by a growth of sage at the edge of the road. The man, seeing he could discover nothing from her, gathered up his reins.

"Well," he said, "I can't run no risks with the finest team in the state of Nevada. I'll have to walk 'em up and down till Mr. Barclay gets here. He said he'd be before time, and he's nearly fifteen minutes late now."

He chirped to the horses, who immediately started on a gentle trot. The dust muffled their hoof-beats, and noiselessly, with something of stealth and mystery in the soft swiftness of their withdrawal, they receded into the blackness of the night.

June stood for a moment looking after them, then turned to where the town sparkled in descending tiers of streets. Its noise came to her ears, the hum of human voices, and suddenly the misery that had held her in a state of broken acquiescence all day, that had been growing in her for weeks, rose into a climax of terrified revolt. The full horror of her action burst upon her. In a flash of revelation she saw it clearly, unblinded by passion. Her repulsion toward Jerry's wooing surged up in her in a frantic desire to escape, to get away from him. She feared him, she longed to creep away and hide from him—the terrible Jerry, her merciless master, before whom she cowered and trembled.

She cast a fearful look into the darkness behind her and made out the shape of the buggy just turning for the backward trip. It would be beside her again in a few minutes. In front, stretching to the town, the road lay dark and deserted. She gripped her bag and started out toward the blinking lights, running at first, lightly and noiselessly on the trodden vegetation that edged the path.

Her engrossing thought was that she might meet Jerry. In the condition of nervous exhaustion to which the long strain of the past months had reduced her, she had lost all confidence in her power to direct her own actions, and resist the dominating man who had had her so completely under his control. If she met him now it would be the end. He would not cajole and kiss her. He would order her into the buggy and ride away with her into the night.

Several times she met men, dark figures against the lights beyond. At the first glance she could see by their build or gait that they were not Jerry. One, of lighter mold and more elastic walk, caused her to pause for a stricken moment and then shrink back in the shadow of a cabin till she saw her fears were unfounded. As the lights grew brighter and she entered the sparsely settled end of C Street, she slackened her speed and gazed ahead, alertly wary. She did not see but that he must come this way, unless he chose the longer and more secluded route, among the miners' lodging houses and cabins, climbing up from there to the road above.

She had started to return without any fixed idea of her goal. As she advanced she thought of this and immediately the Colonel arose to her mind as a rock behind which there was shelter, his lodgings as the one place where she would find protection. In the bewilderment of her mind she forgot that he was not due to return yet, only remembering his original statement that he would be back on Friday night. If she could reach his rooms without meeting Jerry she would be safe. She felt like a child who has run away to find adventures and is suddenly stricken with the horror of strangeness and the wild and piercing longing for the familiar things of home.

The evening turmoil of C Street had begun. Looking up its length, roofed by its wooden arcade, was like looking into a lighted tunnel, swaying with heads. The glare from the show-windows, the lights from lamps, and the agitated flaring of lanterns on the street hawkers' barrows, were concentrated within this echoing tunnel and played on every variety of face, as the crowd came sweeping down on June. It seemed to catch her in its eddies and whirl her forward, a dark shape, furtive-eyed and stealthy-footed in the fierce, bubbling buoyancy of the throng, silent amid its hubbub.

There seemed to her more noise to-night, more of a seething, whirling froth of excitement than she had ever noticed before. She thought it a reflection of her own fever and hurried on, her eyes gleaming through her veil in peering looks sent ahead for Jerry. She was nearing the short street which led down to the Cresta Plata, when from two miners, almost running past her, she heard his name. Her heart leaped, and for a second she flinched and shrank back into the doorway. As she stood there a group of men brushed by in the opposite direction and from these, as they paused for a second at her side, she heard a question and answer:

"How did he come to fall? Did he slip?"

"Yes, on the iron plates. He stepped back and then slipped, and before Black Dan could get him he was gone. It was all done in a minute."

"Lord!" came the ejaculation in a tone of horror.

She started on and from a cluster of men standing in a saloon doorway she again heard his name. The perspiration broke out on her face. At the mouth of the lane that led to the Cresta Plata a crowd with restless edges, that moved down toward the hoisting works and swayed out into the roadway, made a black mass, expanding and decreasing as its members dispersed or drew together. It was too early for the day shift to be coming up, and she looked at it with sidelong alarm. It was part of the unusualness of this weird and awful night. And again as she threaded her way through the scattering of figures on its outskirts she heard his name, twice in the moment of passing.

What was the matter? Why were they all talking of him? The sense of horror that weighed on her seemed to increase until it became threatening and tragic. She felt as if she were in a nightmare, with the Colonel's rooms and the Colonel the only place of safety and means of escape. She forgot to be cautious and started to run, pushing her way through the crowd, dodging round the edges of excited groups, brushing by knots of women collected at the foot of stairways, and from every group the name of Jerry followed her.

Suddenly, between the massed and moving figures she saw the glare of the colored bottles in the window of Caswell's drug store. It was over this store that the Colonel lived. At one side, outside the brilliant radiance of the bottled transparencies, a small, dark door gave on the stairs that led to the floor above. From its central panel a bell-handle protruded. She tried the knob first and found that it yielded. Opening it softly she looked up the dim stairway and saw in the hall above a light burning. She ran up, her steps subdued on the worn carpet. A narrow corridor divided the floor, passing from a door that opened on the front balcony back to an anterior region where the landlady lived and let rooms to less illustrious lodgers. Of the two suites in the front that on the left was occupied by Rion Gracey, the other by the Colonel. June had often been in these rooms. She opened the door and looked in.

The door gave into the sitting-room, empty of occupants and unlit. But the Colonel's landlady had not been advised of his change of plans, and in expectation of his return a fire burned in the grate and cast a warm, cheering light over the simple furnishings and the arm-chair drawn up in front of it. June crept in and shut the door. She fell into the arm-chair with her hands over her face and sat limp and motionless in the firelight. The noise of the town came dulled to her ears. She had escaped from Jerry and the pursuing echo of his name.

A half-hour later the Colonel found her there. After a hurried search for her through the town he had been seized by the hope that she might have sought shelter with him.

As the opening of the door fell on her ear she raised her head and looked up. He saw her in the firelight, all dark in the half-lit room, save for her white face and hands. An exclamation of passionate relief broke from him, and as she rose and ran to him he held out his arms and clasped her. They said nothing for a moment, clinging mutely together, her face buried in his shoulders, his hand pressing her head against his heart. Then she drew herself away from him and tried to tell him the story in a series of broken sentences, but he silenced her and put her back in the chair.

"Wait till to-morrow," he said, kneeling down beside her to stir up the fire into a redder blaze. "You can tell it all to-morrow. And, anyway, there's no necessity to tell it. I know it now."

"Do you know what I was going to do—nearly did?"

"Yes, all about it. I got your letter."

"Do you despise me?" she said faintly.

"No," he answered.

The fire began to burn brightly. They sat for a moment looking into it; then leaning toward him over the arm of the chair, she said, almost in a whisper,

"Where's Jerry?"

"Jerry?" he answered with a sudden slowness of utterance. "Jerry? Jerry's somewhere."

"As I came along everybody seemed to be talking of him. I heard his name all along the street. It seemed as if it was following me. I'm afraid of Jerry."

"You needn't be any more. You won't see him again. There's—he's—I'll tell you about that to-morrow, too."

"Will you let me stay with you?" she continued. "Will you let me live here, somewhere near you? Will you take care of me?"

He took her hand and pressed it, then held it out, cold and trembling, to the blaze, nodding his answer without looking at her.

"I have nowhere else to go. I don't know where my father is. Uncle Jim, I can't live up in the Murchison mansion alone. It's full of ghosts and memories. I'm afraid of it. I'm afraid of Jerry. I'm afraid of myself."

"You needn't be afraid any more. I'm going to take care of you now. We'll get some rooms for you back here with the landlady, and by and by we'll get something better. You're never going back to the Murchison mansion."

"I was so close to dreadful things there," she murmured. "It was so—"

A man's step sounded on the stairs, mounted quickly and then struck a resonant response from the wooden flooring of the hall.

"Who's that?" she whispered, with hurried alarm, her figure drawn alertly upright as if to rise and fly. "Is that some one coming in? Don't let them. I don't want to see any one now."

The Colonel, after a listening moment, reassured her.

"That's only Rion," he said. "You needn't bother about him. He lives just across the hall."

She murmured an "Oh!" of relieved comprehension and fell back in the chair.

They were silent for a space, both looking into the heart of the fire, its red light playing on their faces, the woman leaning back languidly, sunk in an apathy of exhausted relief; the man possessed by a sense of contentment more rich and absolute than he had hoped ever again to feel.